NSA
UNZIPPED AND EXPOSED

To Sally

Best Wishes

Owen Richards

NSA
UNZIPPED AND EXPOSED

WREN RICHARDS

ARCHWAY
PUBLISHING

Archway Publishing books may be ordered through booksellers or by contacting:

Archway Publishing
1663 Liberty Drive
Bloomington, IN 47403
www.archwaypublishing.com
1 (888) 242-5904

ISBN: 978-1-4808-7144-1 (sc)
ISBN: 978-1-4808-7143-4 (hc)
ISBN: 978-1-4808-7145-8 (e)

Library of Congress Control Number: 2018964540

Print information available on the last page.

Archway Publishing rev. date: 01/25/2019

PROLOGUE

The expansive, live oak tree sunk its roots into the Texas soil, where the earth's cool, moist depths sustained human calmness and stability, radiating the source of its creation. The tree lived five hundred years and witnessed the lives of many humans that now rested beneath the expanded canopy. This is one story.

CHAPTER 1
CHILDHOOD

I don't really know who I am. My birth name was Angelo Orlando Andres Lopez. I was born in Costa Rica on May 27, 1962, to wealthy parents: my father, Giovanni Orlando Andres Zuniga, and mother, Gabriela Illeana Andres Lopez. My parents accumulated enough wealth, through clever planning, hard work, and an inheritance, to raise six children. I was one of the middle siblings: I was the third boy born of the four brothers and have one older and one younger sister.

Because I assumed hundreds of identities in my lifetime, I acquired personality traits, mannerisms, and unique knowledge with each new identity. The three traits I know are my own are my love for my mother, my Catholic faith, and the power of my mind.

One of these three traits, the invisible, intangible love for my mother, was constant and unchangeable. My mother was the composite of every type of love, especially God's love and universal love. She was the love center of our family.

My mother and father had a fairy-tale love story, and their life together was a happily-ever-after marriage until my father's passing in 2010. If a book had ever been written with my parents in mind, it had had to be *The Great Gatsby*, except that my parents' love for each other was requited.

My mother loved my two sisters like the mother in *Little Women*, for she understood feminine love, taught it, and administered it to my sisters. For us boys, my mother's love was like June Cleaver's in *Leave It to Beaver*. This kind of love gave us guidance, understanding, and good cookies.

My father was the product of an indigenous Matambu tribe who lived in Costa Rica. He was working as a gardener at a private school for wealthy girls when he became aware that Gabriela was watching him and trying to make eye contact. He was shy and hid in the bushes where Gabriela couldn't see him.

They eventually became friends, and their friendship lasted six years. During Gabriela's last year at school, Giovanni asked Gabriela to marry him. Gabriela told him that he had to ask her father for her hand in marriage. If her father said yes, he must ceremoniously ask her on bended knee in front of the entire family. First, he needed to ask her father for permission to speak with him at her house.

The only way Giovanni could accomplish this was to use the public pay phone next to the school building. Giovanni had no coins for the telephone, so Gabriela gave him her lunch money to make the call. Giovanni pushed the coins into the round spaces and when her father answered, became so nervous, he hung up. Giovanni tried to work up his courage many times while Gabriela continued to finance the calls with her lunch money.

She did not eat lunch for an entire week until Giovanni finally completed the connection. Giovanni soon met with Señor Fredrico Lopez, who told him that he could not marry Gabriela until he had the means to support her. When Giovanni left the house, Gabriela's uncle Enrique pulled him aside, gave him money, and told him not to return until he had doubled the amount.

Gabriela and Giovanni continued to meet secretly while her family introduced her to prospective wealthy young men, whom she refused. Luck was in Giovanni's favor. He and his four brothers were given a piece of land that they must share. The two older brothers divided the land into parcels and kept the choice ones for themselves, leaving Giovanni and his younger brother, Roberto, each with one tiny parcel.

Giovanni knew that he and Roberto hadn't received a fair share, but ignored the discrepancies and put his agricultural skills to work. He taught his younger brother to plant pineapples. They had a wonderful harvest, bought more land, planted more pineapple, and harvested even more. They continued their work until Giovanni had enough money to returned to Gabriela's home and present her uncle Enrique with three times the amount he had received.

After Giovanni obtained Señor Lopez's blessing, on a bended knee, he properly asked Gabriella for her hand in marriage, and they were married in a beautiful Catholic church. A few years later, Gabriela inherited a vast amount of money while Giovanni continued to expand and invest in pineapple, bananas, and coffee. He eventually became one of Costa Rica's largest and wealthiest growers.

The two older brothers became alcoholics while Giovanni and Roberto continued to be partners until later in life when both were wealthy and moved into their own interests. Roberto was interested in restaurants, municipalities, and the government while Giovanni and Gabriela developed mushroom and orchid plantations. My parents became owners of Costa Rica's most premier chain of grocery stores called Grande Comida.

The second pillar of *who I am* is my Catholic faith. During the beginning stages of their wealth, Giovanni and Gabriela began to raise a family. We were six privileged children, with a choice lifestyle, and raised to embrace our Catholic faith and to respect its doctrine. We celebrated religious holidays with strict reverence and without gifts.

My mother explained that our normal everyday life was lavish and that on holidays, we were to be mindful of God, to honor Christ, and to give gifts to the poor. This was the other component of knowing myself. I was a cradle Catholic. Whenever life punched me in the face, my church and mass gave me strength.

My parents donated and built churches in the towns where we were raised. Our name was engraved on church walls, stained glass, and fountains. In many churches, our family had its own separate-seating alcove.

However, our parents taught us how to behave and to be humble in the presence of God and in the company of other community worshippers. They taught us to always be humble, even though we were wealthy.

We knelt before God on the hard floor while the community worshippers knelt on prayer benches. We sat on the hard folding chairs while others sat in padded pews. We never exhibited arrogance or disrespected our Catholic church, home, or school.

During the sixties and seventies and while we were growing up in Costa Rica, there was no middle class. People were either wealthy or lived in poverty. I was the envy of my neighborhood friends because I had a bicycle to ride up and down the streets. I quickly learned that because I always had money, bicycles, and new toys, it was my responsibility to pay my friends' ways. The structure of our society taught me to buy and gift things to my friends. Others might view this as buying friendships, but for wealthy Costa Ricans, paying was a way of life.

The third character trait was the power of my mind. When I was five, my mother came to visit my school and sat with me during class. My classmates were a year or two older than I was. The teacher wrote notes on the blackboard as he gave the lesson. My classmates busily copied them down in their notebooks while I played with a deck of cards Uncle Enrique had given to me.

"Why aren't you writing down the lessons, and where did you get those cards?" my mother asked sharply.

With downcast eyes and humility, I answered, "Because I already know it. Uncle Enrique gave me the cards."

Mother took me out into the hall and said, "You give me those cards right now! If you know the lesson so well, tell me what it was about."

"Okay," I said. "How flowers grow. One flower can populate a big field of beautiful wildflowers, and one fallen apple can grow a handful of trees. Flowers make new flowers and plants with the help of nature.

"There are many plants that use wind to pollenate and spread seeds. Grass, weeds, and even big pine trees have pollen spores that are small and light. This makes it easy for the wind to pick them up and blow them on other plants to help them grow."

"Birds, bees, and other insects fly from flower to flower with pollen stuck to the hairs of their legs and wings. As the bugs touch different flowers, some of the pollen falls off, and that pollen helps the flowers to grow."

"Most plants cannot travel, so they rely on animals and wind to help scatter their seeds. Seeds come in many different sizes ranging from the a pinhead to a mango seed or pinecone. Animals, like iguanas and birds, eat the fruit from the trees and spread the fruit seeds on the ground where they grow into new plants."

"Many plants and flowers, such as lilies and tulips, reproduce from bulbs. A bulb is like an underground tank that stores the entire life cycle of itself in the bulb. The bulb has both female and male parts. The parent plant produces buds that split off from and begin living separately as a new baby plant."

My mother stood in the vacant hallway without saying a single word. I thought maybe she was mad at me, but then she knelt down beside me and gave me a hug. "Angelo, I am sorry. I understand now.

You do know your lesson. Tell me what you are doing with those cards."

"I am learning these cards," I said.

"How are you learning those cards?"

I took the cards from her hands. "See? I pile them up like this, flutter them like this, and watch the numbers go by. Now I pile them up again and know their numbers. It's a game."

"Let me see the cards," my mother said. "Let me flutter them, and you watch them. Then I will take them in my hands, and you can tell me the numbers." My mother fluttered the cards, stacked them again, and said, "Tell me the numbers."

"Okay, I like it when you play with me. Red lady Q, black five, black three, red A, black six, black five, red nine, black four, red five, red man K, red five, black two, black—"

"Angelo, that's amazing! You did very well. You got them all in perfect order. Tell me, if you were to watch all the cards as I fluttered them, could you tell me the order of them all?" she asked as she stood up.

"I don't know. Sometimes some of the cards stick together and I can't see them. I don't flutter them as fast as you fluttered them. I flutter them much slower. Mother you flutter good."

She saved the top twelve cards I had just named, took a pin out of her hair, clipped them together, put them in her pocket, and asked, "Angelo, out of those cards you named, how many fives were there?"

"That's easy. There were four cards that were fives: two red ones and two black ones."

"Do you know the names of these cards?" She took out the black ace of spades and then a red king of diamonds.

"I call them A and man K, but Uncle Enrique said he would teach me their right names the next time we played."

Mother knelt down beside me again, took my hand, looked at

me, and said, "Angelo, look at me. Never go with Enrique to The Lucky Spot. You run home if he takes you there. Do you hear me?"

"Okay, but can I play with Uncle Enrique anymore?"

"Yes, of course, but only at home and nowhere else. Let's go back inside your classroom."

After school, Mother talked to the teacher for a long time. The teacher told Mom that he was aware I was able to learn in a special way. He explained that I was already much younger than my classmates and that moving me ahead several grades would be a cruel thing to do because I was socially immature. Girls matured much faster than boys did, and in a few years, the social relationship would be more meaningful to me. She recommended that mother find activities to challenge me.

On the way home, my mother said, "Angelo, tell me what your school lesson was about today."

"Which one?"

"The one about flowers."

I answered with perfect recall.

"Can you tell me the order of the twelve cards?" she asked as she took the cards from her pocket. I answered correctly again.

As an adult, I have total recall, but it has to be something that is important to me or that my job requires me to remember. There have been times when I couldn't remember something like a phone number or date, but if I could visualize the setting, I could remember the required fact. This gift of total recall from God was the third component of my true identity. Total recall could be a gift but could also be the curse of my life.

I became an alcoholic when I was nine. My father wanted his boys to be tough, strong, and able to hold their liquor. We had sumptuous parties at our house, and drinking was abundant. We had a large house, and it was always the center of our extended family during weekend get-togethers. All holidays, weddings, or school-related functions were held at our house. Children were given alcoholic drinks just like the adults were, and my father would laugh and enjoy my inebriated condition.

Our family had many old Spanish traditions from my mother's side of the family. One tradition had the men and boys gather in one part of the house while the women and girls gathered in another. So I don't think Mother knew how much or how often we boys drank. In these separate rooms, we learned to imitate our fathers, uncles, and male cousins. I suppose that my sisters learned who they were by socializing in the female part of the house.

As children, the boys had their own floor of bedrooms, and the girls' bedrooms were on the floor above us. We were absolutely forbidden to go to the girls' floor. Even though I had two sisters, I was separated from them throughout our childhood. I never knew much about girls.

Many times at our family parties, Uncle Enrique had the job of putting me to bed when I was intoxicated or just tired out. He had never married or had had children of his own. My parents had special affection for him since the day he had given my father the money to prove himself as a businessman. Uncle Enrique was a favorite family member, and my parents adored the idea that he cared for us boys. I was his favorite.

It was during these bedtime tuck-ins that Uncle Enrique would touch and fondle me in pleasure. He taught me to reciprocate the feelings to him. Uncle Enrique's bedtime tuck-ins went on for many years. No one ever suspected that anything was out of order in our perfect household where we had every advantage possible.

When I was eleven, Mother traveled to the USA on a shopping adventure. Costa Rica was underdeveloped. Our Costa Rican stores had only basic staples for sale. My mother bought our clothes and any household goods she wanted.

In the American magazines, I saw pictures of Converse high-top tennis shoes. I wanted those shoes urgently. I showed her a picture of black Converse shoes and begged her to bring a pair home to me. I waited and was eager for her to return with my new shoes. She came home and handed me the box. I opened it to find bright red Converse shoes. She said, "I thought these red ones were so cute. Are you happy?" It was cool that they were Converse shoes but *red*? I wore them to school, and my classmates called me *payahso* (clown).

In my teens, I fit the middle child profile and earned my payahso name. I never needed to study or to pay attention in the classroom. I was several years ahead of my peers, so I grew to become the *clown man*. I remained polite and respectful to teachers, but outside of the school, I was the wild child, who had many friends. I found my own challenges, interests, and creative outlets that consisted of thought-provoking schemes, pranks, and entertainment for my friends and me.

Schoolmates always looked for ways to get out of class. The drawback of only getting myself out of class was that doing things alone was not much fun, so I thought up a plan where at least ten of my friends would get out of class with me.

We had a tiny, old female teacher, Señora Galvez, who lived at the top of our school's hill. The schoolyard had a low wooden fence around its perimeter and separated the school property. Late at night, I got ten of my friends together and went to Señora Galvez's house, put her little Renault car into neutral, and rolled it down the hill. The ten of us lifted it over the school fence. The only way she would be able to lift it out would be with the help of the big boys in the school (my friends). This was a fun plan to get us out of class. After the principal asked us to help her return the car to the other side of the fence, we would not go back to school for the rest of the day. I received much praise and slaps on the back for thinking up such a *happy* plan. We all dreamt of fun activities to do during our school absence.

The next morning at school, our plan unfurled. The principal asked for help to lift the car out of the enclosed fence. He announced the names of the boys who would help. My name wasn't among them. I wasn't one of the bigger guys. My friends gave me a wink as they left the classroom.

My mother was aware of the fun I had with all my school amigos and thought it was time for me to learn how to be refined. She taught us correct table manners. When she was finished, we knew where every eating utensil, plate, glass, and cup should be placed on the table. We knew how to correctly place an eating utensil to signal the waiter without speaking to him. These signals were usually code for I want more, I'm finished, or I am ready for the check.

My mother was always strict about our table manners. One time, my older brother invited a girl over for dinner. At the table, my brother gave his girlfriend a bite from his fork, and Mother excused them both from the table without any dinner.

Mother continued to look for ways to teach us about social graces. She invited girls from my class to come to tea. I invited male classmates, but they refused to come. Mom planned, fussed, baked pastries, organized games and music, and taught my brothers and I to dance. Mom was ready for us to practice our new refinements. Only one of my male friends showed up—the one friend who owned a tie. My brothers were required to attend, but none of their friends would come either. My three brothers, one friend, and I were required to dance at least once with each of the twenty girls.

Mom decided this approach was not exactly successful, so she scaled down her teas by inviting only two girls per brother. This time the girls were our own age. We practiced refinement so much that to this day I hate tea. We were required to make conversation with our lady guests. I developed such elaborate conversational skills that I could talk nonstop for over an hour to a tree and if necessary, to a girl. Mom's refinement practice continued until the last tea before I hit puberty and rebellion. At that tea, I dressed appropriately, appeared refined, and escaped out the back door to sit in my older brother's car and listen to the radio.

My two older brothers had been given their own new cars on their birthdays after they had learned to drive. I didn't have a car and wanted to take a girl to a music concert in San Jose (Costa Rica), so I asked my mom if I could borrow her car. She agreed. I bought a large box of condoms and placed them into the glove compartment. I set out for my girlfriend's house in San Jose. The night was a total success in every way, and I returned my mom's car.

My mom had coffee club on Wednesday morning and drove to pick up four of her friends. Before going for coffee, mom stopped at a bakery to get some pastries. She left her friends in the car and dashed inside. One of the friends needed a tissue, opened the glove box, and saw the big box of condoms. Her friends concluded that Gabriela was having an affair. All four of her friends made excuses as to why they couldn't go to coffee and requested to be taken home. My mother was devastated. She called to find out what was wrong, and her friends refused to talk to her. This shunning continued for a month of tears until Gabriela drove to one friend's house and demanded an explanation. Mom realized the condoms were mine.

CHAPTER 2
REBELLION

My drinking and driving days were abundant. One day, Mom was having a club meeting in the lower part of our house. I was drinking and out of choice, drove the car directly through the wall where the meeting was being held. My friends laughed uncontrollably as ladies, tables, cups, and club notes were scattered into the pineapple groves. Lucky for me no one was hurt.

My drinking increased with each escapade. I was drunk even when I went to school, but it went undetected because I was quiet and rarely participated. After school one day when I was inebriated, I talked my friends into joyriding with me. We drove through the streets of San Jose and spotted a parked, unoccupied cop car with its doors open.

"Anyone want a police car to drive?" I shouted as I jumped out of my own car into the front seat of the cop's car. I turned on the siren, drove the car around the block and then back to my own parked car, and coaxed my friends to jump in with me. Two of them did. We continued to drive through the streets with the siren blaring, laughing all the while, until we were apprehended and arrested.

The arresting officer knew my father, called him, and related what had happened. My father replied, "Leave him in jail. Maybe he will learn something." I did learn something. I felt like a lowlife sitting in the dark, dank hole of a room with other drunks. I remained incarcerated until Uncle Enrique came and bailed me out the next day. I was hungry, tired, hungover, and alone and wanted a drink to steady my shaking hands. I resented Uncle Enrique's kindness and knew he expected sexual payment for helping me out. I wanted him to take me home, which he did. However, he made me feel dirtier than the grime from the jail I had left.

I had experienced the pleasure of girls. I knew my uncle was manipulating and using me. He had been doing this for years. The guilt and shame I felt was more than anyone needed to endure. I wanted nothing more to do with him. I refused to speak to him on the way home and went straight to my room to be alone. All I could think about was how Uncle Enrique had made me sin in the eyes of God.

We had a chapel altar in our house. Before dinner, I went to that silent place and asked for forgiveness. My parents thought I was seeking redemption for my behavior regarding the police car, but I had much older and deeper secrets that needed atonement.

At dinner, we were served wine. As I drank it, my shakes grew milder and my head began to clear. I explained that I was thirsty and had several glasses. I was sixteen years old and didn't realize I had become an alcoholic. The dinner was delectable, and I had a new appreciation for my mom and our home. No one talked about the jail incident or how I had disgraced the family.

Several weeks passed by. I attended school as usual, and my friends rallied to reassure me of my popularity. I was witty, entertaining, and provoked laughter, even with the teachers. I learned to become Mr. Charming, hiding my dependence on alcohol.

It was my seventeenth birthday, and I received my third new car. I had smashed all the others. I invited my older brother Cristian to take it for a joyride. He wanted to drive, and I wanted to drink, so we were both content. We went to an area known as Lover's Lane. It was outside of San Jose, above Cartago, and near winding, narrow gravel roads where kids went to prove their driving talents and to make out. Cristian took a curve way too fast. The car skidded and hit a granite stone wall that sheared off his side of the car. He was killed instantly.

My brother's death changed our lives forever. My mother's grief was immeasurable. It grew into a deep depression that affected my parents' marriage. The funeral mass and graveside ceremony were lavish. Alcohol flowed to numb everyone's pain, especially mine, which was now the pain of a survivor's guilt.

During the mass, my father whispered into my ear, "Angelo, why couldn't this death have been yours?" He didn't know that his wish was also mine.

During the funeral dinner, Uncle Enrique stood next to me and put his arms around me. All of this was more than I could withstand. I doubled up my fist and with one punch he was hurled into the food table, knocking him and several guests to the floor. I broke his glasses and cut his nose. Uncle Enrique was an old man. My brother, who was a medical student, thought I had broken his arm.

My father rushed to help Uncle Enrique up and asked, "Why did Angelo do that? What made him so angry?"

Uncle Enrique said, "Oh, I said something I shouldn't have about his girlfriend."

My family couldn't take any further displays of my drunkenness, reckless bouts of rebellion, and disrespect for life. I was to be shipped off to the United States where my father had enrolled me in the School of the Americas.

Father took me to the San Jose International Airport, which was an hour and a half from our plantation home. In his Mercedes, we rode in complete silence. My dad didn't look at me but stared straight ahead. We said nothing to each other for the entire drive. I guess there wasn't anything left to say. In the past, I don't think I had paid much attention to him or had even looked at my dad, but that day, I felt dwarfed by his size.

To most people in our city, he was a giant. His stature reached further and deeper than his height. His success as a businessman, a sturdy pillar of our church, an employer of our fellow countrymen and hundreds of Nicaraguans, a community benefactor, and a devoted family man caused him to be well known throughout Costa Rica. I was his prodigal son like in the Bible's scriptures I had learned so well, except there was no returning home to enjoy the fatted calf. I was the black spot in his golden world.

Most people thought he was distinguished, but my resentful thoughts became obstacles that blocked my sight of anything good about him. He stood at six feet two inches with broad shoulders and strong thighs and legs. He had big feet and hands and the family trait of large ears with fat earlobes. I didn't see these ears as a family trait as much as a family curse. He had a full head of thick, course, black, wavy hair and big, full, black eyebrows.

My own hair was unlike my dad's. Later, my maternal grandfather's balding gene would appear, but at my seventeen years of age, who gave a damn anyway? I had no trouble getting the girls to go out with me, and what else mattered?

My dad's strength came from the physical activities of working on his plantations. I didn't like to work out. Some of my friends worked out with weights, but I didn't need too. I had strong muscles in my thighs and arms, and my girlfriends said they liked my round butt. They told me I looked good without my shirt, and I think they were right. I liked to go shirtless, partly to vex my dad and partly because the girls that worked for us noticed.

Sometimes, I helped out with the coffee pickers, which was

exciting work because the young girls showed off for me. Wow, how they showed off. I had no thoughts of how I could help the business or my dad benefit from what I did. Personal rewards pleased me.

Our large plantation had six weighing stations, which were located around the property, It was my job to weigh the workers' coffee bean sacks. If the bean sack weighed thirty pounds, that person would receive a red chip. If it weighed sixty pounds, that person received a blue chip. At the end of the day, the workers exchanged their colored chips for cash, two miles away at the checkout station, which was managed by my dad.

My weighing station was a small wooden building where I sat on a stool in the shade and read the scale. I determined the weight and poured the beans into a truck, which would then deliver the coffee beans to a broker in San Jose. I returned the empty sack to the coffee picker and gave him or her an appropriate colored chip.

There was one good-looking, dark, curly-haired Tica (In Costa Rica females are affectionately called Tica. This is not a racial slur. National pride is shown in the word Tica and Tico.) more than twice my age who had ample breasts inside her blouse. She usually brought a thirty-pound sack to be weighed. She would open her blouse and show me her large, soft, brown curves in exchange for a blue chip instead of the correct red one. I wasn't brave enough to give her a yellow chip, which would have allowed me to touch her. Neither of us tired of our weighing routine. Sometimes, if I had nothing better to do, which wasn't often, I offered to drive the coffee bean truck into San Jose and bring back a full truck of supplies.

My mind kept reviewing thoughts about my family as my father drove up the departure ramp and over to the "Unloading Only" lane. He stopped the car. I got out as he popped the trunk lid open and lifted out my one bag the school had permitted.

He said loudly, "Good luck, son." I didn't look back, wave, or even acknowledge I had heard him.

CHAPTER 3
ON MY OWN

I took a flight from San Jose International Airport to Houston, Texas, where I went through US customs. I then continued on to Columbus, Georgia, where the Fort Benning army bus would shuttle me to the base where the School of the Americas was located. That was easy!

I arrived in Columbus and went to the baggage claim where a uniformed American soldier held a sign up with my name on it. "Welcome to Georgia," he said, extending his hand, which I grasped extra hard and firm as my dad had taught me. He looked down at me and said, "Please show me your ID." I complied. He looked at it and gave me a pass. "Your shuttle bus is the third brown bus parked in the bus lane outside. We will go when the bus is full, so it might be awhile."

"Gracias," I replied.

"Speak English, young man. This is America, not Mexico."

The truth was, I didn't often get a chance to speak English. The small rural schools of my early education hadn't taught English, but Mom had insisted on living in San Jose where my sisters, brothers, and I received a better education. I grew up attending the best schools available, but it had only been in the latter two years that I had exposure to a foreign language. I had no opportunity to practice speaking it. I guess that would change. That jerk of a soldier thought I was a stupid Mexican.

I got my bag and stepped onto the bus. A few people were already seated, but no one looked like he was on his way to school. I sat in an empty seat in the middle of the bus and lowered the window because it was a hot day in Georgia.

I had left Costa Rica wearing clothing that was appropriate for the cooler weather we had during the winter rainy season. I wore a long-sleeved, light grey, silk-blend shirt with dark, charcoal-grey, lightweight wool- and cotton-blend pants. However, it was July, and the Georgia heat was hotter than anything I had previously known.

The heat of the bus prompted me to seek a cooler spot while waiting. The bus didn't look like it was leaving anytime soon, so I grabbed my bag, spotted a nearby bookstore, and made my way to its pleasant air-conditioned, book-lined walls to seek comfort and to keep my shirt from soaking with sweat. The contrast from the cramped, non-air-conditioned Costa Rican stores and American stores was startling. I stared and thought wow, abundance, spacious, and lavish.

I strolled through the aisles and spotted a book entitled *Everything You Need to Know about Fort Benning, Georgia*. I bought the book with the twenty dollars my sister had unobtrusively slipped into my pocket while I had been on my way out of the house that morning. Now all I had left was two dollars and seventy-five cents. Poverty didn't make me feel very grand.

I returned to the waiting bus and reclaimed the vacant seat I had occupied earlier. There were a few more people onboard, but they were older men. There was no one near my age or anyone who looked to be a student. Eureka! I got it. I must be on the wrong bus. I leaned across the aisle and asked a man in English, "Is this bus going to Fort Benning to the School of the Americas?"

"Yes," he replied with a Guatemalan accent.

"To the School of the Americas?" I repeated.

"Si," he said in Spanish, extended his hand, and introduced himself. "I am Colonel Jose Efrain Rios Montt. I am going to the School of the Americas to take a class in Irregular Warfare Operations. This is my third time at the Fort Benning base, and I can offer you directions if need them. What course are you taking?"

I extended my hand in greeting. "Angelo Orlando Andres Lopez. I will take the cadet course. Are you from Guatemala?"

"Yes, and your Spanish accent tells me you are from Costa Rica." He stoically reached into his briefcase and handed me a booklet about the School of the Americas. He turned his back toward me and looked out the window, which indicated closure to our conversation.

I accepted the manual, laid it aside, and read the seventeen-dollar-and-twenty-five-cent book *Everything You Need to Know about Fort Benning, Georgia*. The bus continued to fill as I read my new book. Another half hour had passed when a uniformed soldier came onto the bus and announced, "This bus is going to Fort Benning Army Base. If anyone hasn't checked in and received his or her pass, please come forward." Then he sat in the drivers' seat and put the bus in gear. I got a little bit of relief from the heat when a small breeze came through the open window.

I glanced over at Colonel Montt, who was deep in thought and seemed to be anxious and troubled. He was about as old as my dad but not as tall. Everyone on this bus seemed to be older and bigger than I was. My older brothers hadn't grown taller until they had gone to the university. I hoped I would grow soon. I wanted to look like a man instead of a boy. I thumbed through the *School of the*

Americas manual but found myself gazing out the window like the Guatemalan Colonel had.

I couldn't understand why my father had sent me to the School of the Americas. I wondered if he had really understood what this school was about. Their strange classes taught students how to torture prisoners of war and other military stuff. The classes included Psychological Warfare, Counterinsurgency, and Interrogation Techniques. These courses taught military officers and soldiers of third world countries to subvert truth and make war with their own people.

I was not a soldier or an officer. I didn't understand why I was there. Did my father really believe in the principals that were talked about in the manual's mission statement? I was raised to respect capitalism and democracy. Why would my father want me to learn values that opposed Costa Rican ones? There must be some mistake. I thought he wanted me to become a lawyer.

The bus ride was only fifteen minutes long. For as long as I waited on this bus, I could have walked the distance twice over but couldn't have entered the base without military escort.

The driver parked the bus after he presented his papers at the gate, stood and declared, "As I read off your name, form a line here on the left. Colonel Jose Efrain Rios Montt." He continued to read more names.

Colonel Montt stood and said to me, "When you take your entrance interview, stand in front of the officer's desk and don't move until he tells you to. Read the manual before your interview."

I replied with an inaudible, "Okay."

"Everyone remaining will form a line to the right," the soldier shouted.

The American soldier called the names in alphabetical order and in time, got to Lopez. I rose from my seat and stood in the line on the right with seven people ahead of me and more still coming behind me. We followed the uniformed GI (I think he was the same one that had called out our names because they all looked alike) to the building that was to be our bedroom. All of us in the line were to sleep in one big ugly room.

"This place could use my mom's flair for color," I said loud enough for the man in front of me (Levino) and the man behind me (Lunna) to hear. Neither man acknowledged my remark, which I thought was funny.

"Every man is assigned to take his bunk in the order it is given. Levino, here. Lopez, this one. Lunna, here," shouted the uniformed GI as he continued to call the names of the men in alphabetical order. Someone with a name that was closer to the front of the alphabet walked to his bunk and tossed his bag down. This angered the GI soldier, and he pushed his way to the bed, grabbed the man's bag, and flung it to the far wall. The bag landed behind my bed with a crashing sound like glass shattering.

"All personal items go into the locker and remain out of sight. Nothing is placed on the beds except your dog-tired asses. Entrance interviews begin in one hour, starting with Abdulla and ending with Zella. Every fifteen minutes, the next person will enter as the previous person exits. Interviews will commence in room 101 at the Americas Hall of Fame across the plaza. Dinner is served in the cafeteria at 1800 hours. Any questions?" There was silence.

The GI left the barracks, and the men silently moved about placing their personal items into their lockers. I leaned over, retrieved the hurled bag, and handed it to Castano, a man in his thirties from Colombia, as he approached my bed.

"It sounded like glass got broken," I said as I handed Castano his bag.

"Yes, my wife packed a jar of mango jelly she made for me. That dirty son of a bitch GI Joe will pay for this. I have a mess inside this bag," he said as he made his way to the sinks.

I sat down on my bed after I had placed the contents of my bag in the provided locker. The men routinely left the barracks to take their entrance interviews, and I waited for my turn. I kept a watchful eye on Levino, who would precede me. I continued to read the *School of the Americas* manual that Colonel Montt had given me and the new book about Fort Benning, Georgia.

Levino left the barracks, and I glanced at my watch to gauge the mandated fifteen-minute interval for his interview. I finished reading the school manual and flipped through the remaining pages of *Everything You Need to Know about Fort Benning, Georgia*. I left the barracks, cut across the plaza, and entered the Hall of Fame. I saw portraits lining the walls of members who had been inducted into the Hall of Fame. I recognized my father's close friend and my paternal namesake, Oscar Andres Arias Sanchez. He would be the president of Costa Rica one day and the head of the social, democratic National Liberation Party. He would loom largely in my upcoming interview.

The door to 101 opened, and Levino came out and said, "Stand in front of the desk when you go in."

"Okay," I said. "What did they ask you?" Levino shrugged and held the door open as I entered.

CHAPTER 4
THE INTERVIEW

An older soldier sat at the desk, looking at some papers. He glanced up at me and asked, "What's your name?"

"Angelo Orlando Andres Lopez," I replied

"How old are you, Lopez?"

"I just turned seventeen."

"Your father knows powerful people in Costa Rica. He paid big money for me to make a man out of you, and that's what we aim to do. Do you want to be a good soldier?" he asked.

"No, sir. I want to be a lawyer."

Colonel Mike Hollander's thick, gray eyebrows raised, and distain swept over his Clint Eastwood-chiseled, suntanned face. "This is Fort Benning not Harvard Lopez. So what do you know about Fort Benning?" he asked.

"Fort Benning," I began, "home of the US Army Infantry, was next to the city of Columbus in southwest Georgia. It had been moved to this location during World War I between 1917 and 1918. Its mission was to produce the world's finest combat infantrymen.

The US Army Infantry School at Fort Benning confirmed its place as the premier school of arms, training, and developing such military leaders as five-star generals Omar Bradley, George Marshall, Dwight D. Eisenhower, George Patton, and Colin Powell."

"About thirty-five thousand military and civilian personnel worked on the installation. It contributed more than $750 million to the area's economy. Fort Benning spent more than $190 million in purchasing and contracting annually. The army post supported more than 120,000 active duty military personnel, family members, reserve component soldiers, and daily renters. Its address was 110 Vibrant Avenue, Cusseta, Georgia, 31905."

"It was built on the area that was originally occupied by the Dawson Artillery during the Civil War of 1861 to 1865. The post encompassed 287 square miles of Chattahoochee and Muskogee counties. Efforts to establish an infantry school date back to 1826, when Major General Edmund P. Gaines persuaded the war department to establish an infantry school at Jefferson Barracks near Saint Louis, Missouri, but the school closed after two years. No further attempts to—"

"Just hold it right there, Lopez. If you think your memorization impressed me, you are wrong. How long did it take you to memorize your little speech, and who told you I asked our recruits about Fort Benning?" Colonel Mike Hollander asked as he stood up behind the desk and exhibited his six-foot-six-inch stature.

I felt small like an underdeveloped country pumpkin but managed to answer. "Colonel Mike Hollander, I didn't memorize anything. I bought a book about Fort Benning at the bookstore before I got on the bus."

"Okay, Lopez, I'll play your little game," he said as he sat back down behind his desk. "How did the infantry school get started?"

"No further attempts to establish a similar facility were undertaken until 1881 when General William T. Sherman, commanding general of the army, established the School of Application for the Infantry and Cavalry at Fort Leavenworth, Kansas, to educate officers. In 1907, at the urging of Lieutenant General Arthur MacArthur, the army established the School of Musketry at the Presidio of Monterey, California, to train soldiers in marksmanship. This training program was often referred to as the origin of the infantry school and led to the creation of Fort Benning."

"So, Fort Benning was considered a spin-off from the musketry school in California? Is that correct?" Colonel Hollander asked.

"No, sir. The California School of Musketry was transferred in 1913 to Fort Sill, Oklahoma, but its development there was interrupted by the decision to send troops to the Mexican border to fight outlaw raiders. The school's operations were curtailed, and the army, overall, suffered from a severe manpower shortage.

"At the entry of the United States into World War I, government officials recognized that Fort Sill was not large enough to accommodate the training of both infantry and artillery units also housed there. A board was convened in May of 1918 to select a new larger site for an infantry school. Because of its climate, terrain, and transportation outlets, Columbus, Georgia, was chosen to house the new school—"

"How did the school get its name?" he interrupted.

"At the request of the Columbus Rotary Club, Camp Benning was named in honor of Confederate Brigadier General Henry L. Benning, who commanded a Georgia brigade in General John Hood's Northern Virginian division of the army in. Benning. General Hood fought with General Robert E. Lee and earned himself the nickname Old Rock because of his coolness in battle."

"When did the Dawson Artillery occupy this area?" he asked.

"I already told you about that," I scoffed.

"Don't get smart with me, Lopez. Answer any question asked of you. Do you understand?" he shouted.

"Yes. This area was occupied by the Dawson Artillery during the Civil War," I answered.

"What year was that?" he asked.

"1861 to 1865."

"Do you understand everything you just told me?" Colonel Hollander asked.

"*No*. Not everything."

"What don't you understand? You seem to be such a smartass," he said.

"I don't know what a musketry school is," I replied modestly.

Colonel Hollander relaxed his shoulders and tipped his swivel chair back while a faint smile and a compassionate look raced onto his face. *Yeah, that's right. How would Lopez from Costa Rica know what such an American antiquity as the musket was. He has an honesty about him that I like*, Colonel Hollander thought.

"Lopez, a musket was one of the first firearms invented—maybe as early as 1560. China used hand cannons during that time or maybe earlier," answered Colonel Hollander. "Do you like guns?"

"No, I don't really have an interest in guns."

"What do you know about the School of the Americas?" he asked.

"It was founded by the United States in 1946. The school was initially located in Panama but was relocated to the army base at Fort Benning, Georgia, in the early 1980s because of the Panama Canal Treaty. President Jorge Illueca of Panama requested its relocation because of Panamanian politics.

"Today, the instructors and students of the School of the Americas are recruited from the cream of the Latin American military establishment. The school trains seven hundred to two thousand soldiers a year, and since its inception in 1946, more than sixty-thousand military personnel have graduated from the SOA. The school has its own goals. Its curriculum includes courses in psychological warfare, counterinsurgency, interrogation techniques, infantry, and commando tactics. Presented with the most sophisticated and up-to-date techniques by the US Army's best instructors, these courses teach military officers and soldiers of third world countries to recreate truth, to manage union leaders, activist clergy, and journalists, and to—"

"Thanks. You've answered my question sufficiently. Do you see the big green binder on the table over there?" He pointed to a book on a table. "Get it, sit down at the table, and take your time reading it," Colonel Hollander instructed.

I did what he asked. Colonel Hollander left me alone while I read the book. Eureka, this was very dull reading. It seemed to be a ledger for the army defense's budget. I continued to read for fifteen minutes and then glanced at my watch when Colonel Hollander returned and reinstated himself into his swivel chair.

"Bring the book to my desk," he ordered. I placed the large green binder on his desk and remained standing there as he turned the book toward himself and asked, "How far did you read, Lopez?"

"I read to page eighteen."

He opened the book and asked, "What was the defense budget this year?"

"The federally budgeted military expenditure of the United States Department of Defense for fiscal year 1982 was as follows:

Components Funding Change 1981 to 1982

Operations and Maintenance: $41.1 billion plus 4.2 percent
Military Personnel: $26.7 billion plus 4 percent
Procurement: $21.2 billion minus 1.8 percent
Research, Development, Testing, and Evaluation: $4.8 billion plus 0.5 percent

Military Construction: $645 million plus 8.4 percent
Family Housing: $398 million minus 12.5 percent
Total—"

"Okay, Lopez, that's good for now," he cut me off as he picked up the phone. "Hi, JoSam. I have a situation in my office that you might be interested in—now."

I remained standing in front of Colonel Hollander's desk without knowing what was happening. I knew my interview had been much longer than the fifteen minutes that had been allocated for each person in my barracks.

"Do you want me to leave?" I asked.

"You have not been dismissed, Lopez," Colonel Hollander barked.

"I thought other people were waiting their turn for their fifteen-minute interviews," I explained. I really wanted to leave. I needed some wine.

Then I saw a spindled, small man, who was not much taller or heavier than I was, enter. I was ready to dart out. I didn't know why this small, wiry man made me feel uncomfortable. I was tired of this interview. It wasn't so much the way this man, who was in his late sixties, looked, but it was his demeanor that made me want to vanish. He looked like Woody Allen, but I didn't feel like smiling or being congenial as I would have, had Woody been there.

"Lopez, this is JoSam," Colonel Hollander said half-heartedly.

I knew the proper thing to do was to shake his hand but didn't want to touch this man. Because he didn't move forward in greeting, I remained stiff where I stood. Colonel Hollander pulled another chair next to his for JoSam.

When I looked at these two men and compared them, I saw an American eagle nesting with a bat-winged gargoyle. The contrast between Colonel Hollander and JoSam was significant.

The colonel donned a military sand-colored uniform complete with colonel insignia, which magnified his heroic Clint Eastwood demeanor while JoSam wore no uniform, and his clothing looked turista. (Spanish slang meaning boastful tourist). He wore tasteful, light blue, Bermuda shorts with a tropical shirt printed in a variable range of blues. His shoes were expensive Italian, light tan loafers, which he wore without socks. His legs were slick with the sheen of suntan oil. I imagined Woody Allen as a flying beast in a bad science fiction movie.

The Colonel's eyes were a steady steel blue. They reflected trustworthiness and confidence while JoSam's eyes shifted, darted, and penetrated into my skull, which sent cold shivers into me even on this hot day.

JoSam was pinkish-red in color. His hair was flouncy, curly, and a reddish color that matched his freckled skin. He didn't sit in the chair but pulled both knees up, placed his feet onto the seat, and rested his face upon his knees.

He stared at me. I stared stubbornly right back at him. I think I might have been glaring. I knew how to play this game of stare down because I had done it with my classmates and friends. I never looked away first or blinked. I thought, *I can stare you down, you beastly creature.*

I could feel little rivers of sweat running down my back under my far-too-warm clothing. This Woody Allen beast in his hunkered position resembled something inhuman. I wanted to leave, but I didn't blink or look away. I craved a glass of wine.

Colonel Hollander reached for the big green binder and flipped through the pages and said, "Lopez." I jumped at the sound of my name. "What was the military budget of the United States in 1983?" he asked. I was so distracted by the JoSam's entrance and my staring down of him, I had forgotten the purpose of this green binder task. I stood there and stared back at JoSam.

"Lopez, did you hear the question?"

"Yes, sir." I reluctantly broke my stare, even though I had been on my way to victory, and looked in the colonel's direction. "What page was that on?" I asked.

Colonel Hollander glanced down at the page and answered, "Page ten."

"Thank you. The military budget of the United States in 1983 was as follows:

Entity 1983 Budget Request Percentage of Total Notes

Army: $122.4 billion; 41.8 percent; in 1983, $10,175,105,015 billion was paid to retire soldiers and survivors, which was about 6.9 percent of the total army budget.
Navy: $69.4 billion; 25.2 percent, excluding the Marine Corps
Marine Corps: $33.4 billion; 10 percent of total budget taken; allotted from the Department of Navy
Air Force: $80.8 billion; 33.0 percent
Defense Intelligence: $40.1 billion; 13.3 percent; Because of its classified nature, the budget is an estimate, and actual figures may not be actual.
Defense-Wide Joint Activities: $65.2 billion; 22.8 percent.

"That's enough, Lopez," the colonel commanded. "Do you want to hear anything else?" he asked JoSam.

"Yeah, I would. Do you have that book of poetry I left on your desk the other day?" JoSam asked.

"Yes, sir. I do. It's in that bottom drawer by you," Colonel Hollander replied.

JoSam fumbled around in the bottom drawer of the desk and brought out an old, faded, blue book. He flipped through the pages and began reading a poem. I had trouble listening to this red, little beast's scratchy voice, which sounded like the squawks of a parrot learning to talk or the cracking voice of a boy during puberty. I needed some wine. When JoSam finished reading, he asked, "Tell me, what did that mean to you?"

I paraphrased. "It meant someone was angry and capable of killing anyone to express himself."

"Do you like poems? Do you like this poem?" JoSam asked.

"I like some poems, but I didn't like this one very much."

"Do you know this poem?" he asked.

"No, but If I could read it myself, I would know it," I said.

"Fine," he said as he handed me the book. "Go ahead and read it out loud."

"*Poems* by Nicola." My eyes scanned down through the titles of the poems: "At Night," "Agonize," "Smash You," "Blood Crusted." I began to read the poem titled "The Gates into Hell" out loud as both men listened.

When I finished reading it, JoSam asked, "Now do you know it?" he removed the poetry book from my hands and handed it to Colonel Hollander.

"Yes, now I know it."

"Go ahead and prove yourself," JoSam smirked.

Eureka! My teacher with the Renault, wouldn't like me to know this poem. I began to repeat what I had just read in the 648 lines of poetry:

> I'll choke you until your last cough
> And push your face in the mud.
> I'm going to rip your head off
> And write your name in the blood.

I was perfectly verbalizing this long, gruesome poem when JoSam interrupted. "That's plenty, Lopez," JoSam said as he stood up. "Put him into my fraternity, colonel."

"His father enrolled him in the cadet course."

"We can work it out," JoSam retorted.

JoSam tossed the book of poetry to me and said, "Keep it, Lopez. We use this book as a textbook in my class. Remember the words of the poem 'I Tolerate No Betrayal.' Be in my classroom, room number 666, tomorrow at 0800 hours sharp." JoSam left the office, but I remained standing in front of the colonel's desk.

"You can go now, Lopez," the colonel said. I went out into the hall where another candidate waited. Recruits must have been taken into other offices for their fifteen-minute interviews because I saw that the man who was now waiting was near the end of the alphabet.

"What happened? What took you so long? What's with the book in your hand?" he questioned.

I shrugged my shoulders and said as Levino had said to me, "Stand in front of his desk until he tells you to move." The next candidate nodded his head and accepted my words.

CHAPTER 5

BEWILDERED

I wasn't sure where the cafeteria was, but my hunger and need for wine propelled the correct direction like a homing pigeon. When I entered the cafeteria, a GI greeted me at the door and asked, "What's your division?"

"I was placed in JoSam's division less than ten minutes ago," I said.

"Are you sure about that? I need to check the enrollment list. What is your name?" the GI asked.

"Angelo Orlando Andres Lopez," I said.

The GI greeter looked through a stack of papers and said, "Well, you sure as hell are. There it is. Who would have guessed? Come on. I'll show you where you're supposed to sit."

As I followed the GI through the cafeteria where men were eating at long tables, I could see that they were not drinking any liquor. He showed me into a room that had red carpet, rosewood paneling on the walls, and was peaceful. The small tables, which sat four people, had black tablecloths, matching napkins, and place cards with names written on them in gold holders.

I was surprised to see a place card with my name on it; only fifteen minutes had elapsed since my interview. Some of the other fifteen tables had two or three people already eating at them, but I was the first person at mine. I needed a drink badly and was hungry. I hoped I didn't need to wait for the others to arrive.

"The other people at your table have been detained, and you will be served without them," the GI said, as if he had read my mind.

"Thanks."

A waiter arrived and served a glass of cool, fragrant, delicious, red wine that I needed desperately. I drained my glass and held it out for a refill. The waiter obliged.

"You won't be able to have another refill, so you had better make it last. If you noticed, there is no wine being served in the cafeteria. How old are you anyway? I don't know if I should serve you wine at all except I know that people from Central America have wine for dinner," he said.

"Wine for lunch and breakfast too," I said.

An older woman brought a plate of food, and the GI was kind enough to top off my wine glass again. "Enjoy your dinner," she said.

Eureka, I had never seen such a plate of food. Our family was wealthy, but the cut of beef on my plate could have fed a family of six. It was the most succulent piece of meat I had ever eaten. The size of the cut was at least ten inches in diameter and two inches thick. It had been hickory smoked to medium rare. It was served with a side of scalloped potatoes, green beans, and garlic toast. I didn't think I would miss Costa Rican food after all. I was glad no one else had sat at my table because I wanted to devour this heavenly food without thinking about manners. My mother would have made me leave the table for eating like this.

The waitress returned and asked if I would like a piece of key lime pie for dessert. I saved the last of my wine to have before I returned to the barracks. The beautiful key lime pie arrived and was quickly consumed. I had just finished the last of my wine when the GI returned and refilled my glass for the fourth time. I drank it more slowly and believed that it would keep me through the night.

I hadn't been aware of my dining surroundings or the other men in the room because my focus on the wine and the food had been such a driving force. On my way out of the main cafeteria, I noticed what everyone else was eating. They seemed to be eating regular American food. They had been served fried chicken, mashed potatoes, and corn casserole. I wondered if my extra-special dinner with wine would disappear in the days to come.

I walked back to the barracks alone. I tried to sort through the interview and what it meant. Even if these extra privileges ended tomorrow, I knew I had enjoyed that satisfying meal and that I was content with the extra wine.

There was a note taped to the top of the locker, which read, "You have been moved into JoSam's division and will be sleeping in building number six." I looked at the map they had provided me with. Building number six was not that far away, so I walked to my new sleeping quarters. I was baffled by what all of this meant.

I arrived at building six and was surprised by its elegance. It was a white, southern, plantation-style house, which was typical of homes I had seen in pictures. In the grand, marbled entryway, a directory listed names and room numbers. I found that my name had been assigned to room number seven. I opened the door with the key that had been provided and found my clothes hanging neatly in the closet of my own private room.

Eureka! I had my own private quarters. My Mom would have loved this room, which was not large but was completed with my own bathroom. It had big casement windows, which had been cranked open to catch the evening breeze. The room was white with dark wooden baseboards and crown moldings. The navy blue duvet looked good with the linens and towels, which were of a lighter contrasted blue. The floor was made of light colored hardwood. The bed had a dark hand-carved southern style headboard. I think it was an American antique.

There was a desk equipped with a reading lamp and the very first computer I had ever seen. I was excited to see the computer but was also tired. I didn't even need to unpack because it had already been done for me. I took a long, pleasant, cool shower and went to bed. I couldn't believe how special I felt at the School of the Americas.

CHAPTER 6
ADDICTION

During the night, I suffered from alcohol withdrawal symptoms. I knew I was sick but didn't know the cause. The four glasses of wine from dinner didn't quell the required alcohol need my body had known since it was nine years old. I thought it was the previous night's rich dinner, which I had consumed before bed. I sweated profusely, even though the night's breeze had cooled the room from the day's high temperatures, and the crisp, navy blue sheets were no longer fresh. I was burning up with heat, and my body jerked, writhed, shivered, and quaked. I was hot and cold at the same time.

I was badly dehydrated and tried to drink as much water as I could keep down, but my stomach rejected it and caused me to vomit repeatedly. The thought of eating breakfast was out of the question. I trembled my way into the shower, barely aware of the cold water that cascaded over my shaking limbs. The words from Nicola's poem, which JoSam had had me read yesterday, filled my mind.

I tolerate no betrayal;
No tarnished loyalty.
If my trust in you does fail,
You die like dethroned royalty.

The poem propelled my energies forward. I had to get dressed and find the classroom. I picked up my map in hopes that my eyes could focus long enough to read it. The classroom number was 666 in building number six. My bedroom was in building number six! All I needed to do was to go upstairs to the sixth floor. I would make it.

I fumbled through my well-organized closet, removed a light-weight pair of blue pants, and grabbed a white T-shirt and loafers. I reached out for the sides of the doorway for support as I left my bedroom and groped my way down the hallway walls. I pushed the elevator button, the doors opened, and I stepped in and held onto the railing.

The elevator was lined with mirrors, and I glanced at myself. I looked really sick. My hair was wet and matted from the shower. I ran my hands through it and tried to comb it into place. I adjusted my T-shirt. My skin looked gray, so I pinched my cheeks the way my sisters had to give myself a healthier looking complexion. By the time the elevator arrived at the sixth floor, I looked a little bit better. I found room 666. I reached JoSam's class by 8:00 a.m. The door was open, and I entered.

The room was arranged in a semicircle around a lectern. The chairs were overstuffed, made of soft fabric, and staggered in rows of four. I dropped into the first available chair closest to the door and farthest away from the speaker's stand. The deep-cushioned chair hid my shaking body from view.

Men in their early thirties to men in their later years sat in the chairs. Some of the men were in their countries' uniforms. Some talked to each other. I didn't care. I felt retched and rested my head on my arms which were supported by the rounded curve of the dark blue padded chair. I wanted to be left alone and hoped I could get through JoSam's class. My awareness was fuzzy, and I was nauseous. I closed my eyes and rested until class began.

When I opened my eyes again, all the chairs were filled, and a door at the front of the room opened. The small, red, gargoyle, JoSam, entered. My San Jose, Costa Rica, school days etiquette kicked into gear, and I promptly pushed myself up with the help of the chair's arms. Other men in the room saw me do this gesture of respect. They also stood while JoSam walked into the room and took his place at the stand. This gesture of respect pleased him. Once he was positioned at the stand, I fell back into my chair, and the other men repositioned themselves and were ready for the lecture. JoSam began speaking.

CHAPTER 7

THE SCHOOL OF
THE AMERICAS

"Good morning. My name is Joseph Samuel Blake. You may address me as JoSam. I have no rank or title. I began my career when I was nineteen and developed it into a fifty-year career. I am a world renowned strategist. I hold classes and seminars for many groups all over our planet, and today, I have the privilege of addressing Central America. Our goals are simple.

"1. We are engaged in a plan involving world infiltration. Infiltration is how we will survive. As you have experienced, all your countries are led by people who have big egos, are greedy, and have undeveloped, unsophisticated minds. They continually sink their countries into chaos, poverty, disease, debt, and corruption. Each country becomes a mess of bickering politics without any resolution. Each thinks its narrow, egocentric strategy is correct. This point is exemplified and labeled as Democrat, Republican, Conservative,

Liberal, Communist, or Socialist. We know it is all pointless and futile. We plan to unplug ourselves from this deadly current of electricity."

"2 Our courses teach military officers and soldiers to subvert the truth, to muzzle union leaders, activist clergy people, and journalists, and to make discord and dissonance within countries to cause internal wars. Third world countries—your countries—are our easiest targets because they naturally suffer the most unrest.

"3 It is our goal to promote our countries' military relationships, to harmonize with each other, to serve the naturally gifted and naturally selected men who have great abilities."

"Today, every country continues in a downward spiral with each new political successor. In the future, we will have entire blocks of countries crumbling into financial indebtedness together. Europe, in years to come, will bind together as one unit with one currency and one trading market, erasing country boundaries for better business. However, it will sink into financial ruin, destroying itself country by country, with artistic, culturally rich Greece being one of the first to become bankrupt, followed by Spain, Poland, Holland, and so on. Germany and France will be the last countries to go. Perhaps the Scandinavian countries will be able to save themselves. Bickering groups of people are all over the world and have not progressed."

"Each one of you sitting in this room today is special and unique. You possess a unique gift that needs to be shared. You therefore will be treated differently from the common ranks of uniformed men, who exhibit their rank of commonality. You will dress as you want, be served the best and healthiest food available in our fine dining halls, and sleep with comfort and ease because you are all the rare jewels of our planet. Because you are rare, you will conduct yourselves in a manner of royalty. You aren't of the common class and shall not associate yourselves with commoners. This is who you are as an individual."

"This group makes up a very special force. You are not a unit, a division, or a company. You are a special, forceful *fraternity*—an order of the gifted man. During this three-month course, you will learn to accept your own uniqueness. You will discover and use the gifts from others to your own advantage. You will learn to work together as a refined, highly efficient, highly technical, creative, precious, and secret machine."

"This secret machine will work even after you have finished the course and have returned to your own countries. Our privately funded fraternity can be found in most countries. We will eventually be established throughout Asia, the Far East, the Middle East, the northern hemisphere, and the western hemisphere. Today you are the representatives of Central America. You will take home the knowledge from our fraternity to run your country as you envision."

"Tell me, Mr. Angelo Lopez, do you remember, from the manual, how the school was founded?" Jo Sam asked:

I was startled at being addressed but pulled myself together and promptly answered. "Yes, sir. The School of the Americas was founded by the United States in 1946. The school was initially located in Panama but was relocated to the army base at Fort Benning, Georgia, in 1980 because of the Panama Canal Treaty. The president of Panama requested its relocation because of Panamanian politics—"

"That is what the manual stated. Now I will tell you the rest of the truth. The school was kicked out of Panama—*kicked out* because they feared what we taught," JoSam forcefully interrupted.

When JoSam asked me another question, I shook as I tried to stand. "What was the distribution of graduates? Do you know, Lopez?"

"Yes," I responded as I attempted to control my shaking limbs. "Argentina: 931; Bolivi: 4,049; Brazil: 355; Chile: 2,405; Colombia: 8,679; Costa Rica: 2,376; the Dominican Republic: 2,330; Ecuador: 2,356; El Salvador: 6,776; Guatemala: 1,676; Honduras: 3,691; Nicaragua: 4,6693; Panama: 4,235; Paraguay: 1,084; Peru: 3,997—"

My shaking grew stronger, and I heard one of the men whisper near me, "Oh look, I think the kid has stage fright."

I continued. "Peru: 3,997; Uruguay: 931; and Venezuela: 3,250."

"That's right," JoSam said. "When our students returned to their home countries, graduates of the school held a special and unique ..." I continued to shake and grabbed the arm of the chair for support as I tried to remain standing. "Lopez, are you all right?" JoSam asked.

"No, Sir. I am not feeling well," I said as I sank back into the chair.

"Colonel Montt and Montgomery Summers, you two get him to the infirmary! Stay with him until he has been diagnosed and return to me with a full medical report," JoSam commanded. The two men took me by the arms, lifted me from the chair, and supported my shaking body as we left the room and then the building.

"Hang in there, kid. I have a car in the parking lot, and we will drive you to the finest doctor in the United States," Montgomery Summers assured me.

"You did a good job of learning the manual I gave you on the bus, huh, kid? Your study paid off, and now JoSam used you to teach the class. Very impressive," Colonel Montt said smugly.

"Thanks for the manual," I replied.

"Don't need any thanks," Colonel Montt mocked.

I didn't remember much about the ride to the infirmary because I felt bad. I recollected that I rode in the back seat while Montgomery Summers drove.

"This is Angelo Orlando Andres Lopez," Colonel Montt told the nurse. "He is from JoSam's division."

"JoSam's fraternity," corrected Summers.

"Oh, right! We have directions to wait here at the hospital for Lopez's medical report," Colonel Montt asserted.

"You may go to the waiting room. I will take it from here," snapped the nurse.

Inside the doctor's office, I was immediately given a complete medical exam, with blood, urine, and saliva tests. My blood pressure was taken, and my heart was monitored. Then I lay down on a gurney where an IV needle was put into my arm. This all happened quickly and was indicative of an emergency room that was experienced in responding to war injuries.

"We gave you benzodiazepines interveniously to relive your withdrawal symptoms and reduce the risk of seizures. You just lay quietly now, and in a few minutes, you should start to feel better," Dr. Andrews explained.

What a relief! I closed my eyes against the bright lights and enjoyed a more controlled body returning as the liquid dripped into my arm. After fifteen minutes, Dr. Andrews, who seemed like a parish priest in his mid-sixties, returned and asked, "How are you feeling?"

"So much better. Thank you for helping me," I replied.

"That's good. How old are you, Lopez?"

"I just turned seventeen," I said as I lay on the gurney with the hanging bag.

"Okay, son. I'm going to give this to you straight. You are an alcoholic, and you are suffering from withdrawal. We are treating you as an outpatient and will give you a supply of medicine for four days. You should be able to return to your classes and to perform normally, but you will still have cravings for liquor. Under *no circumstances* are you to consume any alcohol: no beer, no wine, no cocktails—*nothing*. This medication is sensitive, and when mixed with alcohol, it can be fatal. Do you understand?" asked Dr. Andrews.

"Yes."

"You may suffer irritability, agitation, and mood swings. You may experience great hunger. Go ahead and eat. We will deal with your weight gain later. One of the great dangers with alcohol is that it kills brain cells. You are too young to waste your opportunity for an education because liquor has killed your ability to learn. You will be sent home with diazepam that you will need to take every two hours. Take your medicine strictly as directed and make an appointment with the nurse to return in four days. This won't be easy, son, but we will do our best to help."

"You will also be enrolled in AA. We made an appointment for you to attend. They will schedule your meetings through JoSam. He will tell you what classes to take that will work around the AA meetings. Do you have any questions?" Dr. Andrews asked as he removed the bag of liquid going into my arm.

I sat up and felt like I had returned to normalcy. "What is AA?" I asked.

Dr. Andrews looked surprised and answered, "It's an organization called Alcoholics Anonymous, and they have experience in helping people deal with their dependence on liquor. Have an early and long lunch with your two friends, and you should be fine to attend your regular afternoon classes."

"How do I pay for your services?" I asked.

Dr. Andrews smiled and replied, "JoSam pays for everything."

I walked into the waiting room and saw my new friends. What a secure feeling I had knowing they were waiting for me.

"How are you feeling, Lopez?" asked Montgomery Summers.

"Almost normal, but I am hungry because I missed breakfast this morning."

"We were told to take you to lunch and to stay with you until our next class. First we have to take your medical report back to JoSam's office," said Colonel Montt.

"I feel much better. I can find my own way to the cafeteria."

"We are used to doing what we are told. That's what the Guatemalan army does to you. We will drive you back to JoSam and then walk you over to lunch," Colonel Montt demanded.

"I'm sorry you guys missed the rest of JoSam's class."

"Are you kidding me? JoSam asked us to take you because we already heard his lecture," amended Montgomery Summers.

CHAPTER 8
NEW FRIENDS

Montgomery Summers looked like an American. Besides being strikingly good-looking, he had thick, wavy, blond hair, big blue eyes, and angular facial features with dimples. He also had a slow, easy smile that revealed his perfectly sculptured, white, shining teeth. He was exceptionally tall and muscular. I think girls liked the way Montgomery looked.

When we arrived at building number six, Montgomery ran the medical report upstairs to JoSam's office while Colonel Montt and I waited on the front steps. When Montgomery came back, he was accompanied by JoSam. The four of us walked to the cafeteria.

"I see you're feeling better. I hope you stay that way," JoSam remarked.

"Thank you. I don't like being sick and intend to stay healthy."

When the four of us entered the big room of the cafeteria while in route to our private dining room, heads turned and watched us parade through. I now had friends who were grown, respected men, unlike the ones from my childhood, whose friendship I had to buy.

When we got to our dining room, Colonel Montt and JoSam went to their designated table. I went to the table that had had my name card on it the night before and noticed that Montgomery Summers was following me. He had been assigned to my table. I was pleased to have someone to talk with during lunch.

"I am glad to have you at my table, Montgomery."

"It is no random happening, Lopez. You will learn that everything in our lives happens by JoSam's design."

The GI waiter from the night before approached our table with a full glass of wine.

"I have your wine, Mr. Lopez."

"Oh, no thank you. I will have a glass of lemonade."

The waiter whisked away the wine and asked, "What will you be drinking at lunch, Mr. Summers?"

"I'd love sweet tea," he said in his Georgian southern drawl.

"What did you mean our lives happen by design?"

"Lopez, you might not have heard JoSam say in the morning lecture that he is a strategist. He designs everything down to the minute detail. We were meant to become acquainted for some reason. I don't know why yet, but perhaps it is for social reasons or that we both have skills to share with each other on some future mission. Hell, I don't know! JoSam is an extraordinary strategist. His plans extend so far into the future, only he understands them. He orchestrates the whole show. We are gifted puppets on his strings. This doesn't stop us from controlling our own destinies, but after you have spent more time here, you will realize the many personal benefits you get by sticking with his classes."

"Look at the changes he has given to you in just one day. You have wonderful food, great sleeping quarters, and a chance to improve your health and to change the course of your life. You are lucky, Lopez. I am twenty-seven years old, and it wasn't until last year that he invited me out of the ranks of the enlisted infantry to take his course."

"How long were you in the infantry?"

"A year and six months, and I don't know why I was invited to join the fraternity. I think it is because of something that happened when I was on maneuvers with my unit. Anyway, it's a long story."

"Do you mind answering some questions? I don't understand anything that goes on around here."

"Not at all, Angelo. We'll get to know each other because we want to and not because JoSam has designed it. I take the infiltration class. The way it works is that a student studies one class all day for three months. Then he chooses another class or goes back to his country. We have special teachers for each subject who are astoundingly knowledgeable and have practical experience. I haven't been disappointed with any teacher I have had so far," he explained.

Our dinner salads arrived, and we continued our conversation. "When you finish the infiltration class, what other class will you take?" I asked.

With a mouth full of salad he answered, "Infiltration."

"I thought you said you are taking that class now."

"Yeah, you got it right. I am studying corporate infiltration. My first class was on general infiltration. Next I will take communications infiltration, weather infiltration, transportation infiltration, military infiltration, media infiltration, education infiltration, religious infiltration, and when I finish all that, because our societies change so rapidly, there will be more classes to take."

"Did you say weather infiltration?"

"Yeah, I did. We have newly invented equipment that we will use to create natural disasters. What could be more efficient than wiping out a country's economy with a single storm, seeding the clouds for more rain over a country that is prone to landslides and flooding, or causing clouds to evaporate and provoke drought in countries already suffering from dry, desert conditions. This is the latest science, and we have been experimenting."

"I just don't get it, Montgomery. You are an American, right? What will you do with all this infiltration education?"

"I will be paid a *big* buck's salary working for the FBI, CIA, National Security Association (NSA), or for JoSam's Fraternity, if he offers me a position. I will also have the option of being an FAO (Foreign Area Officer). I can start an operation to infiltrate any county, depending on who is hiring. I am receiving a great education, all at the expense of the good old US of A. The School of the Americas is funded with American tax dollars," Montgomery explained spiritedly. I remembered the budget report Colonel Hollander had me read in his office and now understand why the army's budget was so large.

Our anticipated lunch arrived. We ate soft-shelled, blue crab, scalloped potatoes, a side of broccoli, another side of seasoned green beans, and a big basket of corn muffins with creamed butter and a flask of maple syrup. We both ate heartily.

"Why did you choose infiltrations, Montgomery?"

"JoSam recommended it. Maybe he saw a future for me. Hell, I don't know. These classes are stimulating, and I have excelled with honors. I love this field."

"Montgomery, what do you think JoSam has in mind for me?"

"Lopez, only you will be able to answer that in time. I can only give you my narrow opinion based on one day's observation. I should keep my mouth shut, but I think he will groom you as his successor. You are seventeen. He can spend more time in his position if he relegates more of his workload to you. After five to seven years as his apprentice and with your natural maturation, I believe he will use you to replace himself if you stick with him."

"I want to confide in you Montgomery. I don't think I like him very much," I said in a whisper. Montgomery laughed out loud.

"Lopez, nobody likes him very much. He isn't likable."

I looked at my watch and saw that I had a half an hour before I could take another pill. I craved a glass of wine. I asked, "Are you going to eat those remaining muffins?"

"No thanks, Angelo. I'm full." He pushed the basket in my direction. "Please finish them up. Anytime you want more of anything, the dining staff will bring what you request."

"Do they always bring dessert?"

"Always," he assured me.

I ate the remaining muffins with the butter and flask of syrup. Then I asked, "I read in the manual that the school taught torture. Will you take that class?" I asked.

"I don't think I have an interest in that. I would rather be involved mentally doing problem solving than be physically involved. I have talked to some of our American GIs who took the class, and they claimed there was a psychology involved in applying the right torture for the correct personality," he stated.

The waiter arrived with a large tray of desserts to choose from. I chose a big piece of chocolate cake with fudge icing.

"What tortures are taught? Do they use live people to practice on?"

"They use horrible methods straight from the torture chambers of medieval days. Let's not talk about this stuff during lunch," he said.

When I had finished the cake, JoSam, Colonel Montt, Montgomery, and I walked back to building number six together. I went back to my room to take my medication in private, only to discover, I had left my key inside the room that morning and was locked out. JoSam and Colonel Montt had continued up the stairs to class.

"Montgomery, where would I go to get another key for my room?"

"I'll open it for you."

"Does your key open my door?"

"No," was all he said as he stepped up to the door, closed his eyes, ran his hand over the plate behind the door knob, did it again, twisted the knob a tiny bit this way and that, and then suddenly twisted the knob twice to the right jerkily. The door's lock released, and the door opened.

"How did you do that? I can't believe you did that!"

Montgomery gave me a coy smile and said, "I'm in *infiltration*, remember?"

"Did you learn to do that in your classes?" I asked.

"Only partially. I have an acute sense of touch. With this lock, I felt vibrations coming from one metal rubbing against another, sensed the tripping mechanism's device, and knew what pressure would release it. Nothing special."

"I once opened a door with a girl's hairpin, but you didn't use anything. Can you open any lock?"

"There haven't been any so far I couldn't open, but who knows, maybe there are new locks that have been made that l need to learn about. I do vehicles too. They are fun because makes and models are all different. Combination locks are the easiest. I can really feel the tumblers. Not only can I feel them, but I can hear them. Never use a combination lock if you need something kept safe," he said.

"I think I have a new name for you. I will call you The Key," I said.

"You'd better not, or I will retaliate and call you a Kodak, Country, Catholic, Cunt Kisser. I'll see you upstairs."

CHAPTER 9
SPECIAL GROOMING

I went into my room, took my pill, grabbed my key, shut the door, and climbed the stairs rather than taking the elevator. I assessed how I felt, which was surprisingly good. In room 666, nearly everyone had returned, and I found that the same chair I had been sitting in during the morning's session was vacant, so I took my place and waited for the teacher with the others. JoSam again entered from the front of the room. I sprang up, and the rest of the class was much quicker to stand this time. JoSam looked in my direction and gave a slight nod. I nodded back in return.

The afternoon session consisted of the distribution of individual schedules and the book of poems that I had already received and listening to an introductory speech from each member of the class. I became aware that there were four more Americans besides Montgomery who were taking the infiltration class. Three men were taking communications infiltration while one man besides Montgomery was taking corporation infiltration.

A few students were studying psychological warfare, but the

most popular class seemed to be the one on counterinsurgency and irregular warfare, which was the class Colonel Jose Efrain Rios Montt was taking. When it was my turn, I reported that my curriculum was yet to be determined because I didn't see the need to report that my only class so far was AA.

"Would you help distribute this stationary and these envelopes to everyone, Angelo?" JoSam asked.

I went to the podium, took the stack of paper and envelopes, and distributed them. As I did this task, many of the men told me they were glad to see me feeling better. When I handed the paper to Montgomery, he gave me a thumbs-up and said, "I think I may be right about your destiny." I shrugged and plopped back into my chair as JoSam gave the next assignment.

"I want each of you to write a letter to someone from your home country. It can be your parents, wife, girlfriend, friends, or anyone else you choose. Address the envelope with your choice. These letters will be written each Friday, and I shall mail them. When you finish, put your letters in this box. There should be forty letters. This letter writing is mandatory. This project concludes today's class."

I addressed the envelope to my father, carefully folded an empty sheet of paper, inserted it inside and sealed the envelope, placed it in the box, and went outside to sit on the front steps to wait for Montgomery. When he came outside, I walked with him and asked, "What is the letter-writing exercise all about?"

"Think about it, Lopez. JoSam is a strategist! What better way to get personal information about his students' private lives than this letter-writing scheme taking place every Friday. He learns about all the class members' lives just by reading the names and addresses on the envelopes. He needs to thoroughly know his students and their potential military, social, political, and business connections. It is very clever, if you ask me. Kid, I am on my way to our frat cocktail hour. I would invite you to go with me, but I know you aren't feeling all that great. I'll see you at dinner," he said as he quickened his steps and cut across the plaza.

I wanted a drink badly and knew that being alone was the better choice for me. I didn't want to betray JoSam or to mess up this opportunity he had given me. I wondered if Montgomery knew what my medical report had said. It was time to go to my room for another pill anyway, and then I would explore the base on my own until dinnertime.

My walk around the base helped me with my addictive cravings. I found a well-stocked library, a military museum, and a cool gym and pool complex. I had entered the pool area just to look around when the pool attendant, Sergio Rodriguez (on his name tag), welcomed me.

"You came to swim today?"

"No, not today. I am just looking at your facility. This is a very large pool."

"Yeah, it is an Olympic-sized pool. We have another pool, but it is reserved for our special division," he informed me.

"What division is that?" I asked.

"It is only to be used by fraternity members on the base."

"May I see that pool?"

"Sorry, son, it is a private fraternity."

"I think I may be a part of the fraternity."

"He laughed and said, "Good try son, but that fraternity is an older men's club," he explained.

"Do you have a roster with the names of those who can enter?"

"Sure do, and I look for the name *plus* an ID."

I gave him my name, and he found it on the roster. "Well, yeah, but let's see some ID," he demanded. I showed him, but he was still doubtful.

"Do you want to see the pool?"

"Yes, please, and may I also see the gym?"

This pool was smaller but far more elegant with small tables, chairs, complimentary white towels and robes, and private rooms for massage. The facility looked very inviting, but I was feeling a little rough and restless. I walked into the gym and looked around. It had many workout machines lined up along the walls of the air-conditioned room, which also had an indoor track.

"Thanks for showing me. It looks like a guy can get buff in this place. I'll be back to swim another day."

"I'd like to see that happen," Sergio said as if he thought I was a sight-seeing tourist and not a member of JoSam's fraternity, but I knew that Sergio and I would soon be friends.

I walked a bit further and found the military museum. I didn't go in but would explore it when I had more time. For now, I wanted to go back to my room and see if I could make the computer work. What a gift this highly technological invention was, and it was in my own room. I thought I'd learn a great deal from the School of the Americas.

At dinner and for the first time, all the chairs were filled at my table for four. Montgomery, his two friends David Allen and Russ Warren, and I were there. David Allen had a burly-bear build, a beard, and voluminous, dark, curly hair. He was in his forties, was from Minnesota, and spoke very slowly, which I appreciated because my mind still processed words into Spanish. Mr. Allen was over six feet tall with large bones and plenty of flesh to go around.

As a child, my mother had read books about a folk hero named Paul Bunyan and Babe the blue ox. Mr. David Allen reminded me of that character. He wore denim bib overalls and a short-sleeved, plaid shirt, which revealed his farmer's tan and made him seem like he belonged in the country on a farm.

He was the instructor for the communications infiltration class that Montgomery would be taking in the future. They had many common interests and filled our table with conversation while I remained quiet, wanting to grab Russ Warren's glass of wine straight from his hand.

The waiter arrived and asked for our drink order. Montgomery and David Allen ordered a mixed drink while Russ Warren sipped his remaining wine. He ordered a refill when the waiter asked.

"Would you like a glass of wine tonight, Mr. Lopez?"

"No thanks. Sweet tea would be great. When I come here for meals, please do not ask me for my drink order. Just bring me lemonade or sweet tea," I instructed.

"I'll remember your order next time, Mr. Lopez." The other men enjoyed their drink orders while I suffered with my desire.

"Mr. Allen, do you also teach computers?" I asked.

"I teach all the communication infiltration classes and computers. Are you interested in learning to use a computer?" he asked.

"Yes, I am interested in acquiring computer skills. I have an Apple Lisa computer in my room and would like to learn about it," I boasted.

"I would be happy to get you started. What is your course schedule?" he asked.

"I am free the next three days because my course schedule has not yet been determined. I only have one class, each evening, starting on Wednesday. I can use the time I have now to learn, if you can teach me," I suggested.

"Lopez, I don't have a computer in my room. How did you manage that?" Montgomery sputtered.

"It was just there. I didn't ask for it."

Our dinner arrived, and they told me that it was typical Georgian cuisine with southern fried chicken, grits, greens, corn on the cob, and a basket of corn bread.

"I love American food," I said.

"What do Costa Rican people usually eat?" asked Russ Warren, the skinny, shy man who didn't seemed very sociable.

"Costa Rican food is quite bland. Beans and rice are served for every meal. You eat meat if your family is wealthier. We ate mostly beef because my father had a cattle ranch as well as coffee and pineapple plantations, but I never saw a cut of beef like the one I was served the first night I arrived," I said.

"Steak is the American choice. Southern fried chicken is delicious and my choice," Russ Warren declared.

"When we finish our dinner, would you feel like taking your first computer lesson?" David Allen asked.

"Yes. I realize I sound childlike, but I want some dessert," I said.

"Me too," chimed in Montgomery

The dessert tray arrived, and I ordered American apple pie a la mode. The conversation during dessert with these men was natural, easy, and relaxed. When we got ready to leave the dining hall, Montgomery was standing next to the bear-of-a-man, David Allen, but still was at least four inches taller than he was.

"For crying out loud, Montgomery, you are so tall, you can go goose hunting with a rake," David Allen chuckled.

We walked back to building number six. I opened my bedroom door, and David and I approached my Apple Lisa, who waited like a girlfriend. David sat at the desk while I stood beside him and learned. His lesson had been going on for an hour when he said, "For crying out loud, you're a quick learner. Do you think you can remember these procedures? Do you have any questions?" he asked.

"No, I think I have it. I am eager to practice."

"That's good. I'm going up to the card room and joining the others. Do you want to come along?" he asked.

"Sure. I would like to get acquainted with the men." David Allen and I went up to the fourth floor, and I spotted several familiar faces.

"Hey, kid, come join our game," shouted Colonel Montt. "How much money do you have?" he asked as he pulled up a chair for me.

"I have two dollars and seventy-five cents," I replied.

"Okay, guys. The kid has two dollars and seventy-five cents, and it's a dollar a game, so ante up. Let's teach him to play. Do you play poker, kid?" Colonel Montt asked as he winked at his fellow players.

"I'm not sure I know the American rules," I responded as JoSam stepped forward.

"I'll tell you fellows something. If Mr. Lopez wins, I'll enrich the pot by twenty dollars, you must never call him kid again, and you'll refer to him as Mr. Lopez. If he loses, the twenty dollars goes to the winner, who will teach him how to play. Do we have a deal?" demanded JoSam.

JoSam strolled over to our table, laid his twenty in the center, and said to me, "I'm counting on you Mr. Lopez." Then JoSam said as he was leaving the room, "Colonel Montt, limit the ante to a dollar per game so he can at least play twice."

Colonel Montt chuckled and asked, "So what's your game, kid?"

"I don't know. I will play by your house rules," I said as the other men hooted with laughter.

"Okay, the game is on. Let's play seven-card stud high," Colonel Montt said as he shuffled the cards.

"Everybody ante up. Pot's in the middle." I put my dollar on top of JoSam's twenty. That had to be good luck.

Colonel Montt served as dealer. Montgomery Summers, David Allen, and Colonel Hollander pulled up chairs to play at our table. Colonel Montt dealt cards to each of us, starting on his left, which was Montgomery. He put two cards facedown (in the pocket) and one card faceup.

Colonel Montt dealt the cards very slowly, which was a great advantage to me. I was next to the last person to receive cards. He dealt to himself last. Montgomery had a black queen of spades, David Allen had a four of hearts, Colonel Hollander had an eight of hearts, I had an ace of diamonds, and Colonel Montt had a nine of clubs.

We all peeked at our in-the-pocket cards. I had a Jack and a six of diamonds. This was a great beginning.

My mind did the math. I added up the cards that were showing and then divided the numbers by fifty-two. I closely watched the dealt cards. David Allen had the lowest number showing, and he was required to start the bring in.

"You betcha. I will stay with a dime," he said as he dug into his pocket and placed a dime into the pot.

"I'll raise a nickel," Montgomery said as he added his fifteen cents to the pot.

"I'll stay," Colonel Montt said and added his fifteen cents to the pot.

"I will stay also," I said, betting very cautiously and adding my fifteen cents to the center. Colonel Montt dealt the fourth street or turn card face up as I watched and counted. Montgomery received a nine of spades, David Allen got a ten of clubs, Colonel Hollander received a ten of hearts, I received a queen of diamonds, and Colonel Montt dealt himself a nine of hearts. I knew that three queens had been dealt, three nines were out, and two tens were showing. With thirty-two cards remaining in the deck, my chances were looking steady.

"Okay, kid. You are showing highest. What is your bet?" Colonel Montt asked in accented English.

"I'll raise another fifteen cents," I said, tossing my change from the bookstore into the pot.

The second highest person was Colonel Montt with a pair of nines showing. He said, "I'll meet your fifteen cents. You are getting brave, kid," Colonel Montt warned.

"I'm in the game," said Montgomery as he tossed in his fifteen cents.

"Me too," echoed Colonel Hollander, tossing in his coins.

"Things are looking better. I'll stay in too," said David Allen.

"Okay, gentlemen, fifth street, over the river, card face up. Now we'll see what our lady has in mind for us," said Colonel Montt as he dealt the cards. He dealt Montgomery a king of spades. David Allen showed a ten of spades. Colonel Hollander received a three of hearts, I received a ten of diamonds, and Colonel Montt gave himself a six of hearts.

"Ace. Queen of diamonds is highest. Kid, you bet first again," Colonel Montt said.

"I'll go another fifteen cents," I said, tossing in more change.

Colonel Hollander was the next highest bidder with his possible flush. "I'll stay in. Here's my fifteen cents," he said.

"Well, for crying out loud! Mr. Lopez grabbed my chances of three of a kind. I'm folding, dontcha know," said David Allen.

"Here's my fifteen cents just to keep Mr. Lopez honest," teased Colonel Montt. Then he said as he dealt, "The sixth card is faceup, a seven of spade goes to Montgomery, David Allen is out, Colonel Hollander received a five of hearts, [now showing a flush], and what does Mr. Lopez receive? A four of diamonds. The dealer takes a queen of hearts." I bid first, again, since I held a high-ranking position.

"I will bid thirty cents," I said, leaving less than one dollar in my pocket.

"You won't scare me away," Montgomery drawled as he tossed in his thirty cents.

"Me neither. I'm staying," Colonel Hollander said.

"Too many hearts showing for my comfort. I'm folding," said Colonel Montt.

"All right. Three players remaining. Here we go. Last card is down and dirty," continued Colonel Montt as he dealt. Montgomery received his card and peeked at it. Colonel Hollander was given his card, and a small frown appeared on his face. (I saw his tell) I received my card facedown and glanced at it. It was an eight of diamonds.

Eureka! I had received the eight of diamonds. I had just missed a royal straight flush by one card.

"All right, Lopez. What's your bid?" Colonel Montt asked.

"I will bid another thirty cents," I said.

"I'll get a look at your cards for thirty cents," Montgomery dared, tossing in his coins.

"Me too," said Colonel Hollander.

"All right, gentlemen, let's see your cards. Montgomery's got a king, queen, high-spade flush, Colonel Hollander has a jack, ten high-heart flush. Mr. Lopez has an ace, queen, jack, ten, eight-of-diamonds flush. That wins the pot," said Colonel Montt.

"Dontcha know? Mr. Lopez, you just missed a royal straight flush by one card. Good try," complimented David Allen.

I picked up my poker pot and excused myself to go the bathroom so that I could take another pill and also count my winnings, which was twenty-eight dollars and seventy-five cents. Now I could play a little stronger.

"Hey, Mr. Lopez, don't you know it's impolite to stop on a winning hand?" shouted Colonel Montt.

"Yes, I know that, and I am coming back! Shuffle them up Colonel Montt. You could deal and play a little faster. That was a dreadfully slow game."

I was afraid Colonel Hollander might fall asleep," I shouted from the bathroom. The room rang with laughter. When I came back for the second game, six more men had joined our table. We had a full table.

Our table had a new dealer who looked like Howdy Doody. He was Leonardo Romeo Suazo from Honduras (He would be helpful during a Honduras assignment in the future). The game was much faster, and there was no idle conversation. As it became rapid, it was a challenge but also great fun.

I won the second game also. We played many hands for a couple of hours, and I won most of them. Montgomery and David Allen won the games I had lost. The betting was much higher, and instead of fifteen cents a bet, we now bet dollars. The more games we played, the more practice I had counting cards and the faster I played to win more money.

After another two hours, I needed to go to my room to take my pills. I stood to leave, gathered my winnings, and said to Colonel Montt, "I know it is impolite to leave after a winning hand, but tonight, most of my hands were winners, and Lady Luck was kind to me as a beginner. I think we need to play again." The men shook my hand and patted me on the back.

"Glad to have you with us, Mr. Lopez," Colonel Hollander said.

"Please call me Angelo."

David Allen shook my hand and said, "Congratulations, Angelo Lopez. Would you like to continue with your computer lesson tomorrow?"

"Yes, please. I would like to practice and to make sure I learned what you taught me tonight before our next lesson. When would you be able to teach me?"

"I can't come until after dinner. Would that be all right with you?" he asked.

"That would be perfect! It would give me time to be with computer Lisa most of the day."

Everyone went to his room, and Montgomery walked with me down to the first floor. "That was a fun night of cards, Angelo. Do you always play that well?" he asked.

"I play much better, but because I was new, I was nervous, and the pills made me a little groggy. I was glad no one noticed."

"I don't think I want to play against you when you are in top form. See you tomorrow," Montgomery waved.

CHAPTER 10
THE FRATERNITY

I went into my quiet room, feeling a contentment I'd never known before. It wasn't just the three hundred and fifty dollars in my pocket that made me feel good. It was knowing I had carved out a place where I belonged.

Six weeks had passed since I had become a student at the School of the Americas and my introductory card game. I had thirty-six classes of AA under my belt without one single drink and felt mentally more alive than I had with all of my seventeen years combined. I had sent six empty letters to my father.

JoSam had created a special three-year curriculum for me serving as his apprentice. I had yet to learn the true nature of this position. I knew it was far more than teaching and planning the curriculum. I took classes in counterinsurgency, and most of the students referred to these classes as coin classes. I did well in those classes, which involved topics about propaganda, psychological operations (psych ops), and assassinations. This class taught many different facets of military, paramilitary, psychological, economic, political, cultural, and civic actions. I was privileged to receive these classes with an emphasis in communications.

What I liked most about these classes was learning from history about the successes and failures of counterinsurgency, all the way back to the French occupation of Spain during the Napoleonic wars. I studied the counterinsurgency of the Philippine/American War, the Shining Path in Peru, and many more wars ending with Vietnam. There were many counterinsurgency theorists like B. H. Liddell Hart, Santa Cruz de Marcenado, and David Galula, who painted colorful histories of world counterinsurgency.

There were over forty coin classes. My favorite, so far, had been information operations. Public diplomacy within information operations required that a person know the country's culture. I would soon take a test on the cultural traits of Guatemala, which required me to travel there for one week to formalize a list of cultural traits by my own observations. My computer lessons helped me comprise this list.

Six weeks of computer classes from David Allen had resulted in me being able to master the Apple Lisa. Now I was hungry for more expertise to whet my appetite. Speaking of appetite, I had gained over thirty pounds to no fault of the computers. The fault lay in the wonderful, social, eating experiences that our private dining hall afforded.

Montgomery Summers and I had walked to our dining hall for the evening dinner and found that we were the only two who would be occupying our table, which was good. It gave us a chance to discuss our school and its students. Montgomery always talked to me straight. I learned to trust his insights and his experiences.

The waiter brought lemonade and Montgomery's wine. After he left our drinks, I asked Montgomery, "Why does Colonel Jose Efrain Rios Montt act like he resents me?"

Montgomery raised his eyebrows, gave me a faint smile, and

said, "Because he does resent you. Angelo, you proved to be a dyna-
mite poker player, and he continues to lose his money to you. How
much is it now, $3,000? More?"

"Colonel Montt has lost $5,300, but others have lost too and re-
main cheerful, good friends," I countered.

"Colonel Montt is unique, and you need to be cautious when
dealing with him. He is a deadly force to be avoided. It is a compli-
ment that he resents you."

"Yeah, but when we first met on the bus, he gave me the manual
and tips for taking the interview. Why would he resent me now?"

"Angelo, look. You won the favor of the most powerful man,
JoSam. Colonel Montt can't gain the favored limelight you hold. You
have youth, a unique mind, diplomacy, and manners. Your future is
whatever you and JoSam desire it to be."

Montgomery continued to talk about Colonel Montt after our
meal of fresh Maine lobster had arrived at our table. "Don't you see?
Colonel Montt baited you with his helping ways until he realized you
didn't need his help. He would have used you as his errand boy, but
you established yourself as an equal man among us. You occupied
the position he envisioned for himself with JoSam. He is too old to
be considered for a leadership role, but you aren't.

"He doesn't know that JoSam is no one's friend or companion.
They are two individuals cut from the same fabric but with different
styles. JoSam is about elegance, and Colonel Montt is a rough cut."

Montgomery finished his lobster, leaned back in his chair, sipped
his wine, and continued his explanation. "Colonel Montt was trained
by the School of the Americas and educated by the CIA in explosives
and sabotage during the 1960s, after his participation in the Bay of
Pigs invasion. The Inter-American Commission on Human Rights
wants to prosecute him for murder in association with many massacres. Right now, they suspect that he led a genocide in his own country against Mayan natives. His name is on the State Department's

list of gross human rights abusers, but he remains free because he is useful to the USA."

Montgomery ordered another glass of wine with dessert as he continued. "This is the way our wars are conducted today. It is no longer black and white or right and wrong. The lines became diplomatically, politically, and economically blurred. The military is much different from the way our fathers knew it to be. It is about intelligence, counterinsurgency, chemical warfare, and espionage. We have replaced the antique battle positions and strategically placed weapons General MacArthur and Eisenhower knew with intellectual artillery. It is a different game altogether. Our military personnel are strong and fit but most of all, are trained to be smart.

Our future will be a war that uses robots and computers and saves human military lives for other advantages. I know our government had been working on unmanned aircraft, submarines, missiles, and tanks. "Unmanned," he whispered. "Can you get your mind around that?

"We are creating a *Star Wars* military. This is 1982. This is our future, and I am excited to be a part of this era," Montgomery enthusiastically orated.

"I was raised as a strict Catholic and was taught the commandment, 'Thou shalt not kill.'"

"Angelo, in time, you'll get over that. This is our job. We don't want to kill, but it is our occupation to do so. It is our job to kill. We trained to protect our country, and that makes us different."

"I was shocked as I read about what the classes taught, but now I find them interesting—almost fascinating," I explained.

"Yeah, I know what you mean. The school is still very young here in the States, even though it has existed since 1946. Americans don't know what is being taught here, but in time, they will. The school is already controversial among some congressmen who know about it. Several newspapers' have called the school a 'School for

Dictators,' 'School of Assassins,' 'Nursery of Death Squads,' and other names. The statistics show that countries with the worst human rights' records send the most soldiers to our school."

"Montgomery, how do you feel about this school?" I asked.

"This is what *new war* is all about, baby. We adjust to our changing times. I learn cutting-edge warfare, the school treats me well, and I am challenged mentally and conditioned physically. I am respected among my peers and enjoy wine, lobster, and good friends at dinner! What more do I need for happiness?"

"Maybe a girlfriend," I said as Montgomery laughed out loud.

"Oh, yeah. Plenty of that awaits wherever I go."

An approaching soldier interrupted the eating of my almond, chocolate dessert. "Mr. Lopez?"

I looked up in surprise. "Yes," I answered.

"When you're finished with dinner, a visitor is waiting for you in the conference room of building number six. I told him that you would arrive in a few minutes," said the soldier.

"Who is it?"

"It isn't my job to inquire," he responded.

I finished my desert, excused myself from the table, and walked to the conference room of building number six, which was my building, my bedroom, my card game room, and my new home and school. I thought about how contented I was and whom the visitor might be as I walked up two flights of stairs and into the red-carpeted, walnut-paneled room with large bay windows, which allowed the evening breeze and setting sun to stream into the room.

I caught sight of the waiting man and gasped in surprise. "Dad, what are you doing here?"

"Hello, son," Giovanni Orlando Andres Zuniga said in greeting.

We both stood awkwardly, in the middle of the conference room, in complete silence, not knowing what to do or to say. Neither one of us stepped forward to offer the traditional tico greeting nor to even shake hands. I didn't think he wanted to show affection, and I knew I surely didn't want to be amiable. The fact was that I resented his presence and that he had interrupted my new life.

"Son, I am surprised to see how tall you have grown in the last month and a half, and you have gained at least twenty pounds," he said as he attempted to diminish the tenseness. I stood defiantly and remained silent.

"Angelo, I came to apologize and to ask for understanding about the terrible mistake I made in sending you to this school. This way of life is not what your mother or I wanted for your future. My friend Oscar Andres Arias Santanez, the Social Democratic Minister of Planning of Costa Rica and whose picture I saw hanging in the school's hall of fame, recommended this school. Later, I discovered the school's tyrannical intent of teaching men to become rebels and terrorists. Why would a school exist to cause world turmoil and hatred?" he asked.

During my continued silence, I was aware of the love and gentleness my dad was showing to me. I never thought my father was capable of such feelings. My observations of men's emotions were now wiser because of my training courses. I saw a man who stood before me, wanted to control my talent and my spirit of self-direction, and used warm emotions to gain his ground. I was also aware of how much older and fragile my father looked. Maybe he was tired from the airplane trip. I wasn't caving into this old approach of offered kindness. I was seventeen and now a man who could determine his own life.

"The school is being deceptive by being under the US government because it is a country known for being concerned with human rights. Something is very wrong, and I want to take you back to Costa Rica with me to erase the past. We can find a new direction for us. I reach out to you, Angelo, to make amends," he said.

"I am staying here. This is where I belong."

"You most certainly do not belong here, and I will not pay any more money for this subversive type of education. Please, Angelo, I am begging you to come home. I promised your mother I would bring you home."

"Well, you have lied to Mother," I challenged.

"The School of the Americas will turn you out when I stop paying your tuition. You should get your clothes and come home with me now."

"I can make my own way. I don't need your money. I have over $12,000 in a savings account and will be offered a place in a work-study group. They train and pay me a salary for going on deployments, and I will pay for my own classes. I no longer need your help. I am on my own now." I left the room as my dad stood alone on the red carpet.

I felt good about ending my family ties, which I had learned were nothing more than family restraints. I had crossed over the line to adulthood and had become a man—not the boy my father had come to visit.

I climbed the stairs to the sixth floor where the card room was crowded with men gambling. Men's voices cheered and welcomed me in the way a rock star received applause.

"Hey, Angelo, it's about time you showed up," Montgomery said.

"Come sit at this table to make it more interesting," Colonel Hollander echoed.

"Lady Luck is riding on my knee, and I am going to win back what you took last week," Colonel Montt stated in his Spanish-accented English.

Standing in the middle of a room full of my friends, I announced, "I have played your poker game for six weeks now, and I am bored. Who wants to play blackjack?" I knew blackjack was my game and could count the cards up to seven decks. This group of men would start to play with only two decks, and I would fleece them for over a thousand dollars tonight. I was emboldened and strong.

Five men changed over to my table and played my game of blackjack. Now they would learn what I could really do. I made the right choice regarding my father and where I wanted to be. I belonged here with my new friends as my family.

CHAPTER 11

FIRST ASSIGNMENT

O n the Monday following my dad's visit, JoSam sent word that he wanted to talk with me after my counterinsurgency class had finished for the day. I stepped into his bizarre, eccentric office, where the walls had been painted with jungle trees, flying parrots, and dark eyes peeking from behind tropical plants. I found JoSam standing on his head, on a tropical colored yoga mat, in the center of the room, facing the door.

"Come on in and sit in the grass," he said as he remained standing on his head. "I'll be with you soon."

I saw a patch of green turf grass behind his yoga mat, eased down into it cross-legged, and waited for him to become upright. This was especially different from the other army offices I had visited. Was JoSam, the red gargoyle, all right in his head?

"Everyone should spend ten minutes every day standing on his head. It's good for the brain cells," he said as he uprighted himself and landed on the grass turf beside me.

"You have adapted to the School of the Americas quite well. I received a handwritten letter from your father, stating he would no longer pay your tuition, and he left money for your return airfare to Costa Rica. What do you want to do about this?"

"I want to stay and continue my classes. The letter I write to him during Friday's class time should contain a return of his airfare money."

"Fair enough, but you know everyone must pay his tuition. How do you intend to accomplish that?"

"I talked to Montgomery Summers, and he is on a work-study plan. May I do the same?"

"Montgomery is nearly ten years older than you. He fills his work portion by completed missions and deployments. Are you willing to do that? Are you old enough and man enough to be reliable on a mission?"

"I am reliable."

"The missions can be rough. Can you handle death and destruction?"

"I think I can."

"Your first mission will be a test to learn if you can endure the savages of war. Your mission will be a three-part assignment. First, you will write a report on Guatemala's cultural traits for your counterinsurgency class from your own observations. Second, you will attend an elitist dinner party with Colonel Montt and charm the daughter of your dinner host. Third, you will serve as a messenger delivering documents between two contacts."

"Let me clarify this," JoSam continued. "First, your Guatemalan cultural traits report has no mandated requirements except that they must be your own observations. Second, you will be an invited guest of a Ladina, (The Guatemalan term for a wealthy landowner) named Antonio Raul Yon Sosa. This will be your night of recreation, and you are to have fun and to keep the landowner's beautiful twenty-three-year-old daughter Venus busy. Third, you will fly with

Colonel Jose Efrain Rios Montt to his home country of Guatemala and serve as a silent messenger.

"You will transfer documents that are handed to you by Bishop Juan Gerardi, a human rights campaigner who had told us that he would only give the papers to an innocent, uninvolved youth. The papers are the 1982 Guatemalan army records. Bishop Gerardi will meet you at the fountain in the main square of Antigua at 10 a.m. It will take you two-minutes to walk the distance to deliver the documents to Unidad Revolucionaria Nacional Guatemalteca (URNG). The delivery contact's name is Marco Otto Posada. He will be waiting on the church steps in the square of Antigua City."

"Colonel Montt will be your driver. He will drop you off and be your guide because he knows the city well. You need to have a reliable watch, and it can only take you *five* minutes between points of contacts. During those five minutes, you will read the report as much as you can so that you will make a timely delivery. When you read the report, don't allow anyone to see you reading it. After your mission, Colonel Montt will take you to our airplane at La Aurora Airport in Guatemala City. He will remain in Guatemala, but I will wait for you inside the aircraft to receive your three-minute report of the army's document as we fly back to Fort Benning, Georgia."

"You leave in the morning. Pack your bag for a three-day trip. You will be fitted for a tuxedo for the dinner party tonight, and it will be delivered before you depart in the morning. Here, take this Minox B camera and snap pictures of everything you don't have time to read. Do you have any questions?" He handed me the small, gold, metal, espionage camera, which was between two and five inches in length and easily fit in my pocket.

"I understand what I am to do, but I know Colonel Montt resents me. Are you sure he is willing to accompany me?"

JoSam's face swelled like a balloon and turned violet with rage. He sprang three feet straight up in the air from his sitting position like his legs were spring, steel coils. His eyes popped out of his head, and purple blood vessels bulged around his temples like drainpipes, which emptied red blood into the whites of his blue, watery eyes. He became a flying gargoyle.

"God damn it to hell!" he screamed at me. "You're not applying for Mr. Congeniality. You're going on a mission. Colonel Montt resents you? Of course he does! You are both doing a job! I don't believe I have ever heard such self-centered dribble. Lopez, I don't want to see you until we meet on the airplane leaving for Guatemala. Get out!"

JoSam's outrage was unexpected and shocked me. I wouldn't have guessed my question would provoke such an outburst. I quickly got up from the grass turf. I went to my room and waited for the tuxedo fitting. I carefully packed my bags to include the proper garments needed to complete the assignments JoSam had outlined.

In my supply of clothes brought from Costa Rica, I had included black patent leather shoes that my mom had given me for dance lessons, which had been worn during her inviting girls to tea phase. Those shoes, which were now a bit too small and painful, would complement the tuxedo. I could endure the pain of pinched feet for a couple of hours to court Venus. I applied the lessons I had learned during the past two months, particularly the drill to pay attention to detail.

I walked to the commissary, which was open until 9 p.m., and bought a small bottle of amber-colored glue. It fit into the pockets of my carefully selected, baggy, blue slacks, which made me look like a youth. I returned to my room and continued to concentrate on the contents of what would go in my bag.

The tuxedo arrived at sunrise (without shoes), and I carefully placed it into a garment bag after I had tried it on. It was a good fit. Colonel Montt tapped on my door shortly after breakfast. "Let's go," he ordered. Colonel Montt wore his full Guatemalan army uniform with its colonel insignia. His uniform enhanced his stature and his significance, which prompted him to assume a commanding demeanor with me.

CHAPTER 12

INFORMANT

C olonel Montt and I walked to the far end of the army base to a private aircraft. It was a Gates Learjet model fifty-eight and was all white with no visible insignias. We climbed into the comfortable interior cabin with its two cafe booths and small tables. There were also four recliners.

I selected one of the recliners and so did Colonel Montt, who seemed to be acquainted with the attractive stewardess. He held her hand each time she checked on our comfort. When she delivered his rum and coke, he surprisingly patted her on her shapely behind, and she didn't take exception. I ordered a coke minus the pat on her ass.

During the flight, I went over JoSam's instructions for the document pickup and delivery. Guatemala's current events circled in my mind. The current president of Guatemala was supported by the United States, who had supplied his government with arms and equipment to protect its interest in the elite American business investors of his country.

The land consisted of mountains and valleys. Over the years, the government had taken this land from the Catholic church and the Mayan Indian population. The expropriated lands were used as plantations to grow crops for exportation, and the majority of these lands' owners were Americans. Later, I would discover the reason for my assignment to court Venus.

Most of the inhabitants were Mayan Indigents who had been displaced from their culture and their land. The Unidad Revolucionaria Nacional Guatemalteca (URNG) had been a sympathetic nonviolent group that had tried to support the civil rights of the Mayan people, but its force was too small and weak to fight against the Guatemalan government army (also supported by the USA). It was my assignment to transport papers from the human rights activist Bishop Juan Gerardi to URNG after reading and photographing the contents for JoSam. My first assignment was to be a spy and an informant.

After my thoughts covered the current events of Guatemala, my curiosity was peaked to include the assignments of my travel companion Colonel Montt. After I experienced JoSam's outburst yesterday, I didn't think I should ask the colonel any direct questions. Maybe he would tell me his assignment without prompting.

"Did you bring any blackjack cards?" he asked.

"No. I didn't think about that. My mind was focused on our trip. Did you bring any?"

"No. My mind was also busy," he replied and closed his eyes. I might as well give up trying to find out information because I was curious. I will give that thought a rest. I pulled the lever to settle back into the reclining seat.

After three hours, we arrived at La Aurora International Airport in Guatemala City. Our plane landed at the far edge of the airport. The stewardess told us that our bags would be delivered to the Casa Santo Domingo, a five-star hotel in the nearby city of Antigua.

Colonel Montt exited the aircraft first, after a provocative stewardess hug while his hands traveled over her body and he whispered something in her ear. We walked a short ten meters to a military helicopter that waited for us. I followed him into the four-seater plane. Colonel Montt chose a seat beside the pilot, and I sat behind him.

"Where are we going?" I shouted over the roar of the noise.

"To a small hamlet called Dos Erres. When we get there, wait inside the plane. I need to be there no more than an hour," Colonel Montt yelled over his shoulder.

It seemed to be a very short ride of thirty minutes or less. The colonel climbed down from the chopper, and the pilot turned and gestured to the mountain range. "This is the volcanic highland of the Sierra Madre's. The village is very isolated, and its inhabitants mostly use trails to reach it," he said as he reclined into his seat for a nap.

When he was asleep, I stood up and went out the open door into a wooded area so that I could have a look at the village. I walked only a few yards on a knoll that overlooked the hamlet below and stopped abruptly. I counted fifty-eight men dressed in guerrilla combat clothing, but I knew they weren't guerrilla fighters because they saluted Colonel Montt as he approached. I was horrified at what I wasn't meant to see.

I found out later, these fifty-eight Kaibiles were an elite special force of commandos from the Guatemalan army (the country's USA backed army that supplied equipment and guns). They were in the middle of an operation called Scorched Earth. These Kaibiles were flown into this area in guerrilla disguise and had orders to kill all inhabitants. This village was considered to have guerrilla sympathizers, but a soldier reported to Colonel Montt. "A through search of the village found no weapons or no guerrilla propaganda," the soldier said.

"Continue with the vaccinations," Colonel Montt replied.

At two thirty in the morning on December 6, 1982, the Kaibiles seized the hamlet by placing the men into schoolhouses and the women into churches and lining the children against a wall, beginning with the smallest, and bashed their heads in against it. The soldiers bashed the next group of older children's heads by using hammers.

I watched the men gather up the small bodies of the tiny children from the first group and toss them down a well before beginning the head bashings of the older children. The Kaibiles then brought the men out of the schoolhouses and the women out of the churches. Then they raped the young girls or the ones they wanted. After this, they stood the girls against the wall and subjected them to the head bashing until unconsciousness or death crumpled their bodies for transport to the wells. The men experienced the same death.

I watched no more, returned to the open door of the helicopter, and slid into my seat behind the napping pilot. One hour and fifteen minutes passed before Colonel Montt returned and found me asleep. If there was ever a time when I needed a drink, it was now. My stomach was a coil of knotted pain, and the images of the children's faces were burned into my brain. The worst part was the fact that I had recognized four of my classmates from the School of the Americas among the guerrillas. Soldiers Manuel Pop, Reyes Colin Gualip, Daniel Martinez Hernandez, and Lieutenant Carlos Carias had been there. Of course, Colonel Jose Efrain Rio Montt had been there as well.

The trip back to the Guatemala City Airport was a deliberate disconnect and escape into a void far from Colonel Montt and the helicopter ride. I remembered that JoSam had asked me if I could accept the ravages of war. What I saw was not war but genocide.

After the chopper landed, we took a taxi to Casa Santo Domingo Hotel in the beautiful city of Antigua. I excused myself, explaining that the flight had given me airsickness and that I wanted to get some exercise and explore the city. Colonel Montt's room was across the hall from mine, and he escaped by explaining how tired he was. We completed our separation in mutual agreement by telling each other lies.

The Hotel Casa Santo Domingo was quaint old world wrapped with restful, elegant country charm, void of the metropolitan high-rise chrome and shine. It was of a Spanish colonial design with lush gardens, walkways, and a pool. The interior was made of rustic wood with river rock walls and fireplaces. I felt that I could stay there for a long time. It helped erase the images of the day from my mind. I had the remainder of the day and part of the next to myself—up until the dinner party tomorrow evening.

I validated Montgomery's description of Colonel Montt and confirmed the information about his participation in massacres. I had heard Montgomery's words but hadn't grasped the reality of them until today.

After I had removed the tuxedo from the garment bag and had hung it up so that it would be wrinkle free, I searched for a restaurant. I opened my hotel door with the intent of finding a restaurant and exploring the city when I caught a glimpse of the stewardess's ass going into Colonel Montt's room. Sex seemed to be the way the colonel released stress and cleared ownership of the brutality of his morning's campaign. The only choice I had to erase mine was to take a walk.

The very satisfying lunch of roasted chills relleno, rice, and beans (without wine) gave me renewed energy and cleared my mind as well. It made me realize how much I missed my own Central American food. When I finished lunch, I decided to find the town square, to check out my route for the pickup and delivery of my third assignment, and to survey of the area.

The town square and the Cathedral San Jose were very close to Hotel Casa Santo Domingo. I got directions from the front desk and walked the easy six blocks. From the hotel, the church was located at 1A Avenida Sur and then another three blocks to 5A Calle Oriente. I assumed that JoSam had wanted me to be dropped off in case someone was following me or so that Colonel Montt could not tail me.

I approached the Antigua town square and spotted the large, ornate, cement fountain standing majestically in the center. I strolled by the many trees that graced the square and leaned on the rim of the misting fountain where tourists tossed coins into the refreshing, cool water.

Over fifteen people enjoyed the fountain, but how difficult would it be to spot a Catholic bishop? I glanced at my watch and quickly proceeded to the cathedral steps. Things had been planned well. It was exactly a two-minute walk as JoSam had said it would be. I needed to find a place to read the document where I wouldn't be seen. I retraced my route to the fountain and spotted a public restroom a few steps off the direct pathway to the church. It would be the perfect place for complete privacy.

I stood up from my perch on the rim of the fountain and sauntered to the public restroom. It took me thirty-seconds to locate the men's room, and this day's search would save me thirty- seconds the next day. I entered the men's room, went into a stall, and closed its door, which made it private for document reading. I was confident this would be a stress-free assignment.

I returned to the fountain and observed the townspeople. I went back to the church steps but checked my watch first. I walked with long strides without appearing to be rushed. Good! It only took me one and a half minutes. Yes, this time, I had been much faster without seeming to be in a hurry. The extra thirty-seconds would give me sixty-seconds more to read the documents.

On the return to the hotel, my mind filled with Nikola's book of poems, which JoSam had given me as required learning.

> I tolerate no betrayal:
> No tarnished loyalty.
> If my trust in you does fail.
> You die like dethroned royalty.

I questioned whether this mandated poem was a form of brain-washing or if my focus on doing a thorough job was the motivation. I concluded that I wanted to do a good job. I did a little sightseeing and stopped at a barbershop on my way back to the hotel.

"How much do you charge for a Jon-Jon haircut?" I asked the barber.

The barber looked up and said, "All children's haircuts are five dollars."

"How much would you charge if I wanted a Jon-Jon?"

"Are you asking for a haircut that is styled like the young John Kennedy's during the 1960s or maybe the Beatles?" he asked.

"Yes, exactly."

"Most young men your age want to appear older not childlike, but if that's what you want, it will be an adult-priced haircut of ten dollars," he said.

"Do I need an appointment? How long will it take to cut my hair in a Jon-Jon?" I asked.

"We can make you an appointment, and it will take about thirty minutes," he said. He walked to his appointment book and asked, "When do you want your appointment?"

"The day after tomorrow at 8:00 a.m. Is that okay?"

"It's fine. What's your name?"

"Angelo," I declared and left his shop. I walked a few blocks more, spotted a flower shop, and bought a bouquet of yellow roses and a box of chocolates to take to the dinner party. It was the custom in Central America to always bring the hostess a gift.

I returned to my room and noticed the "Do Not Disturb" sign was still hanging on Colonel Montt's door. I guessed he had a mammoth-sized level of stress to release. I entered the coolness of my room and placed the bouquet on the table. The flowers made the room smell good. I showered and went to bed.

The next day, December 7, 1982, was time for the second

assignment—to court Venus. I was prepared. I had my gifts and the tuxedo. I was free until five p.m.. I was fortunate I could meet with Venus before I received my little kids' haircut. My present haircut was a good length for the tux, and I hoped to appear three years older than my seventeen years.

I spent the day dressed like a twelve year old in sneakers and baggy blue pants and worked at adding more time for reading the documents. I revisited the fountain and path to the church stairs. Long striding in sneakers gained me another thirty-seconds. I now would have four minutes to slip into the men's bathroom and to read as much as I could. It took one minute to walk to the bathroom, without drawing attention to a hurried pace. I believed this was as good as it was going to get.

I ambled back to the hotel and swam in the pool until it was time to get dressed. I needed the invitation from Colonel Montt in order to find the address, but the do-not-disturb sign was still on the doorknob. I phoned him and asked him to push the invitation under my door at his convenience.

"It would be good, Lopez, if you went on ahead without me because I will be a little bit late. I'll write the address down for myself and then give you the invitation since they are friends of mine and don't know you. Please give my apologies for arriving late," he said.

He pushed the invitation under my door. I scooped it up and realized that the party was very formal with a sit-down dinner. I didn't see how it would be acceptable for the colonel to arrive late, but it was his call.

I was ready and concluded that I looked older, thanks to the tuxedo. I gathered up the box of candy and flowers and called a cab. The driver looked at the address and drove only three blocks past the Antigua town square where I had spent the last two days rehearsing. The center of most Guatemalan cities was usually located around government offices and the dwellings of high-ranking persons, who lived in rambling colonial homes. The entrance to our Señora and Ambassador Antonio Raul Yon's grand home was protected by a beautiful, arched wall with iron gates that opened for guests.

A *domestico* in a black suit greeted me at the entrance where I presented the invitation, flowers, and candy. He placed the items, including the invitation, on a gold tray and ushered me through the living room (salon). To the right of the salon was a large formal dining room that had been beautifully set for forty guests. I followed the *domestico* to the central patio garden where he presented the tray to Señora and Ambassador Yon Sosa. They looked at the invitation, and Ambassador Yon Sosa extended his hand to me.

"Mr. Angelo Lopez, welcome to our home. This is Señora Yon Sosa Molina and Señorita Venus Yon Sosa Molina."

I shook their hands in greeting but placed Venus's hand between both of mine, which expressed my affection. I wanted her to get my message of intent quickly. She was extremely beautiful. Señora Yon Sosa Molina noticed my gesture, and I said to her, "Your beautiful daughter is your replica, Mrs. Yon Sosa."

"Thank you for your kind words, Mr. Lopez. The flowers are beautiful, and I see you know that yellow roses symbolize loyalty. What a thoughtful gift for this special occasion. Where is your friend Colonel Efrain Rios Montt?"

"He sent his regrets that he will be a little bit late," I said as I kept my gaze upon Venus. She returned my gaze in a very direct answer.

"May I introduce you to my American friends?" Ambassador Yon Sosa asked as he ushered me to a group of five guests. "You are from the United States, isn't that correct?" he asked.

"Yes, but I am tico by birth."

"I noticed your Spanish is tico," he said.

He introduced me to a group of American landowners from New York, Pennsylvania, and Florida. The Guatemalan army was supposedly protecting these landowners from the Mayans. I participated in the conversation but kept my eyes on Venus. I knew she had to fulfill her role as hostess, to be present, and to greet the guests. After half an hour, I calculated that most of the guests had arrived. I excused myself from the Americans and walked toward Venus.

"Miss Molina, your house is beautiful. Would you be available to give me a tour?"

"It would be my pleasure," she said as she flirted with me.

"I love the Spanish architecture of Central America's homes."

Venus was tall, stately—an inch under my five feet eight inches. Her body was sinewy and agile, and she moved with the grace of a ballet dancer. I followed her through the corridors of the bedrooms and was attracted to her. Her shimmering, silver, long dress was backless to her waist, where the dress draped in folds against the small of her back revealing her flawless, light creamy olive-toned skin and her strong frame. The dress draped just above her behind. From there it hugged and moved rhythmically with each of her steps. Her waist was small, accenting the voluptuousness of her breasts and hips.

Nothing was more beautiful except for the radiance of her face. Her shining, curly, dark blond hair bounced like her derriere when she walked and framed her oval face with its high cheek bones, full upturned lips, and the deepest dimples when she smiled. Her eyes were a soft sea-foam green with long, dark lashes and a cute snubbed nose. I liked everything about her. The corridors widened, and I walked beside her.

"Your home has the features of the architect Agustin Iriarte from the 1930s and '40s."

"You are so correct," she said and turned to me in surprise. "How did you know that?"

"No one but Agustin Iriarte could design a series of arches like those." I pointed to the corridor that lead to the service kitchen with an open fireplace under a large chimney. "I believe the hotel I'm staying in was designed by Agustin as well."

"Where are you staying?"

"Casa Santo Domingo."

"Agustin Iriarte did design them both," she beamed.

"One of the things I love about Central American homes is the gardens that are folded into the interior of the house, unlike US homes where the house is surrounded by lawns. In Central America, you live in the patio gardens like they are part of the house and not outside where they are rarely used."

"I have never been to the States. Will you tell me what it is like to live there?"

"*Abundance* is what I can tell you. Look at me. Before I arrived in Georgia, I was skinny. You cannot say that I am skinny now. The food is sumptuous, rich, and delicious."

"I hope you won't think our dinner is too bland."

"As long as you will be seated at the table, the dinner will be delicious," I flattered.

"Thank you. You say beautiful words," she cooed.

"I want to get to know you better. Can we move into the central patio garden and talk?"

"Yes, we can sit on the little bench away from the music but not in isolation."

When we were seated together on the small bench, I could smell the scent of jasmine. I reached for her hand, and she gave it responsively. She talked about finishing school with a degree in business to please her father but then explained what she really wanted was to be a mother. I felt the warmth of her thigh close to mine, and my heat rose. My tuxedo pants grew tight in the crotch. I hoped she didn't notice my hardness. I reached up, touched her porcelain cheeks, ran my fingers over her full, pink lips, and put my fingers in my mouth. "I am hungry to taste your mouth," I said.

"I want you to know me, but this dinner party isn't the appropriate place. I cannot disgrace my parents in front of their political friends."

"What is the occasion for the dinner celebration tonight?"

"I thought you knew and that it was the reason you appropriately brought yellow roses, which signify everlasting loyalty. You touched my parents' hearts. The dinner party is for invited political entities such as yourself and Guatemalan nationals who have given their silent support for the ongoing civil war. You are young to be a US diplomatic representative, but your presence is important to our country and to show continued support."

"Do you believe your civil war is necessary?"

"Oh, of course! The Mayan population dominated our country, and in the past ten years, they have become educated and strong. They could easily be the ruling class. I have great fear that our Ladina class of Guatemalan people will parish at their hands. My blond hair makes me a visible target in this war."

"Your attractiveness and your beautiful hair make you a target for any male species on earth, and I think I need to remain close by your side."

"You are unlike any man I have ever met, and I find you interesting."

We were interrupted by Señora Yon Sosa Molina, who approached our bench. "Venus, excuse me, Mr. Lopez, but Colonel Jose Efrain Rios Montt has arrived, and I need her help to seat the dinner guests."

I watched Venus's gyrating, shimmering, sleek dress flow in the direction of the dining room. I took a deep breath, stood, adjusted my pants so that I would be more comfortable, and went to find Colonel Montt. I did believe that my new job had its rewards!

The table was laden with fine crystal, porcelain, and gold ware. I was seated on the opposite side of the table and about fifteen people removed from Venus, but I kept my eyes on her so she would be aware of my attentive interest. Beside me was seated another attractive young women, the daughter of a Ladina landowner named Ellsia, who was easily entertained and laughed loudly at my jokes. I caught Venus's glance in my direction when Ellsia leaned in to whisper a private story about another guest. I caught Venus eyes, winked, and smiled to reassure her of her importance. The dinner of delicious Guatemalan cuisine was excellent, but the dynamics of this political affair were even more captivating.

After a lavish chocolate dessert was served and consumed, Colonel Montt, who was wearing his Guatemalan army uniform, stood and gave a short, unprepared speech about how well his army was doing. He reassured the guests that the war was going well and in their favor. He failed to mention the genocide.

"Men, if you care to join your host, Ambassador Yon Sosa, and me in the men's smoking room, I will entertain any questions you have. Also, I want you to know that my young friend, Mr. Angelo Lopez, is an unbeatable blackjack player. You might want to challenge him," he said.

Everyone began to leave the table. I stood to help Ellsia with her chair and then scrambled to the far end of the table. I reached Venus's chair before another man who had been sitting to her left got up. She looked up and gave me an appreciative thank-you. "Can we continue our talk in the central patio garden?" I asked eagerly.

She rose from her chair, and I placed my hand in the small of her back and ushered her to the bench. I wanted to move my hand down to her derriere as Colonel Montt had with the stewardess, but I resisted.

"The dinner was exquisite and not even a little bit bland. Your fears were wasted. You need to trust your mother's experience because it was delicious," I complimented.

The evening was darker and the bench in the garden was even

more secluded now that the guests were in the house. We sat down together, but Venus sat closer to me than before. I put my arm around her trim waist and pulled her toward me. She twisted her upper body and pressed her breasts firmly into my chest, and I kissed her very gently on her soft mouth. She pressed herself tight against me from her thighs to her clavicle as she rotated her weight onto her hip next to mine. I felt her body move in passion. I was electrified and kissed her again with an open mouth, which was harder and longer than the first tender kiss.

My fingers investigated the clasp of her backless halter dress, and I knew she would be bare to the waist in one flip of the clasp. I slid my hands down her back, touched every vertebrate as she arched to meet my touch, which positioned her breasts forward, inviting me in.

I was breathing heavily and wanting more when I heard hard-soled shoes coming on the terra-cotta tiles of the patio. I released her and moved farther from her on the bench. She stared at me in bewilderment because she hadn't heard the approaching person.

"Oh, there you are, Mr. Lopez. I have been looking all over for you. The men have set up your game of blackjack, and this group is loaded with cash. I bet we will clear two or three grand in this little game because I will bet on you. Come on!" Colonel Montt coaxed.

"Thanks for the invitation, colonel, but I'm not interested. I have a different agenda."

The colonel couldn't hide his anger. He realized he had no command over me and began a new strategy. "You should come in and learn about Guatemalan current events from the most prestigious and knowledgeable men."

"No thanks. You go ahead and enjoy yourself," I said, and then he huffed off.

"I don't think Colonel Montt is used to having his invitations rejected," Venus remarked.

I clasped her hand in mine again, looked into her eyes, and pulled her close. "I have other interests now."

Colonel Montt's interruption had shattered the moment. We transferred our passion into interesting conversation that lasted for over two hours. Señora Yon Sosa Molina gave a faint call to Venus before she approached our bench. "Venus, dear, our guests are leaving, and you need to be available at the door. It has been wonderful having you at our home, Mr. Lopez. Please come again," she said.

"I'll be right in, Mama."

Venus stood up, took my hands, and pulled me to a standing position while she waited for her mother to disappear into the house. I put both of my arms around her and pulled her toward me while I pressed my leg between both of hers. I slid my hands all the way down the sides of her body and felt her magnificent curves. I kissed her open mouth and explored inside it. She pressed her full, firm breasts against me, moved, and made soft sounds. Her small movements set me on fire, and I breathed hard while my hands traveled inside the front of her dress and cupped her overflowing breasts.

"I want you so badly."

"I want to be wanted," she replied.

"I don't want you to go. I don't want to lose you." I removed my hotel room key from my pocket and pressed it into her hand.

"Come if you can," I invited.

"Yes, if I can," she repeated.

After she had gone, I sank back down on the bench and waited several minutes to allow the rise in my pants to recede. I was motivated to do this job! No violent poem was directing me. I liked my work.

I crossed to the front entrance where Venus and Señora and Ambassador Yon Sosa were with the departing guests. I waited my turn in line.

"Señora and Ambassador Yon Sosa, I had a wonderful evening.

Thank you for the delicious dinner. I hope we meet again." I wanted to walk the several blocks back to Casa Santo Domingo even though my pinching shoes crippled my feet.

At the hotel, I stopped by the front desk and explained that I had lost my room key and received a new one. Then I restlessly waited in my room one and a half hours before I decided Venus wasn't coming. I showered, turned off the lights, and went to bed. Another hour passed, when the sound of a key unlocking the door woke me up. I sat up and turned on the dim lamp by the bed as Venus entered.

"I am sorry. I was in bed. I didn't think you were coming," I apologized.

"It's okay," she said, as she quietly closed the door and stood facing me. She reached up and unfastened the clasp of her dress, and it fell, cascading to the floor. She stood in front of me and gifted me with a view of her beautiful body, which only had black lace panties on it. Her skin was flawless, creamy, and almond colored. Her erect nipples were light brown even though she was a natural blond which indicated her mixed race.

I scooted to the edge of the bed and held the sheet up for her. The light made her body glow. "You are so beautiful. I just want to look at you."

She leaned over me to turn off the light, and her warm breasts met my heaving chest. My lips nibbled, and my tongue flicked and licked the brown gumdrop shapes of her nipples. Her back arched as my hands touched her lithe long legs, caressed the insides of her thighs, and massaged her V area.

"Oh, how I want you," I whispered.

"I want to be yours. Take me," she moaned.

I kissed her mouth over and over as I positioned myself above her. I was so hard and ready, but I wanted it to last for her. I easily slipped into her and moved to her rhythm. She moved and danced with me, increasing the speed with each soft lunge. I had yet more length to give, and she begged me to dive deeply.

She wrapped her legs around my back and moved her hips softly moaning. Then she gripped me full force, and I felt the throb of her passion. "Yes, yes, oh yes." I felt her release, and I moved with a strong force of my own to find and give her my pleasure. When she felt the warm fountain of my passion erupt, she began again. I satisfied her again and then another time. I lay beside her completed and worn out.

We began to talk about which dinner guests were the best monetary contributors to the war and her predictions as to when the war would end. We talked about our families, friends, and religious beliefs. We talked for hours when she suddenly sat up.

"What time is it?"

"It is 6:06," I announced, after squinting at the precise watch JoSam had suggested I use.

"I am sorry, but I have to go before my parents discover I am gone." She jumped up, stepped into her panties, grabbed her dress, and was near the door before I could get up.

"I will walk you home. Be very quiet because Colonel Montt is right across the hall."

I stood naked beside her at the door as she explained, "You cannot come because someone might see us together or recognize me," she cautioned.

"Please, at least take a taxi home so I know you will be safe."

"I have my own car. Thanks. I will be fine," she explained.

I searched a drawer for a pen and piece of paper and then wrote something down. "Here, take this. It is my address. Will you write to me?"

"Yes, of course," she said. She cupped my naked genitals in her warm hands while I kissed her one last time. Then she was gone. I fell back onto the bed and slept for a few hours before my 8 a.m. Jon-Jon haircut. I was thankful Venus wouldn't see it.

At 7:30 a.m., the morning sun poured through the window hitting me right in the eyes. I bounced out of bed, showered, dressed in the blue, baggy pants, gray T-shirt, and sneakers and was out of my hotel room in less than fifteen minutes. I noticed the do-not-disturb sign on Colonel Montt's door and wondered if the Learjet fifty-eight stewardess, renamed Miss High Diddle-Diddle was inside. She might have been Colonel Montt's assignment, but my gut reaction said otherwise.

CHAPTER 13
MESSENGER

I strutted to receive my haircut feeling like a movie actor. Last night, I was James Bond in my tuxedo and a champion with my successful courtship to the beautiful Venus. Today after I squinted into the barbershop mirror, I resembled a tall-for-my-age waif from the Charles Dickens's book *Oliver Twist*.

I returned to my room, stuffed my passport, camera, binoculars, and glue bottle into my pocket. I checked to see if Colonel Montt's sign was still on his door. Luck was in my favor. The sign on the colonel's door was gone. I glanced at my watch, and it read 8:45 a.m. It was time for my third mission—the coffee routine. I tapped lightly on the colonel's door and heard the rough harsh voice of Montt. "Who is it?" he asked

"It's me, Angelo. May I come in?"

"Si, the door is open," he responded.

"Would you like to get some coffee before you drop me off?"

"God, what have you done to yourself? You looked better last night! You look like a twelve-year-old kid."

"I am nearer to fourteen," I said.

"Oh! There is a great coffee house right next door," he volunteered.

We walked to the coffee house, ordered our coffee, and he began his interrogation. "That was a hot woman you had on the bench last night. How was she?"

"The entire evening was great. Dinner and conversation were both good. I enjoyed myself, and how was the card game?"

"I always do well when you aren't playing against me. I made $650. Not too bad, but the real purpose was to get pledges for upcoming army campaigns, and that was very successful. The largest contributor was American Blane and Connie Blackwood, who donated enough money to carry us for six months into next year." Venus had told me that they would be the biggest donors, and now Colonel Montt confirmed it.

"I love this coffee. I think I will have another cup, but only thing is, it makes me need to pee." There. I was satisfied. I had laid the groundwork for my cover so that I could duck into the public restroom if he was watching me.

"It is good coffee. I guess we have time for one more," he agreed.

We finished our second cup of coffee and drove one block away from the town square where he pointed to the fountain and explained, "There it is. Afterward, I will drive you to La Aurora Airport in Guatemala City. Give me your room key so I can check out of the hotel, pick up your bags, and meet you back at the coffee shop. Then we can quickly be on our way. I am not going back to Fort Benning with you."

"I understand," I said as I got out of the car.

I looked at my watch, and it was 9:50 a.m. I walked quickly to the fountain and spotted Bishop Juan Gerardi.

"Are you Angelo?" he asked. I lowered my eyes and nodded my head like a shy kid. "May I see your ID?" I handed it to him quickly, placing my thumb over the age. "You are a tall kid for your age. Are you twelve?" he asked.

"I am nearer to fourteen."

"These are your first communion papers," he said as he handed me the sealed manila envelope.

"I have to pee," I said. He smiled and pointed to the public restroom on the pathway to the cathedral. I walked very fast, ducked inside the unoccupied bathroom, went directly to the sink, ran the water to generate humidity, and opened the envelope using the skills I had learned in class. With the help of the Central American humidity, it opened without a tear or a wrinkle.

I entered a vacant stall, noted my watch, which displayed 10:01 a.m., and began to read the documents. I glanced again at my watch, which now displayed 10:03 a.m., took the Minox B camera along with a pair of binoculars from my pocket, and began to snap pictures of the documents. I took the bottle of glue, carefully resealed the envelope, tucked it under my arm, and began my one-minute trek to the cathedral steps.

There was a tired looking man waiting on the steps dressed in common Guatemalan clothes. I approached him, and he asked, "Angelo, are you bringing me your first communion papers?"

"Yes, what is your name?" I asked.

"I am Marco Posada."

"I look forward to being a member of the church," I said as I handed him the envelope.

"Your parents raised you to be a good Catholic," he said. He took the envelope, walked up the steps, and disappeared into the darkness of the cathedral. I had high hopes after the success of the third step of my assignment and looked forward to delivering the information I carried in my head to JoSam.

I met Colonel Montt at the coffee shop, and we drove to the Guatemala City International Airport. JoSam's aircraft was parked on the tarmac and poised for takeoff. I entered the plane and found JoSam sitting comfortably and reading the newspaper. He folded it up, laid it on the small table, and motioned for me to sit in the booth across from him. He gave a thumbs-up to the pilot, and the plane's engines fired up. JoSam looked at me and said, "Cute outfit. Let's start with the report from the cathedral papers."

"Yes, sir." I recited the report as I had read it in the public bathroom:

Guatemala Army Report 1982
Compiled by Corporal Joseph Mande Navarro
Under the Command of Colonel Jose Efrain Rios Montt
January 1982

The Guatemalan government, using the Guatemalan army and its counterinsurgency force known as the killing machines, began a systematic campaign of repressions and suppressions against the Mayan Indians who were working toward a communist coup. The army believed Mayan communities were the natural allies of the guerrillas and needed to be held in check by extermination en masse.

The overall plan of annihilation was to systematically eradicate fifty-two villages per month. Guatemalan Army Special Forces known as the Kaibiles were flown into the villages dressed as guerrillas under the pretense of giving vaccinations. The following fifty-two villages were obliterated and all inhabitants were assassinated execution style:

Perdido Nino, Grande Verdad, Machaco Fuerte
El Abandonar, Perdido Aldea, Perdido, Escondrijo

Callejon, Aldea Feliz, La Saludable
La Capaz, Peligro Grande, Matrimonio, Rapido
Casa Divino, Perros Muchos, Perdido al Azar
El Sano Paloma, Azul Lugar Lluvia
Margarita Bonita, Ciervo Rapido, Pistolas Muchos
Agua Grande, Arbol Verde, Grande Intencion
Sol Baile, Tierra Humedo
Saltamontes, Perdido Nuevo
Agradecido, Recien Llegado
Rio Dique, Oscuro Noche
El Cano, Engano Grande
La Saludo, Agua Profundidas
Mareado Machaca, Amanecer
Grande Dolor, El Filo
Sonrisa Abierta, Duquesa de Broma
Pequeno Novio, Futuro Esperanza
Pequeno, Rio Rojo Flora
Profundo, La Cielo
Alto Arbolis, Alta Damas
Querido, Viento Alto

It was estimated that between seventy-seven to one hundred inhabitants were exterminated per village. For January, the total estimate was four thousand villagers. The army took possession of the villages' property and destroyed all structures deemed unusable. There were no prisoners, and the dead were burned in pits. The army's goal was to erase any remnants of village life.

February 1982

It was an administrative decision to reduce the needed ammunition that would help the Kaibiles conduct the executions of the villagers. The Kaibiles were to invent their own means of extermination to comply with the executive decision to save army ammunition.

The Kaibiles were understaffed and overworked. To correct this problem, the army began training paramilitary teams, including the civil patrol of local men who were forcibly conscripted. Many Mayan communities were rounded up or seized when they had already gathered for civic events like market day or celebrations. Many Mayan villagers were forced to witness the executions by their own men in the civil patrol. The February quota of fifty-two villages was achieved, but record keeping by civil patrol and local men was sporadic. The following list was incomplete, and the names of the other villages remains unknown:

El Primero Aventura
Tierra Sazonado
La Esplendido Lugar
Valle Verde
Aldea de Carrino
Viento Fuerte
Blanco Roca
La Amorosa
El ocupado Vive
La Mojer Debil

I handed him the Minox B camera, and he handed it back after removing the microfilm and said, "Keep the camera, Lopez. Your report is much more efficient than waiting for the microfilm to be viewed."

"I am sorry, sir, that the gathered information is so short, but the document was in a sealed envelope that needed special care to open and reseal it. My time was very short, but I was able to snap pictures of its entire contents. While I used the binoculars as a telephoto lens for the document copying, I read that a total of 658 Mayan villages no longer exist. On the last months total report, over two hundred thousand Mayan inhabitants had been slain. I also have my own eyewitness report of a village called Dos Erres, if you care to hear about it."

"Yes, please tell me what you saw." I told him what I had seen in the village of Dos Erres: Tiny children, youth, adolescents, and women were beaten to death. I saw pregnant women's bodies ripped open to expose their unborn children by soldiers who were complying with the reduction of ammunition requirement.

"How did you react to the ravages of war?" he asked.

"I think I can withstand war, sir, but this was not war. It was genocide."

"The School of the Americas teaches the skills of war but is not responsible for how our students use their knowledge. Angelo Lopez, you did well on this assignment. Your school tuition for the remainder of the course is paid in full. You have earned your place to continue your education with us."

"There is something more that might be important to you. I brought yellow roses to the dinner party," I confessed.

JoSam looked puzzled. "That was a gracious thing to do, but why is that something I should know?" he asked.

"Señora Yon Sosa Molina explained that yellow roses were symbolic of loyalty, and the dinner guests were there to pledge their money and allegiance to the army of the Guatemalan Civil War. I inadvertently mislead the hostess with my yellow rose gift."

JoSam laughed uproariously and gave me a high five. "The yellow roses were a very diplomatic gesture without any commitment," he chuckled. "You receive double points for that one, and you will receive a top score in your Guatemalan diplomatic culture class, Lopez. What about Miss Venus Yon Sosa Molina?" he asked.

I blushed as I explained, "I liked that assignment best of all, and it was successful in every way. She told me details about the big money donors and other things, but I don't know what is important to you and what is not."

"As our Guatemalan and US relations grow, your information may be helpful. You are now in a strong position to gather needed information as our informant. Our future with them will one day unfold. I am pleased with your report, and you did extremely well. I am prepared to offer you a position with our organization while you continue your studies. If only you didn't look like such a twelve-year-old kid. Angelo Lopez, you need a different haircut!" JoSam laughed.

CHAPTER 14
STRATEGY

I returned to my classes and newly assigned missions with a triumphant attitude. I knew that because of my intelligence, I would be able to support myself and build a career.

I continued JoSam's letter-writing class on Friday's, but I now sent my mail to a different person. First, I wrote to my mother and thanked her for the social lessons she had taught me during those dreaded teas. Without these valuable lessons, my success with JoSam, Venus, and the fraternity wouldn't have occurred. I devoted one Friday's letter-writing session to my mother and the next to Venus. I received mail from my mother and Venus, which filled in my family gap.

My mother had written that she wanted me to return home for a visit during the Christmas holidays. I had accepted and had agreed to spend a weekend back at my childhood home in Costa Rica. She met me at the airport and commented on how I had grown into manhood. I felt comfortable with the Costa Rican surroundings and my bedroom, which Mother had left exactly as it had been in those dark days of adolescence before I had enrolled in the School of the Americas.

My father attempted to learn about my missions and classes, but my work was considered classified. I was now an agent, and missions remained confidential, so there was little I could share with him. He believed I was purposely remaining cold and aloof because of our past differences, but we both kept the peace between us. The reunion with my brothers and sisters was lively and playful. It was fun to be home.

My mother had a hidden agenda and reintroduced me to a young woman named Isabella Araya Mata, who was a daughter of the plantation owner Rodrigo Araya, whose land bordered my father's many acres. I smiled to myself because my mother had coaxed me back into one of her infamous teas. My letter of thanks to her for teaching me social graces had encouraged her to show me that my lessons weren't quite finished. Maybe my mentioning Venus had made her nervous and realize that she needed to put on another tea.

Isabella was my age, and we had shared our early school days together. She and I had also shared the same status of inheritance. The joining of our lands would mean continued success for our two families, our offspring, our export businesses, and the Costa Rican economy.

Isabella had suntanned skin, thick, curly, dark hair and black, shining eyes, which were shadowed by long curled lashes. No doubt about it, she was shapely and attractive, and I enjoyed our tea conversations.

Mother was jubilant as she observed Isabella's interest in me. For the next two days, our family events of boating, picnics, and the many Christmas masses included Isabella.

I considered my weekend family visit a success, and my mother and her driver took me back to the airport to return to Fort Benning. I learned that my mother had a zest for life and loved being involved in her children's lives. I loved her more than I had realized or had ever expressed.

"Angelo, I am so glad to have you back with us. It isn't right for a mother to be without one of her sons. Will you come back again soon?"

"I had a good time, Mom. Yes, of course, I'll be back!"

"Do you like Isabella?" she probed.

"Yes, I like her. She is beautiful."

"It would mean everything in the world to your father if you had a relationship with Isabella. It would make him feel you had forgiven him and were doing something to please him."

"Consider it done!"

"Do you mean it?" she asked in surprise.

"Yes, I will write to her," I promised.

"Angelo, you have made me a very happy mother. You need to settle down and begin a family. Do you have her address?"

"Yes. Isabella gave it to me yesterday."

"Promise me you will write to her," Mother urged as we continued our drive.

"I want to make you happy too, Mama. I promise I will write to you as well and tell you how our friendship goes."

"You have become a good man, Angelo," she complimented.

"You are my mother, and your happiness is important to me. I love you, Mama. Thanks for the good time," I said as I closed the car door and entered the airport.

I was glad to return to the fraternity and my classes and to experience more missions at Fort Benning. I kept my promise to my mother, and the next Friday, I wrote a letter to Mom and Isabella. I saw the flicker of a thought in JoSam's bulging, rheumy, blue eyes as he noticed the new name on my envelope, but he didn't question or comment on it.

It had only been a few weeks since my trip to Guatemala, but I noted how quickly my life was changing. JoSam assigned me to a bigger and more permanent position in Guatemala. I was a regular certified infiltration agent and worked on Guatemalan highways and bridges gathering information about Guatemalan government transportation. I had two more months of classes at Fort Benning before the Guatemalan assignment began. My family had taken me back into their good graces. I had two girlfriends: One whom I was jazzed about (Venus), and another who was jazzed about me (Isabella).

Our evening card games were the talk of the base. Our by-invitation-only list of players was expanding The room was so crowded with onlookers, Montgomery had established himself as a doorman, collecting a ten-dollar cover charge that he kept for himself. I had a steadily growing bank account with $25,000 socked away. I felt smug about my achievements.

My correspondence with my two girlfriends and my mother was highly active. My mother asked me in her last letter if she could announce my engagement to Isabella. I chuckled at the enthusiasm she had for her role as perpetuator of the dynasty. I had only just met Isabella during the Christmas season! Not causing disappointment was a Costa Rican cultural trait, and certainly I didn't want to disappoint my mom. The announcement would be fun for her and harmless, so I agreed.

During the first day of January 1983, students from our infiltration class—Montgomery Summers, Colonel Mike Hollander, David Allen, Russ Warren, and I—were briefed on an espionage assignment that would possibly take place in Moscow, Russia. JoSam told each of us separately that we would be working as a team but that no one else was to know. Our team was to be called the Special Five. We were never to be seen together except for our daily routine of classes and our normal associations.

Montgomery and I spent time together in class, during card games, and while we were dining. My computer infiltration class with David Allen had not changed. The occasional lunch with Russ Warren joining our table would also not change. Colonel Hollander only socialized with us during card games. It would be easy to continue our normal routines, but the difficulty would come when Special Five needed to meet together in secret without others knowing of our mission.

JoSam invited me to come to the mail room of building number six at 3:02 a.m. on the following Monday. I was excited to attend the briefing and knew anything having to do with Russia was a very big deal because these were the Cold War years. When I arrived at the scheduled appointment, I wasn't surprised to see Montgomery already waiting there with the mail room door, which was normally locked, opened and ready for the Special Five. He had used his special talents to unlock it.

The mail room was usually open by 5 a.m., when the two sergeants, who shared the mail room dispatch position, clerked the room until 9 p.m. Then it was closed for the night. Special Five arrived silently and exactly on time. Montgomery closed the door while we all took our seats around the reading table in comfortable chairs. The lights remained off so that no light could shine through the shutters. JoSam arrived at 3:05 a.m. Once he was inside, Montgomery closed and locked it after him.

I assumed it would be a two-hour meeting, going on until the mailroom opened by 5 a.m. I observed several reasons why JoSam had selected this space for our meetings. The room was central to everyone's location, it was double insulated, which kept our voices from being heard, and it had central air.

JoSam sat in a center chair so everyone could hear him as he spoke in a hushed voice without any papers, files, or notes. He began giving us information.

"The Pentagon has reasons to suspect that a congressman has leaked special military information to the Kremlin. It is our job to track Congressman Theodore Anderson, a Republican from Delaware, to determine if the Pentagon's suspicions have validity or are groundless. Mr. Anderson has booked a flight to Seoul, Korea, next week, on January 7, 1983, just seven days from today.

"We need to gather as much information as possible before his trip. Mr. Warren, please prepare a personal profile on Mr. Anderson for tomorrow's Special Five meeting, which will take place at 3:02 a.m. in this space. Concentrate on minor details while researching his life. Mr. Lopez, Colonel Hollander, and Mr. Summers, the three of you will present a plan for investigating Mr. Anderson's home, law office, Anderson's campaign office, and his congressional office in Washington, DC. We will be looking for any military information he might be passing to someone in Soul Korea.

"Each of you will present your plan at tomorrow's meeting, and we will collectively examine your strategy. If the three of you wish to save time and to start working on this together now, you may use this mail room until 4:30 a.m. Mr. Allen, you will present a communications infiltration plan on Mr. Andrews for tomorrow's meeting. Mr. Summers, you will be responsible for opening, closing, and detailing the mail room after each meeting. Do you have any questions?" JoSam asked.

I hesitated asking my question after my bad experience in his jungle office but then asked it anyway. "Where does his flight to Soul Korea originate?" I asked.

"Good thinking, Lopez. It originates in New York. Any more questions? No more questions. Good. Get some rest and don't miss your classes," he warned.

Russ Warren, David Allen, and JoSam did their post-meeting-observation work and returned the space to its original state before leaving the room. I watched their actions and methods and was inspired by their thoroughness. The carpet was green, plush and left footprints. Russ took out his comb and combed away all imprints, including JoSam's. David used his bandana to remove our hand oils from the polished table where we had leaned, touched, or sat. The three chairs were returned to their exact positions. One of the chairs was even placed at an odd twenty-degree angle.

As the three men left the room, JoSam said, "We will meet here as long as we remain undetected."

Three of us stayed there. Colonel Hollander spoke first and was barely audible. "What do you think of us each taking one of the four locations to be investigated, suggesting a plan, coming back tomorrow, and then adding ideas, doubts, or questions to each other's plans?"

"That sounds like a good idea. I will make a plan for his home," Montgomery offered.

"Okay," I said. "Splitting up the workload gives us more time to concentrate on details. I will make a plan for the congressman's Washington, DC, office."

"Great! That leaves the Delaware campaign office and his law firm to me," Colonel Hollander said.

"I could use a blueprint of the Capitol building, the location of his office, and a city map of Washington, DC," I stated.

"I have most of what you need in my office. I will give it to you in our infiltration class tomorrow. We can also use the media room to make any phone calls to our Washington agents," Colonel Hollander offered.

"It is nearly 4 a.m. Are we ready to close up?" asked Montgomery.

"I'm out of here," the colonel said. He adjusted his chair so that it was back in position, wiped his footsteps from the carpet, and left the room.

"Montgomery, I'd talk to you at lunch," I said.

I stood and followed the same procedures the others had followed. Montgomery took out a can of spray that had a janitorial smell, sprayed the room to remove our human odor, locked the inside lock on the door, took one last look to make sure everything had been cleaned of our intrusive traces, and closed the door.

I made plans for my portion of the assignment and went to bed. I was excited to be part of the new team, and it was all I wanted to think about. I didn't get any sleep but managed to sit through my morning classes while thinking about my project.

Colonel Hollander strolled past my chair and handed me a folder. "Here is the latest list of people who want to be invited to your blackjack games." I took the folder and slipped it into my notebook. Possessing the blueprints information in the folder, I knew my plan would be more concrete.

After the morning classes were finished, I met Montgomery for lunch at our private table in the dining room. I was energized about the congressman's investigation. We were the only two at our table, so we had latitude for Special Five discussion.

"Montgomery, I understand the reason David Allen and you were invited to this mission, but why were Colonel Hollander or Russ Warren invited?"

"Because they both hold the key to our success for this mission. Colonel Hollander knows what to look for when we enter Congressman Anderson's four locations. If I saw some military information, I wouldn't know if it was important or just random congressman junk.

"Colonel Hollander is an aircraft, artillery, and weapons engineer and designer. He has worked with many major military aircraft contractors in the USA and some foreign manufacturers. He knows what to look for in the way of military secrets.

"He has worked for Lockheed Advanced Development Projects, Northrop Grumman, Boeing, Aeronautical Systems Center, Sacramento Air Logistics Center, and these are only a few of the ones I remember. I know he worked for two foreign companies, Raytheon and United Technologies. For most of 1982, he was also a designer-consultant for U. S. Machine Gun Armory, LLC, General Dynamics of Spain, and Fabrique Nationale de Herstal of Belgium.

"He knows every weapon and aircraft the military has ever manufactured, used, or owned. If he saw information concerning military secrets, he would know it," Montgomery continued.

"Russ Warren is an antisocial, odd duck, but he is a linguistic marvel. He speaks over twenty languages fluently without a trace of an American accent and could pass for a national in each of the twenty countries they are spoken in. His major fields are Russian, Mandarin, and Korean. Special Five might need to travel into those countries while tailing Congressman Anderson. Russ communicates in over fifteen other languages, such as Swahili, Malagasy, Nilo Saharan, and Chewa, but his accent is detectable.

"Russ would be our spokesperson because the rest of us would reveal our origin the moment we opened our mouths. I want these two men on my team for sure! I am the lightweight of Special Five," he explained.

"I don't know if getting us entrance is necessary for allowing us to do our work. I think we are a good team and valuable to each other."

My interest in my job had surpassed my interest in the great food we were served in the dining room. I still took the medication and attended AA meetings, but I had conquered my alcohol dependency. My new obsession with my job had replaced food and drink. My new cravings were to meet the presented challenges and to revel in the intrigue of my work. I only looked forward to our meals as a way to gain inside, helpful information for our missions. Montgomery and I finished our lunch and planned on spending the afternoon and evening immersed in our assignment. We both wanted to be prepared for Tuesday's 3:00 a.m. presentation.

Tuesday's meeting began with Russ Warren's personal profile report on Congressman Anderson. Russ was a shy fellow and delivered his report like a nervous schoolboy. He held his body erect, and his head bobbed and swayed with his words.

"Congressman Theodore Anderson was born in Novosibirsk Russia on February 3, 1943, to his poor peasant parents Anna and Lyev Vladimir, who had seven other children. His parents placed him up for adoption when he was two days old to a Swedish couple named Hans and Ingrid Anderson. The Andersons immigrated to the United States during World War II in protest of Sweden's refusal to enter the war.

"Hans and Ingrid Anderson became devoted US citizens. They sent Theodore to private school in Wisconsin. When he was ten, they moved to Delaware. Theodore became student body president of his high school, captain of the football team, and a high school regional delegate for the Young Republicans during his senior year before he was valedictorian in 1961. He attended Harvard University where he became captain of the rowing team, president of his fraternity Sigma Nu, and graduated cum laude as an immigration lawyer.

"He was elected to the Delaware state senate in l966. He married Lorena Belov, a fellow criminal lawyer graduate from Harvard, in 1968. They have no children and are both active in civic organizations and Republican fund-raising. Theodore Anderson is the current national president for the John Birch Society and was elected to his second term as US Congressman in 1980," Russ Warren continued.

"Mrs. Lorena Belov Anderson has ties to Russia through her Russian Belov relatives. Theodore Anderson researched and located his biological Russian family. Both Andersons are direct Russian descendants. I checked out both of their bank accounts, and Lorena Belov Anderson received a $300,000 deposit from a Mrs. Herrick Asimov, which was transferred from International Bank of Korea last month on December 16, 1982.

"The Andersons belong to the Kent County Country Club and the USA Bar Association. Their Anderson and Anderson law office, home, and campaign office are all in Dover, Delaware, and I have the addresses for all of them. The Andersons work out at the Kent County Country Club three nights a week from 7–10 p.m. and row with the Dover City Rowing Team on Saturday mornings and some Sundays. They both have a shower and a closet of clothes at their law office, so they don't need to return home.

"They frequent their favorite expensive restaurants for lunch and dinner and rarely eat at home, except for times when they entertain a variety of political fund-raising organizations. The house is managed by professional housecleaning and landscaping crews and catering services. Their two weekday evenings are spent attending Dover civic meetings and book clubs or working in their law office." Russ Warren concluded his report like an insecure new kid at his first day of school.

"Your report is very complete, Russ," JoSam complimented. "It seems to me that they are a very tight couple, either from love or from distrust of one another. They also go to Soul, Korea, as a couple. Russ, do you have any insights about them after doing your research?" JoSam prodded.

"No," Russ answered, "except that they don't have any social friends. Everything they do is self-serving, work-related, or politically motivated activity. It seems that they don't have a marriage but a machine."

"What about the civic meetings or book clubs they attend?" asked Colonel Hollander.

"It is the same. The book clubs are dedicated to ones on political history. They attend the civic clubs as lawyers meeting with immigration groups or clubs that need criminal legal counsel. It is also self-serving," Russ answered.

"Do the Andersons ever take separate business trips where she must travel for criminal justice and he must meet with immigration?" I asked.

"I found a couple of trips like that, but they went together. Either he or she stayed in the hotel while the other spouse conducted his or her respective business."

"It appears there is no chance for opposite sex romances or extramarital affairs," Montgomery said.

"None that I have discovered," Warren answered.

"Is Mrs. Herrick Asimov their Seoul, Korea, contact, and who is she?" I asked.

"I don't know," answered Russ as he looked in JoSam's direction for a reaction.

"When Anderson's flight leaves from New York, do they stay overnight in a hotel or with friends?" I asked.

"I don't know that either," answered Russ.

"Are there any more questions for Russ?" JoSam asked.

Following a few beats of silence, JoSam continued. "Russ, do a personal profile for Mrs. Herrick Asimov. Determine if she could be the Seoul, Korea, contact, and find out where the Andersons stay in New York. Look for airports or locker rentals where the Andersons might hide documents so that they could retrieve them quickly before takeoff. Have this information for Wednesday's 3 a.m. Special Five meeting. David Allen, what have you got for us?" JoSam asked.

"Dontcha know. I'm announcing that I have *four* new devices available for use on this project:

1. A covert listening device (bug) to transmit live conversation to us from the Andersons' locations
2. A covert listening device (bug) to attach to the phone system that records and transmits their phone conversations
3. A portable handheld telephone to call JoSam or each other without needing to go to a regular phone
4. A covert tracking device (implant bug) to monitor their location when the Andersons are traveling.

"Communications infiltration will be concentrated in the Andersons' three offices and one in their home. The Washington, DC, office, the Anderson and Anderson law office, and the Anderson campaign office will have a telephone device installed that records conversations. We will have someone listening twenty-four hours a day, seven days a week and monitoring each incoming and outgoing call. This person has a direct connection (the new Motorola mobile phone) to JoSam, who will be alerted to any important information that person hears," David continued.

"My plan is to have our Special Five show up as Bell Atlantic installation crews for a fictitious, new cable installation service at each location. If we are questioned, the story will be that new equipment in Delaware's area code 302 is needed because the old cable has been in use since 1947. New, larger cables are needed to replace the worn-out, cracked, aging cable to accommodate the rising population. Not every 302 area code of Dover will be affected—only 50 percent within the 302–674 numbers. The Andersons' numbers are 302-674-2982, 302-674-9907, and 302-674-9897."

"I have Bell Atlantic trucks and uniforms ready for use. The CEO of the Delaware Bell Atlantic is eager to cooperate with us and asks for no payment. I asked a Motorola representative if he would give Bell Atlantic one of the new mobile phones, and he quickly agreed. He indicated that it would be great promotion for the new product. Everyone gets something for free," David explained.

"I believe we should plant the bugs and search for the documents at the same time. My plan is that Russ and I will plant the bugs while Colonel Hollander and Angelo Lopez search for the documents. This will leave Montgomery free to open any locked drawers, safes, lockers, or help the four of us if he has nothing to open." David was excited about his new technology.

"Our communications group has designed the most reliable, smallest, clearest transmission device invented to date, and our

Special Five can install it tomorrow. Besides the bugs, we will be using a new Motorola handheld device known as a cell phone to communicate with JoSam. We cannot all carry them with us because they weigh about two pounds each, but one of us will be stationed to call JoSam or to call one of us if we need to abort or change our plans.

"We designed another device that could be placed in the luggage that Mr. and Mrs. Anderson take when they go on their Seoul trip so that we can follow them more easily and less obviously. The communications infiltration equipment is ready and will be packed for our flight tomorrow," David Allen imparted excitedly.

"David, I have questions concerning the Motorola phone device. How will this work for us, and how long will it take to bug each location?" JoSam asked.

"The handheld devise was invented in 1973, but it took time for it to be refined. It works better than our two-way radios or walkie-talkies. I worked with the designers off and on for several years, and believe they have a product that is worth trying. It is experimental but reliable enough to go on the market later this year at a cost of $3,000 per phone. If it doesn't work, our plans won't be compromised because we can resort to the two-way radios we have if we need too. I have used it and know that it is reliable. It has a clear sound just like talking on the phone at home and can be used to call long-distance. The disadvantage is having to carry around a twenty-inch-long brick, but it is smaller than our radios. Since we will all be together doing this job, only one of us will need to carry the phone to call JoSam.

"Installing the bugs in each location takes ten or fifteen minutes, but looking for documents, unlocking and locking up file cabinets, and cleaning and detailing ourselves, takes about an hour per location if we all work together. We can take as much time as we need as long as we know Anderson's schedule," David explained.

"What about the device for the luggage?" I asked.

"It can be hidden inside the luggage or an outer pocket of the luggage, dontcha know. It is the size of a pack of cigarettes and runs on batteries that transmit a beeping signal to a receiver we have, which also runs on batteries. The signal beep is inaudible from the sending transmitter. If we plant the device too early the batteries might go dead. I think we need to plant it in their luggage before they leave the New York airport," David explained.

"I think the new technology will be great for all of us! The sooner we get the bugs installed, the more information we might be able to gather before their trip. The use of the mobile phone allows JoSam to know what we have found and gives him time to tell us our next directions," Colonel Hollander reported.

"I found out that the Andersons use one janitorial service called Spotless to clean all four properties, including their home. I talked to an overly ambitious employee who will provide us with uniforms and his truck if we pay him $1,000 for four hours," Colonel Hollander continued.

I stated my opinion. "I like the idea of using a service disguise to bug the two offices and home in Dover, Delaware. It will allow us more time to search those locations for documents. Bell Atlantic will give us more flexibility and protection. If anyone were to call the central office and inquire about our actions, the phone company might cover for us. The ambitious janitorial employee from Spotless is in a position to use blackmail against us. With Bell Atlantic, we wouldn't be restricted by a time factor in case we need more time to look for hidden documents."

"I found out the same information as Colonel Hollander about the Andersons using Spotless Janitorial Service, and my original plan was to use it as our disguise, but I feel more secure switching to the Bell Atlantic disguise," Montgomery added.

"We need to take a completely different approach for the Andersons' Washington, DC, office," I said. The state capitol gives tours from 1 p.m. to 4 p.m. daily, with prior reservations. Monday through Friday, the limit per tour is thirty-five people. Their busiest days are Fridays, and the tours are usually booked up. If we use tourist disguises, Montgomery, Colonel Hollander, and I can be the family from Georgia. Montgomery and the Colonel's Georgian accents will authenticate us.

"I get a Jon-Jon haircut again, Colonel Hollander will be my father, and Montgomery will be my uncle. David Allen is of Swedish ancestry and knows the language, and Russ Warren can speak Swedish as well. They will register as Hans and Bjorn Donelson, two brothers from Stockholm, Sweden. We need to present our respective identities when we register," I said.

"If you accept this plan, I can have these credentials created. We will register for a Friday tour because we will be less noticeable in a larger crowd and will have three hours in his congressional office. We can peel away from the crowd as needed to do our work. Anderson's office is on the first floor and is the one nearest to the elevator and men's restroom. I will give everyone a map of the interior later. Most of the tour is given in the La Rotunda and the legislative chambers, with equal time spent in the Senate room and the Congress hall, which are on the first floor near Anderson's office.

"All congressmen's office doors open out to one long hallway. Each office door has the name of the legislator posted on it. Theodore Anderson's office number is twenty-two. We need to take precautions with this because our shadows can be seen by anyone who is inside the office. This can be remedied by using a sheet of opaque paper with an even, soft, white light behind it to give the illusion of emptiness. We will know if Theodore Anderson is in Dover, Delaware, or Washington, DC, from the bugs that are sending information to the listening station and JoSam. Our new Motorola phone will be helpful," I finished orating my plan.

"I like the idea of your tag team so that not all five of us will leave the tour group at once. Each of us can use eye contact to signal when it is his turn to enter the congressman's office. Montgomery will open the office during registration, and we can take turns from there," Colonel Hollander remarked.

"It sounds like a workable plan, Lopez. Does anyone have anything to add?" JoSam asked. When no one spoke, he said, "Montgomery, besides your security duties of entering and exiting, you must make sure each property is left in its original state and with no trace of our intrusion. We can't afford any mistakes on this job that might alert the Andersons. They must not suspect anything. Colonel Hollander and Angelo, when you find something that is determined as classified information, do not remove the papers. Angelo, you read through them, use the Minox B, photograph every-thing, and call me instantly on the new Motorola phone to tell me what you have found. Don't talk to each other in any of the locations. Silence is untraceable, and each of you has an accent or regionalism in your speech. Lopez, find a private location to make your call when giving your report.

"Everyone will wear surgical gloves and shoe covers so that no hand oils or shoe prints are left. Try to help Montgomery keep it clean," JoSam suggested. He paused and then said, "I am thinking that Mrs. Anderson may be more involved with leaking information than her husband. The new technical equipment should improve the quality of our work. How it all works is amazing." As JoSam said this, he shook his head in disbelief.

He remained silent for a moment and then began again. "When and if we find something, I will have Korean passports ready for your overseas trip. I will make all of the arrangements. I think we are ready for the job. Everyone pack your bag for tomorrow's overnight flight to Dover, Delaware, first and then on to Washington, DC. Russ, you will have time to research your assignment in the morning before we leave, and we will discuss your findings on the flight. We leave at 8 a.m. in my plane," JoSam directed.

Special Five executed the mail room's cleansing routine and then left the room by 4:30 a.m. I waited with Montgomery while he surveyed the room one last time and sprayed it. Then he closed and locked the door. As the two of us walked up the stairs to his floor, I whispered to him, "I believe my days are numbered in Special Five. I think I will soon be replaced by technology."

"You and I share the same thoughts, but for now, we still have a job," Montgomery whispered back. I nodded in agreement, turned, walked back downstairs to my room on the first floor, and began packing and mentally running the plans in my mind. I couldn't sleep.

CHAPTER 15

INFILTRATION

The next day at 8 a.m., the weather was a sunny and a brisk forty-five degrees. I walked to JoSam's Learjet 58 sporting my Jon-Jon haircut and met Special Five. We helped David Allen pack the boxes of his new technological equipment into the bay of the aircraft. We boarded and arranged ourselves at the booths with tables. Montgomery sat on my side of the booth, and JoSam occupied one of the center recliners. The stewardess, Miss High Diddle-Diddle, took our drink orders. She saw Montgomery, and electricity ignited her like she was plugged into the wall socket.

"What can I get the best looking man on the planet?" she asked Montgomery.

"Coffee. Black please," He replied, without patting her ass or even looking in her direction.

"What will you have, kid?" she said to me. I felt myself bristle at her words.

"I will have a coke. I can understand how someone of your

vintage years could mistake me for a kid," I answered rebelliously. Montgomery's eyes twinkled, and he smiled.

When she returned, she leaned over Montgomery so his view was directly down her flouncy lavender blouse, but he ignored her completely.

"Montgomery, I think she has the hots for you."

"Yeah, well I am used to women's reactions."

"I don't think if I got that kind of reaction I would ever get used to it. I would race her to a horizontal position on the floor."

Montgomery laughed and said, "It's best not to mess with her kind, besides, aren't you an engaged man?"

"My mother is the one getting engaged. She loves that sort of stuff!"

"I think we need to hear Russ's report concerning the $150,000 that was transferred from Mrs. Herrick Asimov to Mrs. Lorena Anderson's bank account. Miss, if you wish to enjoy your book at the back of the aircraft, we won't be needing your services just now," JoSam said, dismissing Miss High Diddle-Diddle, and Russ Warren began reading his report.

"Mrs. Herrick Asimov, maiden name Claudia Vorotnikov, age thirty-six, is the daughter of the chairman of the Russian SFSR council of ministers, Vitaly Vorotnikov, and half-sister to our Mrs. Lorena Belov Anderson. Lorena Belov Anderson was born to Vitaly Vorotnikov and Tatiana Belov, who was an unmarried woman in 1945. Tatiana Belov and one-month-old Lorena immigrated to the USA in 1945 during World War II because they were suspected of having Jewish ancestry.

"Mrs. Herrick Asimov worked as an assistant press secretary to Boris Yeltsin. Boris Yeltsin deposited a $500,000 check into Mrs. Herrick Asimov's bank account December 4, 1982. I found a reservation for Lorena and Theodore Anderson at the Hilton La Guardia Airport Hotel for the nights of January 6 and January 9, 1982. I found available lockers to rent at the New York airport, but I didn't find out if Anderson rented one. The Hilton where they will be staying has a safe." Russ folded his fact sheet and concluded his report.

"Interesting relationship you discovered, Russ. If we don't find any army classified documents in the Andersons' Dover or Washington location, we can search their hotel before their flight to Seoul. We have four days after we plant the bugs and search the Andersons' properties to infiltrate their communications. We might get lucky and learn helpful information. David what have you got for us?" JoSam encouraged.

"You betcha." David opened his box of Bell Atlantic telephone workers' uniforms, and we dove into the box like kids with Halloween costumes.

"I tried to get correct sizes, so if the one you have doesn't fit, it probably isn't yours."

The Bell Atlantic red coveralls had embroidered names on the chest pockets (Walter, Mike, Bobby, Dan, and Pete) and looked as if they had been through a day's work.

"Hey, David, these are great, but red isn't the best color for my complexion," Montgomery quipped as he donned the coveralls with the name Walter. David smiled and shot him the bird. My red suit had the name Bobby and seemed appropriate for my kid haircut.

"The Bell Atlantic truck will be parked near the runway we will be landing on and is filled with tools we can use at our locations. We will put the mobile phones into the two empty toolboxes when we get there. JoSam, would you like to see yours?" The guys gathered around the beige colored mobile phone, which was thick as a brick and three times as long, and were intrigued by the novelty.

JoSam picked it up and made a complete examination, turning it over from front to back. "David, this would be a good time to show us how it works."

"You betcha. Inside the aircraft, we won't be able to get the clearest reception, but we can try to make a call. Do you want to call your wife, JoSam?" David asked.

"Which one? I just got married to wife number four. I guess I could call her."

"This button is the power 'on' button. Then you press the 'talk' button. Do you hear the dial tone? Punch in the numbers. Do you hear it ringing?" JoSam's rheumy blue eyes met David's face as he turned the phone in our direction and heard a feminine voice say, "Hello."

We were delighted and each wanted a turn. It was my turn after Colonel Hollander had called his wife, Margaret, so I called Venus. "Hi, Venus in Guatemala! This is Angelo. I have been thinking about you. I am calling from a new kind of phone we can carry around with us. I am on an airplane. No, honest it is true. I am glad to hear your voice. Don't forget me."

Montgomery snatched the phone away and made his call to a girl named Myrna. Russ called his brother, and David called his wife, Sally. While we watched and learned, David showed JoSam how to place the phone back in its cradle to allow it to recharge when it wasn't in use. David prepared the second phone and called JoSam. We heard it ring, and JoSam picked up his phone and thanked David for the modern technology. Everyone was reassured to know that the phone system worked.

David gave us a lesson on the use and installation of the bugging equipment. He demonstrated placing the microphones under one of the booth's tables and then set up the receiver in the back of the aircraft near Miss High Diddle-Diddle. We took turns listening to JoSam giving instructions to the pilot.

I had a great time playing with the equipment, and the other guys were high on energy for our job. You would think we had been drinking.

David passed out two sets of surgical gloves and booties. We placed them into the spacious pockets of our red Bell Atlantic coveralls, which were comfortably worn over our own clothes. We would be warm in the forty-three degree, frosty weather of Delaware.

"The live-listening relay station will be in place at Fort Benning the instant we place and activate the first bug. They have our mobile phone numbers and will call JoSam to give us the information they gather from the answering machines or from our placed bugs concerning the Andersons' whereabouts," David Allen continued.

"We should start with their home, dontcha know, since that location poses the least risk of an encounter. We know from Russ's report that they don't spend much time there," David suggested.

"I agree that the home should be our first hit. I have studied the city maps of Dover, Delaware, and have selected the quickest route between locations. I have written down the directions and suggest that I drive the Bell Atlantic truck. Angelo will 'suck up' the maps and my list now so that we can destroy them. We will receive location information from him. Does that sound like our best plan?" Colonel Hollander asked.

We all nodded in agreement. I looked at the map and absorbed its image into my mind. I read Colonel Hollander's list for route selection and concluded it was efficient. "Does anyone else want to see the map or the colonel's list before I destroy it?" I asked. After I received no response, I shredded the list and burned the small scraps in Montgomery's coffee cup with Russ's lighter. Only ashes remained. I handed the map to JoSam and showed him our route.

"I am ahead of you. Lopez, reach into the butt pocket of your coveralls," JoSam said.

I looked surprise and reached behind me. I found one of the new tracking devices. We chuckled and smiled with pride for our well-executed plan.

"Lopez, you will carry the phone in the Bell Atlantic toolbox because you will be the one calling me about the any documents that are found. I won't call any of you except when you are in the Bell truck. A ringing phone would be an endangerment," JoSam instructed.

The Gates Learjet 58 settled down gracefully on the Dover, Delaware, tarmac, and the Special Five left JoSam like we were leaving our mother sitting in a recliner at home. Clad in red overalls, we walked a few meters to the waiting Bell Atlantic telephone van. I spotted the two empty toolboxes and put one cell phone into the first box. Russ placed the second phone (for insurance) into the other box. I rode shotgun while Colonel Hollander drove. We left the airport and merged left onto the freeway.

"You will take exit number eleven, merge right toward Shadow Glen, and drive five miles," I directed. The other Special Five men remained silent. I assumed that they were mentally absorbed in their respective roles for our first hit.

"Colonel, turn left onto Elegant Pebble Path and look for house number 1811," I directed from 'imprint'. We pulled up in front of a beautiful, well-manicured southern colonial home, which resembled building number six at Fort Benning—the place we called home and Tara because it looked just like Scarlett's house in the movie *Gone with the Wind*.

Montgomery whistled and then said, "Nice shack! We're lucky we don't have snow in Delaware. We won't need to worry about covering our tracks in the snow. Lady Luck is with us."

Montgomery, Colonel Hollander, and I walked to the front door while Russ and David walked to the side door under the portico and waited for Montgomery. Montgomery had us inside the house in less than thirty-seconds. Colonel and I entered the pale blue, lavish marble entryway, which preceded the blue, white, and gold French provincial decor of the living room. I checked the small desk beside the fireplace, and two of the drawers were locked.

Montgomery had walked through the kitchen and dining area to the side door and had opened it for Russ and David. Russ and David began placing the bugs under the kitchen counters, and in the wall phone. Then they started up the stairs to the bedrooms.

I was about to leave the desk in the living room to find Montgomery but turned around to find that he was right behind me. He unlocked the drawer, and I carefully leafed through a stack of letters from campaign contributors and spotted a letter from Mrs. Herrick Asimov with a Russian postmark. I carefully removed the letter from its previously opened envelope, read its contents, and photographed it with the Minox B camera. I quickly searched the remainder of the drawer, replaced the letter in its exact location, picked up my toolbox, and left the house. I found a hidden place in the garden beside the foundation of the house while Montgomery was closing and locking the desk drawer.

I pretended to examine cables that were going into the house as I removed the phone from my toolbox and called JoSam. He answered on the first ring. "JoSam, I've got something. It's a letter from Mrs. Herrick Asimov. I found it in a desk drawer. Can you hear me?" I asked.

"Perfectly! Go ahead."

I relayed the letter from the vision in my mind:

> December 4, 1982,
> Dear Lorena,
>
> I hope you and Theodore are well and progressing on plans. Our father has taken new appointment as chairman of Russian council of ministers this year, but his health isn't the best, and I do not know how long he can remain in position. I helping him and will prolong job as long I can do the work for him.

Please excuse my poor English. I want we write in Russian.

I meet you in dining room of the Westin Chosun Seoul Hotel where you be staying, at 13:00 for lunch, January 8. My travel plans place me in city on January 4 where I stay with friends who have apartment near airport or at Westin Chosun Seoul Hotel. I decide later what is best. I think hotel give more privacy. I bring balance of your payment, and we exchange envelopes in Seoul. The contents of envelope you give help Russia end Cold War and help our father to secure a good future with the party or his pension.

Your little sister gained few pounds but can recognize me from last photo. What strange life we sisters have all because Poppa was a frisky fellow!

Claudia

"Good work, Lopez. You were very quick to find this. How is the rest of it going?" JoSam asked.

"I don't know, sir. I will call you from the Bell van while we are in route to the next location. How is the tracker in my pocket working?" I asked.

"It occasionally lights up and sometimes beeps, but I don't know what this means. We need another lesson from David."

"I'll call again." I hung up, placed the phone in the toolbox, and went back inside. The colonel had opened a wall safe and motioned for me to look inside. I counted over $100,000 in stashed US one hundred dollar bills, which were in bundles of $1,000 each. I took pictures with the Minox B camera, and Colonel raised his eyebrows as Montgomery carefully closed the safe and reset the combination lock to its original settings.

Colonel Hollander caught everyone's attention, lifted his arm straight up, and circled in the air to indicate we were finished. Russ and David nodded, and we walked out the front entrance of the Andersons' house in less than twenty minutes. Montgomery wiped off his hand oils from the safe's combination dial with one of his booties because he had removed his gloves to feel the safe's tumblers, checked the carpet for prints, sprayed the air, turned the inside lock, gave one last look, and closed the door.

When we were on the move again, I called JoSam and told him about the cash in the safe. I passed the phone to David and Russ while I focused on our driving route, and they gave JoSam their observations.

"JoSam, this is Russ. You can't believe the anal-retentive state and immaculate organization of the Andersons' house. Every closet had shoes lined up according to style and color, and every drawer was labeled with gold plates indicating its contents. Nothing was done randomly or spontaneously. Every detail of housekeeping was planned and executed. I couldn't detect if Mr. Anderson or Mrs. Anderson was the fastidious organizer. The kitchen had the silverware uniformly arranged in rows and pointed in the correct position. Hold on. David wants to talk to you," Russ said.

"JoSam, David here. For crying out loud, I think the order motor is Mr. Anderson. What man would allow a woman to roll up his skivvies, with the elastic at the top, and all in a row according to color, looking like little white trimmed roses in his bureau drawer? We learned so much about this man's psychological makeup. He has planned for every moment of the day and has his life in complete order until his death, which he appears not to believe in. Uff da! We just ran into road construction and need to deviate our course. I am going to hang up now," David said.

"A roadblock in the best laid plans! Shit! yelled Colonel Hollander.

"It is okay, Colonel Hollander," I soothed.

"Give me a second." I closed my eyes, visualized the map inside my head, and began to redirect. "Take a right onto South Dupont and drive for three miles." Colonel Hollander drove by my verbal directions. "Take a right on Bridge Street, drive for three blocks, and turn left onto Market Street." I opened my eyes to help him find the street names.

"Good! This is good. Travel down Market for four blocks and turn onto Chestnut. Anderson and Anderson's law office should be near the corner. There it is! There is plenty of space to park on the street directly in front of the office. One of us needs to go in to check it out. It is nearly 13:00, and the office probably won't be empty," I reasoned aloud.

"I'll go," Montgomery said as he left the Bell Atlantic van. He bounded back to the van in less than five minutes. "Okay, we're in! The receptionist, Peggy, who is blond, buxom, and very flirtatious accepted my story hook, line, and sinker. I will be sitting on Peggy's desk if you need me. Let's go!"

Anderson and Anderson's law office was a five-room suite, which included a reception area, two offices, a conference room, and a kitchenette. Russ and David paired up, entered Mr. Anderson's office, and placed a covert listening device there. Colonel Hollander and I swept through Mrs. Anderson's office, spotted a locked file cabinet, and called to Montgomery.

"Walter, we could use your help in here for a moment. Seems we have a rusted wire," I said as I entered the receptionist area. Montgomery went into Mrs. Anderson's office, and I took his place entertaining Peggy.

"Excuse me, miss, would it be possible for you to point out an inexpensive diner where I could pick up some sandwiches?" I asked.

"Why, sure thing, sugar! I'll just step outside for a minute and point the way to the best, doable, darling, deluxe, Dover diner," she said in a singsong voice as she giggled at her own alliteration.

Montgomery popped back into the receptionist area and said, "Hey, Bobby, are you cutting in on the cutest chick I've found in Dover?" he asked.

"Uh-uh, no," I stammered. "She was just telling me where I could go to order some sandwiches," I said, recovering.

"I think they need your help inside, Bobby. Peggy, will you show me the way to the diner? Will you do that for me, Peggy?" Montgomery asked as he winked at her.

I returned and stood beside Colonel Hollander. He pointed to a file he had pulled up higher than the others. He used his gloves to remove a document and laid it on top of the open drawer. I took out the Minox B camera, attached a pair of binoculars to it, snapped each page, and began to read. When I had finished, I grabbed up the Bell Atlantic toolbox and headed for the diner. I noticed Russ and David had placed the bugs in the offices, including Peggy's. They were waiting in the reception room for me. "I think we need to go have some lunch at the best, doable, darling, deluxe, Dover diner," I said as Russ looked at me like he was worried about my mind.

Montgomery and Peggy were standing in front of Anderson and Anderson's law office when I passed them. "I am starved. See you later at the diner. Nice to meet you Peggy," I cordially acknowledged with a wave.

I walked swiftly to the diner Peggy had pointed to, and sat at a booth in the back with my back to the door. The diner was sparsely inhabited due to the time of day. Most of the lunch crowd had cleared out. I placed the toolbox on the seat so that it was hidden by the tall booth, opened it, removed the phone, and called JoSam. The phone rang once.

"What have you got?" JoSam asked.

"F-117A Nighthawk Stealth Fighter information and blue prints."

"Oh, my God," JoSam said, startling me and causing me to be silent. "Lopez, are you there?" he shouted.

"Yes."

"Go on, Lopez. We have hit the jackpot. Give it! Give it!"

"F-117A Nighthawk Stealth Fighter information and blue prints," I stammered. "The F-117A Nighthawk is a unique aircraft. Its surfaces and edge profiles are optimized to reflect enemy radar away from its radar detectors. It is coated with radar-absorbing materials. The radar cross section of the F-117A has been estimated at between ten and one hundred square centimeters or about the size of a small bird, making it nearly invisible to enemy air defenses.

"The Nighthawk is powered by a pair of F48 K-N General Electric F404-GE-F1D2 turbofans, which were derivatives of the F404 General Electric 400 engines used to power the F/A-18 Hornet. To keep the aircraft invisible as long as possible, the engine exhaust area is wide and flat with the air intakes on both sides of the fuselage and covered by gratings that have been coated with radar-absorbent material. The Nighthawk's two large tail fins lean outward, obstructing enemy infrared detection and radar returns of the engine exhaust area, concealing tell tale visible exhaust." I continued.

"The Nighthawk has a one-man crew, and the cockpit is out-fitted with a Kaiser Electronics heads-up display. The flight deck is equipped with a large video monitor displaying infrared images from the plane's onboard sensors and a full colored moving map developed by the Harris Corporation. To keep the plane as invisible as possible to enemy detection, the F117A does not rely on radar for navigation or targeting. The plane is equipped with a forward-looking infrared (FLIR) and a downward-looking infrared (DLIR) with a laser designator. These used a Honeywell inertial navigation system.

"Along the front of the aircraft, there are multi-channeled pitot-static tubes with multiple ports along their lengths, which provide differential pressure readings that the flight control computers compare to provide the Nighthawk's flight data.

"When going into battle, the F-117A can carry up to four thousand pounds and a variety of weapons in its internal weapons' bay, including the BLU-109B, low level laser-guided bomb, GBU-10 and GBU-27 laser-guided bomb units, and the AGM-65 and AGM-88 HARM air-to-surface missiles. The F-117A's top speed has been released as high subsonic, with its cruising speed as 684 miles per hour. The Nighthawk has an unlimited range of operations when using aerial refueling. The F-117A Nighthawk is the world's first operational aircraft that is designed to exploit low, observable, stealth technology. The Nighthawk features the unique design of the single-seat F-117A Nighthawk, provided exceptional combat capabilities, and is about the size of—"

"That's enough, Lopez," JoSam said. "Special Five has done a good job. Place the remainder of the bugs into the 'Anderson for Congress' campaign office and don't search for any more documents. We have what we need. David's bugs are already picking up information.

"The Andersons are at the Dover campaign office hosting an event. There is a back entrance off the alley for caterers, and that might be your safest bet for entry. There is a group of five telephones all at one station. Do a quick in and out, and then we can fly to Washington before the Capitol tour hours end. Thanks, Lopez." He hung up. I stuck the phone back into the toolbox, looked around, and saw Special Five in another booth close to the front door of the diner.

"Hey, Bobby, come have lunch with us. We ordered you a cheeseburger deluxe with a large coke," Montgomery shouted. I inhaled the cheeseburger and curly fries with ketchup as I regurgitated JoSam's information to Special Five.

"I pumped Peggy for information about the Andersons' whereabouts, and JoSam's information confirms her story. Peggy expects me to pick her up from work after five," Montgomery said wide-eyed.

"Let's hit the road, Jack. Where do we go 'Oh sage of great

vision'?" Colonel Hollander asked me as we piled back into the Bell Atlantic van.

I looked at the name on my chest pocket and said, "It is Bobby, not Jack," I said, not realizing the colonel was paraphrasing a popular eighties American song. He scoffed at my mistake.

"Go back down Chestnut and take a left onto Morris. Then drive for five miles and turn onto Plumb. The Andersons' campaign office is 7997 Plumb Street. I don't want to meet the Andersons," I said emphatically.

"I don't either. Avoidance and speed are our best allies in the next hit. Gloves for the placement of the bugs is all we need. We can keep them in our pockets like we did at the law office until we need them. Since all the phones are together, I think it is best if Russ and I take care of it so we don't attract attention with five of us party crashing', dontcha know," David explained.

"Agreed! We will wait in the van, and I will double-park so we can rabbit start out of here," Colonel Hollander said as I nodded.

Russ and David took a toolbox, left the Bell Atlantic van, walked into the noisy office, found the table with five phones, which weren't being used, and went to work unobtrusively placing the last communication infiltration devices. As David stood up to leave, a well-dressed woman entered carrying a large tray of chocolates and two bottles of wine.

"We're all finished," he said as he started for the door.

"Thanks for your help! Take a handful of these chocolates for your kids and remember Congressman Anderson," she said to Russ as she handed him the two bottles of wine.

"Thanks," Russ answered in a fluster. Then he went out the back door and into the waiting van, which then sped away with Special Five munching chocolates. During the ride back to the airport, we shed the Bell Atlantic coveralls, folded them neatly, and placed them back in the box David had brought from JoSam's aircraft before we had begun our Dover infiltration. David also added a new Motorola phone to the box, which was in the new, soon-to-be-marketed, colorful packaging and had an owner's manual. He also added a handcrafted thank-you note.

"For you, sir," Montgomery said to JoSam as he entered the waiting Learjet and handed him the two bottles of wine. JoSam looked surprised.

"Let's save these for our return trip to Georgia. Originally, we planned to stay overnight, but the job went so well today, we can return home early. I need to attend a Pentagon meeting tomorrow morning." JoSam touched a button signaling the pilot that we were ready for takeoff. Miss High Diddle-Diddle took our drink orders with her man-catcher antenna poised in Montgomery's direction.

"I'll have coffee, and Mr. Lopez will have a Coke," Montgomery said sternly.

"Since this is a short twenty-minute flight to Washington, DC, I'll get directly to the assignment. Here are the diagrams of the Congress Hall and its offices," I said as I passed them out. "There are only two phones in Anderson's office according to Chesapeake and Potomac Telephone Company. Of course, the Capitol has the information switchboard. One of Congressman Anderson's phones is answered by a part-time secretary, and his private office telephone has an answering machine. I am thinking—"

JoSam, interrupted, "Thanks to bugs placed in the Delaware office we know his office at the Capitol is vacant. Anderson's secretary is helping with the campaign event in Dover, which is only sixty-five miles from her apartment in the DC area. So this needs to be a quick in and out," JoSam said.

"We no longer need to search for documents," I explained. We only need to do the bug placement quickly. I will call the Yellow Cab Taxi service and have a car meet our aircraft at the airport. I will ask the driver to wait for you at the Capitol and to bring you back. I know the phone number. Do you need anyone else besides Montgomery to do this job, David?" I asked.

"You have it correct, Mr. Lopez," David answered.

"Another lucky stroke. It's forty-three degrees in Washington, DC, without snow or drizzle to damage our invisible infiltration," Montgomery beamed.

I called the Yellow Cab Taxi service and gave them the expected time for our arrival. We landed five minutes later. David and Montgomery walked across the tarmac to a waiting yellow cab beside the ground transportation sign.

"Miss, take this credit card and bring back a full dinner for us to eat on the long leg back to Georgia. I want the very best wine, garden salad, lobster bisque soup, filet mignon cooked medium rare, loaded baked potatoes, vegetables, and garlic bread for everyone. Lopez, what do you want for dessert?" JoSam asked.

"Chocolate cake."

Miss High Diddle-Diddle descended JoSam's Learjet with credit card in hand, as I watched her pumping behind move like two Costa Rican monkeys in a tight purple sack until she was out of sight.

The colonel caught my gaze and laughed. "Cool your jets, Lopez. You are only seventeen."

"I beg your pardon, Mr. Hollander. I am seventeen and a half, soon to be eighteen in May. I got this silly Jon-Jon haircut and didn't even use it! No girl over the age of twelve will even look in my direction."

"Don't whine," he laughed. "You are too young for her."

Russ and Colonel Hollander moved into the recliner chairs as I watched JoSam's strange demeanor. He checked to see if the phone was within his reach, pulled his legs up into his chair in his gargoyle pose, and folded his arms around his legs like bat wings. His eyes became vacant of any present awareness.

"Is he all right?" I whispered to Russ.

"Perfectly fine! He has gone into his strategy mode. We need to be quiet," Russ whispered as he reclined his chair flatly to take his nap. I continued to watch JoSam. His eyes were wide open but never moved or focused. I watched him for thirty minutes until my head began to nod and I fell into a nap of my own.

When I awoke from my tiny nap, I saw that both Colonel Hollander and Russ were in deep sleep. JoSam was still in his gargoyle strategy mode, and his eyes looked like bulging, blue glass bowls hanging on a wall. I looked out the window and saw Miss High Diddle-Diddle walking toward the plane with three men following her, as they watched her purple stretch pants and carried sacks and cartons of food.

When I got the front view, I saw that her pants were so tight the V of the crotch was a W. One man entered the rear door of the plane and placed the items in the galley. He wrapped himself around the front of Miss High Diddle-Diddle and rubbed himself against her protruding cleavage. She flirtatiously backed away and handed him her phone number. This woman was so hot, she melted the Washington snow as she passed by. I wondered if she was the kind of woman who could ever be sexually satisfied.

I assessed my own satisfaction and knew I was grateful for my job and friends. I was amazed how well Special Five worked together. We were like a well-oiled machine. I was lucky for this life. Another hour had passed when Montgomery and Russ returned to the Learjet, and JoSam became alert. "How did it go?" he asked.

"Security was lacking! We didn't even register for the tour. We easily followed the diagram of the congressional building that Angelo gave to us. We breezed in, did our work, and walked out, never meeting anyone who questioned us. You would never know there was a cold war going on. David and I found a locked safe. I opened it just out of curiosity and found another $100,000 in stacked bundles of one hundred dollar bills," Montgomery reported.

"Special Five, this has been a good day's work!" JoSam said as Miss High Diddle-Diddled alerted the pilot that we were ready for takeoff.

"What can I get you gentleman to drink before I serve your dinner?" she asked.

"Give us all wine and one Coke," JoSam ordered. I devoured the beautiful steak dinner, drank the Coke, and rested contentedly.

"David, can you come and sit here? I want to talk to you," JoSam said. David moved over to the indicated chair, and the two of them talked for a couple of hours. They both stood up walked to the cockpit, sat in the vacant copilots' chairs, and talked to the pilot for the rest of the flight. That was a curious phenomenon.

I read law books the remainder of the trip back to Georgia and was glad to sleep in my own bed after a successful completed assignment. JoSam had given us the next day (January 4) off, and we could use it for recreation.

The next day, I went to the gym, swam, and worked out. I conversed with the soldier named Sergio who had denied me entrance and had doubted my association with JoSam's fraternity only seven months earlier.

CHAPTER 16
ESPIONAGE

JoSam called a Special Five meeting for Friday, January 5, at 3:02 a.m. in the mailroom. We were used to our meeting routine and ready for JoSam's Seoul, Korea, instructions. I noticed JoSam looked stressed, tired, redder, and more aloof than usual.

"Special Five will be going into Seoul, Korea, almost naked, except for the clothing on your bodies. You will have no luggage, mobile phones, Minox B camera, or espionage equipment. You will carry only a PSS silent pistol. You have been issued your Colt M1911 service pistols and have trained with them, but the PSS silent pistol is the right one for this job. This will be your first assassination assignment. Your targets are the Andersons and Mrs. Herrick Asimov—at close range. Stop by Colonel Hollander's office to pick up your pistol and your new passports after today's classes." JoSam explained everything rapidly so Special Five wouldn't have time to think about what he had just told us.

"The Andersons are confirmed passengers on Korean Air Lines flight 007, a commercial Boeing 747, out of gate 11 in New York City.

They board at 3 p.m. on January 7th, arrive in Anchorage at 12:30 a.m. for a half-hour refueling stop, depart for Seoul, Korea, at 1 a.m., and arrived in Seoul, Korea, at 9 a.m. on January 8,1983. The Andersons have registered to attend the ceremonies being held for the thirty-year anniversary of the US/Korea Mutual Defense Treaty."

"David Allen, you will be on that flight with the Andersons but will transfer to its sister flight, Korean Air Lines flight 015 in Anchorage when it stops to refuel," JoSam explained as he sighed and took a deep breath.

"Special Five, your KAL flight 015 leaves New York at 5 p.m. on January 7th and arrives in Anchorage at 2:30 a.m. for a half-hour refueling stop. David Allen will board your flight then. All of you will depart for Seoul, Korea, at 3:00 a.m. and arrive at 11:00 a.m. on January 8, 1983. Your flight has Senator Jesse Helms of North Carolina, Senator Steven Simms of Idaho, and Representative Carroll J. Hubbard Jr. from Kentucky, who will also be attending the Korean thirty-year anniversary ceremonies," JoSam said as he shifted into his protective gargoyle sitting position.

"Special Five will take a taxi to the Westin Chosun Seoul Hotel dining room where the Andersons and Claudia Asimov will meet for lunch at 1 p.m. You will be waiting. Chosun Hotel's dining room has circular-shaped, large, padded, leather, tufted booths with high backs, which conceal diners who occupy them. The assassinations will take place in the hotel dining room. This meeting with the Andersons and Mrs. Herrick Asimov has been confirmed by the covert listening device you placed in the Anderson and Anderson law office."

JoSam took a tired breath and continued. "My Learjet will take you to New York to catch your 5 p.m. flight. Be at our airbase tomorrow at 2 p.m. for takeoff. David Allen and I will not be going with you to New York tomorrow. David will meet you in Anchorage as we have another project to complete. When you finish your job at the hotel dining room in Seoul, go immediately back to the airport where I will meet you on the runway with the Learjet, and we will all come home together. Do you have any questions?" JoSam asked. We remained silent. "Okay, that's a wrap." JoSam left the mailroom.

Special Five helped Montgomery detail the room while I checked JoSam's chair for any traces from his tucked limbs. The room was pristine, the door was locked, and I heard Montgomery recite Nicola's Poem to himself:

> I tolerate no betrayal,
> No tarnished loyalty.
> If my trust in you does fail,
> You die like dethroned royalty.

I wanted to be alone but couldn't sleep. I didn't want to talk to anyone, not even to Montgomery. I trudged to our dining hall and brought back my breakfast to the quiet isolation of my room. I wasn't hungry but chewed and swallowed by rote. I had questions regarding what I was about to do: *Could I do it? Why was I doing it? How could I have gotten into such a fix?*

I believed that Mr. Anderson had committed treason, but how could he have been a long-term John Birch Society member and still have done this? Maybe he didn't know what his wife had done. Maybe he wasn't guilty. What about the Russian woman, Mrs Herrick Asimov? She may have been considered a Russian heroine, doing what she could for her father and her country. Who was I to judge who was right and who was wrong? Why was I playing God? I had no right to take three lives, but it was my job. I had to do my job! It wasn't personal. I was an employee just doing a job.

I left my room and attended my morning classes, including AA where I was given an award for seven months of sobriety. If it wasn't for the School of the Americas, would I have been a drunken, stumbling, *soapyloatie* (buzzard) on the streets of Costa Rica? Was my next assignment the way to pay what I owed for my acquired sobriety and respect? I agonized with my thoughts.

Before my afternoon letter-writing class, I picked up my mail and went to sulk in my room and to read my three letters from Venus, Mother, and Isabella. My mother had written that she and Isabella were growing fond of one another and had decided the wedding should take place before my new Guatemalan position began in February. She was overjoyed with the wedding plans and asked if February 14th would be a good wedding day in honor of Saint Valentino.

In class, I answered Mother's letter. I was absorbed with the darkness the next mission had cast over me. My mother's happiness and frivolity would not be extinguished by my future task, which remained a dark, ugly secret. How could my mother or wife stand knowing that at seventeen and a half years old, I was a paid assassin?

I accepted the wedding date. What did it matter? My real life wouldn't be the life of a married family man. It was decided that Isabella would stay in Costa Rica with our families until my job in Guatemala was finished. Our union would provide great wealth for our two families, which greatly pleased both of our fathers. My wedding was an act to please my parents because I had quite another life they knew nothing about. My bride would be my job. I would be married to her, and what a demanding vixen she had become.

After class, I went to Colonel Hollander's office and picked up my gun and passport. We both were under the same dark cloud, and no words passed between us. When I got to my room, I looked at my passport and saw that again, I was someone new. My name was Alonzo Coto Martinez from Costa Rica.

I spent the evening playing blackjack upstairs in the card room and received a warm welcome. The card game made me forget my thoughts of tomorrow. The games were lively, and I raked in $1,400 in less than two hours. Montgomery was there as our doorkeeper and house manager, which made me chuckle at his prosperity. He collected a fifteen-dollar-per-person cover charge. I waved at him as I left the card room at 10:30 p.m., for a night of sleep that would never come.

At 2:00 p.m. on January 7th, Special Five consisted of only four men because David Allen was absent. Everyone was sullen and detached and in their own thoughts. Montgomery and Russ chose the recliners near me and discussed their passports. "None of us has an American name or passport. Mine is German," Russ Warren revealed.

The three-hour Learjet flight was a silent vacuum as everyone read or slept. We arrived in New York on time and boarded the KAL flight 015 and found that our seats were dispersed throughout the aircraft. I was glad to be alone rather than bundled together with the others.

It was a nine-hour flight to Anchorage. It allowed me time to read *The New York Times*. We arrived in Anchorage on time at 2:30 a.m. to refuel, but passengers were not allowed to leave the aircraft. Everyone was restless and noisy and took advantage of the time to stand or move about the cabin. I stood up and stretched to get the kinks out and saw David Allen board, but neither of us acknowledged the other. Did he have a Swedish passport? He hunted for his seat, which was located in the back of the airplane, and sat down heavily. He looked terrible—more stressed and tired than JoSam had looked during Special Five's meeting.

Korean Air Lines flight 007, Mr. Anderson's flight and our sister flight, was two hours ahead of us and had already refueled in Anchorage. After taking off from Anchorage, the flight had been instructed by air traffic control to turn its heading to 220 degrees. Approximately ninety seconds later, air traffic control directed the flight to go directly to Bethel, Alaska.

Upon flying over Bethel, Alaska, flight 007 would be entering the northernmost of five, fifty-mile-wide airways known as the North Pacific routes. These routes bridged the Alaskan and Japanese coasts. Flight 007's particular airway was called R-20 and was located just seventeen and a half miles from Soviet airspace off the Kamchatka coast.

At ten minutes after takeoff from Anchorage, Flight 007, flying at a heading of 245 degrees, began to deviate to the right (north) of its assigned route to Bethel, Alaska. It would continue to fly on this constant heading for the next five and a half hours.

Its autopilot wasn't operating in the correct mode for one of two reasons. Either the crew hadn't switched the autopilot on or the computer, for some reason, didn't transition from one mode to another because the aircraft had already deviated offtrack by more than the seven and a half nautical miles allowable by the inertial navigation computer. In either case, the autopilot remained in the incorrect mode, and the problem wasn't detected by the crew.

When KAL 007 didn't reach Bethel at fifty minutes after takeoff, a military radar at King Salmon, Alaska, tracked the flight at twelve point six miles north of where it should have been. The deviation was six times greater than the maximum expected drift if the navigation system had been operating correctly. The inability to establish direct radio communication with the airplane and transmit its position directly, meant that the pilots weren't alerted of flight 007's ever increasing divergence. It wasn't considered unusual by air traffic controllers because of the unreliable nature of their radio systems while aircrafts were in that area.

Korean Air Lines flight 007 continued its journey, deviating 160 nautical miles off course until it entered Kamchatka Peninsula of Russia's restricted airspace. The buffer zone extended a 120 miles from the Kamchatka Coast, and KAL flight 007 was eighty miles from its coast. The aircraft was shot down by Russian Major Genadi

Osipovich, killing 246 passengers, including the Andersons and twenty-three crew members.

Eight hours after leaving Anchorage, our flight 015 arrived at the Seoul, Korea, airport at precisely 11 a.m., and we went through immigration with our new passports in hand without any trouble. We were right on time to keep our appointment. I focused my attention on the whereabouts of the others, but the airport was in a strange state of frenzy. I felt there was an emergency in the atmosphere. Airline employees were running about, and people were yelling at each other. Announcements over the loudspeakers blared. I knew something was wrong and saw Russ talking to a group of Koreans as I walked out to ground transportation.

Special Five regrouped for the taxi ride at ground transportation, but none of us acknowledged that we knew each other. We acted as if we were business men and this was a shared ride to the Hotel. Russ rode in the passengers seat and spoke Korean jovially with the taxi driver. He laughed and enjoyed conversing. I noticed Colonel Hollander smiled, laughed, and looked at both the driver and Russ as if he understood Korean. I followed suit and laughed the loudest. I noticed Russ's smile of gratitude at our efforts.

Russ paid the driver with Korean money, and we went into the Westin Chosun Seoul Hotel's dining room, which was an expansive room with few people. Colonel Hollander led the way and chose a central booth with the exact description JoSam had given at our meeting. The time was 11:45 a.m. by the large oriental clock on the dining room wall. The waiter took Russ's family style order, including coffee and Coke. After the waiter left, we kept our voices low as we pounced on Russ for information.

"It seems Korean Air Lines flight 007 never arrived and vanished from any checkpoints or radar. The airport was a mess because family, friends, and aviation staff needed information."

"This *smacks* of JoSam's work," Colonel Hollander said. We were all silent with our eyes fixed on David Allen.

"You betcha. This is his work, and we need to continue the plan without the Andersons." That was the only thing he said.

"If Mrs. Herrick Asimov is staying at this hotel, she may not have heard the news and is likely to keep the appointment. Russ, you have Korean money, and I think you should pay for our lunch before she arrives so we won't be detained with the bill," I suggested.

"Good idea, Lopez," the Colonel agreed.

The family style lunch arrived. It looked delicious, but I had no appetite and only managed to drink my Coke to settle my stomach. Russ had paid for the lunch when it had been delivered and had explained in Korean that he would leave a large tip on the table if the waiter didn't come to our section again and disturb us until our business meeting had finished. The waiter had been agreeable. The time was 12:14 p.m. I had a queasy stomach and was all nerves.

Special Five attempted to eat and at least dirty the dishes. We couldn't make any plans because everything was live and variable. The time was 12:30 p.m., and I had nervous jitters.

"How difficult will it be to get a taxi when we leave?" I asked.

"Not hard at all. Taxies are lined up, parked outside, and ready for hotel guests," Russ answered.

At 12:40 p.m., my nerves were hair-trigger tight, and I had the instincts of a trapped jungle panther. By 12:45 p.m., a dark-haired, petite, smartly dressed woman followed a waiter to a booth directly across from us. She positioned herself in the middle of the circular booth and put her purse on her lap. I could see her legs from my vantage point. She reached into her purse and laid a white, bulging envelope on the table.

"What a little beauty," Montgomery whispered.

"I want to make sure she is Mrs. Claudia Asimov so we don't make a mistake," Colonel Hollander declared.

"I'll walk over and call her Claudia as an old friend would do in Russian," Russ said as they both slid from their end of our booth and approached her from the left side, still leaving her visible to me. Like lightning, her hand darted inside her purse, but I saw the gun. I stood up and shot her directly in the head. Her body crumpled into the booth where she was totally hidden. When she fell backward into the booth, her gun discharged, hitting Colonel Hollander in the thigh. Montgomery was at the colonel's side in less than two-seconds and shot her again in the chest for insurance.

Both he and Russ put their arms around the colonel to support him. David left the dining room and opened the taxi's door for Russ, Colonel Hollander, and Montgomery. Russ told the waiters in Korean that the food was delicious but that our friend had had too much to drink. I went to Mrs. Asimov's table, picked up the envelope she had placed there, left forty dollars on our table, smiled at the waiter, and pointed at the table to show him the tip was there. I was the last to get into the taxi, and we escaped to the airport.

Russ rode in the front seat, spoke to the driver in Korean, sang, joked, and laughed all the way to the airport while David Allen joined in his merriment. During the frivolity, I whispered to Colonel Hollander beside me. "How are you doing?" I asked.

"Okay," he answered. "I think it's only a flesh wound, but it hurts like hell. Angelo Lopez, thank you for saving my life!" Colonel Hollander whispered.

Montgomery reached over, jerked David Allen's bandana from his overall pockets, unzipped Hollander's pants, pulled them down past the wounded area, and made a tourniquet from the bandana and his comb to slow the blood flow. I removed my undershirt and wiped away blood droplets from the seats and floor. I tried to clean up his pants so we would be able to pass through customs. The tourniquet seemed to stop the blood flow, and I cleaned the stains from his shoes. We accomplished all of this while Russ and David Allen distracted the taxi driver's attention by directing his focus to passing landmarks. Meanwhile, I redressed him and began to laugh and sing in Spanish when we were finished.

The taxi pulled up to airport's departure area, and I mimed to Russ that we needed a bottle of water. Russ asked the taxi driver if he had any water, and the driver reached into his cooler in the front seat and handed it to Russ. I took it from him and gave Colonel Hollander a drink. Russ paid the driver, and the 'partying' Special five climbed out of the taxi while supporting Colonel Hollander.

Montgomery, Hollander, and Russ got in the shortest line of customs while David and I choose other lines. I watched Russ explain to the customs official that he didn't know the other two and that he was helping to get the giant of a man to his correct gate. I saw them fish through the colonel's pockets for his passport and then stamp it. They each presented their own passports, received their stamps, and were waved through the immigration checkpoint.

They continued their party routine of miming throwing a football, dancing, and high-fiveing fellow passengers, until they reached our gate. We all hurried out to the runway as David pointed in the direction of JoSam's plane. I ran up the steps of the Learjet 58, which seemed like a haven of safety.

"JoSam," I exploded. "Colonel Hollander has been shot in the thigh. Would it be possible for our pilot to radio the control tower and ask for a doctor to come on board?" I asked.

"Yes! Go get Russ."

I ran back to the tarmac and took Russ's place of supporting the six-foot-six-inch Colonel Hollander, who was very difficult to balance. We carried him up the stairs, laid him in the recliner, adjusted it to a flat level, unzipped his pants, pulled them off, and peeked under the tourniquet. The wound looked deep, but there was no gushing blood.

Russ spoke Korean to the control tower and asked for a doctor. A control officer responded. "They will send one directly."

We only waited about ten minutes, and a young, small Korean doctor, who looked like he practiced Kung Fu because he was in top physical condition, knelt down beside Colonel Hollander and removed the tourniquets. Miss High Diddle-Diddle brought a bowl of water and clean clothes for the doctor to use.

"Colonel Hollander was partying and accidentally shot himself in the leg. His flight will be at least fifteen hours. What is your best recommendation for his care?" Russ asked the doctor.

"The bullet did not hit anything major, but I can feel it inside his thigh and cannot remove it without taking him to the hospital," the doctor explained.

"Do you think he can safely make the fifteen hour flight?" questioned Russ.

"I have pain pills and antibiotics that should last him until he gets to the hospital, but you need to keep him still so the bullet won't travel deeper," he cautioned. JoSam paid the doctor, who seemed pleased.

We all relaxed into our seats, and Miss High Diddle-Diddle prepared the plane and signaled the pilot for takeoff. Special Five were served good wine and a Coke for me. JoSam raised his glass. "This toast is in honor of Special Five."

"This toast is for the quick action of the man who saved my life—Angelo Lopez," Colonel Hollander announced through his pain. I reached into my jacket pocket, pulled out Mrs. Asimov's envelope, and tossed it to JoSam as I said, "And this is for my boss." Special Five cheered.

"I had completely forgotten about the envelope," Montgomery chuckled.

"For crying out loud! You are a sly dog, Angelo," David said. JoSam took the envelope, looked at the contents, and tossed it back to me.

"No, Lopez, you remembered to pick it up, so it's yours," JoSam said. I caught it in midair and counted its contents, which was exactly $500,000. "Eureka!" I shouted. Each of the packets contained $100,000, and I tossed one to each of the Special Five members.

JoSam, while in route to deliver Colonel Hollander to the Emergency Room at Fort Benning, called in another espionage team to retrieve the planted bugs on the Andersons' property before the airlines released the names of passengers who had been on board the downed flight KAL 007. The removal of the listening devices insured total erasure of any government involvement or suspicion of irregularity. The Anderson assassination assignment was closed forever.

Later that week, I felt exhilaration as I sat down to a scrumptious dinner at our full table. It had been five days since my teammates had been together. Being in their company relaxed and energized me.

"Hey David, congratulations on your promotion and on the new computer lab. You have the very latest computer technology available, and your new position should make you very happy, not to mention the pay raise you have earned," I exclaimed.

David Allen squirmed in his chair as he ate his prime rib dinner and replied with a very modest, "Thank you."

"I have also heard about the new computer technology called XKeyScore you have been working on with Apple and IBM. I know it is still classified information, but it is my understanding that production of computers, for our use only, will be available soon. You have my admiration for your skills of invention," Montgomery congratulated as he raised his glass.

"I am proud to know you," Russ echoed the toast.

"When we finish our dessert, let's go over to the card room for an exciting, long overdue round of blackjack. I think many dollars will flow my way tonight," I invited.

"Dontcha know! You gents will have to rake in the green lettuce without me. I have work I need to finish in my new computer lab," David Allen replied.

Three of us bounced up to the card room as David entered the computer lab. He slowly and heavily closed the door behind him, arranged his desk neatly, and placed the stack of unfinished work in his "In" basket. He placed three newly composed letters in his "Out" basket and settled his bearlike body into the extra-large, new executive swivel chair.

He ran his hands through his wild mass of unruly dark hair and then folded his hands in a prayer position on the partners-style, rosewood desktop with its new maroon-colored, felt-and-leather-trimmed desk set. He reached over and removed a black, heavy-duty, Glad garbage bag from the newly opened box, placed the bag over his head, reached under his shirt for his special issued pistol, opened his mouth, and pulled the trigger.

Because of the Anderson assassination, my bank account soared to over $250,000 and a permanent place was secured for me with Special Five. The assassination raised my importance with teachers and bolstered my inner self-confidence. It definitely established my status as a leader at Fort Benning.

As I took more classes at Fort Benning, time passed into February and pushed me to return to Costa Rica to attend Isabella and Mother's wedding where I was to be the groom. *How did I get myself into such a fix? I didn't want to be a married man, but my mother wanted me to be.*

JoSam told me that another new team needed to travel south and invited me to ride to Costa Rica with them. I picked up my tuxedo, stopped by the mailroom, and found a letter from Venus, which I stuck in my pocket. I headed out to board JoSam's Learjet. In route, JoSam motioned for me to sit next to him.

"Angelo, you are valuable to your team, and I count on you to be a long-term employee. Your position in Guatemala will keep you based in that country, but you will have extensive travel opportunities as you do other assignments. Your primary base job is to serve as an informant. You seem to thrive on change and challenge, which you will have plenty of in your new job. I know you have many questions concerning your last assignment, and I thank you for your silence," he continued.

"My experience has taught me that the end justifies the means. David Allen placed strong magnetic technology in the cockpit of flight 007 in Anchorage to deviate the plane off course. We took the lives of sixty-eight innocent Americans and the Andersons, who weren't so innocent. The job that David Allen and I did saved millions of Americans from a cold war escalating into World War III. I think that sacrificing 268 people versus millions and millions of people dying worldwide was justifiable. We did our job!"

"In the future, you will understand the scope of our work. I want you to know everything because I don't believe in secrets between team members," he explained.

"I appreciate hearing this directly from you. I assumed something similar about the situation but didn't know for sure. I am glad you told me everything," I said.

"What are you going to do with the money you picked up in Korea?"

"I'm going to raise the stakes in my blackjack games," I boasted.

"True words spoken by a seventeen-and-a-half-year-old!" he laughed.

The beautiful, sleek, white, Gates Learjet descended like a loyal homing pigeon. I thought, *Costa Rica, I have returned again!* I walked into my childhood home and couldn't believe my eyes at the transformation. It was lavishly decorated with bows, ribbons, and flowers and gifts, gifts, gifts were stacked everywhere. Mom had invited thousands of people to the (her) wedding. She was beside herself with happiness at the sight of me.

"You have grown so tall and very handsome, Angelo. I don't

want Isabella to see you before the wedding so she will be surprised at what a man you have become." Mom looked at the tuxedo I carried and nodded in approval. I smiled when I thought about the last time I had worn it. The tuxedo wasn't the virgin she thought it was.

"Take your things upstairs and then we will talk!" she said.

Upstairs, I sat down on my bed in my room that had remained the same. I realized I had changed into someone my mother and I didn't know. JoSam's speech on the airplane had made me forget about Venus's letter in my pocket. I tore it open and began to read:

> February 3, 1983
> Dearest Angelo,
>
> You made me the happiest woman in the world. I once told you that all I wanted was to be a mother. You granted my wish. The doctor told me I was about three months pregnant, and this correlated with our meeting in December. In our letters, I told you about my feelings for you, but I wasn't sure if your love for me was as strong.
>
> Would you marry me? You met my family. You know that I come from wealth and that we would lack for nothing in our lives. Your political position would offer our family advantages. Your letters indicated that your new position in Guatemala would be long-term and that would be good for our child. I send my double affection since now I am two.
>
> Lovingly,
> Venus

I folded the letter into my pocket, picked up my tuxedo, bounded downstairs to my oldest brother, Horacio, and asked him to please take me to the airport. While Horacio drove, I thought about JoSam's strategies and his second assignment for me to court Antonio Raul Yon Sosa's beautiful daughter. Had he known this would happen? Was I going to Guatemala because it was the right thing to do, or was I a mere puppet in his grand plan? I think that on some subtle level, Horacio understood what I was doing. I took the letter from my pocket and stuffed it into his hand. "Give this to our Mother. You may read it first and help her to understand."

My mother later joked about the drama she went through returning thousands of wedding gifts. Venus and I were married for five turbulent years. Our union was disagreeable for both of us because I was away much of the time, and when I was home, I needed peace and rest away from the social life she wanted. She lost her curvy shape, and her body was no longer attractive.

Our son's name was Esteban, and I didn't want to be a father any more than I wanted to be a spouse. I expressed to Venus that I was married to my job, but she never understood, through no fault of her own. The 1980s were secretive years when spouses didn't know that their husbands were operatives. Venus believed that I had found someone else and that infidelity was the reason for my absence. We agreed to divorce, and she raised a son I barely knew for eighteen years.

The work in Guatemala ended up being transportation and communications infiltration. I invested my money and built a large civil engineering corporation with fifty-two employees doing undercover work for the US government and JoSam. I continued to be a star performer for Special Five, which had evaporated and reappeared as Special Ten. I had traveled to almost every country doing assignments, deployments, or missions. Whatever I had been asked to do in the past eighteen years, I had accepted and had excelled.

CHAPTER 17

NSA COMMUNICATIONS INFILTRATION

At forty-six years of age, I was promoted and put in charge of Central America and was responsible for information operations, which included transportation and communication infiltration, espionage, interrogation, and special intelligence.

The National Security Agency, a cryptologic organization, coordinated and directed highly specialized activities to protect US information. It produced foreign intelligence information and maintained cryptologic superiority. I was hired to work for it, but JoSam remained as my boss, and I still answered to him. I worked interchangeably for all US military branches and remained intrigued and challenged by my job, which continued to recognize and reward me for my efforts. My job nourished, pampered, protected, entertained, and seduced me like a beautiful, wild, sexy, exotic dancer.

Costa Rica was the central country for Central America and the

logical choice to establish our infiltration base. I had a new assignment working for the National Security Agency. My responsibilities
were to

1.   Secure Property for a communications infiltration base for
     Central America.
2.   Use my civil engineering corporation to obtain Costa Rican
     governmental contracts where information could be gath-
     ered on the country's transportation and communications'
     systems.

This might be my easiest and most enjoyable assignment since
Venus. I knew and understood the culture of Costa Rica, and my
family's affluence would be helpful. My family's name could open
closed doors, present advantages, and provide me with special favors
if I needed them.

The second goal of my assignment had begun with the construction of a new Costa Rican highway project, which extended the
AutoPista Del Sol to Puntarenas. My first goal, to secure a property
for our base, was past due. The property would have to be secluded,
with enough land to permit communications infiltrations from being detected. We had to have the latitude to come and go without
restrictions or questions. The property had to be quiet for clear communication transmissions and for our personal comfort and rest. It
would help us if the property was near our road construction job site.

I saw an unusual advertisement listing an apartment for rent in
the English speaking *A.M. Costa Rica* newspaper. The ad read:

LA URUKA AREA: Looking for a special person who
has a high level of consciousness and loves nature and
Costa Rica, to rent a small 2BD,1BA, beautiful gardens, gated, pool, bar, and rancho. Environmentally

pure, no smoking, no drinking, nor loud music, no
pets.1 BLK to bus. $600 per month. Call 2288-9593.

My school training kicked into gear when the ad smacked me
more as a personal ad than a place for rent. I sensed this person
might be lonely and looking for companionship. This place might be
an easy takeover or an outright property infiltration where I could
acquire the property. I needed to visit this place and have a look.

I drove around the perimeter of the listed rental property of Casa
Ave Hotel and concluded that it would be ideal for our operation.
The property was hidden in a bottom bowl of land filled with hills
and plenty of space around the house for our protection and privacy.
The boundaries had tropical jungles on three sides and a security
gate on the fourth open side. There was a river so that we would
be able to use an electric generator at the back of the property if we
needed extra power for our surveillance equipment.

I ran a personal profile on the owner, Ms. Sun Wren Richards,
and found her occupational background was a professional fine art-
ist. She had been a professor and director of performing arts. She had
been politically involved with the Natural Law Party in 1996. She had
run for the Texas senate but had taken *no* corporation contributions
and had used *no* Political Action Contributions.

This information told me that she was not interested in personal
monetary accumulation but motivated by idealisms. Her financial
history was impeccable, with a credit score of eight and no mort-
gages. She was otherwise debt free. This was to our advantage because the property would be clear and easier to assume.

There was no husband to run interference because she had been
divorced since 1997. It appeared she didn't have any boyfriends and
remained unattached. Her criminal record was as clean as our steril-
ized gloves. She had been doing volunteer work for six years and had
served as a CASA (court appointed advocate for children) for Child

Protective Services in Austin, Texas. This information revealed she had a bleeding-heart, compassionate, easily touched characteristic. An extra plus was that she was a converted Catholic. Most assuredly, I would make a visit to Sun Wren Richards. When I phoned for the appointment, I heard a high-energy, melodic, clear voice that radiated happiness and femininity.

I drove a modest grey-blue 2008 Honda—the car of an engineer—to the gate of Casa Ave and pressed the intercom button, summoning the sunny, friendly voice of Sun Wren Richards. I wasn't surprised by the appearance of this small woman whose body matched with the warmth of her voice. She reminded me of the character Tinker Bell from Peter Pan, with dark hair instead of blonde. Her personal profile said that she was an American, but she could pass for most anything because she looked Italian, Hispanic, Jewish, and German. She had an eclectic appearance, which made her able to blend into almost any race except black and would make her a good spy.

As I followed her around the apartment and grounds, I was fascinated by her agility and grace. I think she had been a ballet dancer for a period of her life. Her age was difficult to pinpoint, but I thought she was between forty and sixty. We shook hands, and I got the unusual message, during this brief physical contact, that her inner spirit was that of a nun or abbess placed in a call girl's body. This combination would drive a man to drink. She looked like a slender dark version of Dolly Parton, and I reminded myself to take extra precaution not to overstep physical boundaries. I was attracted to her, but gaining possession of this property in three years for our Central American headquarters was of prime importance to our operation and JoSam.

Next, I researched what kind of businesswoman she was. I bargained on the six-hundred-dollar monthly rent. After a bit of bantering, she came down to a five-hundred-and-fifty-dollar rent price, and I concluded she was not a strong business type.

I watched her nymph-like moves as she hurried around the kitchen to feed her hungry gardener. I applied my psychological training and learned she was careful not to be inhospitable or impolite but managed to conduct her normal routine and sidestep my presence with the dexterity of a sprite. She was hurried but maintained her gracious composure toward me as an intruder and leapt about as if she could fly. I judged she would be compliant and would accommodate my requests and expectations. I sensed her vulnerability and aloneness.

It was completely beyond my grasp of understanding how this tiny firefly of a woman could be so trusting and unsuspecting and have survived in our crime-riddled world. She never asked me for references or requested any identification. She just handed me the keys to the apartment after I gave her the requested money. She put me off my game with her looks, her weightless, aerodynamic, energetic movements, and her unbelievable openness and acceptance. Could she be real, or was she the one who was conning me? Why would a woman like that come to Costa Rica—alone?

I introduced my bodyguard, Manuel, to Sun, and he immediately liked her. He convinced me that Sun wasn't hiding anything and that she was a pure reflection of honesty that I didn't recognize anymore. I had worked in the dark gutters too long. Manuel was a quick, accurate reader of character and found no dualism in her demeanor. This perplexed me. I would reassess my doubts about her.

Sun had clearly stated in the newspaper classified ad that pets were not permitted. Manuel loved his dogs and had trained many to be guard dogs. He had two favorite dogs named Rex and Tico and he requested permission for them to be guard dogs for Sun's property. Sun relented and invited the dogs to stay with us. We showed her how to place them on guard duty, which was perfect timing because Manuel and I had to set up the equipment for our operation on Sun's property and respond to an impromptu mission.

Our next mission came in from JoSam. "Angelo, how is the new location working out for you?"

"It will be as easy as kissing your new Venezuelan girlfriend. Will you make her wife number eight?"

"Yeah, you guessed it!" JoSam joked. "We have word from the State Department. They have uncovered an assassination plot against Honduras's President Jose Manuel Zelaya. You have a new mission, which will require your performance tonight in Honduras. Take the agency's MH-60 Black Hawk Kilo helicopter, which will be piloted and copiloted by Night Stalkers from the Special Operations Aviation Regiment. Manuel and one other man from your Costa Rican team will go with you. Your assignment is:

1. Circumvent and thwart an assassination plot against Honduran President Manuel Zelaya, which will be taking place tonight at his residence in Tegucigalpa, Honduras at 02:30 hours.
2. Secretly and without fanfare or bloodshed, take President Zelaya back to President Arias's home in San Jose, Costa Rica.

"The MH-60 Black Hawk Kilo is waiting for you now at the San Jose Airport, and you have twenty minutes before departure." JoSam clicked off.

"So much for rest and relaxation!" I sighed as I grabbed the cell phone to call Orlando, one of our team members. "Orlando, we've got an emergency mission, now! Are you on call at the airport?"

"Yes, I am," he said.

"That's great! Manuel and I are heading to the airport. Make sure the MH-60 Black Hawk Kilo has Honduran insignia on it by the time we arrive. It's to be piloted and copiloted by night stalkers from SOAR (Special Operations Aviation Regiment), and you know they will protest the insignia change, but tell them to suck it up. Have it completed in twenty minutes. You and Manuel will serve as President Zelaya's bodyguards when we arrive in Honduras. You will receive details when we get airborne. Ciao," I clicked off.

Orlando was serving on four of our Central American teams simultaneously. He was a polygamist with seven different wives in seven different countries where he served our teams. He often joked that he had a different wife for every day of the week. His paycheck was sizable, and he faithfully supported his seven wives and thirty-five children. Polygamy wasn't accepted in any of the four countries (Costa Rica, El Salvador, Honduras, and Nicaragua) where he had been legally married under the religious sanctions of his beloved Catholic church. Some of the wives knew about and accepted each other. Each of the wives lived in a separate home and country, peacefully knowing that Orlando had other families. They were content to have children, plenty of food, and a good home. These were the highest goals for most Central American women who lived in underdeveloped, impoverished areas.

He had been a polygamist for over thirty years and remained undetected by the law. Central America had poor working relationships with other countries, and Orlando Rogelio Jose Ortiz used a scrambled name for each of his countries. For example, in Costa Rica, he was a citizen by the name of Orlando Rogelio; in El Salvador, he was Jose Ortiz; in Honduras, he was Rogelio Orlando Jose; and in Nicaragua, he was Jose Orlando. The scrambled name made his many marriages undetectable and gave him a peaceful family life everywhere he was assigned.

Orlando was a good-hearted man and was very reliable, but he was attracted to women. Even between assignments, he made extra female conquests. He was a good-looking, older man in his mid-fifties with regulation-cut, short, greying hair and the physical build of a fit Olympic gymnast.

I transferred our computer monitor shifts at work to another monitoring team, shut off the phones and apartment lights, and locked our doors and windows as Manuel grabbed his machine gun from under his bed. We completed our exit in less than five minutes. As Manuel drove the twenty-minute journey to the airport, I made calls and arranged the Honduras operation as best I could, based on the scant amount of information available. "Hello, headquarters? Angelo Lopez calling. Please put me through to my secretary Evea," I urged.

"I am sorry, sir, but she has left for the day," said a plugged-up-nosed, California valley girl voice.

"Are you a new receptionist? Never tell an incoming caller that a secretary is finished working for the day! Get her on the phone *now!*"

I heard her dialing a phone, and then Evea was on the line. "Evea? This is Angelo Lopez. I tried your cell phone several times but couldn't reach you. Why isn't your cell on? I was also slowed up by the new headquarters's receptionist. Would you please talk to her about incoming calls and how she needs to learn to be of service?"

"Oh, Mr. Lopez, sir, I am so sorry. My grandkids threw my cell phone into the swimming pool, and I was just leaving to get a re-placement," Evea said.

"Okay," I said chuckling. "I have an emergency assignment and need contact information for Major Leonardo Romeo Suazo, who is in the 3-16 army battalion at Soto Cano Air Force Base in Tegucigalpa, Honduras, right away. I usually have his number in my cell phone, but it accidentally got erased. Oh, the trials of modern technology! Try to contact him and give him my number. Explain that it is an emergency. I am traveling to Honduras now, and you can reach me at this number. Call me back or text me as quickly as you can. I want his info regardless. Ciao."

Manuel drove our small blue-grey Honda into the Juan Santa Maria Airport parking lot, called our nearby plant site on his cell phone, and gave instructions to have the car picked up. "It is parked at the long-term lot in spot 145. We will have different transportation needs when we return early tomorrow morning. I will make new arrangements by phone when we are in route to Costa Rica," Manuel instructed.

"Airport security, this is Angelo Lopez. I need special classified security clearance for Angelo Orlando Andres Lopez, Manuel Marco Villegas Martinez, and Orlando Rogelio Jose Ortiz. We will be leaving by private military aircraft MH-60Black Hawk Kilo #999900762 at 20:30 promptly. I will send over Officer Shorty Blanco from the president's office with the proper passports and credentials in the next five minutes. I am sorry for the short notice, but this is an emergency. Thank you." I ended the call with the airport security manager, who was used to our routine. I knew he was speedy and efficient.

"Hi, Shorty. This is Angelo Lopez. I need customs and passport clearance for myself, Manuel Martinez, and Orlando Jose Ortiz. Airport security is expecting credential delivery in the next five minutes. Your name is Shorty because you have run your legs off for us," I joked. "If you see President Arias, tell him he will have a houseguest at breakfast. Thanks. Ciao."

CHAPTER 18
THE RESCUE

Manuel and I walked through the parking garage and onto the tarmac where the big black bird waited for us. I saw Orlando inspecting the new Honduras insignia, which had been freshly applied to the Black Hawk's sides and tail. I gave him a thumbs-up, and he cocked his head toward two men who stood there petulantly with nasty attitudes written across their faces. They were the two pilots from the 160th division of the Special Operations Aviation Regiment (SOAR) and looked very pissed off.

I decided that I would attempt to change their pouting faces. It wouldn't be a good idea to be piloted by someone who was angry with us. We needed their help, but these guys had a reputation for owning supreme arrogance.

"Hi! I am Angelo Lopez," I said, extending my hand in greeting. They both looked at me, gave half-hearted handshakes, and only said their names: "Frank." "Dave."

"I am glad you have come to help us. It is a shame we had to change the US insignia to one of an unimportant pissant little country like Honduras, but we are attempting to save the life of its president. It doesn't have aircraft equal to this beautiful bird, and its army GIs will be impressed if they believe it belongs to them.

"We hope to be wearing Honduras army uniforms and infiltrate without them ever knowing we are from the United States. I will be getting an update on the operation in route and will keep you both informed. We hope to execute this operation without any bloodshed. Would you be opposed to wearing a Honduras uniform if it is helpful to our mission?" I asked.

"We had no idea what we were being sent to do. We believe it is a betrayal to say our aircraft belongs to some other country, but changing the insignia in this case makes sense, and we will do our job," the pilot said.

"Thanks. Do either of you speak Spanish?" I asked. They both shook their heads no. "That is not a problem. We can work around it," I quickly said as I climbed into the aircraft behind Manuel with Orlando trailing me.

I introduced Manuel and Orlando as we climbed in and the pilots slid into their seats. "Manuel speaks English if he has to, and Orlando only speaks Spanish," I said. I received a text message giving us clearance. It explained that our papers had arrived and that we were permitted to leave. "We are ready to take off, and we have special clearance. We need to be in Honduras by 2:30 a.m. How does our time schedule look?" I asked.

"We can make it. This little beauty can easily push three hundred miles per hour, as light as we are traveling," the pilot assured. He started the engines and spoke to air control. We rose into the air.

Manuel and Orlando were seasoned agents with assignments and helicopter travel. They marked off their chosen territory and picked beds while they had the chance. The large wide body of this MH-60 Blackhawk Kilo could transport many men. Because there were only three of us, it was easy for them to stretch out comfortably when lying on the bench-styled seats. Manuel used his duffel bag, which contained the machine gun, for his pillow while Orlando had his nose in the newest issue of a girlie magazine. I moved to a seat that was closer to the pilots so that I could more easily communicate with them when my phone rang.

"Hello," I answered.

"Mr. Lopez, I have your information regarding Major Leonardo Romeo Suazo," Evea said.

"That is great, Evea, please text it to me so I have it," I instructed.

"I contacted him, and he expects your call now," she said.

"Thanks, Evea. That is very helpful. Ciao."

I punched in the Honduras number and heard the familiar voice of Leonardo. "Howdy Doody, Are you still dealing blackjack?" I asked.

"Angelo Lopez, my old school chum! I knew it was you when you called me Howdy Doody. Are you still winning at blackjack?" he asked.

"I don't have a chance to play very often these days, but I win when I do. I would win more if you were my dealer. I am impressed by your new rank of major. You must have gotten a good hand in poker to have received that rank," I joked.

"You should know. Rank is the politics of the game. I understand JoSam has recently appointed you as CEO for all of Central America. Are you still married?"

"Nope. It's too difficult to have a wife and this job. How about you?"

"I am lucky I to have a different wife every night or so. A wife for a night is the only way to go. I love it that way. Now that you are my boss, how can I be of help?" Howdy Doody asked.

We enjoyed our conversation like in old school days. "Howdy, do you remember JoSam's classroom lecture where he told us we would be living in a world where the military would be the power

and strength of our decision-making entities within our countries?"
I asked.

"Sure do! The military is the most powerful force in Honduras.
Decisions and changes happen quickly while the politicians sit around
bickering and getting fat from corruption. Look at the Middle East
today! The military and rebel forces are making the changes. Lopez,
do you remember when JoSam told us his goal was to have all the
armies of the world communicate with each other and to maintain
relationships between themselves?" Howdy Doody asked.

"Those words remain clearly in my mind and are the nature of
my call. I am asking for your help, Howdy."

"Shoot, my friend. The air is full of pigeons. Que pasa?" he
encouraged.

"Leonardo, word has it that your President Manuel Zelaya is in
danger of being assassinated tonight at 2:30 a.m. at his home, and I
have an assignment from JoSam to get him out. You are the captain
of our Honduras team, and I wondered if you can help me?"

"Yes, I can! My 3-16 division, which is known to be one of Central
America's most ruthless military divisions, has orders to arrest the
president tonight at 14:30, so we know that much is true. You even
have the time for the arrest correct, but I don't know about any assassination. My boys play too rough sometimes, and I can see how
things could get out of hand with Zelaya. The Honduras people are
divided on his ethics, and it is possible that one of my boys could snuff
him. What are your plans, and how can I help?" he asked.

"I am now in route to Honduras, flying in an MH-60 Black Hawk
Kilo with Honduras insignia. Two of my top Costa Rican team members, Manuel and Orlando, whom you already know are members
of your own team, a pilot, and a copilot are with me. I hope you can
meet us with three Honduras hooded army uniforms. The one for
me should have a colonel's insignia on it so that I will have some

authority. What are your plans for arrest? Why were you given orders to arrest him?" I asked.

"The reason for the arrest order happened because charges have been brought against him by the attorney general. Our orders are to compel President Zelaya to provide a statement concerning the charges from the Supreme Court. I am taking one hundred of my men to storm his house and make the arrest. Hooded uniforms are a good idea and will be much better for my future political career in case he resumes his presidential office," he said.

"That sounds good to me. How about if we embed ourselves in your group of men? Then we can whisk President Zelaya off to the waiting Black Hawk and take him to Costa Rica," I said.

"That is a good method of settling the Zelaya controversy—exiling him. For the time being, I think it would also be best for Honduras, at least until things calm down. It's very tense here now, and we are just a breath away from mob violence," Howdy agreed.

"Howdy, I need to know if the president's residential grounds are big enough to land our Black Hawk in or if we need to land at Toncontin International Airport. The airport will put us ten minutes away from Zelaya's home, and then we will need ground transportation to and from the airport," I reasoned.

"The president's home has expansive pavers in front and on the sides of the house. It is plenty wide for the Black Hawk," he replied.

"Great! That makes everyone's job much easier. Can we set down, or do we need to hover?" I tapped the pilot on the shoulder and made him aware of my line of questioning but then remembered he didn't speak Spanish and had no idea what we were talking about. I continued my conversation with Howdy, knowing about the pilot's language barrier. "What will be the best and fastest method of egress? If we need to hover, is Zelaya agile enough to climb a hanging ladder up into the helicopter?" I asked.

"No. There is plenty of room to set it down. It will be safer for the president than dangling him on a swinging ladder where he would be an easy target," he concluded.

"I think you are right. This Black Hawk has fast lift, which will be faster than waiting for Zelaya to climb the ladder. I'll talk to the pilots and call you back later to firm up our plans. I want to know where you stand on the president's position," I said.

"If you want to know if I am the one who is going to assassinate him, the answer is no. As far as presidents go, I think he does a reasonably good job. He has done many good things for our country, and I'm not optimistic about the alternative candidates. President Zelaya made a bad political mistake attempting to modify the constitution for his own selfish political career, and that is what causes people's anger," Howdy explained.

"Before we hang up, can you give me a personal profile on President Zelaya? All I know about him is that he was democratically elected as the president of Honduras, but I know very little about his personal life. Can you fill me in?" I asked.

"Sure! After all, I have known him for the last twenty-five years, and he has been my boss for three years. President Zelaya is fifty-seven years old, his entire family campaigns for him, with his mother being the most productive and active. The family has a prosperous timber and agroforestry business. His father had a shady past where he was given a twenty-year prison sentence for his role in the Los Horcones massacre on their ranch, which had the same name. He only served two years of the sentence. Manuel Zelaya has only been president since January 27, 2006, but has a long political history. Do you want to know about his political past?" Howdy asked.

"Howdy, I want to learn all I can about the man. I am trying to save his life!"

"He was a member of the Liberal Party of Honduras was a deputy in the National Congress for three consecutive terms between 1985 and 1998. He held many positions within his party and was a minister of investment in charge of the Honduran Social Investment Fund during a previous government. Under his administration, he has managed to lose $40 million dollars. His nephew was hired as the fund's CEO. President Zelaya was accused of embezzling but escaped without being prosecuted," Howdy continued.

"In spite of a number of economic problems, he has made significant achievements. Several of these things I liked. He created free education for all school-aged children, subsidized small farmers, reduced bank interest rates, increased the minimum wage by 80 percent, and caused school meals to be guaranteed for more than 1.5 million children from poor families.

"Let me think. Oh yeah. He placed domestic employees into the social security system, and poverty was reduced by almost 10 percent during his two years of government. He provided state funds for two hundred thousand families living in poverty, and he gave free electricity to the Hondurans who most needed it. Yep, I would say he has done right well as far as a president goes," Howdy expounded.

"Thanks, Howdy. Your opinion is important, and it helps me to be aware of who the assassins might be. Who do you think would gain the most from his death?"

"Right now, Hondurans have hot blood and are ready to be violent just because they can. Anger and tempers are high, even within the ranks of my 3-16 division, and they don't even need political gain. My guys are trained killers and look for prey."

"Can they be controlled long enough to do this job?"

"Yes. They are trained killers, but they are also professionals who follow orders," he assured me.

"Howdy Doody, there is one more thing I need. Can you get me a flight heading that will take us directly to the president's property? Make sure he is inside when we storm. How about the floor plan configuration? Do you know where his bedroom might be?" I asked.

"That's already a known, and we are all set to make a surprise assault on his home and sleeping quarters. Didn't JoSam provide you with flight headings?"

"That's another subject that I need to tell you about, Howdy. I estimate JoSam is well into his late eighties, and I have done the last few assignments by the seat of my pants and without his help because he forgot to follow up. Some other time, I have a number of horror stories to tell you because he has begun to show signs of dementia.

"We are nearly halfway to our assigned destination, and he has made no contact. I need to talk to our pilots and get their opinions and then I will try to call JoSam again. I will call you back if I need any additional information. Please text me the heading. It's been great talking to you, Howdy," I said and clicked off.

I tapped the pilot on the shoulder again and told him what I had learned from Howdy. They agreed it would be best to set the chopper down and let it run while we did our work. I told them about needing a flight heading and directions to guide them into position onto the president's property.

"We can get the information from our own flight control without any trouble. You can also try to get it as a comparison from your sources, which will be good insurance," they amiably offered.

I dialed JoSam and got a sleepy-sounding, old, cracking voice. "JoSam, this is Angelo."

"Angelo who?"

"Angelo Lopez in route to Honduras. I'm on a mission to thwart the assassination of President Zelaya."

"You must have the wrong number." JoSam hung up.

I dialed again. "Hello, JoSam, don't hang up!"

"Who is this?"

"JoSam, it is Angelo, and I need information regarding my assignment," I said.

"Oh, that Angelo! Yes, Angelo, what do you want?" he asked.

"You were going to call me and give me information about the Honduras assignment," I repeated.

"Yes, of course. What do you want to know?"

"Do you have any information about the identity of the assassin?"

"Yes, of course I do," he said.

"Would you please tell me so I can better protect my men?"

"I have forgotten who it is but that isn't important now. The main thing is to get in and get the president out and take him to Costa Rica," JoSam ordered.

"Do I need to worry about an assassin killing my men in the process?" I asked.

"No, your men will be just fine."

"Do you have the flight heading for the president's home so that I can give it to the pilots?" I asked.

"Yes, you cross the river and turn left next to the girl with the green dress," he said.

"Okay. Thanks, JoSam. Goodnight," I said as I hung up and called Colonel Hollander. "Good evening, sir. This is Angelo Lopez trying to get information for the rescue mission of President Zelaya who is going to be assassinated. I tried to get the information from JoSam, who was unhelpful. Do you know who is doing the assassinating, and how I can best protect my five men? Do you also have the flight headings for the president's residence where we will be picking him up?" I asked.

"Good to hear from you, Angelo. I heard through the grapevine that you are doing a great job in your new position with Central America. I will get the heading right away. JoSam hasn't confided in me about the assassin. I will text you back with the heading." The colonel hung up.

I called Howdy again. "Hi, Howdy. It is Angelo Lopez asking if you got the flight heading?"

"Yes, Angelo, I have it," he said.

"Oh, that is great. Can you text me the information so I can instruct my pilots?"

"I will text it right now," he said.

"Howdy, I wondered about the information you gave me on President Zelaya's background. Can you tell me anything about the massacre on the Los Horcones ranch?"

"Everyone in town remembers the incident like it was yesterday. It happened in 1975. Fifteen religious leaders and students were killed by the military in a backlash against the peasants grabbing land in their frontier region. A Colombian priest helped with farmworkers reform farm organizations. He and another US priest from Wisconsin were both killed during their interrogations.

"Five farmers were burned alive in a bread oven, two other priests were castrated and severely mutilated, and two women were thrown in a well alive before it was dynamited. It was a clash between the interests of large landowners and the social activism of the church," Howdy explained.

"I am trying to figure out what kind of person President Zelaya is. He would have been twenty-three years old at the time of the massacre. Do you think his benevolence toward those people living in poverty of Honduras during his term as president was to atone for the massacre? Do you think the violence affected him?" I asked.

"Hell, the violence affected everyone. Our country is violent, and we attempt to find peace in the booze bottle, girlie magazines, drugs, money, or in whatever way we can," he answered.

"Howdy, on the day of the Los Horcones Ranch Massacre, were you there?" I asked.

Silence followed my question and then he answered. "Yes!"

"Howdy, I got your text message heading for the president's house. Thanks. I talked to the pilots, and we will set down. The minute we set down, come aboard with the three uniforms. The pilots will remain in position for our hasty takeoff and won't need any uniforms. I think I will need body armor and shields for me and my four guys since two of them will be the ones in front of Zelaya protecting him. If the pilots take a hit, we will lose our ride home. We all should have armor. Is that possible?" I asked.

"Yes. I will have the armor and hooded uniforms ready for you. It sounds like we are ready to go, and I look forward to working with you," he said.

"I am going to try to sleep, now that everything is organized. Goodnight. See you in a few hours."

My phone beeped with the text message from Colonel Hollander. The flight heading was a match to Howdy's. I showed the numbers to the pilots, and they gave me a thumbs-up. "That's three matches. I guess we know where we're going," Frank said.

I moved to the back of the airplane and stretched out with the other two sleeping men. I had just fallen asleep when the helicopter's blinking red and white lights flashed in my face from the rounded glass of the cockpit upfront and woke me up. I made my way to the nose behind the cockpit and looked out to see the lights of Tegucigalpa below in the distance. The inside of this ride was far from comfortable, even though I was able to stretch out to my full height on the bench seats. The interior of the helicopter was hard, brownish green, and tinny. It smelled like the locker room of a high school gym class.

I wondered why we were using such a big helicopter, which was meant to engage troops in battle, when a smaller aircraft would have been sufficient. I supposed this machine made us look tough and like we meant business. I never knew all the reasons why things were the way they were. Many things were a puzzle to me. My job was only one of the pieces that fitted into the whole.

I woke Manuel and Orlando, who were both still sleep and envied how they looked so refreshed as they sat up and stretched themselves like cats. I was tired, felt like hell, could use a good cup of coffee, which we didn't have, and was grouchy. We didn't even have any water, and it was now time to go to work.

We three sat in the middle of the reverberating, bullet-shaped interior with our legs stretched in the center aisle as I briefed them on the assignment. I told them about their responsibilities. I knew we were ready. I felt the collective adrenaline that was always present before our inner energies sprung to life.

I called Howdy Doody and apprised him of our location, and he said that he saw us. He told me his men were in position. The Black Hawk set down with its blades continuing to rotate. Zelaya's house was surrounded by pavers like Howdy had described, so the landing was easy with plenty of space.

I felt the strong wind from the blades grabbing my hair and shirt as I opened the door and Major Leonardo Romeo Suazo (Howdy Doody) climbed aboard. Orlando took the oversized duffel bag from Howdy. Orlando, Manuel, and I dressed in the bulletproof body armor and hooded uniforms. I introduced the pilots to Major Suazo as I tossed them their bulletproof gear. They put it on without questions or protests. Howdy Doody removed his hood, and Orlando, upon recognition, gave him the traditional tico greeting. Howdy knew Orlando because he was part of the Honduras Team and they had worked together on previous assignments.

We were now appropriately clad. Manuel was armed with a machine gun, and we each had our pistols. We opened the helicopter door. We felt the rotor's blades whipping our hoods as we jumped from the Black Hawk. We ran across the pavers and up the steps to the front door. The president's house looked like the sandstone- and beige-colored Greek Parthenon. There were many Greek ionic pillars all around the front of the house with a large arched entryway accenting the door.

Howdy's one hundred hooded men were stationed around the perimeter of the house and looked like greenish-brown Ku Klux Klan members. There were two armed presidential security guards on duty at the entrance. One pointed his pistol at Major Suazo (Howdy) as he ran up the steps toward the door. Orlando, who was below him on the pavers, shot him without hesitation. His body crumpled, and he fell in the corner.

Howdy and ten men pushed into the house, pinning the second armed guard to the wall and holding him while three of us followed Howdy to Zelaya's bedroom. The house had marble floors, and our noisy entrance and footsteps sounded like thunderous horses. The president heard us coming and turned on the light bedside his bed.

We stormed into his room and pushed the double doors wide open as he bolted upright in his bed, surprised by our intrusion. He wasn't armed, and Orlando and Manuel seized him and pulled him from the bed to a standing position. Manuel grabbed one of the pillows to muffle any shouts for help he might make, but he remained silent. No one spoke a word because there was no need to. I walked in front of the red pin-striped, pajama-clad President Zelaya as Manuel and Orlando stood on each side of him and Howdy protected his back. We rushed the barefooted president to the waiting Black Hawk.

I jumped in first and pulled the president inside while Orlando and Manuel boosted and shoved his plump bottom into the opened doors. Once inside the Black Hawk, we ushered President Zelaya to a space between Manuel and Orlando. We shed our armor and uniforms. I retrieved the armor from the pilots and placed it and our uniforms into Howdy's bag. Howdy remained uniformed and hooded, grabbed up his newly packed bag, waved at us, and jumped to the ground. He ran in a low position because of the Black Hawk's rotating blades as it lifted toward the mountains and left the lighted city of Tegucigalpa. It was completed in less than ten minutes.

We had created a small piece of political history without knowing what we had done in the larger scheme of things. Sometimes our story had no beginning and no ending, and we just did the job of connecting someone else's dots. Did we save him from being assassinated? Maybe we did, but we would never know for sure.

"I am sorry, sir, that it was necessary to take you from the comfort of your bed. We were in such a hurry, we weren't able to get anything for you to eat or drink," I apologized to the president.

I looked over, and Manuel gave me a wink and smiled until his round, bulbous nose wrinkled. He reached behind his back, pulled out a pillow, which he had taken from the president's bed, and handed it to President Zelaya. "Here is your pillow, sir," Manuel said. President Zelaya's laughter revealed that he had a sense of humor.

I wanted to calm his nerves and to assure him that we were not assassins, so I said, "Cute jammies." I reasoned that President Zelaya's friendship might be helpful to my Central American position in the future. We talked and traded our personal histories and bonded as old war heroes during the return trip.

Manuel made transportation arrangements for him to be delivered safely to the Costa Rican president's home in our more comfortable armored car where our staff served us a well-needed breakfast with plenty of famed Costa Rican coffee.

Later, President Jose Manuel Zelaya spoke to the media from his place of exile in San Jose and explained the events as a coup and a kidnapping. He stated that soldiers had pulled him from his bed and had assaulted his guards.

Many times because of secrecy, I was forced to portray the role of the bad guy in some awful B-rated movie, when in my mind, I believed I was valiant and perpetuated life, friendship, and peace. I had to armor myself like an armadillo and not take on the untruth that others perceived of me. If I was continually viewed to be the villain, when would I begin to image myself as the perpetrator, and how long before I started performing as a criminal? I believed this was the agonizing truth David Allen had confronted when he had taken his own life.

CHAPTER 19
BAD DREAMS

I had a hard time falling asleep, even in Sun's peaceful resort. I couldn't help but think about the day's events: the infiltration of the courthouse in San Jose so that I could have a look at Katerina Mesa's law books and my current assignment of securing the Sun Wren Richards's property. I had disguised my offer to help Sun with her citizen's investment residency. Sun's lawyer, Katerina Mesa, had not given her the six legal books she had needed for closing the purchase of her hotel Casa Ave.

I had found that Katerina Meza's criminal activities had included 210 unsuspecting foreigners. These innocent, successful foreigners had come to Costa Rica looking for paradise and had ended up losing their life savings and destabilizing their retirements.

I had helped Sun secure and regain her property and had added her case to the many solved cases in my resume. However, I had been thrown off balance because she had given me cause to reflect on the consequences of my job. I had lost my footing and had plunged into a depression because I knew I cared for her beyond the range of a protected witness.

The help I had given Sun caused her to be compliant and compelled her to trust me without question. I had put myself in a good position to confiscate her property as JoSam had instructed for his strategy and plans for Central America, but the discomfort I felt was new. I was sure that this doubt would become an obstacle for my future successes. I had experienced success in past assignments because I had believed that the end justified the means. I had no conscience that had prohibited me from barreling through the destruction of humankind, if the end had resulted in my better personal future.

I now suffered from my past actions and was tortured by the things I had seen and done. Sun's unusual philosophy and Honduras president's humanitarian programs had given me new thoughts regarding good stewardship for humanity. JoSam's had said, "Nice guys finish last." Was he right? My body flopped from one position to another, trying to push my mind to a quiet place of treasured sleep, but thoughts about Sun kept intruding.

I would rescue Sun's property from the property-scamming criminals and then take it from her because I could. I punched my hard pillow a few times hoping to find comfort and sleep and then turned onto my side. For many years my mind had gone without sleep, and it was difficult for me to sleep even when I had the chance. My thoughts drifted back to sixteen years earlier in 1991 when I had lived in Argentina and had just been divorced from my wife Venus.

JoSam, Russ Warren (the antisocial, odd duck and linguistic genius), and I were to travel to Vienna, Austria, for a highly classified assignment from the US president's office. Russ and I had no idea why we were going to this country.

We had worked on the Anderson assignment together, some years before that. I knew of Russ's self-taught linguistic talents, which had been developed by the sheer number of years he had spent alone. Russ was aloof and difficult to get to know, even though I saw him regularly in the dining room and he was on my team. His strange eccentric mannerisms kept him apart from the group of men that played in the card room and worked out in the fitness center. I believed that his shyness accentuated his geekiness.

Russ had a slight build—in truth, he was downright skinny. When he talked, he barely opened his mouth and kept his head lowered. His voice seemed to come out his eyes or from the inside of his glasses, which sat on the end of his beak-like nose. His face was ruddy and pockmarked due to a teenage case of acne. He had a long neck that was too thin for the shirt collars he wore. It left gaps of vacant space at the top of his shoulders. He was gangly like the Ichabod Crane from *The Legend of Sleepy Hollow*, which Señora Galvez had made us read in school. His hair was medium brown with tuffs of grey, which gave his head an irregular shape. It was greasy and slicked down with patches of frizz standing up, which made his head look like a molting bird. His overall appearance was scruffy yet clean-shaven. He wore outdated clothing and smelled of older men's cologne.

In spite of being uncool, I liked him even though he was more than twice my age. I felt his kindness, and there was something sensitive about his nature. He was easygoing—so easy you never knew he was around. He was thoughtful. One time on a mission, he walked five miles in the heat of a sandstorm to retrieve a folder I had forgotten, which could have fallen into suspects' hands and placed our team in jeopardy. He was polite and had refined table manners but sat with his legs crossed like a woman. He always wore dark sullen colors, which matched his bland energy. Russ's only family was a mentally retarded brother, which he supported with his agency paycheck and lived in a special home in California. He didn't date any women and made no friends.

The trip in 1991 to Vienna, Austria, in our Gulf Stream IV

aircraft, which had been constructed five years before it would be marketed to the US public, had an interior like my mom's living room. The plane's plush interior didn't shorten the many miles I flew with Russ the introvert, esoteric JoSam, who had withdrawn into his folded, wing-wrapped gargoyle stance and had squatted into the cream-colored executive chair, and ten strangers who looked like businessmen or politicians and spent their travel time engaged in conversation with each other.

A couple of hours passed before JoSam unwrapped himself from his tangled position, placed his feet onto the floor of the aircraft, returned from his vacant stare, and acknowledged our presence. He slid into the aircraft's conference table booth and began making introductions. None of the men looked American, but they represented the US oil industries of Exxon, Shell, Texaco, Standard, Conoco, Chevron, Phillips, Gulf, American, and Mobil. He introduced each of the men by name to us and told us which company they represented.

JoSam explained, "The United States and our President Bush has a vital interest in crude oil from the Persian Gulf. We are going to Vienna to attend the OPEC [Organization of the Petroleum Exporting Countries] meeting. The OPEC group is an intergovernmental organization comprising more than twenty-four countries and serves as an oil cartel coordinate for the policies and prices that help countries export in a fair way to benefit all their members. There will also be non-OPEC members attending today's meeting as observers.

"Our assignment is to negotiate individually with selected countries and to bargain for the best possible price for US oil Companies. The countries attending the meeting today are Egypt, Syria, Israel, Lebanon, Jordan, Iraq, Saudi Arabia, Kuwait, Qatar, Iran, Turkey, Yemen, Bahrain, Oman, Russia, the Netherlands, Brazil, Angola, Algeria, the United Arab Emirates, Nigeria, Gabon, and Cyprus." JoSam handed out office supplies as he talked.

"We have two days to set up forty-five-minute meetings with these countries' representatives during OPEC session breaks and breakfast, lunch, and dinner. You oil industry men need to select the country you will be negotiating with and coordinate the meeting times with Mr. Warren, who will be your spokesperson," JoSam clarified.

"Mr. Warren speaks all of these languages like a national. We don't want any of the OPEC members to know we are Americans. Our nationality will remain unknown, and Mr. Warren will act like he is a national investor from their countries. For example, if you bargain with Egypt, Mr. Warren will become an Egyptian investor, and each of you will attend your designated meeting with him. You must talk to Mr. Warren without the OPEC members overhearing because many of them understand English. You can reach your individual objectives as well, so that you may receive the best price possible for your corporation," JoSam emphasized.

"It is important for you to be at the meeting location on time. Each day, Mr. Lopez will receive a schedule of countries, meeting times, and locations. If you forget where to go or what time you need to attend a meeting, Mr. Lopez will give you that information. Once a meeting has been confirmed, there should be no changes. If the country changes the time or place, we will make adjustments, but, hopefully, there will be no changes. If a change is needed, it might be better to cancel that meeting and choose another country to fill the vacated spot because one change will be disruptive for all. Once your meeting is over, don't hang around. Go be a tourist and enjoy Vienna," JoSam ordered.

"While we travel to Vienna today, choose the country you wish to negotiate with. Each day, there will be six times to meet: breakfast, the morning coffee break, lunch, the afternoon coffee break, dinner, and after dinner. Each of these breaks last forty-five minutes except for the meals, which last one hour," JoSam clarified.

"You will choose amongst yourselves who will receive the meal hours. Each of you needs to plan your negotiating strategies and goals so that you use your time to its best forty-five-minute advantage. This means that each of you has one meeting. There will be two extra spots available in case an OPEC member is a no show or is late and needs to reschedule. The after dinner spot each day is reserved for that purpose. If the day goes smoothly and the after dinner spot is available, that time slot is granted on a first request basis, scheduled with Mr. Angelo Lopez. Mr. Russ Warren will need to know your targeted countries, and Mr. Lopez will keep the schedule flowing. We will never be rude by making an OPEC member late for his regular OPEC session. Mr. Lopez will signal to Mr. Warren and his representative (US oil man) to tell him to end the meeting. It is your responsibility to conclude negotiations during your meeting," JoSam advised.

"Have your contracts and papers in order before each meeting and make sure you have an extra pen for signing. I arranged a small conference room for your needs. We will change different rooms for each meeting to avoid suspicion. Mr. Lopez will know the rooms' locations and will signal a five-minute warning so you will know the meeting will be beginning and can be in the room before your OPEC member arrives. Mr. Lopez will give a five-minute warning to end your session as well," JoSam outlined.

"Get together with Mr. Warren before each of the meetings to explain your oil price and agenda. Mr. Lopez will help get the OPEC member to the correct conference by signaling, and Mr. Warren is to usher him into the room," JoSam instructed. "If you don't have any questions, please begin working on your plans. Remember to leave the building after your meeting!" JoSam cautioned as he distributed a stack of invitations for Russ Warren to address after the US oilmen selected their choice of OPEC countries. JoSam moved back into his executive chair and drank his coffee.

My assignment was lightweight on this Vienna trip. JoSam invited me because I was definitely being groomed for his position in future years. This trip was my classroom to learn his procedures. When the oilmen resumed their planning, it became apparent that I needed to be a mediator. Bickering over who got the longer meal breaks became their coveted goal.

"Okay, gentlemen, lets allow destiny to be our guide," I said as I took out my deck of cards. "The first position will be the breakfast invitation today. Russ has time to distribute and confirm the invitation after our arrival in Vienna this morning. Everyone draw a card. The highest card will be the winner of the first breakfast position," I explained as I shuffled the deck. Each man drew a card, and Mr. Texaco won the first draw with the ace of spades, and he chose Saudi Arabia as his breakfast date.

The selection process continued until the meals for both days were allocated. I made a list of all the available time slots, and Russ wrote each invitation in the language of the invited OPEC member. I carefully read the list, imprinted it on my mind, and gave it to JoSam. The US oilmen ate their in-flight breakfast and drank their coffee as they worked silently on their business plans for the meetings.

I had traveled with JoSam to many countries, and our trips had always been elegant and comfortable. This time, we stayed at the old-world hotel called Palais Hansen Kempinski Vienna, which charged a rate of $300 per night. Each of us had our own room, and there were thirteen of us. JoSam never pinched Uncle Sam's pennies and gave us the best of comforts. Our teams worked under stress and diplomatic pressures, and we deserved these special amenities.

I enjoyed traveling to the European countries, and this was my first time in Austria. Vienna was embellished with old-world architecture. The buildings were ornate and majestic.

We arrived two hours before the official OPEC session began. The extra time allowed us to settle into the magnificent hotel Palais

Hansen Kempinski Vienna, which provided us with personal com-
forts. I walked down the hallway to Russ's room and knocked on his
door, which he answered promptly. "Russ, can you use my help in
distributing today's invitations?"

"Yes, I can use the help!" he replied nervously.

"You are finally in the star role with this assignment, and it is
about time you got recognized for your talents."

Russ and I scooped up that day's invitations from his hotel bedside table and left his room to walk to OPEC's main meeting room.
OPEC's headquarters had to be the ugliest building in all of Vienna.
It had been designed like a square box with vertical lines, making
it look like an American correctional facility. It didn't fit into the
historic flavor of Vienna's gentility and definitely wasn't posh. This
building was all about making business deals and money, smashing
your competition, and climbing the financial ladder without one
concern for making its inhabitants feel comfortable.

I felt Russ's tenseness as I walked the few blocks beside his stick-
like body to the OPEC Center. I could tell he had given extra attention to his grooming and had attempted to choose business clothing
for today's meetings, but nothing was working for him.

"Hey, Russ, let's duck in this men's store and get you a new shirt
and tie," I said jovially.

"I think that's a good idea. I will wear whatever you think is
best," he uttered compliantly. I could feel his gratitude, which was
hidden under the pile of his jangled nerves. He had never had anyone
who had cared enough to help him before.

"Did your Mom ever take you shopping?" I asked.

"My brother and I were raised in an orphanage. We never had
parents that I can remember. I was only two months old, and my
three-year-old brother remembers nothing because his mind is ab-
normal. I don't think he knew our parents either," Russ stated. Russ

was now dressed in a light blue, well-fitting business shirt with cuffs and a conservative yet jazzy tie that complimented his navy-blue suit.

"Russ, now you look the part you play. You look great! How does it make you feel?"

"It makes me feel *loud*," he admitted.

"Loud is perfect for a petroleum investor. Let's go!" I laughed.

The OPEC meeting room had the members' names on plaques, and it was quick and easy to distribute the ten invitations with Russ's cell phone number as the RSVP contact. Russ kept Mr. Texaco's breakfast invitation for Saudi Arabia in his pocket to be delivered and confirmed by the hotel room service concierge.

JoSam suddenly appeared in the OPEC hallway to show Russ and I where the ten meeting rooms were located and reserved for our oilmen. He noticed Russ's new clothes but withheld his approval. We walked to the hotel where Mr. Saudi Arabia was staying. I paid the concierge to deliver the invitation and to wait for confirmation. We waited in the lobby. I thought we were making a mammoth assumption that these OPEC members would accept our invitations.

"These oil producers will break a date with a Playboy centerfold to make a yearlong contract," JoSam boasted. We waited ten minutes for the concierge, who returned with the confirmation.

"Russ, I will notify Mr. Texaco that the Saudi Arabia meeting will take place in this hotel dining room while you usher your OPEC member into place," I directed. Russ long stepped down the hall.

"JoSam, I am amazed at how your decisions are always golden," I said.

"It is from many years of experience of knowing the temperaments and greed of humanity," JoSam justified himself as he walked into the dining room and selected a table in a far corner.

My thoughts troubled me as I walked to Palais Hansen Kempinski Vienna to escort Mr. Texaco to the first meeting of the day. I had learned to second-guess JoSam and his strategies. I mulled the reasons for JoSam to be out working in the field that day instead of his regular mode of operation, which was directing the show from his hotel room or airplane. I knew that the US was slipping into a recession where gasoline prices had fallen and that the Pentagon assignment was to buy as much oil as possible at a price that was lower than the US could produce on its own. This was one possibility.

Another reason could be that the Pentagon assignment was more importance than I knew it was. It could also be that JoSam wasn't trusting his agents. I agreed that Russ had no confidence in himself to be a star player. All these ideas were reasonable assumptions why JoSam was out today.

I pulled out my cell phone and called Russ. "Russ, you look better than Bill Gates today. Just remember to be calm! I know your Arabic is flawless, and you will do great." I hung up. I reached Mr. Texaco's room and walked him to the dining room where Russ and the representative from Saudi Arabia hadn't yet arrived.

"Mr. Texaco, when you finish your meeting, stand and shake the Saudi Arabian representative's hand but don't speak a word and be the first to leave," I instructed.

"Yes, I will do that."

"Good luck," I said as I left the dining room to usher Mr. Mobil to his space in OPEC headquarters, which was a short walk away from the first coffee break meeting of the morning. I encouraged Mr. Mobil to use his time to prepare while he waited for Russ.

I waited for Russ in the courtyard outside and enjoyed the warm sunshine. I could see the walkway leading to OPEC's headquarters. After fifty minutes of the designated hour had passed for Mr. Texaco and Saudi Arabia, I walked toward the hotel dining room to tell Russ it was time to end the meeting when I saw Russ walking toward me.

"How did it go?" I asked.

"It went great! Texaco got his full contract at a bargain. My Arabic was flawless, and I think he liked my shirt," Russ laughed.

"Eureka! Mr. Mobil is waiting in the conference room for you now. I think he wants to spend time going over his plan while he waits for the OPEC member from Russia. I will give you a five-minute warning when I see OPEC getting ready for their morning coffee break."

"I have forgotten which room we are in for this coffee break meeting because I am nervous about JoSam hanging around," Russ declared.

"Yes, that would make a Chinese person on opium nervous, but not to worry. *Tranquilo.* I will get you where you should be. You just watch your language," I joked, scolding like my mother.

"Why do you think JoSam is watching me?" he asked.

"He probably went to the dining room to get out of his own room because it smelled like cleaning chemicals or something. You know how meticulous he is." I glossed over his question.

Russ and I walked to the conference room where Mr. Mobil and Russia would meet, and I saw JoSam going into the OPEC morning session. It was unusual that I didn't see any of his protection tracking team with him. Russ was not the problem. I suspected that JoSam was the one with a change in his behavior.

I stepped into the Mr. Mobil/Russia conference room before their meeting began and signaled to Russ. He came to the door. "Russ, I have been thinking about your question regarding JoSam. You don't have a problem. There is no need for you to give the matter anymore thought. JoSam is behaving differently. I hope this news gives you support so that you can concentrate on your job."

"Thanks!" Russ said as he returned to Mr. Mobil's negotiating plan.

I entered OPEC's meeting room and sat on the perimeter where I could see both the speaker of the meeting and JoSam. I tried to determine what was strangely different about JoSam. He seemed to be jumpy and agitated, and I wondered if this OPEC job was pivotal to his position with the Pentagon. I observed JoSam sweating, mopping his face, squirming, sitting on his feet, readjusting his position in his chair, leaping up to go to the water fountain, returning, fidgeting, and searching his pockets for something. JoSam's exhausting, perpetual movement lasted throughout the morning session.

I couldn't stand to watch his neurotic behavior anymore. It was beginning to affect me. I saw the OPEC member from Russia. I needed to direct Russ there. I peeled away from the crowd of visitors, who were sitting in chairs, to signal Russ the five-minute warning and to reveal the Russian member's location to help save time. Russ entered the dispersing OPEC meeting and escorted his new Russian client to the secluded conference room where Mr. Mobil waited. I watched JoSam to see where he would go during the break. JoSam jumped straight in the air and stared intently in Russ's direction.

I intercepted JoSam's path. "Good Morning, sir. Russ performed like a true professional and has everything under control."

"Stay out of my way, Lopez!" JoSam snapped with wild hatred in his eyes as his mouth snarled out the words. This man was to be feared. I stepped aside and watched him go into the men's room, where he remained for the full forty minutes, and didn't follow him. Maybe JoSam was having a bad day or perhaps he was sick.

I walked to the private room where Russ was meeting with Russia and Mobil. I signaled Russ with his five-minute warning. Russ looked up and then gave me a big smile and a thumbs-up as Mr. Mobil and Russia shook hands.

This was how it went throughout the entire day. Russ performed brilliantly! He met Mr. Exxon and the Iranian OPEC member for lunch and conversed in Persian. He met with Mr. Phillips Oil and Mr. United Arab Emirates and articulated in Arabic for the afternoon coffee break. Dinner was devoted to Mr. Norway and Mr. Gulf Oil, where he spoke Norwegian. The day's schedule went so smoothly, Russ told me he felt great and wanted to use the last slot of the day for Mr. Chevron and Mr. Iraq, where he would speak Kurdish-Arabic.

After the last evening meeting with Mr. Iraq, Mr. Chevron

stopped me in the hallway of OPEC's headquarters and expounded on his happiness with Russ's help to secure his corporation's contract.

"Mr. Warren is a credit to our country," Mr. Chevron said.

"I agree! He seems even more amazing when he speaks Arabic, Russian, Persian, Norwegian, and Kurdish-Arabic. I will give Mr. Warren your compliments, but it is best that the Iraq OPEC member doesn't see or hear us speaking together." Mr. Chevron nodded and left the building. I waited for Russ to finish his conversation with Mr. Iraq, and then we walked back to the hotel together.

"Russ, you were absolutely astounding today! You did your job *brilliantly*. You didn't need to worry about JoSam. I think he might be sick. He spent forty-five minutes in the men's bathroom, and I haven't seen him this afternoon. Have you?"

"No! He scares me shitless! He makes me feel so apprehensive, I can't be fluent with my language."

"I watched JoSam during the morning session. I wouldn't be able to do your job with him lurking around and behaving so abnormally. Russ, did you notice he doesn't have his protection team?"

"No, I can't think of anything except my job."

"That's perfect. Stay focused for one more day. Mr. Chevron wanted me to give you his thanks and his admiration for the great job you did for him. Did you want to go shopping in the morning for another shirt and tie?"

"Yes please, as long as a new shirt doesn't change my good luck," Russ smiled.

"Not at all! It will only make it better."

The Vienna morning was crisp and clear as Russ sported his new light-yellow shirt with a dark-yellow and cobalt-blue striped tie, which made his worn navy-blue suit look snappy. The cobalt blue in the tie complemented his eyes and made him look years younger. I looked forward to the end of this OPEC operation to see if Russ's success would make any change in the way he related to other team members.

After we finished his shopping, we walked to another hotel's coffee shop to wait for Mr. Shell Oil and Mr. Kuwait for breakfast where Russ would speak Arabic.

"Russ, if today goes as well as yesterday, we would have two extra positions to give away to two of our US oilmen. I would like to get them together while you meet Mr. Kuwait to see who wants those positions. Is that agreeable with you?"

"Yes. Two of those companies will get another chance to negotiate price with two more countries. Go for it!" Russ cheered.

I left Russ in good spirits and waiting for his clients and contacted the US oilmen. They were exuberant to learn two US companies would return with bonus contracts. We agreed to decide the positions with the luck of the card draw. Mobil and Gulf won the draw. I knew Russ could make a grand salary working for any of the US oil companies to secure their future contracts. Russ had a bright future.

I returned to the hotel coffee shop and gave Russ his five-minute warning, and he responded with another thumbs-up. This started the day out just right! Russ and I walked to OPEC's headquarters, chatting like two old women about the day's schedule. Breakfast with Mr. Shell and Kuwait went unexpectedly well.

"Angelo, you will never guess what happened at that meeting. Kuwait offered me a job negotiating oil contracts for the entire country of Kuwait. Can you believe that? He offered me a salary of $220,000 a year! I could bring my brother to Kuwait and work for the government." Russ cheered like a young kid at a pep rally. I had never seen Russ so enthusiastic about his job or his life.

"Congratulations, Russ! Only thing is you have a problem."

Russ sobered his frivolity. "What problem do I have, Angelo?"

"Your problem is that you are not a Kuwait national. You are American, my friend."

"Oh yeah, I forgot," he laughed heartily.

"You played your part so well you even fooled yourself! Russ, you can be hired by any of the US oil companies you served yesterday. I believe they would gladly pay you $220,000 to work for them.

"Okay, here is today's schedule. Breakfast was Mr. Shell Oil and Kuwait where you spoke Arabic. The morning coffee break will be with Mr. Standard Oil and the little known country of Bahrain in the Middle East where you will be speaking Arabic again. Lunch will be Mr. Conoco Oil and the country of Venezuela where you will chat in Spanish. Do you want me to take that slot? I speak Spanish, remember?"

He looked at me in earnest. "Angelo, do you want to?" he asked.

"Not at all! This is your job, and I speak Costa Rican Spanish, which would be a dead giveaway because Cost Rica has no oil to buy or to sell. Afternoon coffee is with Mr. American Oil and the Netherlands where you will speak Dutch."

"Dinner will be a second bonus meeting for Mr. Gulf Oil, who won the card draw, and the country he chose was Gabon in Africa. You will be negotiating in French for this meeting. And drum roll please … your last meeting of the day and second bonus position goes to Mr. Mobil Oil and the country of Angola where you will speak Portuguese. Should we make this meeting for 19:30 hours?" I asked.

"19:30 will work best because dinner is at 17:00 hours. The meeting should be over by 18:00, giving me an hour to meet with Mr. Mobil, locate and escort Mr. Angola, and get to the next meeting," Russ explained.

"We've got a plan! Russ, since I need to be there to end the meeting with a five-minute warning, do you want to have your meeting at some little tavern where I will reserve a table for the three of you?"

"Yes, that would be relaxing. Last night, I didn't eat much at dinner because my mind was on the last meeting, which lasted until late. Tonight, I feel like celebrating. Thanks."

CHAPTER 20
ASSASSINATION

The day's schedule flowed in perfect harmony with a repeat of the previous day's performance of success. Our US oilmen were high-fiving each other in the hotel lobby when I walked in at 5 p.m. They stopped me with spirited antics and wanted to invite Mr. Warren to dinner. I explained that they needed to wait until we were inside our aircraft returning home to avoid being seen because their contracts could be retracted if OPEC members became suspicious. I also suggested that they become invisible until all OPEC members were gone. They nodded their understanding as they dispersed.

"I will tell Mr. Warren about your invitation, but he has two more meetings to finish. One is with you, Mr. Gulf, at 17:00 for dinner with the country of Gabon at the Plaza Restaurant, where he is waiting for you now. Mr. Warren will speak French. Did you forget?"

"No Way! Mr. Warren and I met earlier this afternoon to put our plan into place, but the guys are pumped up pregnant, and they are ready to deliver," Mr. Gulf joked as he ran off to the Plaza Restaurant.

"The evening meeting will be at the Vienna Waltz Tavern, one hundred meters north of here with you, Mr. Mobil, at 19:30 hours. Would you like to join us for dinner at 18:00? It would be helpful to Mr. Warren and acceptable if we were to be seen by other OPEC members. However, it wouldn't be good if we were seen to be having a party," I cautioned.

"Thank you! I accept your invitation for dinner at the Tavern, which will give Mr. Warren and I a chance to go over the negotiating plan before our meeting with the OPEC member from Angola at 19:30," Mr. Mobil reasoned.

"I know Russ Warren will be pleased to have your company. He may have already eaten with his previous appointment, but maybe not," I invited.

I made reservations at the intimate, quaint Vienna Waltz Tavern at 18:00 hours, and I sent hotel room service to notify Mr. Angola of our meeting place at 19:30. I directed the concierge to wait for his reply. I waited in the lobby where I saw JoSam sitting in a blue, overstuffed chair as if he were waiting for someone. He stared at the imperial designs on the carpet.

JoSam was dressed in tourist island clothes, which were out of place in this inner-city European environment of Vienna. His hair was a matted mass of red frizz, which accentuated his vacant, dilated eyes. His face looked distorted as if it had been misshaped by a stroke that had left his mouth hanging open, slobbering, and unappetizingly wet. His freckled shin was an unhealthy mauve color with violet-colored trim around his nostrils, eyes, mouth, and ears. If I hadn't known him, I would have labeled him as deranged.

The polite thing for me to do would be to acknowledge him. I waved in his direction, and he gave no response. Maybe he was sick and needed my help. I walked across the lobby to his chair. "How was your day, sir?" I asked cheerfully.

"Leave me alone, Mr. Lopez!" he said through gnashed teeth and in a raised voice as people around us turned their heads to stare. I didn't speak another word and returned to my place near the desk to wait for the concierge who was coming out of the elevator. He handed me the note confirming our evening meeting at the Vienna Waltz Tavern, and I tipped him for his errand. I needed to give Russ Warren his five-minute warning and then wait for him to finish his 17:00 appointment with Mr. Mobil and Mr. Gabon.

Russ met Mr. Angola in the lobby of our hotel, and he felt victorious because the previous dinner meeting had finished with a flourish of goodwill. They chatted in Portuguese during the pleasant walk through the hotel's manicured gardens where an orchestra played classical music for guests to enjoy in the pleasant night air. The OPEC member from Angola was a tall, stately, fit-looking, handsome, dark man, who presented himself to be well educated. He and Russ entered the dimly lit tavern where our Gulf Oil man waited at a small table.

Russ could see that JoSam was sitting alone at a table directly in his line of vision. Our successful linguist began to sweat and tremble, and both of Mr. Warren's guests noticed his sudden change in demeanor from the professional he was. Russ became an inept character like one of the three stooges. He upset a glass of ice water all over Mr. Mobil's folder as he took his place at the table. Russ was flustered and could utter no words at all. He knew he needed to make introductions, but it was like he was in a bad dream where his mouth moved but nothing audible came out.

His guests looked confused, and Mr. Gulf gave a small visible shrug to Mr. Angola as they waited. Mr. Gulf signaled the waiter to bring a round of wine, and Mr. Warren sat gazing back at JoSam, who gave him a wicked stare. The three sat in silence until the round of wine was served, and then Mr. Gulf raised his glass in greeting but remained silent. Russ lifted his glass, drank half of it at once, and opened his mouth with a gush of Arabic that rushed out and slammed into the ears of both guests who were expecting Portuguese. Mr.

Angola's face registered his realization that he had been duped. He rose from his chair and left the Vienna Waltz Tavern. JoSam had sat in the corner waiting for failure to happen. He was enraged when he received his prize.

"Mr. Warren! What happened? We were well prepared, and you negotiated professionally at yesterday's meeting. What happened?" Mr. Gulf asked.

"I spoke the wrong language." The two men sat in silence until Mr. Gulf Oil gathered his papers and left the tavern.

JoSam seethed with anger, leapt from his dark corner, pushed the heavy hand-carved ironwood chair back against the wall, took out his wallet, placed an American twenty dollar bill on the green-and-rust-colored paisley tablecloth, and rushed to Russ's table with bulging, dilated watery, violet-rimmed eyes like a winged beast. His tasseled Italian loafers barely touched the eight-inch-wide, planked, highly waxed, ironwood tavern floor.

"Get up, Mr. Warren! You are through here," JoSam snarled.

"I must wait for the bill," Russ Warren replied, barely audible.

"It's paid! Let's go," he growled as he slapped down two more American twenty dollar bills onto the soft paisley tablecloth and shoved Russ ahead of him through the heavy wooden and stained-glass door the waiter had just opened for them.

"Have a pleasant evening," the waiter said.

JoSam's wrath mowed down every beautiful sprout of green grass that lined the rust-colored, old brick walkway between the tavern and the hotel. His eyes singed the petals of the rose bushes as he passed. His breath, which was full of hatred and anger, flared from his violet-edged nostrils and stunned insects and birds alike as he passed. It was evident that no creature would live through JoSam's rage. His facial and neck skin glistened with sweat and caused his tropical shirt to stick to his shoulder blades. He resembled a striding vulture with his big redheaded, frizzy hair protruding forward in front of his body as it cut through the air like a knife causing a deep wound. JoSam's bile-soaked attitude caused people to move away as he flung open the elegant, ornate Victorian doors of the Palais Hansen Kempinski Vienna and forced Russ to obey his wordless directions from the sheer strength of his ferocity.

I had been waiting in the lobby for the end of the Mr. Gulf and Mr. Angola meeting when I saw JoSam herding Russ into the lobby. "Russ, what's wrong?" I asked as I fell into step with him.

"I spoke the wrong language," Russ said.

"You're coming with us," JoSam gnashed at me as his face blazed like a colored neon light ignited by his wild vehement frenzy.

"Okay," I said, knowing that I should keep quiet during one of JoSam's temper tantrums. I followed the boiling gargoyle across the blue imperial-designed carpet and past the blue, overstuffed, satin chairs in the lobby. All the while, I felt the heat from JoSam's wired body. The trodden marbled floor echoed the clicking sound of JoSam's shoes like vulture talons striking the hard surface. Our echoed footsteps cut the silence of the hotel's hallways into shreds as JoSam's turbulence blew the back doors of the hotel open.

We stood outside its old brown stone walls, which formed a tight passageway with another tall cement building not more than five feet away. Russ and I stopped as the hotel's arched glass doors closed behind us. Russ's face reflected his fear.

"Take everything out of your pockets," screeched JoSam.

We reached inside of our pockets. "Not you, Mr. Lopez. Only Mr. Warren," JoSam snarled.

I didn't know what I should do. I couldn't guess what JoSam had in mind. I was helpless and only knew that I should follow his orders. I stood outside the back door of the hotel and looked down the block-long passageway between the two rough pockmarked surfaces of the brown walls. Russ handed JoSam his wallet, passport, room keys, and scraps of notes from today's meetings.

"Walk down the passageway, Mr. Warren, and when you get halfway to the end, stop and get in a prayer position on your knees," JoSam's voice reeked with his hostility.

"Sir, I want to apologize to you right here," Russ whispered.

"I said walk the passageway. Follow me. I will go first. You stay there, Mr. Lopez," JoSam said with sharpness. JoSam led the way, stopped, and said to Russ, "Okay, Mr. Warren, on your knees facing Mr Lopez." I heard their every word as the walls channeled their voices to me clearly in a strange, hollow, empty, surreal way. I knew that humiliation was what JoSam had chosen for Russ's punishment. What was happening? What should I do? What was JoSam doing, and what was my role?

Russ lowered himself to his knees as he was ordered, and I watched him remain there facing me while JoSam stood behind him. I can't adequately describe the blackness of the evening overhead against the grayness of the walls and the light of twilight beginning and ending at both ends of the tunnel-like passageway. The light at the far end silhouetted Russ's kneeling figure with the deranged beast-like form of JoSam behind him. The vision looked like a black and white photograph, which burned deep into my mind. It was indescribable because it was a sight that ate at my core rather than a visual that flashed before my eyes.

Now that Russ was on his knees facing me, we could see each other. I shrugged my shoulders and extended my hands, gesturing to him that I didn't know what to do and that I didn't know JoSam's plans. Even in the shadowy dim light, I read the bewildered innocent expression on Russ's face. I wanted to tell him the oilmen had been pleased with the job he had done for them. I wanted to shout to him that I was proud to have him on my team. I felt compassion to the boundaries of its meaning as I watched.

"Mr. Warren, I want to hear you recite Nikolas's poem, 'The Gates to Hell.' JoSam's voice resonated infuriation with hatred

between the two walls. I heard myself reciting the poem with Russ
and knew he understood I was showing him that we had bonded in
friendship.

> I tolerate no betrayal,
> No tarnished loyalty.
> If my trust in you does fail,
> You die like dethroned royalty.

"Good job, Mr. Warren *and* Mr. Lopez. Now say it in every language you know, Mr. Warren." JoSam's ill-tempered voice amplified
with the help of the gray, towering, concrete, tomb-like walls. Russ
returned the message of friendship with a slight nod in my direction,
showing me he had received my compassion.

I joined Russ again, reciting the poem in my native language
of Spanish. Russ continued alone, speaking in German, French,
Polish, Russian, Hebrew, Swedish, Norwegian, and Arabic. When
Russ began to recite in Portuguese, JoSam reached under his sweaty
tropical shirt, groped for the black leather body holster that held his
service-issued pistol, slowly drew it out, aimed at the back of Russ's
head, and pulled the trigger. I watched Russ's body remain in kneeling position for a few seconds before it fell over on its face with its
arms dangling relaxed behind it.

JoSam stood there for a few seconds, and I thought he was going
to shoot me too since I was directly in line with his pointed gun. Fear
pounded in my chest, and abhorrence filled my mind. We stood there
and looked at each other for an eternity. Were we finishing the stare
down we had begun when we had first met? I knew he had cunningly
planned what he had in mind for me, but he wanted me to know the
decision was his. He slowly put the gun back into his body holster,
and I stood in place, not moving until I was instructed to.

JoSam needed to pass back over Russ's body to reach the back door of the hotel, but the lifeless heap took up nearly all the width between the walls. JoSam was agile enough to have leapt over the body, but instead, he stepped directly onto Russ's outstretched arm and casually walked the remaining way as a rested, calm, transformed teacher of strategy.

I now remembered these images from my past, and they became the avalanche of thoughts that prevented sleep. My bed and boxer shorts were soaked with sweat from the memories of Russ Warren and the OPEC operation. My body felt stiff as it shifted from side to side, front to back, and side to side again, waiting for the pleasure of sleep. I got up, changed into dry clothes, and went out the back door of my bedroom to sit on the balcony. I felt the cool night breeze drying my wet skin. I looked at my watch, and it read 3:30 a.m. I debated about trying to go back inside to sleep, but sitting on the balcony steps, I remembered what JoSam's next OPEC directive had been.

"Mr. Lopez, notify the oilmen to be at the Vienna airport in one hour. We are leaving!"

"Yes, sir," I replied as I opened the door for him and exited the OPEC assignment.

On our return flight, JoSam joined in the frivolity and provided steak dinners, champagne, and chocolate cake for everyone. The oilmen were spirited, victorious, and generous. I remained aloof, drained, and grieving.

"Mr. Lopez, why isn't Mr. Warren with us?" asked Mr. Gulf. My heart was in my throat, but I lied, "Mr. Warren sends his apologies that he can't be with you, but he has another job in Vienna next week."

"I am sorry to hear that. I wanted to personally thank him for the great job he did and to tell him that even though the Angola deal didn't work out as a bonus, it was of no consequence because Gulf Oil will do well next year due to his efforts."

"I am sure your words will mean a great deal to him," I said as I swallowed my grief.

Mr. Standard stood, raised his glass, and toasted, "To Mr. Warren."

My grief was unmanageable, so I moved into the bathroom to compose myself. It took a few minutes before I rejoined the group.

"Mr. Lopez, we want to give Mr. Warren a tip for his help. We want to donate $1,000 each as a gift. Will you see that he gets it?" Mr. Shell asked as he handed me $10,000 in an envelope.

"I am returning to Argentina, but JoSam will deliver your appreciative words and see that he receives your gift."

"No, Mr. Lopez. You will see Mr. Warren in the dining room before I will. Take it!" JoSam demanded.

I reached up, grasped the envelope, and said, "For Mr. Warren. Thank you for thinking of him." The ten US oilmen applauded.

It was the second time I received money for someone's life. The first time had been in Korea after the Anderson assassination, and now I was receiving money for the death of my friend Russ Warren.

I felt the night breeze on my unclad body as I returned to my bed. I felt as if my mind needed Rotor-Rooter to unplug the sludge of memories that clogged my path to sleep. I needed to extract the Russ Warren assassination from my mind. I went back to my bed and slept.

I sprang out of bed with my feet touching the polished, cool, burnt-orange-colored tiles as I grabbed up the clock to focus on the time without my contacts. I couldn't believe it! I had slept until 8:30 a.m. I reached for my cell phone and saw I had three missed phone calls from JoSam. I quickly punched his button. "Sir, I am sorry to have missed your calls."

"Where were you, Mr. Lopez?"

"The truth is, I was sleeping,"

"Hmm. That's unusual for you. I want the property secured for our operations. Now! We are behind."

"I am taking care of it today. I will call you when it is completed."

"Good," JoSam said and clicked off.

CHAPTER 21
MISSION ACCOMPLISHED

I looked toward the hotel windows and saw Wyoming moving about. I knew Sun was doing her morning meditation, which gave me time to swim. The pool was always clean, cold, and refreshing when I plunged in and swam laps. From the pool, I saw Sun opening her bedroom curtains and knew she was finished with her morning of silence. Sun saw me and waved while I clutched the soft, aqua-blue towel around me and dripped my way up to her patio. She struggled to open the heavy, mahogany-framed, sliding-glass doors, and I reached up to help her.

"Thanks. I love seeing people use the pool. How was your swim?"

"It was great! You look full of light. Do you have time to brunch with me this morning?"

"I wondered how I could get out of weeding the flower gardens today. I would love to have brunch because I haven't eaten. When do you want to go?"

"How about as soon as I get dressed?" I invited.

"Perfect! I will meet you in the lobby. Come when you are ready."

I opened the grey Civic Honda door, and Sun gracefully sat down and swung her long slender legs in. I noticed the curve of her attractive white pants, which accentuated her figure. She wore a loose-fitting, purple, draped blouse that attempted to minimize her ample chest. I was attracted to her understated sensuality combined with her sense of elegant style. She was sexy. I needed to keep my mind on my job.

We drove a short way to the TinHo Restaurant, which offered a sumptuous Asian buffet brunch. I selected this restaurant knowing that Sun loved flowers. I thought the charm of restful waterfalls, fountains, and outdoor pathways with bridges, which led to tables under flowering trees, would impress her.

"Angelo, this place is spellbinding and straight out of a story-book. You know so many wonderful places, and I see that your job taught you to impress your clients. I'm not even a client, but I'm delighted by this place."

"I love your company." I pulled out her chair as I watched her glide gracefully onto the small Asian piece of furniture. "Do you want to order from the menu, or would you like the buffet?"

"I want the buffet. I love to taste new foods." I escorted her from her chair, and we made our way to the many artistically displayed food tables. I became aware of her tiny size as she barely reached below my shoulders in height. Her well-shaped, rounded behind and her long legs moved to the food tables. She had an Asian body type with small delicate bones and with curves. Her hands were small with long fingers and French-manicured nails. She made her way around the food tables, and it appeared she was enthusiastic about food. I had once heard that if a woman ate unselfconsciously in your presence, she would be good in your bed. I wondered if that was true.

We sat back down at the table, and I said, "I notice you meditate twice a day. Why do you do that?"

Her big emerald-green eyes looked at me with surprise, and

she laughingly said, "To become the most evolved person that I can become." I noticed that she was proficient at eating with chopsticks.

"Why is being evolved important?"

"I believe evolved people are happier and more productive. I want to reach the highest level of consciousness, stay grounded there, and live my life from that level."

"Sun, what level of consciousness am I?"

She laughed and said, "We are in the first stage of consciousness."

"Only the first one?"

"Yes, the first state of consciousness is the awake state. We are awake now," she laughed. "There are seven states of consciousness: the awake state, the sleep state, the dream state, transcendent, cosmic consciousness, God consciousness, and unity consciousness. It's possible to move in and out of these consciousnesses without boundaries, and many people do. The more developed we are, the more we become more stabilized in a higher state, but my goal is to be permanent and to live from unity consciousness."

"How do you know when you are in one of the higher states?" I asked.

"You feel better. Each level of consciousness has its own set of signposts. You become aware of your self-evolution, which is also known as self-referral. For example, people who experience the transcendent level of consciousness have higher levels of energy, have more proficient work ethics, get sick less, have a better sense of humor, enjoy themselves and other people, are more likely to be thoughtful toward others, and make better choices for themselves and nature."

"What about unity consciousness? What is that like?"

"Oh, that's the best. Unity consciousness knows everything from a level of total integration. It's experiencing and not intellectualizing. It is knowing from the level of experienced creativity and the source of creation. It is knowing every detail of being, about our universe,

God, natural law, our environment, and understanding that we are all *that*—we are all from the same Source and are all *one*," Sun emphasized and continued her explanation.

"The sleep level is important too. Your body and mind must have between seven and eight hours of adequate sleep each night. The time you go to sleep is also important. People who have night jobs and sleep during the day don't get proper rest because the sun keeps their body cells enlivened and active, even in a dark room. The most profound sleep happens between 10 p.m. and 2 a.m. During sleep, the brain has time to restore damaged brain cells. If the body has ample sleep and is well rested, it sends and receives clear signals from the source of creation.

"Taking impure substances like alcohol, nicotine, or drugs into the body obstructs clear channels to reach cosmic consciousness, God consciousness, or unity consciousness."

"I find this topic interesting, but you are also an interesting person."

"Thank you. I think you have been given a rare and wonderful mind, and I want good things for you. I see other goodness you were born with and want you to make life-enhancing choices for yourself," Sun complimented.

"Will you allow me to help you get your legal papers in order?" I asked.

"I welcome any help that would allow me to understand the Costa Rican legal system of running a hotel. I don't know if I am doing things correctly and legally or if I'm in violation. I want to learn and to do things correctly," Sun said determinedly.

"Conducting business in Costa Rica isn't easy. For one thing, there is some sort of tax due on your corporation and property once a month. They are small annoying taxes, usually between $100 and $200, but it is time consuming, and going to government offices takes a long time. They make you stand in line and wait your turn with many other people. I can easily pay both of our taxes when I pay for my construction company."

"That's kind of you. I appreciate your help. I can devote my time to the tourists."

"The necessary paperwork requires you to give me a limited power of attorney. This is easy to do, and we can get it on the way home if you like."

"What is a limited power of attorney?"

"It means you give me permission to pay your taxes. It will be like a permission document."

"Will this power of attorney document be expensive?" she asked.

"No, it is free. On the way home, I will run into the courthouse and pick up a form. We can take it home, and I will translate it into English for you so you will understand it before you sign it. I will take it and have it registered with the public registry. I will present the signed paper at the tax collectors' many offices when it is time to pay. I can check to see if your taxes are up to date as well."

"Angelo, thanks. I want you to make a list of my taxes, my due dates, their location of payment, and the amount of tax to be paid so I become self-sufficient, especially since you cannot be around all the time."

"Since we met, I have enjoyed being around you and am going to stay nearby more often."

Sun smiled and said, "That might be fun." She conveyed her sincerity as she raised her green-eyed gaze to meet mine. "What are your future plans concerning your job?"

"I started with the company when I was seventeen years old, and I have been told that I am being groomed to replace JoSam when he retires. This job is all I know. I believe I would feel very insecure doing anything else," I said truthfully.

"I believe men associate their value with their occupation. I don't think it's the same for women. Women find their value within. They don't need the measure of their self-value to come through business, however, our women going into the workplace and women's equality changed all of that. I'm not sure that change was good for anyone. Being other directed rather than inner-directed places too much stress on both sexes' nervous systems and causes illness. Women used to live longer, but now the longevity between men's and women's life-spans is shrinking. Stress of any kind damages individuals."

I knew JoSam was waiting for my call and felt his pressure. "Sun, if you are ready to go, we can talk more on the way to the courthouse. I hate to end our time together, but I have to work this afternoon."

I stopped at the courthouse, picked up the power of attorney form, and went back to Sun's mini resort where I smoothly changed a few words in the translation. She signed it.

"Thank you for brunch, and thanks for helping me," she graciously said.

"Thanks for your wonderful company," I responded as I walked to my apartment. I felt uneasy again as I thought about JoSam and my job. JoSam and Sun seemed to be diabolically opposed to each other. I thought about Sun's brunch conversation. She said it was important to make life-enhancing decisions! My work, JoSam's continued support and rewards, and the status of my position could be called life enhancing. Did my job give me the happiness I was looking for? I liked the thrill of the chase, the surge of energy when I made a conquest, the adrenaline rush that I felt with each new case and was rewarded by promotions and money. All that seemed like happiness to me.

It had been JoSam's highest priority for months to find the perfect location for our Central American communications' base, and now I'd found Sun Wren Richards's property to be the ideal location for our operation. She was my conquest. It was our goal to infiltrate, set up an undetected worldwide communications' system to use for our agency's projects, missions, and long-range goals. We needed this central location to be in operation for at least three years.

Once this system was established, we could signal any of our aircraft, nautical vessels, ground vehicles, and personnel without going through regular Costa Rican channels of entry. This infiltrated country wouldn't know we were here. We would construct our own nearby airport for our helicopters and private jets. We would succeed with this arrangement because it would be disguised as part of Sun's private residence. The thick jungle vegetation near Sun's property would serve our purpose of obscurity. I had bought enough land near her hotel to begin building our airport and compound.

I reached the privacy of the apartment and made my call. "Hello, JoSam, this is Angelo. It is done. I have power of attorney and placed a $350,000 lien on the property. I know Sun can't pay it off, and the lien is big enough to keep her from selling the house to someone else. She won't know there is a lien on the property for a long time. I used the money I received from the lien holder, Leonardo DeLancy, one of our own agents, for our airport construction costs. Sun unknowingly contributed to our goals."

"This is good for our agency, Angelo. You have done well," JoSam complimented.

"Sun Wren Richards is a quality person. I find her attractive and like this assignment."

"Forget those ideas, Mr. Lopez. You are doing a job, so don't get hung up on some woman."

"You would like her. She's an interesting lady."

"All women are interesting. Stay out of the bedroom. Do I make myself clear?" JoSam clicked off.

CHAPTER 22
INVESTIGATION

I t was a cool morning, and a pleasant breeze soothed my skin as I stood in the open doorway of my apartment in my undershorts. I listened to the creaking stands of bamboo moving in the zephyr and sounding like a violinist tuning up for a concert. Everyone was still asleep, even the birds and Sun. It was another short night with less than two hours of sleep. I had dressed, packed, and downed the remaining coffee.

It was still dark as I left Sun's Costa Rican mini-resort, Casa Ave Hotel, on that early morning, to meet my NSA Colombian team of seven men, who would be searching for connections between ticos (the Meza family) and Colombian people who were involved with the purchase of Sun's property. In Costa Rica, property must be incorporated. Often property has an exiting corporation and in Sun's case she bought a corporation consisting of foreign board members. These persons of interest included Colombians: Mauricio Machado Santos, a board member at large; Leonardo Garzon Serpa, vice president; and Valerina Pachona Uribe, president, who was recently murdered.

The day Katerina Meza's secretary, Marianela, gave Sun and I the books, I placed a complete communications' surveillance on Ms. Meza's electronics, which led to an interesting phone call involving Mr. Serpa, one of the Colombians and vice president on Sun's corporation board. It appeared from the phone conversation that the Meza Family worked for the three Colombian board members. The purpose for this trip was to determine the nature of their employment.

Our Colombian NSA seven-man team had begun a communication surveillance on Mauricio Santos and Leonardo Serpa and had faxed personal profiles on both men. The profiles were in my briefcase to be read on the airplane in route to Colombia. The Costa Rican NSA three-man team traveled with me as protection trackers until we reached Colombia when I transferred to the Colombian team. Manuel would stay with me in Colombia, but Joseppe and Geraldo from the NSA Costa Rican team planned to return home. I was never alone and relished my few moments of morning breezes and bamboo serenades before my flight to Colombia.

I settled into the comfortable executive seat of the new NSA supersonic, private twenty-two-passenger Gulf Stream G650, which traveled nonstop across the Atlantic Ocean at 704 miles per hour. It was fully equipped with a galley, bathroom, and dressing room. Our agency, in 2009, had the first aircraft of its kind, and production for the public wouldn't begin until 2013. I was given many advantages because I worked for progressive agencies of the US government. During my career, I had experienced the use of *firsts*. I used the first cassette tape recorder, computer, cell phone, and facial-recognition technology. My job remained successful because of innovative, clandestine inventions, which were developed daily for our use.

It was a pleasure to ride in the comfort of the Gulf Stream G650 compared to the hard tinny interior of helicopters. I opened my briefcase and read the prepared personal profile for one of Sun's former board members. Mauricio Machado Santos, age fifty-seven, born to agricultural laborers from Cali, Colombia, and educated by a village priest until the fifth grade. At eleven years old, he joined his family in the vegetable fields where he continued his self-education of agriculture, fertilizers, chemicals, and farm marketing. Mauricio Santos started making his own fertilizers, pesticides, and insecticides from the family's back porch at age twelve.

Today he was one of Colombia's wealthiest executives. He owned two fertilizer plants, five chemical plants, and forty-two laboratories, which served many hospitals and clinics throughout Colombia. Mr. Santos was the employer of 2,300 Colombians, who worked in his fertilizer and chemical plants. The number of employees excluded the many people who worked in the privately leased health care laboratories.

In the last twenty years, Mauricio Santos began another business called The High Green Vegetables Transport Corp, where he contracted out farm-to-market truck transports. He owned 250 trucks and employed another five hundred truck drivers. Mr. Santos's longtime interest in agriculture led him to become a major farm real estate investor, where he owned one-third of Colombia's farmland and employed another three thousand farmworkers. The crops produced from his farms were one of Colombia's largest sources of food.

Mauricio Machado Santos married *Elle* magazine's top fashion model, Felicity Farrow, in 1980 and had five daughters ranging in age from eighteen to twenty-five. Three daughters had modeling careers. Mauricio Santos raised his family to be Catholic but rarely attended church himself. He and his family lived near his childhood home in Cali, Colombia.

The second name on Sun's former board was Leonardo Garzon Serpa, another of Colombia's most wealthy people. Leonardo Garzon Serpa, age fifty, had been described in interviews as "a charming high roller." He was the only son born to a Colombian commodities trader in 1959 in Bogota, Colombia, where he was educated in private schools until he graduated.

After graduation, Mr. Serpa studied communications at Boston University. In Boston, Leonardo Serpa made many connections with the sons and daughters of moneyed families from Latin America, Europe, and the United States, who furthered his investment business. After graduation from Boston University, Mr. Serpa's oversized personality turned him into a mega salesman for the investment company Money Grow Green, which lost $7.1 billion of his clients investments but supplied himself with an apartment in Manhattan, a mansion in London, another in Madrid with a butler, a chauffeured car, and a private jet.

Leonardo Serpa married and became the flamboyant son-in-law of Walter Hill, the founder of Money Grow Green hedge-fund investments. He married Hill's oldest daughter, Rene, in 1990 and became managing partner of the firm. Serpa and his wife flew around in jets, gave elaborate costume parties, hunted pheasant with European royalty, and yachted with models. Rene Hill was a carefully curated Connecticut graduate from Boston University with business and finance masters' degrees.

Leonardo and Rene Serpa were owners of an impressive art collection. They entertained from their $52 million dollar yacht, which was anchored off the Colombian coast in the port of Santa Marta. They sold their US mansion in Manhattan and bought another mansion in the port town of Santa Marta and a town house in Bulgaria. They went from country to country on their yacht named *High Tide*.

Leonardo and Rene Serpa were parents to twin boys, Ramon and Renaldo, born in 1992 in Bogota, Colombia. Their sons attended Southern Methodist University in Dallas, Texas. Mr. Leonardo Serpa brokered commodities, investments, and real estate from his Santa Marta home or while traveling in his yacht.

I closed the files and asked the three Costa Rican team members

Manuel, Joseppe, and Geraldo to join me for an in-flight meeting. "It is important for the Costa Rican team to work closely with our seven-man Colombian team. Share your ideas or thoughts with them and give them any evidence you think may or may not be related or any incidents, activities, or movements that have occurred involving Serpa and Santos. Geraldo what have we learned from the communications surveillance placed on Ms. Katerina's electronics?" I asked.

"Ms. Katerina Meza communicates frequently by e-mail with Leonardo Serpa. It appears that Lawyer Meza represents him in his Costa Rican real estate dealings. She filed the purchase and ownership papers for the Costa Rican properties he bought. Mr. Leonardo Serpa was the original property owner and has held the mortgage for the sellers of the Sun W. Richards property, Tony Lopez and Rodney Lewis, since 1990. There was a $7,000 balance owed to him at the time of Sun's closing. Sun's deposit ($60,000) and property closing money ($350,000) was paid in cash directly to Mercedes Meza Hernandez's personal account and distributed to Tony Lopez and Rodney Lewis, minus Mercedes's $15,000 commission. Mercedes Meza Hernandez was Pablo and Katerina's 23 year old daughter who became Sun's tour guide, friend and realtor.

Pablo Meza was involved in the sale of the property in 1990 when Lopez and Lewis bought the property from Mr. Serpa, which indicates his longtime business relationship to the Costa Rican Meza family. Katerina Meza did the legal paperwork and represented Leonardo Serpa while Pablo Meza served as his Costa Rican real estate broker and developer. Mercedes was employed as the errand girl. She opened and deposited money—perhaps even laundered money—into accounts in foreign countries.

This next event is interesting. Mercedes, our suspect from Costa Rica, opened four new accounts in the countries of Nicaragua, El Salvador, Panama, and Honduras under the name of Sun Wren Richards and used Sun's original passport number to deposit twenty dollars in each of the accounts. Do you want me to continue?" asked Geraldo.

"Yes," I encouraged.

"There were phone conversations between Ms. Katerina Meza and the deceased former board president, Valerina Pachona Uribe, about Sun's recently purchased corporation, who was demanding $100,000 of the sale money. Valerina explained that she was owed the money as payment for other sales, and Katerina Meza made her president of the corporation to reassure her that she would receive her salary when Sun Wren Richards closed on the Costa Rican property. In a very heated argument with Katerina Meza, Valerina Pachona Uribe threatened to expose everyone if she didn't receive the money."

Geraldo took a breath and continued reporting. "Leonardo Garzon Serpa, Mauricio Machado Santos, Katerina Meza, Marianela Gonzales, and Pablo Meza served on twenty-two to forty-three corporation boards where it looked like property scams similar to Richards's property had taken place. This could be termed racketeering." Geraldo concluded his report.

"Geraldo, this is good information. Thank you," I said.

Geraldo was a common man, who would fit unnoticed into any crowd or room. This made him ideal for being an agent. He was a tico in his thirties and maintained everything as average. He was an average male with a height of five feet ten inches. He was an average 160 pounds and had a lightly tanned complexion and dark-brown hair and eyes. He was not good-looking but not ugly either—he just looked average. What was not average about Geraldo was his dedication to his team and his diligent, precise work for the NSA. He remained loyal to his job but was happily married to a woman in her early twenties and had one male child, who was a year old.

"Does anyone have comments on the report?" I asked.

"It seems the Costa Rican people serve as Serpa's employees, but is Santos equally involved?" asked Manuel.

"Good question, Manuel. Does anyone have thoughts pointing to Santos's involvement?" I asked.

"When we performed the detailed investigation of Sun's art studio and examined pools of Ramon's blood and dog hair, I found this wrapper unnoticed beneath the sculpture table." Joseppe held up a small plastic bag that contained an empty arsenic package. When I heard Mauricio Machado Santos's personal profile that mentioned he had owned chemical plants in Colombia, I looked on the package and saw it was manufactured in Colombia. It's a long shot, but maybe this could be the connection to Santos," Joseppe offered excitedly.

Joseppe was thirty-two-year-old buff, handsome Italian man from Rome, who had the body and grace of the flamingo dancer he was. He was athletic, agile, and acrobatic. He looked Italian Basque with dark, curly hair, blue eyes, and light-tan colored skin. He wore fitted shirts, which accentuated his broad shoulders and slim waist, and he had the dancer's rounded, developed buttocks and thighs. He had been a professional dancer, trainer, and choreographer with a company in San Jose, Costa Rica, for the past five years. Women adored this man, who commanded their attention, and begged to dance with him. He was a master of competitive ballroom dancing and held many trophies.

"That is a good lead, Joseppe. I will give that piece of evidence to our Colombia team, and they can follow its origins. Maybe you found the Santos link," I said as I reached for the bag and placed it in my case.

"Geraldo, I want you to determine the connection between Santos and Serpa. Are they business associates? Friends? How do they know one another? How do they hold equal status when Santos is from a background of poverty and labor and Serpa is an educated elitist?" I asked.

"When I took my shift to monitor Katerina Meza's electronics last week, I saw an invitation to a Serpa party. Do you think this invitation might be helpful to us?" questioned Manual.

"Bingo! This will be our needed step to party crashing or infil-tration," I shouted. "Manual, make us five invitations. We can go as Katerina's guests. Find out if she plans to attend and get the details. Please investigate this now so we can make use of this opportunity," I excitedly requested.

Manuel smiled until his bulbous nose crinkled. He moved to the back of the aircraft, made his call to headquarters, and returned before I had finished my Coke. "Good news. The invitation given to Katerina is for a party at Serpa's Santa Marta mansion and takes place at 5 p.m., Saturday, on his yacht, which is docked at the mansion's home port. The party requires costumes or tuxedoes," Manuel reported.

"Eureka! This is great, but we have a change of assignments. You three will not return to Costa Rica as planned but will stay and work the case in Colombia," I said.

"Geraldo, you can work out of NSA's Colombian headquarters. Your assignment is to infiltrate Mr. and Mrs. Serpa's bank accounts, accounting systems, and wealth management companies. I want to know if their income is as great as their spending. I want a daily report of their banking activities to determine whether or not they have unreported income and their lifestyle balances with it. Make use of our XKeyscore [USA's clandestine and world's largest com-puter located in Utah] and dig deep into their business activity. Call me immediately if you find any irregularity or a possibility of money being laundered," I requested.

"Manuel, do you want a tux or a costume?"

"Tux, please."

"Manuel, I need you to manufacture an e-mail from Katerina declining the party invitation but explaining to Serpa that she will send him five unrelated, possible investment clients as guests. We will keep monitoring her e-mails to know whether or not she will attend. It won't matter if she attends since she doesn't know any of you and I will be in a costume and a mask. Manuel, you were curious about Santos. Check out his accounting, banking, and financial history. Use the NSA Colombian infiltration team whenever you need too," I instructed.

"Joseppe, your dance background will be valuable for this assignment. You will serve as an informant. Collect information from the females in attendance. They may talk a lot. Find out whatever you can. We have two days before the yacht party. Do you want a tux or a costume?"

"Tux, please."

"Joseppe, you will visit the chemical plants before the party and answer the question of the arsenic wrapper," I encouraged.

"Okay, I guess it is settled. I am mandated to wear a costume. Before Saturday's party, we have much to do. Manual get a list of Santos's laboratories and their locations from the Colombia team. I think we should visit as many as we can, and the rural ones should be first on the list. We need to visit Santos's vegetable farms and Serpa's financial properties and real estate offices. Remember, we are investors," I urged and continued to formulate my strategy.

"There will be seven NSA Colombian team members, and you three Costa Ricans total ten men making visitations on sixty-five properties in two days. My protection trackers will work their regular jobs. We can take more days after the party if necessary. This is a workload of six-and-a-half properties for each of us to visit before the party. We can divide it up and visit what we can. The most rural properties will be the most interesting. Each of us will visit one rural location in combination with the more accessible metropolitan properties. We will finish our visitation plans when we meet with our Colombian team, and we will meet each day to report our findings before Saturday's party." I saw that these young men were fully engaged in this project.

"We will stay in Santa Marta, Colombia, at the Santorini Hotel and Resort. You will be fitted for your tuxedoes in your rooms before

Saturday. It is important for us to portray ourselves as independent investment clients who don't know each other, to gain a wider swath of information. We can keep in touch with our secured cell phones, and you can call me anytime. Call me immediately if you find something. Do you have any questions?" I asked.

"Why are you emphasizing that we research the rural areas first?" asked Geraldo.

"Oh, Geraldo, I don't know! Call it a hunch or a gut feeling, but I think the high life Serpa has lived weighs more than their income has produced. Maybe Daddy-in-Law helped cover the bills, or illegal unreported activities were going on to supply the cavalier attitude of Serpa. —Maybe not.— Maybe their business is good, but why are they on so many corporate boards in Costa Rica unless they are money-grubbers or are hiding something. It would be easier for them to operate illegal activities in rural areas.

"My skepticism jumped up and down and is the reason I want you to examine their financial records. If we can't find answers out in the field, maybe you will find them in their records. Does anyone have anything else to ask or to add? No more questions? This is an investigative assignment, and we can relax a bit and enjoy our jobs. Use headquarters XKeyScore equipment and our plane if you need too. Work independently but pool your resources and information. Some of the properties may be in the same areas, and you can use the same vehicles. Let's go party!"

We left our plane and joined the waiting Colombia team, that took us to the Santorini Hotel's secluded conference room for our Special Ten strategy meeting. By the time we arrived, Manuel had received the needed information concerning Santos's laboratory locations. The Colombia team was overloaded, so I decided to help out. The team quickly divided the site visits between the ten of them, and we dispersed.

CHAPTER 23
MY BLUNDER

Dressed as a tourist, I took a commercial flight from northern Colombia's Santa Marta and Serpa's mansion to Cali in southern Colombia, known as Santos territory. No one but I had property assignments in that area, so I forfeited use of the plane to the larger group of investigators.

After I arrived in the city of Cali, which was located on the fertile Cauca River and was surrounded by enormous sugar fields, I rented a car, picked up a couple of sandwiches, and drove to the most remote of Santos's vegetable farms. It was located high in the Andes with a gradation elevation starting at two thousand to three thousand feet above sea level. The car was a cool green in both color and *wappa* (Spanish trendy slang meaning cool). I enjoyed being alone. Not really alone for I knew my protection team was there, but driving alone was a pleasure.

The road that led to the farm was well maintained, graveled, and narrow but passable for two vehicles. I met two High Green Vegetables trucks, which came down the hill as I went up it. I tried to see the contents of the transported goods in the trucks' beds, but the trucks were covered with canvas tarps. The trucks looked almost new and were well maintained, as were the tarps. Judging by the transport vehicles, Santos was no slouch of a farmer. I continued to drive until the road widened into a parking area beside a tan-colored stucco Spanish-style farmhouse with lush flower gardens. I assumed this home was the farm manager's place.

I parked the car and watched the farm activity. There were an abundance of farm laborers who carried baskets of asparagus to a large shed. There were tables and water sprayers where over thirty women washed the asparagus. Thirty more women crated the clean spears while men loaded the crates onto the waiting High Green Vegetables trucks. There were trucks coming and going frequently. When one truck was fully loaded, another empty truck took its place. Santos's business looked prosperous.

It looked to be a well-managed farm with washing sheds set up for a variety of crops. In two other sheds, workers were washing a mountain of potatoes. A dump truck with High Green Vegetables logos displayed on the doors dumped potatoes onto the shed's washing tables where women and men washed and crated them. I was impressed with the work ethics of this farm, and I judged it to be a clean operation.

Then, I spotted a man who was holding a machine gun and was guarding the entrance to a one-vehicle graveled road, which led to a much higher elevation of farmland. Once you got up the hill, you were at an elevation of five thousand feet. The "NO TRESPASSING" sign and a man with a machine gun would be deterrent enough for any lost tourist, but why would Santos need a machine gun to guard asparagus?

I knew what I needed to do, and my thoughts made me smile. The protection tracking team wouldn't like what I had in mind. The foreman in the farmhouse came out, and I waived and shouted,

"Nice farm," as I started the car, turned it around, and returned down the same road. I found a thick grove of coffee bushes and hid the car.

I saw that all the sheds had trucks loaded with cargo and that any truck entering needed to wait their turn or to drive up to the higher farm fields. I waited for a slow-moving, empty High Green Vegetables truck that I could grab onto. I needed to be on the passengers' side away from the man with the machine gun. Otherwise, I had to sneak past the posted sentry on foot. I didn't know how far I would need to walk before I got to the higher fields, and the walk would be uphill.

My best choice was to grab onto the passengers' side of the truck. I could stay crouched low on my knees under the view of the side mirrors where the running board and the door handle gave me the best support. Once I was on board, I would adjust the side mirror so that the driver could see the back of his truck but not me. I heard a vehicle crunching its way on the gravel road toward me. Lightning fast, I moved a large log across the road to stop the truck. I would then be able to grab onto the truck. I quickly placed the log, ran back to my hiding place, and waited for the truck to arrive.

The only thing was——it wasn't the right truck! It was my guys. They got out of the car, and were slowly dragging the log off the road when the High Green Vegetables truck pulled up behind them and stopped. I made my move and latched onto the passengers' side of the truck. Roberto from the Colombian team explained to the farm driver that they were tourists who wanted to see the farm. The farm driver and Roberto chatted for a while, and I wanted everyone to start moving. In my crouched position, I managed to adjust the mirror to keep myself hidden.

My tasks were completed, but already, my crouched legs were cramping. I thought, *Come on. Let's go.* Roberto finally drove up the road, and the High Green Vegetables truck moved forward. I was glad that the road that led to the narrower, private road could not be seen by the farmworkers in the washing sheds.

The protection team saw the log in the road and knew I had placed it there. They kept well ahead of the truck driver and laughed animatedly. I knew they could see me at a distance since they were directly in front of me. As we got to the parking area, they pulled over and waved to the truck driver, who approached the sentry. My Colombia team quickly followed the truck to the sentry. The sentry knew the driver, waved him through, and became engaged in conversation with my team. I thought, *Good cover work guys!*

The truck picked up speed on the twisting, bumpy, rough, graveled road, which narrowed and was close to the edge of the cliff where I clung. My legs screamed for relief, and my mind calculated the miles toward my unknown end. I was focused on my cramped legs but finally noticed acre after acre of grown coca plants, which were mature enough for processing into cocaine. My painful ride and my hunch paid off.

The truck slowed, and I saw freshly cut raw coca leaves stacked in bundles under a shed where two men waited to load the truck. My mind raced into survival mode. The truck pulled close to the walled side of the shed. I remained adhered to the truck. The truck's backside was open and exposed for loading. I slipped from my crouched position and slid under the truck to hide, but more importantly, I stretched my cramped legs until the truck was loaded. The process went quickly. One man climbed into the empty bed of the truck while the other loaded the bails with a forklift onto the truck. Then the first man guided them into place. I used the sound of the loading tractor to mask my voice for the phone call I made to the tracking team. I punched in Roberto's number.

"Where the hell are you?" he asked.

"Under a truck. We are talking cocaine! Listen, call our helicopter and give the pilot the location of this farm. I want your guys in the helicopter to stay far enough away so that they won't be a threat but close enough so they can use the camera to photograph the evidence. I will grab a handful of leaves from the bundles if I can. There are acres upon acres and tons and tons of harvested coca plants ready for processing. The truck will be loaded soon, and I will hopefully return to my car and follow the High Green Vegetables truck to the lab. I might need your help to jump off this truck when we reach my car, which is parked near the log you drug from the road," I explained.

"Yeah. We spotted your hidden car. How can we do our jobs while you are playing James Bond?" he asked.

"You did fine as a distraction for the sentry, who otherwise might have seen me. Thanks for the good cover. Just help me get back to my car." I clicked off.

I lay directly under a leaking oil gasket, which had made a large, oily spot on my new tourist shirt. *Damn! Some James Bond I am.*

The loading man jumped from the truck as the tractor pulled out and drove to another shed that was full of bailed coca leaves. The man waited for another empty truck to arrive. My driver ambled up to the newly loaded cargo and covered it with a canvas tarp as I slid back into my crouched passenger position, ready to roll. I was exhilarated, and a rush of excitement and pride filled me. It was great. I had proven to myself that I could do a job equal to the twenty year olds on my teams.

On the return trip from my breezy roost and as the wind whistled in my ears, I heard the sound of the helicopter in the distance. My legs were a tight mess of quivering, cramping muscles, and the return trip to my rented car seemed double in length. Luck was in my favor. I saw the sentry in the distance who was on my side of the truck run across the road to the driver's side. He took a white form from his clipboard and handed it to the driver. *I'm saved*, I thought. The truck was put into gear and continued down the hill.

When I could bear the squatted position no more, the truck's bucking ascension nearly jostled me loose from my perch. I felt the truck jolt and heard the thudding, flapping noise from a flat tire as the truck slowed down. The driver coasted down the hill for two hundred meters and stopped one hundred meters short of my parked rental vehicle. *Clever! Just how did the protection team manage that?* I wondered.

The truck driver got out. I quickly dropped and rolled into a swampy ditch while he examined the damage of the passengers' side front tire. He retrieved a spare from under the truck bed, hunted for the jack and tire iron, unscrewed the lug nuts, and finally changed the tire. The ditch smelled putrid, and I nearly lost my digested sandwiches as I lay with my face just inches away from the foul stench of the green slime that had ruined my silk tropical tourist shirt and nicely pressed khaki-tan Bermuda shorts.

As the truck pulled away and turned a curve that hid me from view, I knew I should follow him. I oozed up from the vomit-colored slime. I dripped and sloshed in my Italian shoes and slogged through the stinking ditch toward my concealed car. I couldn't see the protection team anywhere. When I reached my car, I fished my cell phone from the shirt's manure filled pocket and examined its condition. I took off every smelly, saturated piece of clothing, tossed the bundle into the trunk, and placed my shoes in the back seat to dry.

Naked, I slid beneath the steering wheel, rolled down the window, and got a whiff of my own rancid stink. My cramped thigh muscles trembled, and my tired knee bounced involuntarily up and down as I stepped onto the gas to pursue the High Green Vegetables truck. As I closed the distance behind the moving truck, I smiled at the name, which was appropriate for the transported coca leaves.

My exhilaration and humor faded when I saw that my protection team had changed its members and had tracked the truck instead of me. I was embarrassed by our reversed roles. I felt their testosterones' competitive message, which they had pointedly sent to me to prove their youth and vigor. I looked down at my naked shriveled body part and realized my mistake. I was to be a symbol of wisdom and not a stunt man. My swollen pride had shrunken to a short humiliated size.

I followed the truck into the city center of Cali, which is Colombia's third largest city. I pulled over to the curb and parked eight doors away from Santos's laboratory. I watched the truck pull behind the building's twelve-foot-high chain-link privacy fence. A large garage door opened. The truck backed into Santos's laboratory and disappeared as the door closed. My cell phone rang, and I saw Roberto's ID displayed on the damp phone screen.

"Hello," I said.

"What do you want us to do?" Roberto asked from his speakerphone.

"My birthday suit is damp and wrinkled," I said as I heard peals of masculine laughter. "Try to get into the lab and take as many pictures as you can. If you can get into the cocaine processing part of the lab, it would be a bonus. I have the plate number of the High Green Vegetables truck. It is "ARS 22450." While I sit here, I will contact our team and tell them what we have. I will run a check on the driver and record the plate number in our file. The lab and farm are both on my list of properties to investigate so we won't duplicate or overload our team.

I finished everything I needed to do in this area of Colombia and will fly back to Santa Marta to our hotel. It will be very late when I arrive, but Roberto, I invite you to join our team meeting at the hotel's conference at 14:00."

As I sat and waited, I noticed three team members had called. I returned their calls in order.

"Sorry I missed your call, Joseppe. What have you got?"

"I am at Santos's chemical plant and can't talk now but the

Colombia arsenic wrapper was a match, and I have more," Joseppe whispered.

"Great! Special Ten will meet in Santa Marta at the Santorini Hotel conference room at 14:00. Ciao." I clicked off. I felt ridiculous sitting there in the buff. Second thought, I was not naked, I was nude. It seemed more dignified that way.

"Sorry I missed your call, Manuel, what have you got?" I asked.

"I got a good look at his business ledgers inside the chemical factory. Santo is one genius at business. I took pictures of his records," Manuel reported.

"Great! Special Ten will meet in Santa Marta at the Santorini Hotel conference room at 14:00, and you could fill us in. Ciao." I hung up. I became self-conscious as I sat there naked, fearing that a passerby might look down into the car at my undignified state of undress.

"Marco, sorry I missed your call, What have you got?"

"I won the lottery. I found a coca plant farm that belongs to Santos," Marco excitedly reported.

"Bingo. Where did you find it? What is your assigned area?"

"I am thirty miles north of the capital city of Bogota," he exclaimed.

"Have you finished at the farm and did you get pictures?"

"Yes, many pictures, sir," he answered.

"Were you assigned any Santos laboratories?"

"Yes, there are two on my list that are nearby," he explained.

"Can you visit them while you are in the area?" I questioned.

"That is a definite yes."

"Okay, Marco, Special Ten will meet in Santa Marta at the Santorini Hotel conference room at 14:00 to give our reports. I look forward to collecting the information. Ciao," I said, clicked off, and called the rest of the team, disseminating the meeting information. I saw Roberto return to his car, and I called him on the phone. "How did it go?"

"More information than I hoped for," Roberto reported.

"You are invited to give a report at a meeting at 14:00 in Santa Marta at the Santorini Hotel conference room." I paused and then asked, "Roberto, I hate to ask you this, but do you guys have any extra clothes I could borrow?" Peals of raucous laughter exploded in my ears.

"A package will be tossed through your car window," he snorted and chuckled.

"Thanks. I need underwear too," I pleaded. More roars of laughter tumbled out. I clicked off.

I watched three protective team members approach and stand beside Roberto's car while he talked to them. I watched their bodies convulse with belly laughs while they played a fast game of Roshambo (rock, paper, scissors). Roberto appeared to lose and ambled off to a clothing store while the others still laughed.

My phone rang several times with inquiries from Roberto about sizes and colors. The phone rang again, and his snickering voice questioned, "What brand of underwear do you want? Haines, Tommy John, Jockey, Calvin Klein, Performance, Fruit of the Loom, Buck Naked, ManSilk, Hugo Boss, or Under Amour? Do you want men's boxers, briefs, bikinis, thongs, G-strings, knit mini briefs, trunks, low-rise boxers, satin boxers, men's boxer briefs, concealed fly, control top, or high-rise boxers. For patterns and colors, do you want paisley, solid colors, prints, polka dots—"

"Just buy the damn underwear!" I shouted and clicked off.

A few minutes later, a flying package came through the passenger's open window without my even seeing Roberto. I rummaged through the bag until I found the first article of clothing to be donned: Buck Naked, hot pink, men's bikinis, with a concealed fly. I couldn't help but smile. The rest of the clothes were acceptable. I dressed in the car and drove to the rental car return in my bare feet. When I got to the car rental place, I collected my dried Ferragamo

Italian loafers from the back seat. They were hard, shrunken, and pinched when I put them on. I retrieved the stinking bundle from the trunk, stuffed it into the store bag, and tossed everything into the garbage.

I smelled the stench of my shoes, and so did my fellow passengers as I removed them and placed them onto the conveyor belt at airport security. Stink or not, I had a meeting to conduct in Santa Marta.

CHAPTER 24
COLUMBIA INFILTRATION

O ur meeting at the Santorini Hotel began precisely at 2 a.m. The hotel was empty except for our eleven men who were arriving. We sat around the conference table behind closed doors. We were all tired.

"Marco, give us your report on Santos's High Green Vegetables farm," I invited.

Marco was a sinewy light-complexioned, twenty five year old, fresh from Universidad de Los Andes, Colombia. He loved to party but was enthusiastically involved with our agency and his Colombia team. He was resourceful and creative at infiltrating privately secured properties.

"This is an amazing find. Santos's farm is between Puerto Salgar and a point roughly thirty miles north of the capital city of Bogota. It looks prosperous and well maintained. The farm manager's home is well kept and would sell for approximately $200,000. There are six washing sheds with the name Santos written on their roofs, and the helicopter got great pictures.

I counted over twelve truckloads of vegetables that were washed and loaded in two hours. Cucumbers, tomatoes, squash, and many acres of green beans were being shipped. Green beans seem to be the main crop they are harvesting. Well, green beans are the second main crop they are harvesting. The largest fields are hectare [two and a half acres] after hectare of coca plants," Marco said.

"I visited two nearby laboratories: one in Puerto Salgar and the other in Bogota. The security for the labs was intense, but I managed to get into the back of the laboratory where two High Green Vegetables trucks were unloading coca leaves—*bundles and bundles* of leaves. Here are some pictures of the fields and the trucks unloading at the laboratory," Marco explained as he passed around his cell phone.

"You did a good job, Marco. Did anyone else find farms of coca plants?"

Four people raised their hands. "We will get to those reports later. Manuel, you visited one of Santos's fertilizer plants and saw the books. What did you find out?" I asked,

"I was left alone in a room with Santos's business records for almost an hour before I got waited on. I made good use of my time. Mauricio Santos is a business genius. It seems that for every farm he owns, he also owns a laboratory in the same area. The five Santos chemical plants and the two Santos fertilizer plants are used for supplying his farms with needed products for produce production. The books showed that Santos is his own best customer. He bought insecticides, herbicides, and pesticides from his own Santos chemical plant for his own farm's crops. He did the same with the Santos fertilizer plants. He bought volumes of fertilizers for his farms. His chemical businesses sold products to all of his forty-two laboratories," Manuel explained as he sipped his coffee and continued with his report.

"He owns everything, and his profit is 100 percent his. If his farm needs fertilizer, he buys it from himself. If the labs need chemicals, he buys them from his chemical factories. He makes money by being his own best customer. Many other non-owned farms in Colombia also buy supplies from him. If he has a good harvest of asparagus and local and export sales are good, he pays his fertilizer and chemical bills with recorded receipts. He makes profit from the produce. He makes profit from his fertilizer and chemical factories. He is careful to show expenses and profit for each farm. Some of his farms do better financially than others do, but his accounting seems to be clean," Manuel kept reporting.

"From what our investigations found today, his labs process the coca leaves into cocaine, but the books mention nothing about the profit or distribution of the cocaine. I suspect that cocaine is a cash only crop, and Santos carefully spends the cash by reinvesting it into his farms for farm labor salaries and maintenance," Manuel concluded.

"Thanks, Manuel. There are forty-two Santos laboratories. Did anyone besides Roberto find cocaine processing plants?" Six people raised their hands. "Okay, Roberto, tell us what you found," I said.

Roberto at age nineteen was the youngest of the protection team members. He was the biggest man of both of our teams, but he was not a regular on the investigation team. He had been a resourceful protection team member for two years. He had a dark complexion with large Talronas Indian features and large bones. He was a second-year student studying agriculture at the University of Colombia. He was good-humored and a practical joker.

"I followed a Santos High Green Vegetables truck full of coca leaves from a farm in a rural area to a laboratory in Cali, where the truck unloaded for processing," Roberto announced.

"How did you know the truck was carrying coca leaves, and what made you follow it?" Joseppe asked, knowing Roberto usually didn't receive assignments.

"I had a very reliable eye witness, and I infiltrated the laboratory where the truck unloaded. I got the license plate number of the truck when I followed it inside the lab. I saw the bundles of coca plants and took these pictures with my cell phone," Roberto replied as he gave me a knowing glance and passed his phone for us to see it.

"Sir, inside the lab's processing facility, I had an opportunity to see the coca leaves up close before processing, and they are of the Novograntense and Truxillense variety, which contain Colombia's highest values of cocaine alkaloid. This translates into big bucks for Santos," Roberto reported.

"You did good work today Roberto. Get these pictures to head-quarters for the Santos file," I urged.

"I confirm Manuel's report on Santos's operations. My assign-ment was to use XKeyScore and to dig into bank records, financial records, and wealth management or savings accounts. I gleaned much information from this electronic surveillance. Santos's bank account system is clean. Each of Santos's businesses has their own bank account with easy to follow payments and deposits. At the beginning of the spring, the fertilizer and chemical businesses have lean holdings, but at the end of harvest, they swell to grand propor-tions. It is the same for his farms. They have abundant payments for farm supplies seasonally, but the accounts swell during harvest.

"There is no apparent money laundering associated with these accounts, but I still need to investigate the High Green Vegetables trucking company. I found no records of cocaine processing or mar-keting. Since everyone investigated Santos today, I will check on the trucking company and Serpa's properties tomorrow," Geraldo offered.

"In the interest of time and the late hour, do any of you have conflicting reports or confirming evidence that differs or supports the reports?" I asked.

"Just a bit more, sir. I visited Santos's chemical plant in Colombia's second largest city, Medellin, about a piece of evidence that may tie into Sun Wren Richards's case. We found a Colombian arsenic wrapper there. This Santos chemical plant supplied some of the chemicals to a nearby Medellin laboratory to produce strychnine and arsenic. Arsenic is manufactured by distilling arsenical pyrites, FeAsS Oxide, and Ar406 with carbon. It is used in insecticides and weed killers. Inorganic arsenic combined with oxygen chlorine or sulfur is believed to be the most toxic. It is used in rat poison and semiconductors.

"There is a storeroom full of packaging supplies that are an identical match to the wrapper found in the Sun Wren Richards's Costa Rican case. I told you about the arsenic because it ties Santos's chemical plants to his fertilizer plants and laboratories. We have a ring of Santos's businesses supporting each other, and the wrapper links Santo's or a Santos's employee to Costa Rica," Joseppe explained.

I looked around the room at the faces of the tired young men and said, "You did good work today investigating Santos's properties. We need to investigate Serpa's properties tomorrow and discover their connection to our Costa Rican case. Colombia, as you Colombians already know, ranked third in worldwide coca leaf production, with all cultivation being illicit. There is widespread cultivation in the eastern plains region. Santos's area encompasses one-half of Colombia. The heaviest areas are all Santos's farms. Colombia's cocaine expansion takes place in the south and southwest. It seems reasonable to assume that Santos recycles his cash and acquires more land for coca plant production.

"Cocaine is a major business for Colombia. If we stop this production, we stab Colombia's serpent and improve the world's mental stability, but we also harm the country's economy. Should we perpetuate good and force Colombia to remain in poverty? This isn't a discussion or a debate, but it is a question you need to think about. You are Colombians and must decide for yourselves. I accepted this work and will be loyal to her," I said.

"The bundles of coca leaves we found today weigh about twenty-five pounds each. Colombia's bundles are always twenty-five pounds, where Peru's and Bolivia's use fifty-to-seventy-five-pound bundles. Santos knows that the larger bundles retain more moisture than smaller bundles do. The smaller bundles also lose more volume to fermentation. Santos is a smart farmer. Colombia's alkaloid content remains at 85 percent pure. It is diluted to 60 percent by dealers, who maximize their own profits. By the time it reaches the USA, it drops to 30 percent purity." I drank some coffee and talked more about cocaine.

"It takes 450 to 600 kilograms of coca paste to produce one kilogram of cocaine base. In Colombia and in today's market value, it costs between $580 and $780 to buy enough coca leaves that will produce one kilogram of cocaine. The processing of the leaves requires that they convert it into paste. From paste, it is converted to a cocaine base. From a base, it is processed into pure cocaine. One kilogram of cocaine can be purchased in the Colombian jungles for $2,200, where Santos has some competition from indigenous peasants, but their cocaine quality is very poor," I continued.

"If you sell cocaine at Colombian ports, you get $5,500 to as much as $7,000 per kilogram. It increases in value as it travels north. In Costa Rica, cocaine is purchased for $10,000 a kilo. In southern Mexico, you can buy cocaine for $12,000 a kilo. In the border towns next to the USA, it costs $16,000 to buy a kilo. In northern USA— Chicago or New York—you pay $24,000 to $27,000 a kilo on the street. In Europe, they pay $53,000 to $55,000 a kilo. If you want to buy a kilo of diluted cocaine in Australia, you pay $200,000," I related.

"The point of all this is that Santos's real cost is his labor, which is absorbed into the expenses of his corporations. He uses the chemicals like sodium carbonate, kerosene, acid solution (H2S04), sulfuric acid, or hydrochloric acid and potassium permanganate from his chemical corporation. What is the cost of the chemicals per kilo? It is about one dollar and thirty cents. My guess is that he sells the cocaine at the Colombia port market value of $5,500 to $7,000 since he owns his own trucking company, where again, the costs are absorbed into the cost of doing business within the trucking company. His expenses equal one dollar and thirty cents, and his profit is $5,500 to $7,000 per kilo.

"Is there anymore to add? If not, I have some new replenishment supplies for anyone who needs them. I have several new fountain pens that are GB voice memo recorders with extra microphones that have sensitivity for over ten feet." I explained their ease of operation as I laid them on the table. The eight sleek green ballpoint pens disappeared into the young agents' hands.

"Wilber, did you get one?" I asked. He shook his head no, and I handed him one.

"Here are ten fingernail clippers, which are 720 mini digital voice-activated recorders with built-in speakers for instant playback and are compatible for the PC or Mac computers." I laid them on the table.

"This looks like a smoke detector, but it is a computer-monitoring device that is wireless and connects to your computer monitor so you can view what is being typed live from its placement. I only have six available. Take one if you think you will use it tomorrow," I said.

"Here are a few GPS tracking devices. These are tiny cell phone call recorders. This looks like a flash drive for your computer right? It is, but it also records voices and is adaptable for playback on your computer. These are combination key chains that give GPS tracking and record voices." I held out my hand and offered them.

"See this credit card? It is just a hair thicker than a real card and can be kept in your wallet, but look what happens when I gently squeeze the corners and bend it slightly. It opens and provides you with door-unlocking tools. My friend Montgomery Summers has such a sensitive touch, he doesn't need these tools. Marco, you should have one of these," I said as I handed him one.

The thought of Montgomery Summers's ability to open doors unaided by technology made me reflect on Colonel Hollander and Russ Warren. I had trained among those men who had relied and developed their innate special abilities to perform tasks. The new breed of agent knew nothing about developing their natural minds or their five senses that they were born with to do their work. Instead, they relied on trinkets, contraptions, gadgets, mechanical contrivances, objects, gimmicks, and technological apparatus.

I worried that my own photographic mind had been diminished because my superiors and I had used copy machines, recorders, and cameras and hadn't needed the skills I possessed. Keeping the daily codes for the Central American teams was the extent of using my gift. It was rare to find someone who strived to engage in self-development. *Is technology thwarting our human evolution?* I wondered.

"Use of these technical devices helps us greatly for gathering court-approved evidence, but the trick is to retrieve these little helpers after you use them. Remember to think *retrieval* strategy while planning. Don't lose them. Share your new toys with each other. Tomorrow's work will be more research and fieldwork. I want you to:

1. Divide the Serpa properties for visitation
2. Find out where Santos's cocaine cargo goes after processing
3. Look for methods of money laundering.
4. Find the Meza Costa Rican and Colombian connections.
5. Find out who hired the five Colombian assassins who were assigned to murder Sun"

"Use your resources: XKeyScore, Central American Interpol, and headquarters," I reminded them.

"Our Special Ten report meeting needs to change to another location so we don't attract attention. Roberto is invited to be our special guest if he wishes. We will meet at Santa Marta Harbor Beach in swimwear at 16:00 to celebrate Wilber's twenty-second birthday. Get some rest and good night."

"Excuse me, Roberto. Can you stay for a moment? I would like a word with you."

"Yes, sir." Roberto looked surprised.

After the others left, I sat back down and pulled up a chair for Roberto. "Roberto, thanks for your help today. You were good in the field. Tomorrow, I need to work on a case for Nicaragua. I won't be going out much so the protection team will have a boring day. It might be more interesting for you to be in the field. You can participate but you will remain on the protecting tracking team. You may choose how you use your day tomorrow. I just need to know your decision so that I can make tomorrow's adjustments."

"Thanks. I would like to join the team out in the field," Roberto said.

"How did you manage the flat tire today on the High Green Vegetables truck so precisely?"

Roberto laughed. "I grew up in an indigenous tribe of Colombians who are proficient at jungle blow darts. I can hit a two-inch circle at a distance of more than seventy-five yards with the power to penetrate two-inch plywood. I hit the tire perfectly, but the tire going flat one hundred meters from your car was pure luck," he chuckled.

"I owe you one. What would you like?"

"Angelo, I would like for my team and I to have a night with cute girls," he laughed.

"I can arrange that! We need to find the right time. By the way, the hot-pink bikini underwear is way too small in the crucial area," I answered. Roberto left the room cackling.

I rarely had the opportunity to sleep. The ten teams in Central

America needed constant planting, transplanting, cultivation, fertilizing, and weeding. The end of a case always needed careful harvesting. My cell phone always had a call from one team or another, day and night, and my sleep was limited to two hours. I received the Special Ten's team codes from headquarters and dispersed them throughout Central America.

Before my short night of rest, I called Orlando in Costa Rica. "Orlando, code 555mt640#7#929. A $600,000 shipment of fiber optics is waiting at the San Jose Airport to be buried at Sun Wren Richards's property and needs to be installed Saturday of next week. Sun will receive a truckload of plants from Fauna de San Sebastian Vivero. Use your special designer skills to our advantage and make her gardens beautiful when you bury them. This landscaped work is important, and our future depends on the fiber optics installation," I said and then clicked off.

CHAPTER 25
SURVEILLANCE

Morning opened her blouse and radiated warmth like the voluptuous coffee picker I once knew from my early adolescence. Morning revealed Special Ten was vigorously at work, and I had completed a list of errands.

The tuxedoes and costumes for the five members attending Saturday's Serpa costume party arrived at each hotel room. Arrangements for Wilber's early evening birthday party were made, and I texted the directions for our secluded beach party. I shopped with extra special thought and bought Sun a handcrafted vase from Colombia. I replaced my stinking, swamp-hardened, leather shoes and spent the rest of the day working on a case for the Nicaraguan team. At 15:00, I started the short walk to the beach.

I carried an armload of large colorful beach towels, a basket of iced, bottled water, and sunscreen. I enjoyably trudged through the powdery, deep sand in my new flip-flops. This was a rare experience for me since most of my days were spent in strategy meetings or in front of a computer. The sea breeze was cool and perpetually whipped a pleasant, fine, misty spray, which helped us celebrate Wilbur's birthday and mask the true intent of our gathering.

I stuck a cardboard sign that said, "HAPPY BIRTHDAY WILBER," into the sand to give our Special Ten and the caterers a visual of where we were having the party. Within minutes, the beach event planners arrived with tables, chairs, plates, silverware, table-cloths, napkins, glasses, wine, and covered serving dishes, which held the lobster gourmet menu and a sixteen-inch, chocolate cake.

Wilber wasn't our youngest member but was the newest. He had only been with us for a couple of weeks and had trouble adjusting to the group's competitiveness. He had a proven history in his training as being a fast responder to crisis and a creative problem solver but Wilber lacked self-confidence in the mix of the Columbian investigation team's spirited, good-natured, aggressivness. He had come from an abusive family, which made him act like a beaten dog and caused him not to trust his teammates. I hoped the party would give him assured acceptance and enable him to prove his value.

Special Ten plus Roberto arrived, and we indulged in the spread of seafood dishes that were displayed on the long generous tables. The first hour was used for needed stress release and relaxation. It was evident that everyone enjoyed our fraternity. I asked our caterers to leave our event and return in two hours so our group could continue to graze, drink wine, and socialize without rushing. They agreed: I watched their delivery trucks vanish. From time to time, there were a few people who walked by on the beach and shouted *"Feliz Cumpleaños."* Occasionally, a couple holding hands was seen splashing along the edge of the water, but we still had privacy. Our young agents spread their beach towels on the gray-black sand while others draped themselves over the chairs like spaghetti, but the focus was on our strategy meeting.

"Happy Birthday, Wilber. Your team and I welcome you to our

group. Today, many of you requested time to report. Marco, let's begin with you," I suggested.

"Thank you, sir. I will report about my visitation of Serpa's Financial SA. I made an appointment with Mr. Leonardo Serpa for ten o'clock this morning at his Money Grow Green Investments Santa Marta office, which turned out to be an impressive space at his home. The Serpa personal profile was helpful and accurate. I used my new fingernail clippers recording machine. I hope you can hear the recording clearly." Marco switched it on. On the tape, Marco said,

> Good Morning, Mr. Serpa. Your property has an impressive office. Thank you for talking with me about investments. In May, I graduated from college, and my father urged me to get involved with investing in commodities. You have a reputation for making prosperous, bold investments, and your company is touted as one of the best. My father gave me $25,000 to invest, and I wondered if you had a recommendation?"

The voice of a well-educated, arrogant, older man, Mr. Serpa, could be clearly understood from the clippers.

> You are a young investor, and I will give you my philosophy for investment success. I believe in commodity fetishism, which is the perception of social relationships between money and commodities. Don't follow the crowd or use conventional logic. Strike out for the new. The Money Grow Green hedge fund is a good place to begin as a first time investor.

Marco and Mr Serpa continued their conversation:

> Your lifestyle points to your success, and it is the
> reason I chose your company. I need quick results to
> impress my father. I need something to elevate my
> status with him. What commodity is involved with
> the Money Grow Green hedge fund?.

A secret commodity is bringing in quadruple the amount of the
investment. It is a successful fund because it is guided by a simple
philosophy: Public perception of how valuable a given commodity is,
compared to other commodities, is what runs the show. The market
is an independent interpretation of how buyers, sellers, and producers value the commodity. Right now, the exchange rate between the
Money Grow Green fund commodity and money are exceedingly
high.

Is there anything you can tell me about the Money Grow Green
Fund?

Certainly! Here is the Money Grow Green fund's investment
chart. You can see for yourself that its history is nothing but a steady
upward climb.

It doesn't mention the commodity that caused its rise. Is it precious metals?

It is much better than metals. It is agricultural raw materials,
which are organic, natural, and very stable. At the moment, this
commodity is far more stable than metals are.

Please excuse my slowness to grasp the commodity trade, but
why must this commodity be kept a secret?

If everyone began trading in this secret commodity, which has
given us good returns, it would saturate the market, driving the price
down. Then the valued commodity would become common and
lose its value. If you are interested, you need to move fast while the

product is considered to be hot and sought after. It won't be this way forever. Right now, I am reaping its benefits and am recommending it to my clients.

Mr. Serpa, I will think about the things you've told me today. Thank you for your time. I will consider your recommendation about the secret commodity.

You seem like a progressive young man, and I want to invite you to a costume party on my yacht Saturday night at 5 p.m. I have five nieces who are about your age. They are unmarried and the pride of my life, but they are driving me crazy. I would love for you to meet them. Here is an invitation. Will you come?

I wouldn't know what to wear for a costume.

Come as the young Prince William of England. My eldest niece, Monica, is crazy for him.

Marco turned off his nail clippers with a fast snap.

"Eureka!" the birthday party gang hooted. "You have your own invitation to his yacht." Some of the men took this break to refill their wine glasses and helped themselves to another slice of chocolate cake as Marco continued with his report.

"The last part of my report has to do with a cell phone call I recorded at the time of our business appointment. Leonardo Garzon Serpa's cell phone was lying on his desk when the *domestica* ushered me into his home office. I saw it and attached the new cell phone recorder/GPS tracker before he came in to meet with me. I can hook this to my computer so you hear it better," Marco said.

It was a conversation between Leonardo Serpa and Katerina Meza. Katerina spoke first.

> We haven't talked for some time, and thought I
> should call you to explain with regret that I will not
> be able to make your party on Saturday. I hoped we
> could talk when I came to the party, but I represent a

real estate client and need to be in court. Thank you
for inviting me

I am sorry to hear that, Katerina. We have issues to talk about,
and I need answers! Why haven't I received the passports and identities you promised? I haven't opened any new bank accounts in a long
time. Isn't Pablo Meza doing any business up there?

We are busy with the Valerina Pachona Uribe mess. I guess you
heard about her husband?

No. What about her husband?

When he came to Costa Rica to take her body back to Colombia,
he was shot in a drive-by shooting.

Hmm, interesting, but it still doesn't explain why I'm not getting
what we agreed upon.

Leonardo, you need to understand—

No! Katerina you need to understand. People issues are your
problem! Real estate is my business. I bought and sold the properties
with cash. Pablo received his commission for the property contracts,
and you got paid for the legal paperwork. I was to receive foreign
identities after the sale was completed. The sales have been completed for three closings, and I haven't received the identities. I want
the identities of those clients now! Do you understand?

Please be patient, Leonardo. You could show a little compassion
since dealing with Valerina Uribe's death has been emotional for all
of us, and since she was Colombian, you might show more appreciation for what we have done to get your identities and to protect
you. People give you the lives of their employees, and you still ask for
more! Please, let's not fight while the wound is still fresh. My brother
Jorge Vargas will get rid of Sun Richards soon, but like yourself, he
is one of her board members and receives a salary for his work. Have
patience and allow things to heal up and you will get your identities.

I'm not doing any more business with you or Pablo until I get my the three identities you owe me. There is one more thing, Katrina, I sent two capable Colombians to help you with your dirty work, and what did you do? Nothing. You didn't even pay them. Who was supposed to pay them? You were! I paid for them to get there, and you were to pay them to come back to Colombia. So why didn't you pay them?

They were arrested and interrogated by the police. I was afraid to contact them. They didn't do their work. Am I to pay for work that didn't get finished?

Katerina, yes, they told me they were interrogated and tortured. I have kept my side of our deal, now you keep yours! I cannot allow you to implicate me. You need to change things in Costa Rica fast. I don't want any of the properties. You know that. Properties are Pablo's and your gig. You know what I want!

Leonardo Serpa hung up. Marco shut of the recorder and asked us, "Do you think he will make a good uncle-in-law?" The team laughed and gave a good impression of a beach party.

"You made good use of your new service tools, Marco. What is your understanding of the two recordings?" I asked.

"The Serpa investment meeting points to cocaine as the possible commodity of our conversation, but the meeting doesn't give us any definite evidence. The meeting leaves the door open for the possibility of more meetings where more information might be gathered. I think the meeting was a moderate success. The phone call between Costa Rican Ms. Katerina Meza and Colombian Mr. Leonardo Serpa assuredly confirms the two groups are linked. One possible theory for the suspects' plans is:"

1. "Leonardo Garzon Serpa is the money behind the property scam. He is the planner and leader for the two groups. Pablo Meza's role is to look for properties to buy and sell to foreign investors and to serve as real estate broker. Leonardo steals

the identities of the foreign investors to launder his money, possibly from cocaine, into the accounts because he can't spend the money fast enough to keep up with his surplus of stashed cash.

2. Ms. Katerina Meza is the lawyer doing the foreign legal work, but she never files the papers into the National Public Registry. She puts the property into her name or into the names of others who serve on the boards of corporations. They do other work for her while they wait for their payoffs. Ms. Katerina Meza forces the foreign investor to vacate the property or possibly takes his or her life. She claims the property legally because it is never filed with the public registry, or she assigns it to others on the boards. Ms. Meza positions herself to gain a wealth of property.

3. Former board president, Valerina Pachona Uribe of Sun Wren Richards property, was murdered because she lost patience while waiting to be paid or to receive her promised property and threatened to expose the scam.

4. Pablo Meza and Katerina double-crossed Leonardo Serpa and told the seller of Sun's property, Tony Lopez, he could have his property back when they got rid of Sun if he would invest in Pablo's development projects, which he did. The Meza's plan is to take over Leonardo Serpa's operation for themselves, buying and selling property, laundering money, and stealing identities to open bank accounts. The plan is to help their daughter Mercedes ease into the new business by assigning Katerina's brother to steal Sun Wren Richards's identity while Mercedes opens four new bank accounts in other countries so laundered money can't be traced to the Mezas.

5. The reason Mr. Serpa offered me the invitation to the yacht party is because he has two sons who will take over his

billion-dollar golden-hen business but wants to secure his
nieces' futures the same way the Mezas want their daughter
Mercedes to have a good financial future."

Marco concluded his report to the boisterous and hooting team
members, who then sang the "Wedding March' and imitated wedding bells.

"Marco, that was an excellent case probable. Does anyone wish
to debate or inquire into this report? Manuel, do you have something?" I asked as I saw his late arrival.

"I have information to support Marco's report. Today I monitored Ms. Katerina Meza's communication records and found this
conversation at eleven thirty this morning, which I recorded onto
my computer after Marco's appointment." Manuel turned on the
recording between Katerina and Mercedes. Katerina speaks first:

Hi, Mercedes. How was your trip from Spain?

It was okay but the baby fussed the entire way,
and nursing on the plane was almost impossible. I
am exhausted. I plan to nap when he does, but I am
glad to be back. Apollo was a great daddy and tried to
help, but the baby just needed to fuss. What is going
on with you?

I talked to Leonardo Serpa today, and he wants
the three identities we owe him. I am going to call
him back and tell him about the accounts you opened
in Sun's name in Colombia, Panama, Spain, and El
Salvador. I want to tell him you opened them for
him as a gift since we are late in delivering. We can
give him four accounts, and he should be pleased.
He might call you, and I wanted you to know what

was going on. He is eager to deposit money and our gift will quiet him. We can implement the Meza plan later, but for now, we must become bunny rabbits. Mercedes, what are your thoughts?

I think it is a good idea, Katerina, after all, none of us has any money to deposit anyway. Later when the accounts are full, it might be the time to claim the accounts for ourselves.

We think alike Mercedes! Give him the account numbers if he calls you. Ciao.

Katerina clicked off. Manuel turned off the recording and continued his report. "I think that recording confirmed the Costa Rican Meza and the Colombian Serpa connection. It also supports the personal profile report that states that Serpa only has a business office in his home and on his yacht.

"I took this afternoon to fly from our hotel in Santa Marta to Cali, where I rented an old jalopy to follow three of Santos's High Green Vegetables trucks from the laboratories back to the Cali Santos farm to pick up a load of vegetables. I watched these three Santos trucks make deliveries to Colombia's most important import-export port of Buenaventura near Cali and I saw them unload their cargo of vegetables onto the docks.

"I stretched out on the dock to eat a sandwich while I waited thirty minutes for the produce to be loaded onto Centurion Air Cargo before it departed. The empty trucks remained on the docks without their drivers. I wandered over to take a look at the bill of lading left on the windshield of one of the trucks and made a copy. The truck's weight was given and then subtracted from the weight of the vegetable cargo. The difference between the full truck and the empty truck surprised me! Santos must use very heavy trucks! I thought this was a curious observation so I climbed into the empty truck bed." Manuel took a couple sips of Coke before continuing.

"Inside the bed of the truck, I noticed there was a white, eight-inch-thick, interlocking, plastic liner that was hinged at the corners, which could be quickly disassembled. These flat side pieces of the truck's bed lining when disassembled, looked like packing racks or pallets and could be stacked or used for hauling other cargo. They looked like cargo pallets, but I took them apart, and when I looked inside, I found their hollow cavity filled with eight-inch packages of cocaine." Manuel noticed the team listening intently.

"I climbed from the truck and waited. A truck driver arrived, drove the alleged empty truck onto the scale, and recorded the weight while another man jumped into the bed of the truck. Together, the men disassembled the white, eight-inch-thick, plastic liners and used them as pallets to load a shipment of bananas from three other Santos High Green Vegetables trucks. The empty trucks were weighed again without the liners."

"The men on the dock placed the papers on the windshields of the trucks while the truck drivers took a coffee break. The cocaine-lined pallets of bananas were loaded onto an awaiting cargo boat, which then left the port. I sneaked over to the Santos trucks, reread the shipping lading bills, and found a three-thousand-pound difference in the weight of the truck without its liners. Five minutes later, the Santos drivers returned and removed the papers, which I had copied, and drove away. I observed three thousand pounds of exported cocaine.

"My flight was late in returning to Santa Marta. I didn't tell you happy birthday, Wilber," Manuel said.

"Manuel, this is a great discovery, and a giant missing piece in our puzzle. You did well. Thanks," I congratulated. "Does anyone have anything to add or questions for Manuel's report?" I asked.

"Roberto, you jumped up and down like you needed to pee. Do you have something you want to say?" I asked.

"Yes. Yes, I do! Today, I went to the city of Medellin and visited a Santos laboratory. I watched five trucks leave the lab. Three of the trucks had stacks of those white, plastic pallets, which were uncovered in the back of the Santos trucks. I assumed they were empty pallets since the drivers had left their loads of coca leaves to be processed at the laboratory. I didn't know what I had seen. I followed two of the trucks and assumed that they would be empty because they were coming from the lab and returning to the Medellin farm, where they unloaded the vegetables. Cocaine was in the linings of those empty trucks, which returned to the farm for real vegetables loaded for export. The three trucks that carried stacks of pallets had been stuffed with cocaine. Manuel's report told me what I needed to look for," Roberto admitted.

"We all learned something from Manuel's report, and it is good information to learn. Plastic pallets are openly transported. The Santos Medellin farm might be another source for cocaine. Thanks for your addendum, Roberto. It is assumed that a minimum of three tons of cocaine per truck are shipped out either by air cargo or by boat through the Colombian ports. The question remains: Who is the buyer?" I asked.

"I know the answer to your question, sir," Joseppe shouted.

"Tell us what you know, Joseppe."

"I did surveillance outside Leonardo Serpa's home and saw Marco arrive at 10 a.m. He left this appointment at 11:30 a.m.," he chuckled. "After Marco left, I followed Serpa, who walked the short distance to Banco de Santa Marta where he withdrew $14,834,600 in cash and put it into a briefcase. I laid my recording pen down on the counter where Serpa met with the bank teller and recorded the transaction." Joseppe jumped up eager to tell his entire story.

"Serpa walked back home, got in his private plane, and flew

to Cali. I knew Manuel had gone to Cali and to the Buenaventura seaport. I called Manuel, who used his GPS/phone recording device and found Serpa. Manuel saw Serpa meet Santos at the Cali Flamingo restaurant, where they had a late lunch. Serpa left the briefcase with Santos, but Manuel took pictures of their interaction with his cell phone. It appeared that Leonard Serpa paid Mauricio Santos $14 million plus dollars. But we don't know if it was for coca leaves, coca plant processing, or transporting goods. I think it was for agricultural raw materials. Serpa told Marco his secret commodity was agricultural raw materials. Manuel, did you tell Marco how you retrieved his cell phone recording/GPS device?" Joseppe laughed.

"I saw Mr. Serpa lay his phone on the restaurant table, and when I went to the men's restroom, I walked by his table and put it into my pocket. I took it into the restroom and removed Marco's device. I gave the cell phone to a waiter, and told him that Serpa had dropped it and asked him to please return it. This was no big deal. Marco, here is your device that took a trip to Cali today," Manuel explained as he handed the cell phone recording device to Marco.

"Thanks for looking after my stuff, Manuel. I owe you one," Marco said.

Geraldo, sprang to his feet and said, "My assignment was to determine if the Serpa family was spending more money than their recorded income, which would indicate possible money laundering. I monitored bank accounts today and confirmed Joseppe's reports. I found irregularities that were interesting." Geraldo handed me Serpa's bank account records so I could follow his report.

"Leonardo Garzon Serpa's account showed the $14 million withdrawal, confirming Joseppe's report. Cash deposits made by Leonard Serpa totaled $10 million. He has a balance of $6 million in his personal account. I have information on each family member," Geraldo said.

"Leonardo's wife, Rene Hill Serpa's account shows a $2 million check withdrawal and a $3 million cash deposit made by Leonardo

Serpa, leaving a $1 million balance. Their twin sons, Ramon and Renaldo's accounts are in Dallas, Texas, and each has his own account. Both twins' accounts show cash deposits made by Leonard Serpa for $2 million. There was a check withdrawal of $1 million for Ramon and a $500,000 withdrawal for Renaldo, leaving the boys with a $2,500,000 balance. That is a hefty chunk of money for school."

Geraldo explained other communications infiltration. "By 12:00 hours today, I had infiltrated Ms. Meza's phone call to Mr. Leonard Serpa. I have a recording of her telling him about the gift of the four Sun Wren Richards's accounts in the four countries from Mercedes. At 12:00, those accounts only had twenty dollars in each of them. By 16:00 hours today, the time of our birthday party, those accounts swelled to $700,000 each. The purpose of my assignment was to determine money laundering. The conclusion is a strong yes," Geraldo said with exuberance as he continued his report.

"A different pattern of perfect record keeping applied to Mr. and Mrs. Santos' joint account. Every deposit that was made from a variety of sources and withdraws were all accountable, with a balance of $12 million. Felicity Santos Farrow, Mauricio's wife, had her own account of $2 million, with every deposit coming in from a variety of sources and withdrawals accounted for by checks and credit cards. These accounts didn't appear to show money laundering."

"The five Santos girls, Monica, Jessica, Lyndia, Rebecca, and Sandra had separate accounts, and these accounts were very irregular with unaccountable deposits of cash. Withdrawals were usually made by check or credit card. Their bank balances ranged from $400,000 to $1,000,120. Every six months, $400,000 was consistently deposited by Mauricio Santos in each of his daughter's accounts. It appears the girls got money from sources other than their father," Geraldo said as he shuffled through his papers.

"There were two exceptions to Santos's daughters' accounts. Monica's account was pristine like her parents had been, with deposits and withdrawals recorded. Sandra's account had the largest cash deposit of $15 million, which was made by Mr. Leonardo Serpa and was significantly larger than any of her sisters'. This left her with a $14 million balance. I suspected these girls had dealt in cocaine and had perhaps even used cocaine, or they may have just received this income from their modeling careers. I believe we have a good file of financial evidence on Santos and Serpa," Geraldo concluded.

"This case is coming together nicely. Does anyone have anything else? You did a good job of surveillance, investigation, and infiltration, everyone. Since Marco received his own invitation to the party, we can invite one more person. Roberto, would you enjoy going to the Serpa party?" I asked.

"I had a tuxedo ready in case I was invited," Roberto said excitedly.

"We will meet quietly after the Serpa party at 02:00 in my room—number 707—at the Santa Marta Hotel. Your assignment for tomorrow is to look for loose ends and to prepare your own agenda for Mr. Leonard Serpa's yacht party. Work together as a team, but don't get too relaxed or careless and stay alert. During the party, keep in mind that we are investors and do your job! I will be in costume dressed as Zorro. Okay, that's a wrap. Until post-party time!" I said.

CHAPTER 26

EVIDENCE

I felt the party energy of my men build up and knew they were ready for the yacht bash. It was party time. Serpa's silver metallic Aerodynamic, *High Tide* was majestically moored next to the rolling green gardens of the Serpa Spanish colonel mansion. The gangplank was decorated as a Japanese bridge with bonsai trees, cherry blossoms, and a refreshing mist machine that cooled down the guests who were boarding, dressed in their costumes and tuxedoes.

At the top of the bridge, a waiter, dressed as a silver metallic robot, collected our invitations and shook our hands. Another robot served Singapore slings, margaritas, piña coladas, and champagne on large rocket-shaped trays. Six or seven shapely women wearing skintight, silver bodysuits with hoods and whose faces were painted silver handed us tea sandwiches on silver napkins.

I wondered how my nostalgic Zorro would mix with this outer galaxy world of living, shiny creatures that resembled objects. After consuming two or three of the sandwiches, I walked to the top of the bridge and stood off to the side. I intermittently answered my cell phone and observed the guests as they boarded. Most of the women's costumes were gaudy and elaborate, but many women were partially nude while others wore only stilettos and earrings. I admitted it was difficult to keep my mind on my job.

A silver body-suited robot motioned for me to follow her as she gave a tour of the ship. Following the silver undulating hips of the galaxy creature reminded me of the silver dress I had followed twenty years earlier that had caused me to make a mistake with lasting effects. I summoned a little more caution this go around.

Miss Metal Vibration escorted me on a tour of twelve staterooms with private decks, a main salon that included a fireplace, a large dining room with a ballroom, and a library for the designated business area. She explained that the yacht was designed by Fanachelli, the Italian yacht designer. Miss Metal Vibration led me to the reception line and introduced me to Mr. Leonardo Garzon Serpa and Mrs. Rene Hill Serpa, who were costumed in a silver tuxedo and a silver ballroom gown.

"I am Zorro from Costa Rica. Katerina Meza gave me an invitation and recommended that I talk to you about investments. Your *High Tide* is intriguing, and I look forward to talking with you at a more convenient time," I said as I shook Mr. Serpa's manicured hand and relinquished my space in the reception line to other waiting guests.

"Yes, indeed! Enjoy the fruits of my bounty," Serpa said as he gestured toward the dining area and bar.

"Mrs. Serpa, your dress reflects the space goddess within you, and I hope you saved a celestial dance for me."

"The night wouldn't be complete without a dance with Zorro, she laughed.

I moved to the dining area and spotted most of our Colombian team, who were looking around wild eyed at the opulent life before them. I grazed around the buffet table and intermittently answered my cell phone. A magnificent short rooster reached across the table, scooped up *chevichi* with his wingtips, and put it onto his plate while trying to keep his black plumage out of the sauces.

"You must be an American Bantam rooster," I said.

"I would rather be chicken stew than an American Bantam rooster. Look at these speckled feathers around my chest and neck and the big red comb on my head. I am a Spanish Barnevelder rooster. Zorro from Spain should know his Spanish roosters," he said.

"How could I have made such a mistake? Of course, you are a Barnevelder. Now that you've taken your wing out of the fish sauce I can clearly see the Barnevelder in you," I joked.

"It is a pleasure to meet any man who knows his chickens. I'm Mauricio Santos," he said as he extended his wingtips in a handshake.

"I'm pleased to meet you. Your costume is truly magnificent. I'm Zorro from Costa Rica, not Spain," I said, gripping his extended hand.

"Poppa," a beautiful young girl dressed as Queen Isabella interrupted. "Poppa, I am looking for your hen. Where is Mamma?" she asked.

Mr. Santos pointed to a fluffy white chicken talking to a monster and Mr. Serpa. "There she is, but where are your manners daughter? This is Zorro from Costa Rica, and this is my youngest daughter, Sandra, who refused to wear a cute Chicken Little costume," Mr. Santos said.

"I'm pleased to meet you, Sandra. Your mother hen looks to be a Silkie Chinese Wu Gu Ji," I said as I looked across the crowd toward the striking fluffy chicken who was talking to Mr. Serpa.

"Yes, she is a Wu Gu Ji! Poppa, I need to talk to Uncle Serpa too," Sandra said as she swept away.

"Now I am truly impressed with your knowledge of chickens," Santos said.

"Did your daughter call our host, Uncle Serpa?" I asked.

"Yes, Leonardo Serpa is my brother-in-law. Our wives are sisters. Most people don't know this because my wife goes by her modeling name, Felicity Farrow Santos. It is really Felicity Hill, and her sister is Rene Hill. Both are Americans. Sandra gets her abrupt manners from her American mother. Sandra and her Uncle Serpa are in a business project together. It is a diversion for Leonardo, who has a hobby business with Sandra. It has been good for both of them, and Sandra seems to be his favorite niece. I have five daughters who are all unmarried. There is another daughter dancing over there with the Italian young man," Mauricio Santos said as he pointed to Agent Joseppe, who was dancing with Cleopatra.

"She is a pretty girl too," I said as I observed Joseppe clutching his recording keys.

"Her name is Jessica Santos Farrow. Look at them dance."

The orchestra played Bolero, and couples moved to the sidelines to give Joseppe and Jessica (Cleopatra) more space. Joseppe swooped, twirled, and bent with grace as the crowd watched his showmanship and skill.

"Cleopatra, you would be a wonderful dancer, but I think you had too many of those fancy drinks tonight. How many?" Joseppe asked.

"I only had a few Singapore slings. I like cocaine, my handsome swan, and I think you might dance better without me." She whined and then started to cry. "Why don't men like me? I am skinny and rich, and a girl can never be too skinny or too rich. Isn't that true?" she mushed her questions together with a thick tongue.

"How did you get to be so rich, Cleopatra?" Joseppe asked as he touched the green fountain pen in his tuxedo pocket, turning on the recorder.

"My name is Jessica Santos, not Cleopatra," she said arrogantly. "Rich is rich is rich is rich. It's cocaine, cocaine, and more cocaine.

Cocaine makes you rich and jazzy. Do you want some cocaine? You like me, don't you?" she asked.

"You are very beautiful. What about your sister Sandra? Does she like cocaine too? Will she give me some?" Joseppe asked.

"No! Sandra is a stingy bitch and takes it away. She doesn't know how good it makes me feel. Sandra thinks she is a businesswoman and tells me to go straight," Jessica slurred.

"Jessica, thank you for the dance," Joseppe said, helping her to a chair as the crowd applauded.

"Zorro do you see that girl in the red-sequined dress talking to the big guy leaning on the bar? That girl is my eldest daughter, Monica. I hope she likes the man she's talking to. He is the only man that I have seen here who looks capable of an honest day's work," Mauricio Santos stated as he noticed Agent Roberto.

I glanced in the direction he had pointed and saw his tall shapely daughter. The raven-haired beauty, Monica, was talking to Roberto, who twirled his clippers in circles on the bar's counter top.

"Miss Santos, I admire your father's hard work, knowledge, and success as a farmer. He had done very well and has used his skills to accomplish a better life for himself," Roberto said.

"Do you know my father?" Monica asked

"No, I only know about his reputation for making plants grow. He and I have similar childhood histories. I relate to the obstacles he hurtled and respect a man like that," Roberto explained.

"I respect him too and am proud to be his daughter. Poppa thinks of expanding the farms to include more of the northern lands of Colombia. We have heated arguments about his future plans," Monica said.

"Why do you disagree with the expansion?" Roberto asked.

"We don't disagree on the expansion. We disagree about the crops he should plant for the expanded business. I want him to plant Colombia's gooseberry, a native plant of our country," Monica said.

"Are you talking about *Physalis peruviana*, which is not a fruit but is related to the eggplant and tomato and grows to the size of a marble inside a bright yellow-orange covering, inflated by a papery calyx enclosing each berry?" Roberto asked.

"The very one! It is known as an anti-inflammatory, has antioxidant properties used in treatments for lung cancer, and it also has in vitro properties against diabetes. I want the Santos farms to contribute better well-being to our country," Monica explained.

"Miss Santos, I couldn't agree with you more! Pharmaceutical farms are the future, and US Corporations pay top dollar to harvest and contract for their needs," Roberto jubilantly agreed.

"I wish your words could convince my father," Monica said.

"Why doesn't your father agree with you?" Roberto asked.

"My Uncle Serpa has a strong personality and his own agenda. My father is a humble man. Oh, excuse me but I think Prince William of England, my heart throb, wants to dance with me," Monica said.

"Good luck with your plans," Roberto shouted over the orchestra.

I watched as Agent Marco, who held a key chain, cut into Agent Roberto's conversation and asked Monica Santos to dance.

"Miss Monica, your red-sequined dress pales beside the sparkle and shimmer of your beauty," Marco said.

"Very nicely said as the prince of England, but how did you know my name?" Monica asked.

"Your Uncle invited me to this party especially to ask you to dance," Marco said.

"Did he tell you that Prince William of England has my attention?" Monica asked.

"He did, but the motivation behind my actions is my own. When I saw you, I knew you were someone special. You must know that you are very beautiful," Marco said.

"Thank you, but Uncle Serpa wants to derail my forward-moving train with handsome, tuxedo-attired, gallant men. Does that fit your personal profile?" Monica asked.

Marco was taken by surprise by her choice of words. Did she know he was an agent or was it only a coincidence? He nervously wondered.

"No, not really. My name is Marco, and I met your Uncle Serpa a few days ago when I was in his office asking about investments," Marco replied.

"Was he selling Money Grow Green hedge fund investments?" Monica asked.

"Yes, he was, but he wouldn't tell me about the secret commodity within the fund," Marco replied.

"The secret commodity is *cocaine*, Prince William of England, cocaine. It is the commodity ruining my family. Have you met any of my sisters?" Monica asked.

"No, you are the only Serpa niece I have met. Are your sisters here tonight?" Marco asked.

"My name is Monica Santos, and my four younger sisters are being destroyed by Uncle Serpa and his cocaine. Look at them! What you see now is not who they are. It is the cocaine talking. There they are: number one, two, three, and four," Monica said angrily as she pointed to them in the crowd.

"I'm sorry Monica, I didn't mean to upset you. Would you like to go out on the deck for some fresh air?" Marco asked. Monica nodded her head, and Marco ushered her outside.

"One thing I can clearly see for myself, Rooster Santos, is that you and your Mrs. Hen Santos have made some beautiful chicks! You have something to crow about," I said.

"Thank you for saying so. I want my daughters to select good husbands. Zorro, take a good look at most of these playboys, who only want to marry for money," Mauricio Santos said.

"Your problem is apparent. A beautiful woman with money can

be quite an incentive for any man to make his move. Felicity Farrow Santos is still Covergirl beautiful even in her Silkie chicken outfit. Are your girls models too?" I asked.

"The three middle girls, Jessica, Lyndia, and Rebecca, are models, but their careers have suffered because they are party girls. I raised them all to be good Catholic girls, but my three middle girls do drugs and ..." Mauricio Santos stopped talking as he watched a long-haired, slim, stunningly attractive, young woman, whose skin shimmered like she had drunk liquid gold, being carried in the air by two shirtless weight lifters wearing bikinis. They set her down on her feet. One of the men sat in a straight-backed chair. She straddled his lap and kissed his chest. The second man stood behind her running his hands everywhere over her naked gold body.

Mr. Santos left the dining room and walked out on the deck. His face telegraphed the identity of the golden goddess to be either Lyndia or Rebecca Santos Farrow. I stood alone beside the table of artistically presented food. When my cell phone rang, I answered it and watched the progress of the young agents as Mr. Serpa in his silver tuxedo approached.

"Zorro, does my way of partying suit you?" Leonardo Serpa arrogantly asked.

"Everything is perfection," I said as I touched my green recording pen.

"Did you meet my friends by the fireplace?" Serpa asked as he pointed in their direction. "They are English dukes and my clients. The couple by the floral arrangements are Europeans from a royal house and also my clients. Zorro, I want everyone to see the splendid life I have. I have fun, and fun is what life is about. There may be men who have billions, but they don't know how to spend it. Nobody spends it like I can. Do you know why?" Leonardo Serpa asked.

I shook my head no and knew he would tell me whether I wanted to hear it or not. "I know how to invest. Investments make money for spending, and look at all of this. I know how to spend, as well as I know how to invest," he said.

The dance floor suddenly cleared again, fringed with appreciative onlookers, as Agent Joseppe and the silver-gowned Rene Hill Serpa dominated the dancing area. The movement of the crowd retreating caught Mr. Serpa's attention as he watched his wife dance the tango with the stately handsome Agent Joseppe. He was at his peak of dancing form, and she had had a formal dance background as demonstrated by her intricate foot crossing, flicks, drags, and pure moves of sensuality. This couple was fantastic, and Leonardo Serpa's mouth opened like a cave for hidden thieves.

"Mrs. Serpa, you out-ginger Ginger Rogers," Joseppe complimented. We need to become a dancing duo and compete professionally," he said, clutching his recording key chain.

"This is the most fun I have had in years," she beamed.

"Do Mr. Serpa's parents still live in Colombia?" he asked, searching for possible money-laundering havens.

"No, both of Leonardo's parents are deceased. My mother and father have been both of our parents for years," Rene Serpa said.

"Are your grandparents still alive?" Joseppe asked.

"No. My parents and my sister Felicity are the extent of our family," Mrs. Serpa confirmed.

"Mr. Serpa seems especially fond of the youngest Santos daughter, Sandra. Is she also your favorite?" Joseppe asked.

"No, I love all my nieces, of course, but Monica is my favorite. Sandra has a mind for business, and her father gave her a couple of farms to play with. My husband taught her about commodities, which is the business he understands. Leonardo buys Sandra's crops and exports them as a commodity for his Money Grow Green hedge fund, which was originally founded by my father. What goes around comes around—now for a third generation," she laughed.

"Are your twin boys interested in the business?" Joseppe asked.

"Not in the least. They want to become doctors! Twin doctors; now that could be humorous for their patients, don't you think?" she chuckled.

"Who are Sandra Santos's and Mr. Serpa's biggest export buyers?" Joseppe asked.

"The best market is Europe, and Sandra has done well using the Money Grow Green hedge fund with my husband as her rep. Leonardo also has a client in Costa Rica, which is a developing market," Mrs. Serpa explained.

"Are Pablo, Katrina, and Mercedes Meza his clients?" Joseppe asked, taking a bold risk.

"That is correct. What a small world we live in," Mrs. Serpa twittered.

The orchestra tango music swelled to a high crescendo as Agent Joseppe and the glamorous Mrs. Rene Serpa tangoed into a full Milonguero style, where they were very close while embracing with full upper body contact.

He spun her into a *mordida alto*, and she caught his knees between both of her legs. The watching crowd gasped in delight. Joseppe then escaped by doing the needles, which was an adornment done by working the foot vertically with his toe pointed into the floor while pivoting and doing a windmill. Meanwhile, Mrs. Serpa danced a grapevine in circumference around him, stepping as he continued to do a triple pivot at the center.

Suave handsome Joseppe continued his next steps as syncopation cut the music beats in two, stepping on the half-beat while Mrs. Serpa in her silver fish dress followed his rhythm to perfection. The crowd cheered loudly while Joseppe stopped her syncopation by placing his foot into a *passada* next to her foot, which forced her to step over his placed foot. He then did a *saltito* jump, and she did an ultra *patada*, kicking one leg high onto his shoulder while he supported her back.

She ended the dance with a beautiful and graceful back bend standing on one leg with her other leg on Joseppe's shoulder.

The Santos girls clapped and cheered, "Bravo! Bravo!" for their Aunt Serpa, and the crowd of guests went wild with admiration and disbelief. The guests on the decks and balconies had come back inside to watch the tango dancers. The improvised dance was a work of art, depicting what tango should be.

I looked into Leonardo's raging jealous eyes and could see the contempt he felt toward Joseppe. I quickly pushed the red alert button on my cell phone, which connected all our agents. "Get Joseppe out of here—now! It is time for us to leave," I said into the phone.

"I need to teach that bastard a lesson. He danced with my wife," Leonardo Serpa exploded.

"Mr. Serpa, your lifestyle appeals to me, and I want to invest $100,000 now!" I said as I grabbed his arm to distract him. "I need to go back to Costa Rica tonight, but I would like to meet with you on your yacht later. Can we make an appointment?" I asked.

"The $100,000 would be worth my time. I will meet you at midnight," Leonardo Serpa replied. Mr. Serpa plodded abruptly toward the dance floor with the movements of a mule, compared to Joseppe's grace. I waited five seconds, looked around, and saw no agents except for my own protective team of Roberto, Manuel, and Geraldo, who watched Zorro leave the Serpa yacht.

Our post-party meeting in room number 707 was packed with eleven tired men, talking in whispers, who had successfully completed their assignments. I began the meeting with an announcement. "When we finish this strategy meeting tonight, the Costa Rican team and I need to travel to El Salvador," I told them. "The Sun Wren Richards Colombia-Costa Rican case is big, and its success for arrests depends on our restrained caution. It is important that all arrests happen simultaneously, and that includes the Costa Rican arrests. We need help from other NSA teams. Take as long as you need to complete this case. Coordinate with other agencies and our Costa Rican team. Finish up any loose ends before our criminal roundup begins. My best guess is that this pre-roundup work will take at least a month to prepare. This case involves hundreds of people, and keeping your cover takes extra caution. You need to involve:

> Cali and Santa Marta local police
> The Drug Enforcement Agency (DEA)
> Local firefighters for the cocaine crop burn
> The National Transport Agency for the seizure of Santos's High Green Vegetables trucks
> Colombian national import and export inspectors for air cargo export arrests
> Interpol for freezing bank accounts
> Colombian and Costa Rican coast guards for arrests in ports that export cocaine
> US warships for seizure of cocaine on the high seas."

I looked at the wide-eyed agents and explained again about caution. "Anyone of these agencies can be on the take from the Mezas, Serpas or Santoses. Watch your back and the backs of your teammates. Do not group together in hallways, dining rooms, cars, lobbies, or bars. Do your work separately but communicate with each other. Share evidence and remember that the end of a case will be the most dangerous. Call me anytime, day or night, and stay safe."

CHAPTER 27

NARC-DARTS

I t seemed like only yesterday that I had left Colombia, but an entire month had passed since Special Ten had spent an evening on the Serpa's party yacht. Now we were returning again to finish our investigation of the Sun Wren Richards's case.

Team members Manuel, Geraldo, and Joseppe traveled from Costa Rica to Colombia. They provided security for me and were familiar with the case. I had been absent because I had been working on a border-dispute case between Nicaragua and Costa Rica, but the Special Ten Colombian investing team had made good progress on their own. They had collected information concerning the Meza Family, Mauricio Santos, and Leonardo Serpa.

Teresa Jimenez, Sister Rosa Diaz, and Danelle Ariza were three of our regular Colombian team members who had coordinated cocaine information with the Colombian Drug Enforcement Administration (DEA). These women had trained with the Narc-Darts.

The US National Security Agency and War on Drugs Department had their own narcotics' submarine to help them detect the hidden maritime drug-smuggling operations of the Central and South American drug cartels. The NSA and its community partners had created its own submersible vessels called narc-darts. Drug smugglers had been using submarines to elude fast coast guard boats for years. However, Tum Tumbuku (known as Tutu) had created narc-darts in the Borders and Maritime Security Division of the US National Security Agency. Narc-darts were housed at Eglin Air Force Base near Fort Walton Beach, Florida, and were maintained by the air force's forty-sixth test squadron. Narc-darts could submerge and reemerge at double the speed of drug smugglers' submarines, which were mostly from Colombia.

Our government agency also had a semi-submersible narc-dart named Pluto, which US airplanes used during practice to detect drug smugglers from the air. Pluto was over forty-five feet long and could only travel a maximum of ten knots. The practice sub could have a crew of three or four people, but usually operated with only one. All three of our Colombian women team members had operated this replica of the full-sized narc-dart and understood the logistics of drug submarine apprehension.

Teresa Jimenez was captain of our regular Colombian team and our oldest member. Teresa, aged fifty-two, was large-boned and taller than most of our team—she was six feet tall. She had an attractive Colombian face with deep dimples when she smiled her lopsided grin. She had dark, curly hair and dark skin. She also had a bold brassy attitude, which kept the team working together. She was stubborn in her ways, and we had crossed paths more than a few times when I had had to use my rank to make my point. She followed orders as long as she understood the goals of the project.

Sister Rosa Diaz, age forty-four, passionately wanted to rid her country of drugs and crime. She believed drugs were ruining her native Colombia. She was brave beyond good judgment and took too many risks for herself and her team. Rosa, a Catholic nun, was short and thick bodied with dark hair and eyes. She had a tireless energy that matched that of a caged tiger. She believed her job was to be of service, helping God clean the mess humanity had made for itself.

Danelle Ariza, age eighteen, had been rescued from forced prostitution when she was only twelve years old. This happened when I worked in Honduras on a human-trafficking case. Danelle was slowly learning to trust her male teammates. She was very reliable and loyal to the women team members she worked with and who protected her. She and her teammate Wilber, who had celebrated his twenty-second birthday last month, shared the same beaten dog characteristics. Danelle had dark hair and eyes, was small in stature, and didn't want to be attractive or to draw attention to herself.

The three women worked well with the other team members Roberto, Marco, Wilber, Manuel, Joseppe, and Geraldo, who were also working the Serpa-Santos case. The team had secured a small hat shop and used it as an office and work area in the capital city of Bogota, which was located near central Colombia.

The space was located near Bogota's central city's rapid transport system at the Old Savannah Train Station, a large antiquated 1800s beige-colored building located on Calle Trece (avenue number thirteen). Our space was designed by our three women as a shop for a hat maker, so the front of the office had a display of handmade hats. The train building and the hat shop worked well for our team headquarters and allowed our agents to come and go unnoticed to and from the busy train terminal.

Manuel, Joseppe, Geraldo, and I walked into the expansive room with a high-vaulted ceiling that echoed the crowd's din over the amplified loudspeakers, which announced the arrival and departure of the train. The interior smelled of travelers' warm bodies, suitcases, and pipe tobacco, which wafted from the nearby open door of the tobacco shop. We walked to the center corridor and spotted the plate-glass window displaying colorful men's and women's hats.

I opened the beveled glass door, entered the hat shop, and discovered what looked like a real operating business with cash register, desk, drawers, fax machine, telephone, computer, and advertisements from the hat designer. Danelle recognized me. She gave a little wave, ducked behind the counter, resurfaced with a large "CLOSED" sign, and hung it on the front door. We moved into the back rooms away from the hat shop's window as Danelle turned off the lights.

The team members talked softly while seated around a large wooden table, which had been used for cutting bolts of fabric or laying out patterns. I received handshakes and greetings from the sprawled and relaxed young Colombian team. Teresa Jimenez ushered me into an comfortable chair in the middle of the room, facing the team.

The table held bottles of water and platters of sandwiches. Marco lifted one of the platters and offered it to me and the Costa Rican team. He then watched as the platter of food disappeared into the mouths of our hungry team members. Marco placed three more platters of meats, breads, and cheeses on the table. He invited the team to make their own sandwiches. Afterward, Roberto replenished the empty platters with pies, cakes, and cookies.

"Angelo, this mangy crowd is glad to see you. We have some sticky spots that need your help," Teresa Jimenez announced.

"Ms. Jimenez, would you like to start first?" I asked as I finished my sandwich.

"I will catch us all up to speed, and everyone can help me fill you in. Marco, we should start with your report first," Teresa blurted.

"Okay, I am glad you are back with us, Mr. Lopez. I returned to the Leonardo Serpa investment meetings on the *High Tide* yacht. On my fourth meeting and after I had invested $25,000, I learned that the secret commodity was cocaine and have recordings of our conversations. Mr. Serpa is exceptionally cozy with me because he believes his niece Monica Santos may be romantically interested in me. He hopes to distract her from her plans with the Santos's northern land expansion. He believes that if I am in his camp, Monica will be persuaded to plant more land with cocaine instead of her current plan for natural herbs.

"He also told me on tape that he was the only buyer of Santos's cocaine. Santos produced the coca leaves and manufactured them into cocaine, but Serpa was the distributer and Sandra Santos was the marketing director. He guaranteed that I would triple my $25,000 investment in three months. I have a written shareholders' document from the Money Grow Green investment fund, which is proof of his racketeering," Marco factually concluded as he presented the shareholders' document.

"The next fact of interest is your report, Wilber. Tell Mr. Lopez what you found," Teresa proudly said.

"Mr. Lopez, I found a Serpa special bunker," Wilber said shyly.

"Tell me what that means, Wilber," I urged

"Lords in the drug-transporting business like Serpa need a safe place to store cocaine until it can be sold. Such storage places are called bunkers in both Spanish and English," Wilber humbly explained.

"Yes, I understand about bunkers, but why is this bunker special?" I prodded.

"It was my job to do surveillance on Sandra Santos, Leonardo Serpa's niece and business partner. She has a degree in business and continued her education to receive a master's degree in business marketing at the National University of Colombia, right here in Bogota," Wilber explained in sudden animation. He became a different person as he took on his surveillance role.

"I followed her to the modern high-rise campus that looks like an American condominium. It is located at the Francisco de Paula Santander Plaza," Wilber continued, explaining and sneaking around the room as if he was a villain in a B movie.

"I became Scott Black, a student at Sandra's university. I dressed in khakis, a polo shirt, Dockers, and a new backpack. I sat in the back row of her class as a student auditing the class and followed her everywhere for one month. At last, she went to her rented locker next to the large university stadium and soccer field and ..." Wilber lowered his voice to a whisper during his suspenseful description. "I found the key to the gold mine," Wilber continued, as the team members were sucked into his antics.

"When Sandra went to her next class, I used my credit card that was full of tiny tools for unlocking door, and voila, I opened her locker and snooped around. I found these," he said like a magician pulling a rabbit from a hat. He held up pictures of cocaine wrappers displaying an ornate "SERPA" printed in bold fancy script. "I only took photos of these and left her locker in perfect and undisturbed order so she wouldn't suspect my surveillance," Wilber elaborated.

"Cocaine business is Colombia's big business, and I guess when you're in the business, you have no shame. Serpa sells the best cocaine with the purest, highest grade and touts, advertises, and markets with the Serpa name in accordance with Sandra's marketing plan. I kept a close watch on her, and she led me to the special bunker. Inside the bunker, there were floor-to-ceiling, built-in shelves stacked with cocaine. All of it was wrapped, marked, and displayed with the Serpa brand label and advertised as number ten graded cocaine," Wilber explained as he came to the climax of his story.

"Now here comes the big prize!" Wilber exaggerated as he pulled another picture from his bag of tricks. "Serpa's drug smugglers use sophisticated drug-packaging machines. I found a hydraulic press and a series of design stamps that matched the hand-drawn designs found in Sandra Santos's campus locker. These designs were pressed into the face of the package and designated its origin. Serpa brand is advertised as the best quality number ten." Wilber continued his charades.

"Their ego and vanity will put them in jail. They don't fear apprehension, and I assume the payoffs to officials must run deep. I don't think it is right to call Leonardo Serpa and Sandra Santos smugglers." Wilber comically exaggerated and said the word *smugglers* as if he had a mouthful of smelly fish. "They don't hire low-life people as drug couriers. They sell only in bulk to upscale businesspeople in Holland, the USA, and Costa Rica. I have many pictures of the pressed and stacked Serpa kilos. This is a proud, professional business company. Serpa and Santos should instead be called curators for custom, cosine, cocaine contraband," Wilber said as he took a magician's bow to his chortling, applauding crowd, who shouted, "Bravo! Bravo!

"This was a helpful discovery, Wilber, and I enjoyed your presentation," I chuckled. I had just seen Wilber overcome his lack of trust and prove himself as a valued team player.

"Sister Rosa Diaz, you are up next," Teresa Jimenez said, imitating an announcer of a television show.

"Eureka! You're making me follow the stand-up comedian," she quipped. "I guess I need to start my report by saying three Hail Marys." She did as the group chanted with her. When she finished, she quickly began with her report.

"I have discovered that Serpa's custom, cosine, cocaine contraband," she smiled as she used Wilber's words, "has a direct hotline, which connects the exporting docks to air cargo for future tapping. The phone number is 011-57-2443-6996." At this, the team grabbed pencils and took notes. "Serpa calls the laboratories to tell them about arriving transports from Santos's farms. He advises the export docks about cargo coming from the labs. He keeps close watch on the transporting process.

"He also has a sophisticated tracing system for his cargo at sea and in the air while it travels to the USA, Holland, and Costa Rica. Serpa knows exactly where his cocaine shipments are through his communications and tracking systems. He also has four submarines that elude the coast guard. The submarines, while packed with cocaine, can also be used to protect the regular transporting boats, which are carrying cocaine, by alerting them of the locations where drug police or coast guard members are. Serpa also has a website cunningly worded to sell Money Grow Green stock. I believe the website can be used in conjunction with Marco's stock document, proving that there is racketeering involved," Sister Rosa Diaz said as she sat down and continued her report.

"Teresa, Danelle, and I, under the authority of Mr. Angelo Lopez, contacted the National Security Agency, the Drug Enforcement Administration, the Department of War on Drugs, and the Eglin Air Force base forty-sixth squadron. We directed them to the exact underwater locations of Serpa's narc cargo submarines. Eglin Air Force sent three narc-darts to Colombia to confiscate the drug cargo, and Teresa, Danelle, and I were individually invited to ride in one of the narc-darts as they seized the Serpa underwater vessels.

"Each of us dressed in combat gear, including the army-issued machine guns deployed with the US narc-dart two-man crew while Roberto and Marco relayed surveillance teams' real-time information to us, and we served as translators for our individual narc-dart crews," Sister Rosa demurely continued her bold story. It seemed incongruent to see Sister Rosa elaborate on her fierce actions against the drug captains of the narc submarines, but she gave factual accounts of the seizures.

"Marco and Roberto gave us timely and accurate locations of the departing drug vessels. Our narc-darts had time to position themselves while we waited for the cargo to reach intercontinental waterways where they would be captured. We were aware that Serpa knew of their capture, but he didn't suspect our local Colombian infiltration. It appeared to be random acts of high seas police patrol, and we kept our cover intact," Sister Rosa continued and then sipped her bottle of water.

"After we had our targeted suspect who had operated as a one-man crew on our radar, the three narc-darts surrounded the Serpa cocaine-laden submarine. One of our darts intercepted its forward movement and positioned it horizontally and directly in front of the vessel, so it had to stop. Our other two narc-darts paralleled the cocaine sub on both sides. The narc-darts' crew prepared themselves in combat gear while I gave the drug runners the command in Spanish to surface or be entombed inside a sunken vessel. Our paralleled narc-darts surfaced more rapidly than the contraband vessel and waited for the criminals while the horizontally positioned narc-dart surfaced last to keep them from escaping," Sister Rosa faltered and paused in her account of the capture.

"Our horizontal narc-dart had a faster emerging rate than the cocaine-stocked vessel, and when Serpa's sub surfaced, we floated topside. I quickly opened the hatch and sprung out like a caged lion before my commanding officer gave the order. I was humiliated and chastised for my rash actions, but since I already stood in arrest position, my commanding officer gave me the order to translate his orders, which were, 'Throw all your weapons out the open hatch!' I ordered in the same harsh tone as my commander. A machine gun and pistol slid out across the deck. Without waiting for orders, I quickly retrieved them and handed them to one of the other narc-dart captains from the paralleling submarines. My captain bellowed, 'Wait for orders, Diaz!' I responded with a tiny voiced, 'Yes, sir,'" Sister Rosa continued.

"Teresa Jimenez now stood on the captured submarine's deck and brashly said to the officer, 'Ask for the detainee's machete!' He gave an indignant look in her direction and refused, returning her insulting stare. Teresa, in her boldest brass voice and in Spanish, gave the command, 'Toss out your machete.' The words were barely out of her mouth when out of the hole erupted a hand-crafted, black-handled, deadly sharpened machete that skidded across the deck and sliced through the combat pant legs of one of our officers.

"'He still has his boot knife, sir. Shall I give the order to throw it out?' Rosa respectfully asked the commander. 'Yes, ask him to throw it out the hatch,' the commanding officer ordered and displayed his authority."

Sister Rosa Diaz imitated Teresa Jimenez, gave her a sly, knowing wink, and bellowed, "'Toss out your boot knife.' An opened switchblade zinged out the hole and pegged a life preserver, which was hanging on the metal railing.

"Teresa said, 'I think that should be everything he has.' 'Okay, ask him to come out slowly,' the officer barked as he strutted the length of the topside deck. The officer's words were translated and repeated. The smallest mouse-like Colombian in his twenties emerged from the hatch, looked timid and scared and revealed his cowardice. The nine of us, who were twice his size, thought the unequal show of our strength was funny. Without waiting for the officer's command, Teresa and I lunged upon the little man and cuffed both his hands and feet without allowing him to see our faces."

"'Jimenez and Diaz, you will be written up because you did not wait for my orders,' the officer smugly stated. 'Sir, we had no time to wait for your orders. The detainee was ready to throw himself overboard,' Teresa retorted. The commanding officer didn't write up our insubordination, but he did report my infractions," Sister Rosa Diaz reported.

"The officer asked, 'Ms. Jimenez, how do you know the detainee's intention was to abort the ship?' 'Sir, I know and understand the Colombian culture!' Teresa snapped back in our defense. One air force man from each of the three narc-darts waited for the officer's command to enter the Serpa vessel, and they reported finding one ton of stashed Serpa hand-designed, machine-pressed, stamped one-kilo packages of cocaine, which will be excellent evidence for the Serpa's and Santos's arrests and trials," Sister Rosa brightly reported.

"The small mouse-like Colombian drug runner who was hired by Serpa to operate his submarine was taken aboard the narc-dart by two air force men and turned over to the Drug Enforcement Administration while Teresa, Danelle, and I returned to Bogota with the remaining two narc-darts. The three air force men waited for a US warship to pick up the one-ton load of seized cocaine. The Serpa submarine was delivered to the Elgin Air Force Base in Florida to be remodeled, equipped with new technology, made into another narc-dart, and added to their fleet," Rosa Diaz concluded.

"That was a good piece of teamwork," Angelo congratulated.

Roberto had originally been part of my Colombian protection team but had joined the Sun Wren Richards's case a month earlier and had remained doing surveillance investigation until this case closed.

"Roberto, do you have something to add?" I asked.

Roberto, who was our largest and youngest team member, stood tall and reported, "I should go next with Serpa's and Santos's boring-but-needed facts. Santos has eleven farms, and out of those, six grow hectares of coca plants. Those farms are in Cali, Barrancabermeja, Bogota, Puerto Salgar, Medellin, and Villavcencie. The farms produce tons of cocaine that is exported by Leonardo Serpa. If any of you have evidence that there were others, please let me know. I spent hours at Santos's farms and laboratories and believe the other farms and labs are clean but could have missed some," Roberto graciously invited.

The team members began to take notes for their own research from Roberto's factual report and scribbled as Roberto continued. "There are seaports that Serpa and Santos use regularly. They are in Cali, Santa Marta, Barranquilla, Cartagena, and Buenaventura.

There may be more, but these have been documented as Serpa's exporting cocaine ports," Roberto explained.

"Mauricio Santos has forty-two laboratories, and today, we know that twelve of these process coca leaves into cocaine. I have pictures of trucks loaded with coca leaves arriving at the laboratories and then departing carrying stacks of the white plastic pallets that Manuel discovered were hollow containers used for storing one-kilo packages of cocaine marked with the Serpa logo. The cocaine-processing laboratories are in Mocoa, Cali, Barrancabermeja, Bogota, Puerto Salgar, Medellin, Neiva, Manizales Quibdo, Tunja, Villavcencie, and Florencia. These twelve cocaine-processing laboratories gave two places per farm for more efficient and quicker processing.

"It is my guess the other non-cocaine laboratories will be opened as processing factories as coca plant farm production is expanded. It is possible that more of the forty-two laboratories are involved, but I believe they are legal, serving only the vegetable producing farms and Colombia's health clinics and hospitals." Roberto helped himself to three more cookies as he continued.

"The last part of my report involves tracking Santos's 250 High Green Vegetables trucks. I have pictures and the license plate numbers of 120 trucks transporting coca leaves and racks of pallets and pallet-lined trucks transporting vegetables. Any truck transporting cocaine or the production of cocaine has been documented," Roberto reported while he swallowed the cookies.

"There are 130 trucks parked in a locked storage parking lot on the Santos's northern Mocoa farm that seem like they have not been used until recently. It is my assumption that these trucks were originally used for US and northern transportation of cocaine until Serpa bought his fleet of sixteen cargo ships. When the Drug Enforcement Administration began to seize his cargo ships, he invested in his four narc submarines. These have now been reduced to three because of Ms. Teresa Jimenez's narc-dart project," Roberto continued.

"I noticed the removal of thirty trucks from the parking lot after Ms. Jimenez's arrest. I documented the license plate and registration of these thirty trucks and with the help of Interpol, tracked the trucks to Chicago, New York, Atlanta, Dallas, San Francisco, and Mexico City. I believe that transporting by truck to the USA isn't as profitable as exporting by water or air cargo to Europe. In the beginning of the Santos-Serpa cocaine business, they most likely trucked everything, but as their business knowledge improved, so did their methods of exporting. Now that Serpa's tons of cocaine have been seized, he will again resort to ground transportation and engage the dormant truck fleet," Roberto said, reaching for three more cookies and sitting down with the other team members.

"Roberto, your report wasn't boring and revealed good, hard work. We all thank you," I encouraged him. "Come on now, Ms. Jimenez, it is your turn to tell us what you have," I begged laughingly as large Ms. Teresa Jimenez pried her wide bottom from the sides of the plastic armchair, which entrapped her lower half, and reluctantly stood in relaxed attention.

"My report will be a short, simpering, whining one because I am frustrated," she bellowed while pulling her own tangled hair. "Danelle Ariza, Sister Rosa Diaz, and I spent this past month working for the capture of six Serpa cocaine-exporting cargo boats and one narc submarine. We coordinated our work with the National Security Agency, who furnished us with American warships for hauling Serpa contraband. The air force at Elgin Air Force Base in Florida helped us seize a total of nineteen tons of cocaine." Teresa drew a deep breath and continued.

"We seized six cargo ships carrying three tons of cocaine. Each load was a legal capture. We used the narc-darts and transferred the contraband onto the American warship that held the nineteen tons of Colombian cocaine. The seven apprehended Colombians from the six Serpa cargo boats were turned over to the Colombian Drug

Enforcement Administration, who knew that Leonardo Serpa was a major drug lord. It is my fear that the DEA or Serpa's captured boat captains receive payoffs, suspect our local operation, and have informed Serpa and Santos. Even though we were careful to make our arrests appear as random acts of drug enforcement, we might be the targets of the informers. I am uneasy about our operation and sense danger," she explained intently.

"The biggest problem, which forces our efforts into slow motion, is the US warship that is carrying nineteen tons of Serpa-marked kilos to Costa Rica. The US warship's cargo is to be used as evidence in the Sun Wren Richards's case, but Costa Rican congressmen won't allow the ship to dock in their ports because it is a warship and they are concerned about American aggression. Presently, our strongest evidence is floating around out there unable to dock, and Serpa continues to find new ways of exporting," Teresa concluded in exasperation.

"You have done a superb job with this case. It is understandable you are frustrated, Ms. Jimenez. I validate your feelings. There are a few things that will hasten progress," I encouraged. "I hope to relieve your stressful situation soon, Ms. Jimenez," I reassured as I continued with the assignments.

"Marco, I would like you to prepare an evidence presentation packet, combining Roberto's truck transporting investigations and Teresa's high seas investigations to prove this case is intercontinental. Serpa and Santos clearly transport cocaine over foreign boundary lines and on the high seas. Please have the packet ready in the next two days," I explained.

"I will make a presentation, requesting that the Costa Rican president and congressmen open their ports to receive our evidence-laden American warship. Marco, I will take your file with me when I return to Costa Rica. Marco, another difficult task, before our day of arrests, is for you to get a list of all Money Grow Green stockholders.

If Serpa told you the commodity is cocaine, it is reasonable to assume that other stockholders also know cocaine is the marketed commodity. This list will be necessary to support our charge of Serpa's racketeering," I continued.

"Roberto, I would like for you and Wilber to begin working on an arrest list, starting with Santos's and Serpa's family members. We need names, identification numbers, and locations for each listed person. The arrest list should be inclusive to all of Santos's coca plant farm supervisors. We need a list with the names of every export dock's foreman where cocaine has been exported, every air cargo manager that has shipped cocaine, and every Santos laboratory manager who has processed coca leaves into cocaine. We want the names of Santos's truck dispatchers, and the names and locations of 150 truck drivers who have been hauling cocaine even for short distances.

"The arrest list includes Santos's five chemical plants and two fertilizer plants, but Santos's clean vegetable farms are exempt from arrests. Roberto, when arrest day comes, there will be many arrests, and we will need to enlist our full teams from Colombia, Venezuela, Honduras, Guatemala, Nicaragua, Ecuador, and Panama. Costa Rica needs their own teams to make arrests on the Meza Family," I elaborated as I drank my Coke.

"Joseppe, right now, much of the evidence we have connecting the Costa Rican Meza family to the Colombian drug lords Santos and Serpa is the phone tapes and the empty Santos fertilizer wrapper you found in Sun Wren Richards's art studio. We need to know if the Colombians that Katerina Meza hired to assassinate Sun Wren Richards and the arsenic placed in her swimming pool were the same men. You need to work with the Costa Rican Fuerza Publica, Roberto Zamora, and the chief inspector of the Judicial Investigating Organization.

"This is a difficult assignment and a longshot, but maybe you can find out something. The other important thing to remember is that your face is well known to the Serpa and Santos families, and they will remember you. You must keep your distance from them, but Wilber can help you," I pointed out, as Joseppe took notes.

"Wilber." Wilber looked up and was startled as I said his name. "You have your own assignment besides helping Joseppe. When arrest day is announced, you will be in charge of the Santos cocaine crop burn. You will coordinate the dates and times of the fields to be burned with the Drug Enforcement Administration. This must happen simultaneously with the farm supervisors arrests. All crops should be burned at once. We need to surprise the farmworkers to avoid giving prior information that will aid their escape or causing workers to defend the cocaine crops. All arrests and crop burns will add to the three-ring-circus effect and will help protect our team members who are engaged civically," I elucidated to Teresa as she waited intently for her assignment.

"Teresa Jimenez, you and your teammates do important work on the high seas with the narc-darts. Continue working with Danelle and Sister Rosa as they both are valuable to you. Keep up the pressure and organize seizures on Serpa's and Santos's trucking ground-transporting fleet. Serpa only understands the power of money and economics, so let's squeeze where it hurts him by drying up his moneymaker. Choose your cocaine-seizure locations carefully. Choose countries that will support your efforts and protect your teammates," I directed.

"We need to work very fast. There are many people involved with this case, and it is possible that leaks will happen and that rumors will spread and compromise our operation. Don't group together in public. Help your teammates. Protect your cover and your identity." I concluded the Colombia briefing meeting.

CHAPTER 28
DEFECTED

The following two days were a scramble of fleeting tennis shoes, pots of lukewarm coffee, unfinished bottles of flat Coke, wastebaskets of overflowing scribbled notes, ten cell phones ringing or being clicked off, and anxious agents waiting their turn for the computer. The hat shop had empty bakery boxes of cookie crumbs, piles of stacked papers where yarn marked the boundaries of someone's territory, and lost pens, cell phones, notepads, and sun glasses. Floors were strewn with stale, half-eaten bags of potato chips.

The "Sorry we are closed" sign hung on a constantly opened door. There was a flourishing of backpacks being zipped or unzipped and scattered folding chairs sitting upright or toppled. This was what happened to the usually sedate hat makers shop in the Old Savannah train station when young agents were completing their assignments.

Roberto constructed his extensive report with efficiency. He handed me the list of the names, IDs, and locations of six Santos farm supervisors to be arrested and twelve Santos cocaine-processing laboratories' managers with documented evidence for arrest. He listed five foremen along with clear pictures of their faces at the exporting docks where Serpa contraband had been shipped. He also listed 120 High Green Vegetables truck drivers with locations of their six dispatchers, which totaled 149 arrests. The Colombian team had nearly finished preparing the arrest day details, and Roberto had finished his list and had handed it to me before I left for Washington.

Roberto finished his excellent concise report and made time for his own agenda. He was gone for ample periods. When he left, he looked crisp and clean-cut, and when he returned, he was relaxed and content. The team respected each other's privacy and didn't inquire or intrude. Sometimes Sister Rosa teased a little bit, but Roberto walked away from the grimy, black-and-white-tiled floor of the hat maker's shop with a determined strut.

The black-and-white-tiled floor of the Fast Connection internet cafe was shiny and clean, compared to the neglected one at the hat maker's shop. The long, curved, glass cases filled with freshly baked tarts and cupcakes made this cafe a popular place for the intercity residents who lived in central Bogota. It was quiet in the separate, red-colored dining room with white crown molding. Roberto was glad the cafe was open and ready for breakfast, coffee, and pastries. He had been planning this meeting for days.

Roberto took special care to be well groomed and stylish before he arrived fifteen minutes earlier than the agreed meeting time. He saw her and gasped at her beauty. Monica Santos wore a violet, draped blouse with matching violet tapered pants, which complimented her small, shapely figure. He had been attracted to her at Serpa's boat party, but now in the daylight, she was even more stunning with her dark black hair and thick long lashes.

"It is good to see you again, Miss Santos. I didn't know if you remembered me or if you would agree to meet me for coffee, but I am glad you are here," Roberto said sincerely as he pulled out Monica's black wrought iron chair, which matched the cafés decor.

"Are you hungry?"

"Please call me Monica," she invited. "I am not very hungry. Are you?" she asked.

"I am always hungry. Will you share some pastries if I get us some? How about some coffee?" he asked hospitably.

"Both are welcome," Monica replied.

In his absence, Monica remembered the conversation she and Roberto had had on the Serpa party boat, and she was inwardly excited he had taken the initiative to reconnect. She watched him move around the curved-glass display counter as he carefully made his selection. Monica liked the way Roberto looked. He was solid in stature, confident, and strong without arrogance or pretentiousness. He was educated without looking or seeming bookish. She knew he would be a man who would stand up for what he believed. Monica wanted a man who worked hard for the principals he carved out for himself.

As Roberto approached their table, Monica said, "Oh, that looks inviting. Maybe I am hungrier than I thought, and the coffee smells good too."

"You are the most beautiful woman I have ever seen. Our conversation on your Uncle Serpa's party boat was short, and I didn't know if you would remember me," Roberto said while stirring his coffee.

"I felt we had a like-minded connection that night, and in that type of party environment, it was rare to share meaningful words with anyone. Our conversation was short, but it was one of substance. Do you honestly enjoy gardening or was that only party talk?" Monica asked, doubting any man would choose such a vocation.

"I like plants and farming. I want to own a place of my own someday, and when you talked about your plans for your father's northern lands, I felt the rush of a shared energy. I majored in botany and worked in the rainforest as a forest ranger to earn enough to pay for my classes. What about you? What is your major?" Roberto inquired, genuinely interested.

"I hold a degree in pharmacy, and planting crops for healing is my passion. At Uncle Serpa's party, you mentioned you and my father had similar childhood histories. What did you mean?" Monica was curious.

"I know your father as a local legend. We were both raised in remote areas by poor people. I want to use my innate abilities like he has done to become a successful farmer so the entire country can benefit from it," Roberto explained honestly.

"Did you know, Roberto, my father came from the Chanco Indigenous Western Colombian tribe?"

"Yes, and I come from the Amani Central Colombian tribe. That is why his story is important to me."

"My poppa saw us talking at the party and asked me who you were. What should I have told him?"

"You could have told him that I am the man who would make your dreams come true."

"You say that with such certainty," Monica mused.

"Yes, I do, Monica. You will plant your northern lands with Colombia gooseberry, and maybe some of the other Santos farms will grow bitter melon," Roberto declared, believing his own words.

"Are you a prophet or a tribal shaman?" Monica teased.

"Something like that, Monica. I know I want good things to be yours."

"You have already given me good things. These cakes are divine," Monica said as she licked the sugar from her perfect mouth.

"Can I see you again?" Roberto asked.

"Would you like to meet my poppa?" she asked with big blue, hopeful eyes.

"Yes, when the time is right," Roberto answered honestly.

"I believe in living in the present, and this Sunday, dinner at my house after mass is the future present." Monica's fast-thinking rhetoric poured from her heart-shaped lips, and Roberto was surprised by her assertiveness.

"Right now my job is an obstacle. I cannot see you on Sunday, but I can meet you in Bogota for lunch or dinner during the week, if that is possible," Roberto offered.

Monica and Roberto agreed to meet, and they saw each other regularly while Marco held meetings of his own with Uncle Serpa. Marco kept his connections to Leonardo Serpa well tended. He nourished and pampered the relationship to gain information that would help progress the Sun Wren Richards's case.

"Mr. Serpa, thank you for giving me your valuable time," Marco said as he entered the *High Tide* yacht's lavishly furnished business office.

"I will always make time for friends," Leonardo Serpa said as he handed Marco a Bacardi with Coke and motioned for him to sit on the white-upholstered settee on the deck that opened out to the midday sky while calm water lapped against the bow.

"It is much too soon to have any prediction about your investment, if that is what you have come to talk about," Mr. Serpa clarified, as he stretched his tanned legs onto the matching ottoman.

"Oh no, sir, that isn't the reason for our meeting," Marco laughed. "I'm learning from your example of progressive business ventures and have been contemplating how best to reinvest my original principal from my Money Grow Green fund. I have an idea I want to talk to you about if I have your permission," Marco explained as he sipped his pleasant rum drink in the cut-crystal glass.

"You always have permission to talk business, Marco. What's on your mind?" Leonardo Serpa asked as he lowered his leg to the deck floor and leaned forward showing interest.

"I want a list of the other Money Grow Green stockholders who share the same commodity as I do. I think it would be prudent for me to buy out their stock as my investments mature. Each time I receive a dividend, I could invest to own more of the business, and eventually, I would be the only stockholder besides you, of course. I want to know your thoughts about my plan," Marco emphasized.

"You have a good business mind, Marco, but the stockholders and I maintain an unspoken trust of confidentially. Mr. Serpa paused, finished his drink, and ambled to his bar to pour himself another. Marco, I had dinner with the Santos family last Sunday. Monica told me that she sees you regularly and that she is very fond of you," Mr. Serpa remarked.

"Did she? Did she say my name?" he asked, realizing his mistake and knowing Monica had been keeping company with Roberto. "Monica is usually a private person, and I am surprised she told you about me," Marco elaborated.

"Well, she said she had been seeing someone she met on my party boat, and of course, I knew you were her Prince William of England," Serpa remarked coyly.

Marco laughed. "Yes, Monica has too much pride to admit you were instrumental in our meeting," he improvised.

"Your relationship with Monica pleases me, and it brings us closer than friends. I want you and Monica to do well together. Since we might be family someday, I don't see the harm in giving you the stockholders list you want," Mr. Serpa construed as he went to his desk, riffled through papers, and presented Marco with the coveted document.

"Please realize, Mr. Serpa, the arrow from cupids bow may not strike me as you want," Marco spoke decisively.

"Oh, my young protégé, of course. Love is a crapshoot, and that's just the way the dice rolls. If it worked out, you have my blessings. If not, we gave it one helluva try, didn't we?" Serpa clarified as he patted Marco's back. Marco left the *High Tide* with the document Angelo Lopez had requested.

Marco raced back to Bogota on the next available flight and protected the list from public view. He hopped into the first available red taxi to the Savannah Railway Station, hastily paid the cab, skidded into the protected hat maker's shop, opened the heavy beveled-glass doors, rushed inside, and sat down among his focused teammates. Marco unfurled the easily won trophy of the Money Grow Green stockholders list.

There were thirty-six names, all alphabetized by the last name of each stockholder. Marco started with the name of Ariza and then read names through in alphabetical order to see if it contained any names he might recognize. His eyes scanned the list, recognizing no one until he got to the letter M. There it was, another monumental break through. Neatly listed on the crisp cream-colored, gold-embossed Serpa letterhead were the names in script: Katerina Meza, Pablo Meza, and Mercedes Meza Hernandez.

This was the Colombian-Costa Rican connection Angelo Lopez had been looking for. "Eureka!" Marco shouted as he jumped up and shook the wooden table, which made his focused team members leap like frogs and protest the disturbance. Marco was so excited that he read the investors list aloud. "Mercedes Meza Hernandez, CINS #77858, total amount of investment $15,000. Katerina Meza, CINS #35799, total amount of investment $50,000. Pablo Meza, CINS #22164, total amount of investment $50,000."

"Mercedes Meza spent her commission from the sale of Sun Wren Richards's property on Serpa's racketeering project. She invested in the Money Grow Green hedge fund two hours after Sun Wren Richards closed on the property. According to the posted dates, Pablo Meza bought his Money Grow Green hedge fund stock when Sun Wren Richards paid $60,000 in earnest money. Katerina Meza bought her stock from Serpa one day following the Sun Wren Richards's closing," Marco finished reading aloud. He quieted down, rummaged through his backpack, found his cell phone, and called Angelo Lopez.

"Good afternoon, Mr. Lopez. This is Marco. My assignment is completed. The ground-transport evidence packet contains photos, truck registration numbers, and license plates' numbers. I tracked the trucks through several Central American countries to three US cities as their final destination, and the report is well documented. The same is true for boat and air cargo. The documents show good evidence with bills of lading and photos. The evidence packet is ready for you to take back to Costa Rica and for congress to review in order to persuade them to allow the warships to deliver the nineteen thousand tons of cocaine," Marco continued talking into his small gray phone, "And here—"

"Good, Marco," Angelo interrupted. "It is good to know I can make a strong presentation—"

"Yes," Marco interrupted, "but wait. Let me tell you about the surprise gift. I have the list of stockholders for the Money Grow Green hedge fund, and all three of the Meza family members are stockholders. I am so excited to give this to you," Marco wildly delivered the news.

"EUREKA! Marco, you got the list so quickly? Good for you! Your findings have propelled us to the finish line for the Colombia arrests and ending this case. Good work, and thanks for calling to let me know about the Mezas. This is great news. Thank you. I have made plans to travel to the USA, but I will stop at the hat maker's shop to pick up the folder you have prepared for the Costa Rican congress. Ciao," Angelo clicked off.

I had been called to the USA for our regular Pentagon meeting on foreign affairs. I returned to Colombia a few days later. In my absence, the team prepared for arrest day.

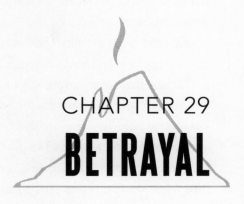

CHAPTER 29
BETRAYAL

Most mornings, work for the Colombian team began early. Teresa Jimenez, Sister Rosa Diaz, and Danelle Ariza traveled to seaports, dressed in fishing clothes and carrying fishing gear. The team was cautious to vary the reason for their seaport departures to reduce the risk of establishing patterns that might easily be tracked. Sometimes the team targeted Santos's Cali farms and the Buenaventura seaport like they did on this day. At other times, they used different ports. The other team members watched the cocaine-transporting High Green Vegetables trucks and notified the narc-darts when a shipment of cocaine left the dock.

Teresa Jimenez and her two female teammates were especially careful to use a different disguise every time. Last week in Cartagena, they were sunbathing tourists. At the Santa Marta seaport they were marine biologists. Today they were fishermen. Their departing motorboat, driven by another team member, took them out to sea. There they waited for the three narc-darts to surface. The three women boarded the narc-darts and waited. When the surveillance

land team had given them the departure time and destination of
Serpa's cocaine cargo, the three narc-darts were ready to capture it.
Today land surveillance reported that the cargo boat had doubled the
size of its crew and had armed guards for their contraband.

Their procedure had been successful for the last six Serpa drug
busts, but Teresa knew that Leonardo Serpa was angry over his
losses and that her teammates would inadvertently be the targets
of his revenge. The fleet of High Green Vegetables trucks hadn't yet
traveled to northern countries. When the land surveillance team had
followed the trucks that had cocaine, Serpa had continued to export
by air or by sea. Teresa had plans arranged for ground travel for when
Serpa chose that mode of transportation, but until then and with
Sister Rosa's prodding, Teresa and her narc-dart team stayed vigilant
and stopped as much cocaine as possible from reaching the streets.

Inside the waiting narc-darts, the crew members exchanged fishing attire for combat gear and masked hoods while they waited for
the Serpa cargo boat of cocaine. Teresa never entirely rid herself
of the claustrophobic effects the vessels permeated. She resented
her large size, and it was even more pronounced inside this tight
forty-five-foot space.

Teresa sat with her face toward the quartermaster's panel on
the small sub and watched the controls unnecessarily, as this small
vessel was operated easily by a one-man crew. However, it gave her
something to do as she looked at the interior floor-to-ceiling, flashing
lights and dials of the instruments. She filled her mind with the me-
chanics of propelling the submarine. She reviewed her training. Each
crew member was required to know how to operate the vessel. The
captain from the air force base in Florida was an excellent navigator.
She felt relaxed and contented to watch his movements. She knew
that in a crises, she could operate the vessel.

Teresa didn't engage in social activities or in conversation
with the men on the narc-darts. The air force men thought they

were supremacists, and she avoided contact to preserve her own self-esteem. In her past, Teresa had been attracted to men but nothing had ever been reciprocated. She had been twice the size of the boys in her class during her school years, and it hadn't been until her late twenties that she noticed some men were her physical equal.

Occasionally, Teresa saw a man who was larger than herself. Teresa wouldn't have objected to a size disparity, but there had never been any man interested in her. Teresa taught herself to use her size to its full potential. She liked being strong as any man and liked being competitive, aggressive, and confrontational.

The Serpa private cargo they were waiting for was a less-than-a-hundred-foot, shallow-hulled boat that carried only three to six tons of Serpa cocaine and had a crew of six on its way to Mexico or Texas. It seemed to Teresa that the cargo boat was taking longer than they had anticipated it would to arrive at its predicted route. She assumed the cargo boat had been prepared for combat. The Colombian coast guard had been alerted and patrolled the legal boundaries of its region. For the high seas arrests, they used a US warship to pick up the cargo.

The warship would wait for permission to dock in Costa Rica. Today's contraband would be picked up by the Colombian coast guard within its legal territories. Teresa expected the Captain of the Serpa cargo boat to show his bravado and strength, which would be different from the last arrest. Teresa explained all of this information to her team. She emphasized the importance of wearing their hooded masks. They each prepared their captains so that their arrogance wouldn't deafen their warnings.

Teresa's narc-dart captain suddenly called out, "We've got company."

There were three Serpa narc subs under the cargo boat. The subs had a two-man crew. That was a total of six combatants plus the six crew members aboard the cargo boat.

"We are outnumbered, but we have the help of the coast guard," the Captain reported with challenge in his voice.

"Sir, I advise you to abort this mission. Do you have the coast guard sighted on your radar?" Teresa asked forcefully.

"Yes, they are keeping their distance behind the cargo boat," he emphasized.

"Sir, I am restating my advice. Abort! Abort this mission! The coast guard is now in international waterways, and they will not help us. Abort! Abort now!" Teresa demanded.

"Not on your sweet sister's virginity," the captain retorted with adrenaline and testosterone pumping into his veins. "We can do this," he challenged.

"Sir, the coast guard is out of its territory, which means they are paid by Serpa, will protect the cocaine, and will not help us. The narc subs are most likely packed with maximum loads of cocaine. Abort! Abort now! We must think of the safety of our crew," Teresa screamed.

"The coast guard is the coast guard, and of course, they will do their job," the American air force captain shouted back.

"This is the Colombian coast guard, and they work for the highest payer. It doesn't matter who paid. Abort, please Abort," Teresa pleaded. She knew his mind was made up to accept the lopsided challenge.

"Okay, if that's your choice, we have half a chance if we surface and seize at top speed," she said with bitterness in her voice as she assumed the sub's planesman position and took over the diving and surface steering controls. She knew the other two narc-darts were listening on the secured, low-frequency radio and would surface with her. The captain knew Teresa was correct and accepted her forcefulness. Teresa's mind raced with the rapid surface speed of the narc-darts, and she knew they were twice the speed of Serpa's narc subs.

"If we seize the cargo boat before Serpa's subs emerge, we might be able to persuade them and the coast guard to withdraw." She pulled on her hooded facemask and was ready for the Serpa cargo invasion.

The little US forty-five-foot metal narc-dart surfaced in seconds. Teresa and her two air force crew members sprang aboard the cargo boat and held the Serpa captain at gunpoint. Masked Sister Rosa Diaz and her two unmasked air force crew members leapt over the seized boats side railings. Rosa reached into her combat pants, pulled out hand and feet shackles, shoved the cargo boat's captain to a deck railing, and restrained him in less than two minutes.

Teresa turned to the air force captain and asked, "Shall I give the order for the other Serpa crew members to toss out their weapons?" she asked, acknowledging his unspoken egoism.

"Yes, give the order to relinquish all weapons," he commanded.

Teresa executed the command in Spanish. Six machine guns and six pistols spun out from the stairwell that led out of the boat's shallow hull as she and her male crew members gathered up the weapons and tossed them onto the narc-dart's decks.

"Tell the six Serpa crew members to come out of the cargo hull one at a time and at five-second intervals," barked the air force captain.

Teresa followed his orders. Each Serpa crew member was garbed with expensive protective equipment. They wore bulletproof body armor and riot helmets. The first detainee was a large Colombian, and the air force crew from Danelle's narc-dart quickly apprehended and placed him in cuffs and shackles. They restrained him on the opposite side of the boat away from the Serpa cargo captain.

The second combatant climbed the boat's hull stairs as the three Serpa narc subs popped up like floating corks. Fast-thinking, small but agile Danelle jumped onto the surfaced Serpa narc sub and used her handcuffs as a padlock by slipping them into the latch holes of the hatch to lock it down, entrapping the Serpa crew. Danelle's air force crewmen imitated her actions but were too late.

The third Serpa sub crewman came out of the hatch and shot his light ninety-six machine gun. The shooter sprayed a round of bullets that pinged everywhere. He shot without focus or aim, and none of the narc-dart crew suffered from his desperate attempt.

The air force crewman from Danelle's boat shot him in the head before he was able to crawl entirely from the hatch. Danelle jumped onto the second sub where its crew member had been shot, shoved his body back down the hatch into the sub, closed the hatch's heavy metal door like a lid on an open can of tuna, and fastened it closed by wedging her knife through the holes. Danelle knew it wouldn't hold him for long, but it might buy enough time to finish restraining the combatants of the cargo boat. The two air force crew members from Sister Rosa's narc-dart stood on top of the hatch door on the third Serpa narc sub to hold the hatch closed.

Sister Rosa took her position beside Teresa to hasten the capture of the cargo boat's crew members. There were three cargo men left on the hull's stairway when the coast guard arrived next to the surfaced Serpa subs and opened fire on everyone and everything.

The coast guard officer sprayed the cargo boat with bullets like he was using a paint sprayer. The bullets plunged into the bodies of Serpa's cargo crew, the air force crew, and the hooded, masked agents alike. The goal was to take human life and reclaim Serpa's cocaine.

Teresa lay as still as death while the spraying continued. She didn't think she had been hit but dropped to the deck by trained reflex. Teresa felt Sister Rosa next to her but couldn't take the chance of moving while the shelling sounded like the roar of thunder with the ear-piercing pings of bullets hitting metal. Teresa's body was motionless, but her mind was on overdrive and was planning her next move. Her face was against the rough timber planking of the Serpa cargo boat deck, and the smell of diesel fuel from the coast guard's boat made her eyes water as she tried to assess her situation.

The Serpa Cargo crew had either been slaughtered or had retreated into the hull of the cargo boat, and their weapons were out of their reach on the deck of one of the narc-darts. Danelle had locked the hatches of two Serpa submarines. They had submerged and were no longer an immediate threat, but where had they gone? Had they returned to a Colombian harbor, or had they continued to their delivery destination? From her position, it didn't matter, as long as their retreat lessened the danger for herself and her teammates.

Teresa forced herself to lie still. She heard the stealthy steps of the Serpa cargo crew members sneaking up the steps. Their motion was detected by the coast guard, who shot another round, hitting all three of them and leaving them splayed on the steps to the deck. Teresa was positioned in such a way that she couldn't see Danelle or any of the air force's crew. She knew the coast guard would resume their shelling if they saw any movement. Teresa remained still while the coast guard waited and watched. She could almost touch Sister Rosa's hand, but now wasn't the time to test the watchful eyes of her predators. Was Sister Rosa making herself lay as lifeless as possible?

Teresa assumed that the coast guard would not come aboard. They could not transport the cocaine cargo themselves but would report to Serpa that the cargo had been saved. They radioed for another captain to move it to its destination. The two Serpa subs resumed their travel and left only one narc sub behind. Serpa would assess his damage as minimal and would replace the crew with fresh men who needed the work.

Was she the only survivor? She planned for the return to Bogota. Teresa heard the coast guard's boat switching its gears in reverse, but she remained motionless. She lay like a stone as the menacing coast guard's vessel prepared itself for travel to its own legal territories. Teresa lay on the deck holding her machine gun. *Please leave now*, she thought. The boat retreated from the bloody scene. *Be still just a little longer,* she told herself.

The murderous coast guard left, and Teresa reached out her hand to grasp Sister Rosa's outstretched fingers and squeezed them for comfort and love. Teresa thought the touch was returned.

"Sister Rosa, can you hear me?" Teresa sobbed as she sat up next to her friend. She scooted her bottom closer to the round, crumbled frame, which had collapsed where they had both once stood. Teresa removed her own hooded mask. She carefully and gently removed the hood from Rosa's ashen round face. Teresa leaned over her friend's neck and touched it to see if she could find a pulse. It was there! Teresa felt a heartbeat.

She put her face next to Rosa's to detect any words and thought she felt Rosa's breath. Teresa moved onto her knees to inspect Rosa's body for injuries and saw the gaping wounds in her chest and abdomen. Teresa jumped to her feet in search of a blanket so that she could improvise a stretcher and remembered the first aid area within the narc-dart.

Teresa lowered herself quickly through the hatch of the narc-dart and heard Danelle release a surprised screech. "Thank God, you are all right, Danelle!" Teresa sobbed, hugged her tightly, and saw the air force captain.

"Is the coast guard gone? Are we three the only survivors?" Danelle lamented.

"No, Sister Rosa needs our help quickly. She is barely alive. We need to get her to a hospital now. We have to move fast," Teresa commanded as she grabbed a blanket and retraced her steps back to the deck. The captain and Danelle followed.

The air force captain had medic training and knew the best way to transfer Sister Rosa into the narc-dart with the least amount of movement. Teresa flung items to the floor to clear a wide shelf to support Sister Rosa's short stature and rounded frame. She improvised a seat belt, even though the narc-dart rarely moved when submerged.

"Danelle, get her out of those combat clothes, redress her in fishing clothes, and change into fishing clothes yourself. Captain, come with me. We will look for other survivors," Teresa ordered. Teresa and the captain made their way around the Serpa cargo boat and looked for survivors but found none.

"I will help you load your dead air force crew into the second narc-dart, but let's move it!" Teresa ordered coldly.

"Thank you," the air force captain shamefully replied.

"When we finish loading the remains of your crew, we three will return the narc-darts to our original position for pickup. Our agency's motorboat will pick us up, but without your crew, I don't know how you will get the narc-darts back to your secured hiding place. Don't underestimate Leonardo Serpa. He has all the money he needs to find your subs. It is best for us to get out of here fast before the coast guard returns or Serpa sends a new crew," Teresa clearly emphasized.

"Ms. Jimenez, I am sorry about your sister. Was she your younger sister?" he asked.

"Sir, the time for you to hear my words has passed. Sister Rosa isn't my relative. She is a Catholic nun doing a wonderful job as an agent against crime. Your ego is what got in the way of her life, and maybe that is the lesson she wants you to learn. Ego seems to run rampant in the air force. You can start working on your ego problem by giving Sister Rosa medical help before we prepare to propel the narc-darts home. I expect you to help Danelle with operating instructions for the third narc-dart. She is trained, as you know, but she has less experience than Rosa and I. If you ever disregard someone's experience or knowledge because you evaluate that person to be less than your rank as you did with me, I will be there to slit your throat some dark night, and that is a promise. If Sister Rosa dies, I promise I will order the entire Franciscan nunnery to place a hex on you, and you will never be able to humiliate anyone again. Do you understand my words flyboy?" Teresa curtly expressed and then called the Bogota hat maker's shop.

"Marco, this is Teresa. We are in bad shape here. We are leaving the area of Serpa's cargo boat now. You have our heading, and we will come back to the point of our original departure as of this morning. Please be there waiting for us. Call the nearest hospital's ER and have an ambulance waiting at the dock. Sister Rosa has chest and abdomen injuries from machine gun wounds. The story is that we were fishing, and a drive-by drug runner tried to steal our fishing boat. You were there, right?" Marco knew that she couldn't be sure it was a secured call.

Teresa clicked off, slid through the hatch, and changed into her fishing clothes. Teresa would do whatever she could for Sister Rosa. The captain and Danelle were hunched over Sister Rosa and were applying gauze. Danelle looked up tearfully as she said, "It is really bad."

"Can we reach a hospital in time?" Teresa asked the captain after he had seen the extent of Sister Rose's wounds.

"We should leave now. Come on, Danelle. I'll get your sub started and headed in the right direction. All you need to do is keep it on course. I know you can do it," he encouraged as he climbed out the hatch to navigate two narc-darts home.

Teresa sat at the controls of the third narc-dart, effortlessly turned it around out of Danelle's path, and set her course on full speed ahead. "Sister Rosa, I know you can hear me," Teresa bellowed in her official brassy voice. "Please hang on until I can get you to the hospital. I will drive this little black bean as fast as it goes, and Marco is waiting for us. Rosa, I love you as my sister. You are a wonderful agent, and when we work together, I am blessed you have my back. Your bravery is an inspiration to our team.

"You must listen to me. Just listen, okay? If our world was as good as you are, God would have nothing to do. Let me tell you, I gave our arrogant SOB of a captain his lesson from God. I delivered it in your name, so you can be sure that you did your nunnery work for today. Your efforts have changed one air force captain into a decent man, if there is such a thing," Teresa spoke her tear-soaked words.

"Sister Rosa, this is for you," she said as tears ran down her dimpled cheeks. "Hail Mary, mother of God. Blessed are thou amongst women and blessed is the fruit of thy womb Jesus. Hail Mary, full of grace, pray for us sinners now until the hour of our death. Hail Mary, mother of God, blessed are thou among women and blessed is the fruit of thy womb Jesus. Hail Mary, full of grace, pray for us sinners now until the hour of our death. Hail Mary, mother of God, blessed are thou amongst women and blessed is the fruit of thy womb Jesus. Hail Mary …"

Teresa continued her chant the entire time until she surfaced the narc-dart at the agency motorboat pickup location. She held Sister Rosa's hand as Marco sped them to shore where an ambulance waited at the dock. Two days passed while Sister Rosa's life clung to its fragile perch on the edge of earth, but Teresa sat vigilant every day beside her friend.

Teresa looked beautiful in makeup and her black sheathed dress with high heels as she walked ladylike up the steps to St. Catherine's Hospital. Sister Rosa's room was full of the brown and sand colored habits belonged to the sisters of her Franciscan order. The priest conducted Sister Rosa's last rites.

Teresa bent over and whispered into Sister Rosa's ear as she held her hand. "You have been the best friend I have ever had but don't stay here because of me. You go where you belong," she said as she felt Sister Rosa Diaz's slight grip release her hand.

CHAPTER 30

DECEPTION

That morning, at the Pentagon in Washington, before the foreign policy meeting started, a very unusual event occurred.
JoSam always wanted to be in his chair before a meeting began and
insisted on arriving one hour prior. Being there before the meeting
started permitted socializing with members and laid down political
groundwork, which could be beneficial. That day before the meeting, a strong, sturdy man in a snappy gray suit with a lavender shirt
and violet tie greeted JoSam. The man was in his early thirties and
had blond hair, blue eyes, and the build of someone with a German,
Scandinavian, or Russian heritage. He had large bones and straight
white teeth.

JoSam turned to me and said, "Mr. Lopez, I would like to introduce you to your newest member of the Special Ten team. May I
present Mr. Russ Warren, who I don't believe you have met before."

My stomach wretched. My heart pounded, and my entire nervous system filled with fire. My nightmares shouted Russ Warren's

name as I remembered witnessing his death in the wake of JoSam's wrath. "I'm sorry, what was your name?" I asked.

The big man in the gray suit extended his hand. "My name is Russell Warren, but I like being called Russ. I am glad to meet you. I have heard glowing accounts of your work, Mr. Lopez," he said as we shook hands.

"Tell me about yourself. I always enjoy getting to know the men on my Special teams," I encouraged.

"I welcome this opportunity! I was raised in an orphanage from the time I was two months old. I have a brother who is three years older and is mentally challenged. Neither of us remember our parents. I am a linguist and speak many different languages. I know you are from Costa Rica. Would you like to speak in your mother tongue?" he gushed.

"No, that won't be necessary. I have US citizenship and prefer to speak the language of the place I am in. Tell me about your brother," I said.

"Thank you for asking, but there isn't much to tell except that he is in California where our US government donated $10,000 to a home where I send my agency monthly paycheck for his care," Mr. Warren elaborated.

"That is a kind thing to do. It is good to meet you. The committee speaker is calling us to order, but I look forward to talking with you later," I abruptly turned my back and took my seat.

"What do you think of our Mr. Russ Warren number two?" JoSam asked as we moved into our chairs for the meeting.

"He seems to be sturdier," I responded.

I assumed we had needed an identity for this new gray suit, whom I believed to have been a Russian defector or a fugitive from justice. He possessed the same special skills as Russ Warren number one and that our agency needed. Russ number two needed a new identity. Russ's death had been a planned strategy for this new man.

I remembered how nervous Russ number one had been because of JoSam's close supervision the day of his death. Now I knew that JoSam taking Russ's life hadn't happened entirely from anger. It had been a planned strategy,

Today, at forty-eight years old, I stood at a crossroads. I realized I'd been groomed since I was seventeen to replace my mentor JoSam. This morning we sat around the large semicircle conference table at the Pentagon for a foreign policy meeting like we had for many other meetings over the years. I sat next to JoSam. For the last three years, my job had required me to keep him awake, prompt him to answer questions correctly, and lately, to provide entire strategies for him. JoSam's intelligence had never dulled, but he was in his late eighties. His life had been full of stress and not enough sleep. His reaction time had slowed, and his attention span and social awareness had been cut in half. He just wanted to sleep.

JoSam sat in his gargoyle strategy mode position with his eyes wide open but unfocused. He was asked to report on our Asian team's infiltration but didn't break his unfocused stare. Under the table, like many times before, I pinched his thigh, yet his eyes still remained vacant. I reached over the back of the chair and whispered into his ear but detected no signs of breathing. I touched his shoulders with a little shove and realized that Joseph Samuel Blake was dead. Nicola's poem ran through my head and sprang to my lips:

> I tolerate no betrayal.
> If my trust in you does fail,
> You die like dethroned royalty.

A nearby Senator heard my words and flatly asked, "Was that a eulogy?"

"Yeah, I guess it was," I responded unemotionally. Shortly after I had uttered the poem, the committee chairman made a phone call.

JoSam's body was zipped inside a thick padded black bag and wheeled away on a gurney.

"Attention please, committee members. We have a very full agenda today. Can we get back to the business at hand? Mr. Lopez, can you give the Asian team's infiltration report?" the undeterred chairman asked impatiently.

"Yes," I responded, realizing my new position had begun. I was staggered by the lack of emotional response this group of foreign policy makers had shown for the passing of JoSam. There was little emotion, concern, or respect for his lengthy career in government. He had sacrificed eight marriages, endured eight divorces, and neglected two daughters for the sake of his job, and there was no acknowledgement or appreciation expressed for his service. I examined my own empty emotions regarding my longtime mentor. I knew him better than these policy makers, and yet I too felt no emotion. The players had changed, but the job went on.

An original Russ Warren had been replaced by Russ Warren II, and my mentor of thirty-one years had been replenished by me. The next day without hesitation and while I was still in Washington, I addressed Teresa's team captain of Colombia problem. I met with NSA and DEA officials concerning Costa Rica's refusal to allow US naval ships to dock.

"Good morning, Mr. Jackson," I greeted as I extended my hand.

"Good to see you again, Mr. Lopez," he welcomed as he directed me to sit on the opposite side of his unadorned office desk.

"I won't take much of your time. I have a sticky situation on a case in Costa Rica and Colombia. The Colombian team coordinated seizures of drug-laden boats, planes, and transporters on the high seas and international airways. Our US teams worked closely with the Colombian and Costa Rican Drug Enforcement Administration. We have confiscated more than nineteen tons of cocaine. A US naval vessel picked up the evidence we need to present our case to the

Costa Rican courts, but the Costa Rican legislative assembly disallowed the vessel to dock because it was a US warship. If you can help with clearance, the Sun Wren Richards's case would end."

"This could be the break you have been looking for to escalate your infiltration into Central America. We have other US naval vessels carrying 120 tons of cocaine that need to dock in other Central American ports to show evidence. What better way than to have these vessels penetrate, infiltrate, and complete your goals? Can you help?" I asked the interested director.

"Mr. Lopez, you are a genius to see this opportunity. I will call the Costa Rican president today," he announced.

"I have a packet with documented supporting evidence for our case, if you would care to look at it," I offered.

"It won't be necessary. I will make the appointment with the Costa Rican congress and president. You can present the evidence packet to them and be our representative. This is a lucky break for my department. Thank you, Mr. Lopez." He stood and shook my hand.

The following week, I remained in Washington. I accepted papers that my superiors expected me to sign regarding JoSam's position. I tried to understand the new requirements for this promotion. This fast transition was difficult for me to grasp. A mere two months earlier, this committee had chastised, demoted, and humiliated me for mistakes I had made on the Sun Wren Richards's case. Now, I was being promoted without question to fill JoSam's vacant chair. I didn't understand this powerful country or its confusing politics.

A portion of the new position required me to become a highly paid strategist. The job description called for planned infiltration terrorist attacks on our own country as well as foreign countries. The United States appeared to foster, augment, and encourage terrorism under a campaign against terrorism disguise. Many of my US colleagues had prepared resignation papers or had already resigned.

I excused myself to return to Costa Rica. I needed to supervise a large Colombian arrest case where I had lost a valued agent, and another sensitive political case in Nicaragua needed my attention. The truth was, I wanted to talk to Sun about these transformational changes in my job. I took JoSam's plane back to Costa Rica and realized it was no longer his plane. It was mine. From the San Jose Airport, I went directly to Sun's mini resort. It had been weeks since Sun and I had talked. We met in the lobby, and I took her hands in mine as we sat together.

"Sun Wren, I am glad today is Saturday. Your staff is gone, and you have time to talk with me."

"I have very little to do except for regular routine stuff now that I'm not taking tourists' reservations. You look like you haven't slept. Would you like some coffee?" she asked as we sat in the lobby at Casa Ave Hotel.

"No thanks. I don't have time, and I want to talk with you before I leave for Colombia. We need to speed up our criminal roundup in Colombia because one of our agents was killed and it won't be long until the undercover investigation team is exposed. It is your case, Sun, and it is huge. There are 149 criminals to be arrested for drug production, transporting, marketing, money laundering and racketeering. I will be sending one of my agents, Joseppe, to work on the Costa Rican roundup. Sun, I have your phone records. Mercedes Meza contacted you two days ago at 10 a.m.," I confronted.

"Angelo, you spied on me, and you violated my privacy," she shouted as she jerked her hands away and jumped up. "It is my responsibility to make these decisions. You overstepped your boundaries. I'm not a child. I am not your suspect. I am an American citizen, and you disregarded my rights. You cannot make decisions for me. Why have you put me under your surveillance?" Sun emphatically questioned as she did angry bird hops around the hotel lobby.

"Yes, I have stolen your privacy in exchange for your safety.

Mercedes called you at 10 a.m., and you called Chief Inspector Mario de Luisa of the Judicial Investigating Organization at 10:10 a.m. He called me in Washington at 10:15 a.m., and we discussed strategy. He called you at 11 a.m. and asked you to invite Mercedes Meza, Katerina Meza, and Katerina's secretary, Marianela, for a visit to your hotel on Monday at 9 a.m. You called Mercedes at 11:30 a.m. and gave the three of them the invitation to visit," I calmly explained as Sun finished her angry flight around the lobby and sat back down beside me.

"Sun, this is one of the things I want to talk to you about. The JIO set you up to be case bait. When these women come to visit with the intention of murdering you, the police will arrest the three of them. Other officers will be simultaneously arresting Pablo Meza, Tony Lopez and the escrow bank manager Mr. Gonzales but not Rodney Lewis because he recently died of AIDS. The three women in one place makes their arrests easier, but you are the decoy on the pond, and I wanted to make sure you understood the risk you accepted."

"Thank you, Angelo, for your explanation, but I understood perfectly before I made the invitation to Mercedes," Sun assured.

"Okay, I didn't want you to be involved if you didn't want to be," I continued to disclose the plan. "Sun, before your guests arrive on Monday, one of my men, Joseppe, will be here to instruct the JIO on the execution of the arrest plan to insure your safety. After the arrests are made at your hotel, I want you to accept this plane ticket to Austin, Texas. I need to be in Colombia and can't be with you. We no longer have a protection team for you. You should go to Texas and stay with your long time friend Molly until we get this case closed and these people go to trial and prison. I don't have enough men to protect you and to make the Colombian arrests. It is best for you to be gone for a few weeks," I emphasized as Sun nodded her dark, curly head in understanding. She no longer seemed perturbed with my poking into her private life.

"I wanted to come home to talk to you about the future. I was promoted to a good position, which will grant me a great lifestyle, social status, recognition, travel, and money enough for whatever I want, but the job requires me to do things I know are morally wrong—taking the lives of innocent people and other things that are ethically unacceptable. The position is for me to be a highly paid US strategist for terror. I considered resignation, but I only know how to do this job. I don't know what else to do except open my own engineering firm, but it would be a lower standard of living," I said to Sun, who was quiet. I felt her compassion.

"Angelo, I will share whatever I have with you, but committing immoral acts will destroy your happiness, peace of mind, and your mental and physical health. The rewards you spoke about—money, power, position, and social acceptance, are all food for your ego and have nothing to do with inner happiness. Those things are superficial and become what our society believes is important, but I know they aren't the source of real happiness. When you perform acts against natural law as you would be paid to do, you gain monetarily and receive public recognition, but you suffer from a lack of fulfillment," Sun explained.

"When I know I have done wrong, I give a present in God's name for his forgiveness and to make things right. Not long ago, three young boys got in the way of our targets, and they died, so I gave a boy's foundation $230,000. I do something good for every bad thing I have done. Can't I erase my mistakes that way?" I asked.

"You can't bargain with God, and those wrong actions lodge in your physiology."

"Do you think I should resign?" I asked her.

"Yes. Why are you hesitant about resigning?"

"I feel lost and detached. I believe resignation is the right thing," I agreed.

"The lost feeling only exists when you don't understand that you have the power to place your thoughts in the universe, and it gives you what you want. You should do what you know is right. If your nervous system is healthy and well rested these feelings of what is right will be clear. I know you would have spontaneous right actions, if only you could sleep," Sun encouraged.

"I resent the horizontal, dormant, inactive body position that never brings the promise of rejuvenating my mind," I lamented.

"When was the last time you slept?"

"Two hours in the last three days," I answered truthfully.

"The human body feels dis-comfort and dis-ease when it needs sleep. Sleep is the flow-er of energy. It is the cleanup time for the brain, and without it, humans get dirty brain diseases like Alzheimer's or dementia. I will make you a natural sedative of hot milk, honey, and a few drops of an herb liquid melatonin. I will bring it over to your apartment. You need to take some time to sleep. Can you take a few hours for yourself?"

"I think I would like to try." I surrendered with a sigh.

"Angelo, you have been through great changes that have placed your nervous system in a state of imbalance, and you need to give your mind permission to stabilize. You need to learn to meditate. I will make up my special brew and deliver it as room service. Would you like me to give you a wake-up call?" Sun asked as she gave me a hug.

"Yes, please. I will drink your brew and try to sleep," I said as I left for my apartment. No one since I was ten had cared for my well-being. They had only cared about the output of my work. JoSam did this, and where did it get him? No one even cared about him, not even me. I liked the way Sun pampered and nurtured me. It made me feel great. Even if I didn't sleep, I could at least rest.

I slept deeply and couldn't believe Sun had a hard time waking me up. She was right when she said that sleep helped a person to think more clearly and to feel better. I was grateful for her thoughtful help and realized she was a special woman that I was fond of.

CHAPTER 31

COLUMBIA PREPARATIONS

I continued to think about Sun as I walked into the Colombian hat maker's shop. My Costa Rican protection team, Manuel and Geraldo, each carried two heavy suitcases and looked like train travelers. When we arrived, everyone gathered around the pattern-cutting table, which we used as our buffet, ate spaghetti, French bread, salad, and drank Coke.

"Welcome Mr. Lopez," Teresa shouted above the din of the passing train. We are ready for the roundup. When do we begin?"

"You all seem like a pack of hungry wolves ready to pounce on a rabbit. Is everyone ready for his or her part tomorrow at 08:00?" I asked.

A resounding *"Si!"* reverberated off the cement walls.

"The Costa Rican president and congress have relented and given us permission to dock the US warships at all Costa Rican ports so that we may deliver the nineteen tons of Serpa-stamped, one-kilo packages of cocaine to the courts as evidence. The warships have been successful in confiscating a total of 120 tons of cocaine from

Central America. Our Serpa evidence was delivered to the courts yesterday and indicates our readiness for the Colombian roundup.

"Joseppe is in charge of organizing the Costa Rican arrests and won't be with us." The Colombian team members listened intently to my every word because they knew that danger lurked around our teams and our surprise attack.

"Ms. Teresa Jimenez, I gave you an assignment to gather evidence against the Colombian coast guard. Did you have enough time to establish an indisputable case against it?" I asked as I noted her strong exuberance and passion for this assignment.

"I am more than ready, sir! Every shred of gathered evidence has been dedicated in memory of Sister Rosa Diaz. I traced the coast guard's boat that turned traitor on our operation. I have the names of the coast guard members responsible for the debauchery and slaughter of the Colombian citizen crew, which was hired by Serpa, and the US air force's fallen men, who gave us the use of their narc-darts and who gave their lives to fight the war on drugs. I have a strong case for murder to add to the charges against Mr. Leonardo Serpa, and I have a team ready to arrest the guilty coast guard traitors with a smooth, well-executed, practiced, and drilled plan." Teresa delivered her report as she stood at attention before our Special Ten team.

"Have all of you had enough time to brief, practice, and execute your individual arrest plans using the foreign country Special Ten teams sent to help you? Does everyone know exactly what is expected?" I asked the serious young faces that had traces of spaghetti and stared wide-eyed at me.

Teresa Jimenez again jumped to her feet and announced, "We are ready, sir!"

"Okay, all teams will rendezvous and be in place precisely at 08:00 tomorrow morning," I commanded. At eight a.m., Marco's team will make the first wave of arrests on the Santos and Serpa family members. Wilber is in charge of the teams that will torch the six Santos farm coca crops and the related drying and bailing sheds. Marco is also in charge of arresting Santos's farm supervisors and will confiscate all trucks used for transporting cocaine. Marco, you will activate the XKeyScore equipment just before 08:00 to jam or disconnect all communications of every family member. That includes family members not arrested, farm supervisors, and their family members. All communications include computers, cell phones, landlines, Skype, radios, and their televisions."

"Local Colombian enforcements will be in place in each of the six coca-documented Santos farm areas by 8:30 a.m.. Those included will be local fire departments, the DEA, and Fuerza Publica. Besides the six Santos farms, local enforcements will be in attendance for each of the twelve Santos laboratories and seaports with documented evidence of the transporting of drugs. One official from the Ministry of Transportation will be present at the six port docks and at the six Santos High Green Vegetables truck dispatches that have evidence of cocaine." I paused for the team to reassess their positions.

"Tomorrow everyone will wear full combat gear and be masked and hooded without insignias to protect your identity for future work," I ordered. "Does each team leader have enough man power to cover their area of arrests?" I asked the intense assembly that looked more like a rock group than the professional agents they were.

"We are all nicely covered, sir," Teresa brightly responded.

"Okay! You have done an excellent job of keeping this operation undetected. Are there any questions?"

"Yes, sir. I have a request, not a question," Teresa bravely stated.

"What is it, Teresa?"

"Would it be possible to have our team leaders wear bulletproof vests tomorrow?" she asked.

I couldn't conceal a sly smile as Manuel and Geraldo made direct eye contact with me. I gave each of them a nod of my head. They stood up and opened the heavy luggage they carried as the group gave an elated and impressive sigh.

"For once, Ms. Jimenez, I am one step ahead of you."

The agents lightened the weight of the suitcases and placed the bulletproof vests under their clothes or into their backpacks. Manuel and Geraldo closed the empty cases and resumed with their disguises of train travelers.

"I have two more items of order," I said, regaining the distracted team's attention. "You will not travel, eat, socialize, or telephone each other until seven days after the arrests are made. Do I make my order clear?" I asked.

"*Si, señor,*" Ms. Teresa Jimenez responded while the others nodded assent with multiple echoes of *"Si, señor."*

"One more thing. During your days off, discretely dismantle this location. Come alone and remove what you can without attracting attention. At the end of three days, I want to see this hat maker's shop gone. Before you leave tonight, coordinate this job with Danelle, who is in charge of dismantle."

"Get some sleep! The human body feels dis-comfort and dis-ease when it needs sleep. Sleep is the flow-er of energy. It is the cleanup time for the brain. Without it, people get dirty brain dis-eases like Alzheimers or dementia. If you can't sleep, here is a recipe: hot milk and honey with a few drops of liquid melatonin. Here is a bottle that each of you can take home with you," I offered.

The reaction from my agents to this nurturing commentary was primarily one of disbelief as they departed the hat maker's shop, one by one. They dispersed into the sea of travelers and were absorbed in their own thoughts, plans, and apprehensions of what tomorrow would bring.

Before Marco infiltrated communications, Roberto felt he must connect with Monica Santos. Roberto had been spending time with Monica since they had met at Serpa's party. It was a miracle that

Leonardo Serpa hadn't discovered that it was Roberto who had attracted Monica's attention instead of Marco, who he had confided in. Roberto made his call to Monica.

"Hi, Monica, I miss you so much. My forest ranger job keeps me very busy, but I have some vacation time, seven days from tomorrow, and I wondered if you could meet me in Bogota for lunch on Thursday?" Roberto asked as he walked home from the hat maker's shop.

"What a wonderful surprise to hear from you, Roberto! Yes. I work at the Bogota pharmacy on Thursday and could take an extra-long lunch hour to be with you," Monica joyously accepted.

"I have a forest rangers' convention this week, and my cell phone reception will be terrible up in the forest, but I want to see you after the convention. I want you to know your life may have some darkness for the next few days, but it will clear, and your dream of the health herb farm is in your future," Robert elucidated.

"Roberto, I live by your psychic prophesies," she laughed. "I am at work with a long line of people waiting for their prescriptions, and I must go. Please remember, my heart is yours. Ciao," she answered and clicked off. Monica's words made Roberto a mighty man for what he had to do the following day.

CHAPTER 32
ARREST DAY

The light of the new day stretched its long fingers across the tropical lands and fulfilled the promise of life in the hearts and minds of the young agents. Marco, in his hooded mask and gear, walked the familiar manicured pathway to the Serpa *High Tide* yacht where he spent time working to gain Leonardo Serpa's confidence. Marco knew that Serpa and his niece Sandra would be enjoying morning coffee and muffins as they talked over future business plans.

The walk was pleasant, and Marco felt well rested. He was aware of the strong smell of the salt and sand as the sea breeze glided over the hood that covered his face and neck. Two *fuerza publicas* with arrest warrants in their hands walked on each side of him.

It was difficult for Marco not to feel empathy for Leonardo Serpa. Maybe he had allowed himself to become too aligned with his subject. He was glad he was at the end of this operation. His compassion for Serpa faded as he thought about Sister Rosa Diaz. The masked man and the two officers boarded the yacht as if it had belonged to them, and Marco led the way to Serpa's morning sundeck. Leonardo

Serpa was relaxing on the white deck's settee and wearing his blue lounging jacket with white pants. Both he and Sandra sat with their backs to the deck door. They faced the open sea as its gentle waves licked the *High Tide*'s bow.

Marco's maleness enlivened as he saw Sandra's beautiful backside draped in a gold-yellow sundress and with her long dark hair flowing over her shoulders. She was a Santos, and all the Santos girls were works of art.

Marco prompted the officer to speak. "Leonardo Serpa, you are under arrest," the officer bellowed as Marco grabbed him from behind and had his hands in cuffs before Serpa's startled face could swallow his muffin.

"Sandra Santos, you are under arrest." She stood up and upset a crystal stemmed glass full of orange juice, which shattered onto the white deck.

Marco stepped out of hearing range and called the patrol car for pickup as the other officer placed the heavy handcuffs on Sandra's delicate wrists. The two criminals were quiet as the two officers and the masked man marched them off the yacht and into the waiting patrol car. By the time Serpa reached the police car, he was all mouth with high volume.

He exclaimed, "There is a big mistake, and you officers are going to be beaten for your transgressions!" The Serpa arrest was over in less than five minutes.

It was unbelievable to imagine that this operation was taking place throughout Colombia and that many arrests were being made simultaneously. Marco didn't ride in the patrol car with Mr. Serpa but instead, climbed into a car that took him away from the yacht and toward the nearest seaports of Santa Marta and Barranquilla, which was according to the team plan, and he assisted other arrests.

Wilber's team spread across the country and torched Santos's coca plant crops in Cali, Barrancabermeja, Bogota, Medellin, Puerto

Salgar, and Villavicencio. He wore a bulletproof vest for protection from the armed guards that were stationed at the Santos cocaine farms. Wilber's team fearlessly charged the guards and took them into custody. He directed the firefighters to surround the perimeter of the fields.

Wilber walked over the moist, rich, brown soil as the coca plants brushed his combat gear and felt a deep sense of peace being so close to nature on this glorious morning. As he walked, he felt a trickle of perspiration under his hooded mask, which reminded him that he was part of a large operation and was doing his assignment. He cast his eyes toward the horizon of rolling hills covered in lush dark green coca plants and watched the local Cali firefighting department take their position while holding their lit torches high over their heads. He thought he was watching a choreographed theater production of dancers wearing dark blue dance jumpsuits as they waited for the last dancer to take his place.

He checked his watch. It was exactly 8:30 a.m. Wilber raised his arms like an orchestra director and brought them straight down to his sides, giving the signal to ignite the crops. The flaming plants belched out white smoke in protest as the heat of the flames touched their dampness, but the flame of the torch won the contest. Soon the field was engulfed in bright orange-red tongues that licked the blue of the sky.

The Drug Enforcement Agency's official stood beside Wilber, silently giving proper legal approval for the colorfully planned sizzling production.

Wilber spoke above the hissing fire. "Sir, I am glad our agencies are working together to rid our country of this crop, which causes destruction in the world. The fire department is watching over the fire. If you care to, we can walk back to the buildings that were used for drying and storing the coca plant leaves. We have a warrant to destroy any building connected to cocaine production." Wilber removed the papers and presented them to the DEA official who nodded his approval.

They walked with their backs to the heat of the flaming fields and toward the drying and storage sheds where Marco's team had already arrested the farm's supervisor. Most of the Nicaraguan farmworkers had scattered like chickens when they saw their superior in handcuffs being taken away.

The DEA official and Wilber stopped beside the pile of torches and other fire supplies, which belonged to the firefighters, and picked up two torches. Together they lit their torches, walked to the drying sheds like two Olympic torchbearers, and ignited the stack of drying plants. The combustion happened fast, and Wilber was startled. The heat was intense and they both backed away and watched in awe as the building quickly burned to the ground and the flames died into red coals.

The two cocaine gladiators grabbed two more torches and continued to the coca-plant storage sheds, which held a full supply of bailed plants that were to be taken to the laboratories for metamorphosing into cocaine. Wilber expected this building to burst into flames even faster than the drying sheds, so he tossed his torch up onto the roof and slowly backed away.

After Wilber had thrown his torch, he had heard a pathetic whimper like a scared cat and had peered into the dark corners of the shed. He saw the shadowed small form of a dark-haired, crouched child wearing diapers and sitting in the stacked bundles toward the back of the shed. Wilber darted in, scooped the child up, and held him around his little torso. The DEA's torch had already touched the stack of dried plants and had ignited it into six-foot flames. The raging, hot barrier of flames surrounded the child and Wilber, who were trapped inside. He thought he was in the belly of the devil's inferno. He saw nothing as the heat caused his eyes to sting and blur.

Wilber felt the singe of the fire on his mask and knew the only way out was through the prison wall of flames.

He tucked the child inside his combat jacket and barreled through the flames toward the open front of the shed. Wilber was confused about which direction he should go but knew he had to make a decision and to trust his instincts. The DEA officer saw the bundle of human flames surging out of the building. He knocked Wilber to the ground and covered him with dirt to extinguish the flames when the child crawled from under Wilber's jacket into the DEA's outstretched arms, crying as loudly as any child could.

The DEA officer helped Wilber and the child get into his car and rushed them to the hospital. The child belonged to the farm supervisor, who had been arrested while the child's mother had been away. The arrest of the father meant the child would be alone but kept at the hospital until his mother arrived. The baby's burns were minor, but Wilber was sent to the burn center for special care.

Wilber's assignment was declared a complete success with the simultaneous destruction of the six Santos coca farms. Young agent Danelle had special feelings for Wilber. She had been working with Teresa's team to close the twelve Santos's cocaine-manufacturing laboratories. She was stunned when Teresa told her about Wilber's condition. Teresa knew Danelle wanted to go to Wilber's hospital, but she repeated Angelo Lopez's instructions about staying away from each other for seven days after the operation had been completed.

Marco and Roberto managed to impound 120 High Green Vegetables trucks and showed cause to arrest fifty-two drivers and six dispatchers. Except for Wilber's misfortune, the Serpa and Santos operation had been executed smoothly and successfully. The hidden hat maker's shop was carted away, one piece at a time, by team members who used the train, bicycles, cars, and carts. The Serpa and Santos Colombian cases were closed.

Seven days passed, and Roberto and Monica kept their lunch

date. It was a beautiful, pleasant, sunny day when Roberto reserved a patio table at a sidewalk cafe in Bogota. He waited for Monica and saw her drive up in her BMW. He watched her long bare legs emerge from the opened car. She was gorgeous, wearing a white sheathed dress, which showed her tiny thin torso, waist, and rounded breasts and hips. When she stood beside her car, many heads turned to look at her radiance as she glided toward Roberto and the empty chair that waited for her. Many curious eyes had wondered who the lucky man receiving this woman's attention was. Did he deserve to be in this woman's life? Roberto doubted it. If she would have him, he would devote all of his being to make her happy. Roberto stood and gave Monica a passionate and sincere hug.

"Monica, I missed you so much!" he said as she slid into the hand-crafted, quaint wooden cafe chair under the sun-yellow tablecloth.

"I wanted desperately to talk to you all last week and even cried myself to sleep one night because I wanted to share my devastating experience with you," Monica lamented.

"I agree we need to make changes in our lives so I can be more accessible. What happened?" Roberto inquired.

"Roberto, you are the only person I feel close enough to share my family's shame with. My father was arrested and charged with cocoa plant production, cocaine manufacturing, and the transporting of cocaine. Sandra was arrested and charged with marketing cocaine. Some of Poppa's fields, sheds, laboratories, and trucks were destroyed or seized. I am not sad about the property loss because it is only right, but I feel so miserable about of my poppa's loss of dignity." She unfolded as the tears cascaded down her creamy almond face.

"I am very sorry for your father, Monica, but now is the time he needs to hear your dreams for Santos farms'. You must visit him and describe your vision. He needs a new future for his hard work. How proud your poppa will be when he knows his oldest child will be the strength of the family and provide new directions. Monica, your stellar ideas are good for everyone. You must give him your plans so he feels the family's forgiveness." Marco looked into the surprised eyes of beautiful Monica.

"What makes you such a wise and strong man when you are still so young?" Monica asked as she dabbed her tears away.

"Monica, I love you and want to help you! Will you marry me?" Roberto boldly proposed.

"I think you are the person who will bring new strength to our family," she said.

"I want to resign from my job so I can devote myself to you and your dream," he added excitedly.

"Roberto, yes, I will marry you, and I want you to come with me to visit my poppa when the time is right. If you visit him with me, he can get to know you as I do. We make a good team with our life dreams, plans, and existing heritages. You have your agriculture, botany, and desire for digging in the dirt. You have the necessary drive for hard work." Monica's sadness transformed into brightness.

Seven days had passed since the operation had concluded. I commuted to and from the burn center at the Colombian Bogota Hospital, which was a surprisingly bright and cheerful facility. I had placed a protection team there for Wilber's safety while he recovered. I served as messenger for his teammates, who sent gifts, letters, and special thoughts to him during the time of no social contact. The team members were compliant with the security rules but managed to convey their concerns.

"How are you feeling today, Wilber?" I asked as I entered his sun-filled room.

"Much better, Mr. Lopez. I think I am to be dismissed soon," Wilber said in muffled words beneath the wrappings on his head that matched the ones on his face and hands.

I pulled up a chair closer to his bedside. "Wilber, the doctors told me your face and hair damage will be minimal when the burn wraps come off. I want you to know our agency will pay for whatever cosmetic surgery you want. You did a great job with your assignment, and saving the child was heroic." I conveyed my thoughts to him as best I could.

"I won't be able to accept your offer until I get a chance to see myself, but I appreciate it. I am glad you are here to talk to me," Wilber's muffled voice continued under the gauze.

"What's on your mind, Wilber?"

"Sir, I want you to accept my resignation. I have thought about my twenty-two years, and doing this kind of work provides no life-embellished rewards for me. I want to experience the goodness of what life has to offer. Since I have been an agent, I have seen too much of the dark low-level scum of life. It seems that we manage to clean up one area of crime, and instead of good things flowing into the cleared area, more low-level crimes pour into the newly opened cavity. It seems futile. It is like taking dirty water from a hole and watching it fill with dirty water again. It would be better if I experienced the positive side of life rather than wallow in the muck of crime," Wilber orated clearly beneath his bandages.

"Wilber, I accept whatever you decide for yourself! I asked the team not to visit you in the hospital to help the protection team safeguard your stay. There are things that have happened in my job that give me pause to think about too. I may not be doing this work much longer either, because I will accept a promotion or I too will resign. Do you know what you want to do now that I have accepted your resignation?" I asked.

"I think I will go into the high tech field. I am interested in inventing a new type of electrical power for our planet's demanding consumption," Wilber emphasized with an enthusiasm that couldn't be hidden.

"I envy your gusto for something new. I haven't any idea what I want to do. This job is all I know," I explained as I rose to leave at the nurse's request. "Wilber, thanks for the good work that you did for us, and please feel free to call me anytime." I waved goodbye and walked the short distance from the hospital to a small coffee shop where I met Teresa Jimenez.

I selected a table for two and waited for her arrival. When I saw her, I thought she was in disguise but realized that her disguise was an attempt at femininity.

"Good to see you, Ms. Jimenez," I greeted as I stood and held her chair. She looked at me in surprise and sat down opposite me.

"Would you care for something to eat or drink?" I asked.

"Just coffee, Thank you," she replied as she tugged at her skirt and brushed her hair into place. She wore a casual summer print dress and Latin American high heels.

"You look as if you have lost weight, and it is very attractive," I complimented.

She blushed a little but was grateful someone had noticed. "Thank you, Señor Lopez," she said. "I wanted to meet with you to explain my plans." When I nodded, she continued. "Sister Rosa Diaz's death affected me greatly! Rosa was a pure, good-intentioned person. She was trying to make Colombia a better country when corruption from our coast guard took her life.

"People we trusted to look after our safety took her life because they were paid a higher price than their regular honest salaries. I despise the fact that Colombian honor is for sale to the highest bidder. I don't think Colombians know the value or meaning of the word honor anymore. I want to give you my resignation papers," she said, holding out a folder.

"Have you thought about this carefully, Teresa?" I asked, reaching across the table to accept it.

"I am definitely doing the right thing! I opened a charter school for children and young teens to teach them ethics, honor, mediation, art skills, and creative problem solving. Living life without honor is a wasted life, and I want children to know they contribute to our culture just by being honorable. They may be poor but they are also honorable! I want children to know that if they possess honor, they own everything that is important. If all they have or wanted is money, they have nothing. This is what Sister Rosa Diaz wanted me to teach," she sniffled and wiped the tears that filled her dimples.

"I find myself in the position of possible resignation myself," I confided.

"Resign, sir. We put many years into this job, and the only thing we gained was weight," she laughed. "You and I both need to find our honor," she declared as she finished her coffee and then walked determinedly east in the direction of the Franciscan church.

What had happened to my agents? What was this turn of the tide that made them think about the quality of their lives and the worth and consequences of their jobs? Was there a lesson I needed to understand from each of their resignations?

I walked up the steps of the library where I met Danelle. She had reserved a reading room for us. I looked into the designated space and saw her waiting alone. At a glance, Danelle was the type of girl you expected to see at a library with her stringy long brown hair that covered most of her face and hid it from life. Her faded purple cardigan was pulled tightly around her body with the sleeves hanging past her fingertips. She was sitting with her head drooping almost to her flat chest when she saw me and sat up straighter.

"May I come in?" I asked.

"*Mucho gusto*, Mr. Lopez," she softly said.

"Danelle, did you ask me to meet you because you want to give me your resignation papers?" I asked.

"Yes, sir. How did you know?" she asked in surprise.

"Because I received four others. Danelle, did you know about the other resignations?" I asked.

"No, sir. I only knew about Teresa's because she had been

working on her charter school application and plans for several weeks," Danelle answered cautiously.

I pulled out a chair across the table from Danelle and asked, "Why do you want to resign, Danelle?"

She laid her face in her hands, looked up at me with trust in her eyes, and answered, "Sister Rosa Diaz was one of God's perfect people, and now she is gone. There is no end to this job we do. The criminals are selfish, mean, and rotten, and I don't want to be around them anymore. I want to be with good people doing whatever I can to live on the brighter side. Most of all, I want to be with Wilber if he will have me. I want to be there when they remove the bandages to tell him I don't care what his face looks like because it is the character inside him that I want to be with. He needs a true friend, and I want to be there for him," she said with conviction.

I picked up her little folded piece of paper. "Thank you for telling me your feelings, Danelle. You are a valued agent and deserve to make your own decisions about your life." I placed the chair back under the table and walked the seven blocks back to the Bogota Hotel, lost in thought.

I wished I could take back the years of this job until I reached the age of my young Colombian agents and could make a choice like they had. I committed many atrocities in the name of my job, and choosing another career would be refreshing, but I wasn't in my twenties anymore. I was far from it, but it would surely feel good to walk with the lightness of their youth. I listened as my footsteps clipped on the marble floor of the Bogota Hotel and then took the elevator up to the second mezzanine. I selected a comfortable over-stuffed chair at the back of the room to wait for Marco. Would he also be handing me his resignation too?

I waited in the mauve-colored, carpeted, mezzanine lobby at the farthest point away from the elevator doors, where I would be able to clearly see Marco's arrival. I looked at my watch and knew he was a few minutes late. The hotel was adorned with crystal swag chandeliers and shapely cocktail waitresses. One beautiful girl took my order for a Coke as I waited. Within minutes, the round-bottomed waitress bent over me to serve the refreshing drink.

I was taking a few sips of the Coke when the elevator door opened and I glimpsed Marco. Then I heard loud unsilenced guns blast through the hotel's serenity and saw people screaming and running. I watched Marco's body crumple into a heap at the door of the elevator. I felt Manuel jerk me to my feet and knew Geraldo was covering my back as they pushed me down the service stairway to the entrance of the main lobby. Geraldo hailed a cab as Manuel pushed me into the back seat between the two of them. Manuel gave the cab directions to drive fast to the airport.

In route, I called our aircraft and told them to be ready for a quick departure to Costa Rica. As our plane took off, I tried to make sense of the scene I had witnessed. It seemed Leonardo Serpa had finally discovered Marco wasn't Monica's chosen man in whom he had confided and had believed would be a new family member. Serpa took his revenge when Marco was in the hotel elevator. Even though Leonardo Serpa was jailed, his money and power still worked for him.

Marco's stellar performance had cost him his life. The Colombia case had closed, but crime, death, and hate continued. The flight back to Costa Rica afforded time for me to prepare my resignation. I told Manuel about my intentions and discovered that he too had made the decision to resign. I called headquarters and heard the familiar voice of Colonel Mike Hollander.

"Good afternoon, sir. I called seeking your advice on a personal matter," I greeted.

"Whatever you need, Angelo Lopez. You know I've always been there for you," Colonel Hollander graciously offered.

"Sir, I want to resign," I declared forcefully.

WREN RICHARDS

"Angelo, you know your request is impossible, don't you?" he asked.

"No, sir, I don't. I lost two valued agents who were gunned down. Five agents have given me their resignations. I need to completely rebuild the Colombian team because right now, we don't have a Colombian team, and many of my own coworkers in the US have resigned. I want the same for myself," I reasoned.

"Your position was different from the beginning, Angelo. You have been given special tutelage since you were seventeen years old and have been groomed for your new position for over thirty years. Yours is a lifetime position, and I can't accept your resignation," Colonel Hollander returned my emphasis with a reverse spin.

"I need to start the resignation process with the National Security Administration," I parried.

"Yes, that would save you the time of being denied once from the top rather than being told four times in the process. Why do you have pangs of morality now after thirty years of service?" Colonel Hollander probed.

"None of the other victims of our projects are quality people, and now Sun Wren Richards is our prey and doesn't deserve unethical treatment, even if our Central American communications infiltration project is strategic to our world plan. She doesn't deserve to be our target and suffer economic loss," I pleaded.

"Angelo, do you have the hots for this woman?" Colonel Hollander asked.

"Your language is too common for her stature," I defended.

"Wow, I guess you have a strong case on her."

"Sir, I ran a total background check on her, and she has never caused harm to anyone. In her criminal background search, I couldn't even find an overdue parking ticket. She is angel pure, and it isn't right that she should know poverty because we can easily take her earned wealth."

"Angelo, the end justifies the means," he reminded me. When I helped you with your JoSam problem in Costa Rica a few weeks ago, I owed you one, but I also protect the agency's goals."

"I no longer believe JoSam's justification was true, sir. I learned that process must be honorable as well. JoSam and Sun have opposing philosophies in their personal natures."

"Angelo, no matter how long we talk on this subject, I cannot accept your resignation," he concluded.

"Will you at least think about my request?" I pleaded persistently.

"No. I'm sorry Angelo. You have no replacement. This Costa Rican communication project is to last another three years. In 2016, come and ask me again, and I might be able to help you find your way out," he offered.

"What if Manuel wants to resign? Is he able too?"

"Yes. I will accept his request, but if you can't resign, are you sure he wants to?" he questioned.

"Yes, I think so. I feel conflicted."

My thoughts raced forward while Colonel Hollander continued to convince me of the responsibilities I owed to my job. My reflections were about Sun. During our very brief time together, I had felt like a refreshed man. She had afforded me glimpses into a life I had never known, where sleep and a restful job were possible. I knew I was in love with her, but giving up thirty years of success and security to fly off a cliff into the unknown, which could end in a wreck, was also a possibility.

I didn't have a good family record. My immediate family of sisters and brothers despised me for neglecting my parents, and my short marriage was a constant battleground that I didn't care to repeat. I was held by Sun's allure, but an unknown future with her provoked inner panic. My job gave me all the opportunities to be at my level of command.

"I feel like I am in displaced suspension."

"Yes, I understand. We are the working, moving parts of our machinery. We continue to operate for the benefit of the total. Angelo, this new communications project you are to install at Sun's property is twenty years ahead of its time. You have been the first to use our newest technology, and you have a great opportunity to advance the US to reach its strategic plans. Sun has gone to Texas, and you and your crew have free rein to get our big project in place. Have you seen the new equipment?" the Colonel asked, derailing my objective.

"I was given the orientation of the new underwater Internet, which uses sound instead of electricity. It is the most exciting invention since the computer. My job of communications surveillance expanded 1,000 percent. This submerged wireless network gives us an unprecedented ability to collect and analyze data from our oceans floor in real time and to make this information available to anyone with a smartphone or computer, especially when a disaster occurs. Agencies like the National Oceanic Atmospheric Administration use sound wave based techniques to communicate underwater. NOAA relies on acoustic waves sent to data sensors on the sea floor to surfaced buoys. The buoys convert the acoustic waves into radio waves and send the data to a satellite, which then redirects the radio waves back to land-based computers." I revealed what I knew about the new science of underwater Internet.

"Come on, Angelo. You don't think this advancement rocked our surveillance world? This new equipment could lead to improvements in tsunami detection, offshore oil and natural gas exploration, pollution monitoring, and other activities Sun Wren Richards would want to make our world a safer and more peaceful planet, wouldn't she?" Colonel Mike Hollander coaxed.

"I want to be part of this new project and its installation," I relented. "I have been privy to most of our newest technology over the years, and it is mind-shattering to know that the underwater Internet system uses sound and transmitted data from existing, undetected, underwater, small forty-pound sensors," I elaborated with ferocious enthusiasm

"Angelo, isn't it possible that Sun won't even know her property is being infiltrated? You explained the lien was only on paper, was without money, and was a protection lien, and she accepted your explanation, right? We will use the property for three years and return it when we no longer need it, without her knowledge. You already have some of our equipment installed into her well systems and in her neighbors' well systems, which gives us greater latitude. You installed over five miles of fiber optics and assisted the installation of land communications devices. This project will only be wrong and hurtful to her if she finds out her property has a $350,000 lien on it.

"In three years, we will remove the lien, and she will be none the wiser. You were correct to call the lien a protective lien since it was for our agency's protection. How could such a technological advancement used to progress our country be detrimental to her? She would probably want to help us if she knew about it. Let me help you with your resignation in three years," Colonel Hollander concluded his case.

"If you see a chance for my exiting the agency before the three years are up, let me know," I stated as I clicked off.

Our new technology was like magic and operated undetected by sending water sound waves instead of the conventional electrical airwaves. The fiber optics helped transport the water sound waves into conventional electric waves and boosted the signal for any type of land device. Our infiltration would be unsuspected for years, using the ocean and well water from property owners. What a brilliant cover! I couldn't deny my enthusiasm to work with this new discovery and knew I would enjoy my new world project.

The rest of the return trip to Costa Rica was devoted to the new underwater Internet systems installation schedule, where our crews had two weeks of free-range movement while Sun was in America.

The Hotel Casa Avenue was a perfect place of inactivity, seclusion, and secrecy, which accepted the world's new equipment.

I was sucked back into the black hole of US espionage. I continued to seek my escape through the Pentagon's dead-end chain of command. Meanwhile, I enjoyed the flavor of using the new technology while finishing Sun Wren Richards's property infiltration assignment. When this project completed, I was to establish residency in Washington, D C and assume my new duties. The NSA had purposely separated me from Sun's influence.

CHAPTER 33

PROMOTION

Sun expressed disapproval over the continuation of my job and ended our friendship. She stated, "I want to be with a person who has strong moral character." Her e-mail turned my unbounded feelings of love and friendship into limitless rage. I felt more anger than I thought possible. My love for her quickly changed into revenge and resentment. My anger propelled a plan for her complete financial destruction.

Her e-mail disconnection made my path clear. I enjoyed the status of being JoSam's replacement in a way the US Agency had never seen before. I became the toughest strategist known to the Pentagon. JoSam was right when he taught that nice guys finished last. My job was the total focus of my life now, and I did it with overkill vigor.

I sent a Memo from Angelo Lopez to the DC office staff:

1. Stop paying the interest on Sun Wren Richards's Costa Rican property lien.

2. Use the Costa Rican property's new underwater Internet surveillance equipment on full power because S. W. Richards won't be back.

3. I want S. W. Richards tailed and her location and activities known day and night. She drives a 2000, green, Tacoma Toyota pickup, with Texas license plate NLP 2796. Put a tracking device on it and give her to the recruit surveillance teams as their assignment. It would be good training for them. I want a weekly report on her.

4. Stop the sale of Sun Wren Richards's Costa Rican property. Give this assignment to the new Costa Rican sabotage team.

With my personal agenda in progress, I fully concentrated on my work associated with the promotion, but first, I needed to fly to Colombia and meet with the new agents for their orientation to tie up the loose ends associated with my former position. I took along my replacement, Sergio Rodriguez, who had been the swimming pool director at Fort Benning, thirty years earlier, who had doubted my membership in JoSam's fraternity. I would brief him during the flight in my Cessna Citation X 2013 aircraft capable 717 miles per hour.

It was equipped with a long-legged, dark-haired, beautiful Miss Chocolate Pie of the Sky, who gave free tastes. I patted her ass each time she brought my drink. I drank up every perk and indulgence the job offered since the simple pleasures of sleep and happiness eluded me. I briefed Sergio, and we were ready for the Colombian team.

Dressed in monks' robes, Sergio and I met the recruits in a vacant chapel behind a monastery on the outskirts of Bogota. This was our headquarters as long as it remained undetected. There were fifteen new agents, and they had a different look about them: scruffier, tougher, shifty-eyed, and slick. Their monks' robes failed to camouflage their con-man, Wall Street demeanor. They reflected the nature of the world they served. I stood at the chapel's sanctuary pulpit and thought how I liked this godly position. It fit my style.

"Good Morning! My name is Angelo Orlando Andres Lopez, but you will address me simply as Angelo. I have no rank or title. I started with the agency when I was seventeen and developed it into a thirty-year career. I am a strategist. I hold classes and seminars for many teams all over the world, and today I have the privilege of addressing the new team in Colombia.

"Our goals are simple. First, we are engaged in a plan of world infiltration. Infiltration is how we will survive. As you have experienced, all countries are led by people with big egos, greed, and undeveloped and unsophisticated minds who continually sink their countries into chaos, poverty, disease, debt, and corruption. Each country is a mess of bickering politics without resolution, and each believes their narrow egocentric strategy is correct. This point is exemplified and labeled democratic, republican, conservative, liberal, communist, or socialist. We know it is all pointless and futile. We plan to unplug ourselves from this deadly current of electricity."

"Second, your job is to work with the National Security Agency and Department of War on Drugs."

"Third, you are to work as self-motivated, cooperative, creative individuals and as a team to successfully complete any order, mission, or assignment given to you. You are required to protect your identity and the identity of your teammates at all costs."

"Your First Assignment is to infiltrate the Colombian drug cartels' economic structure and to look for areas of weakness that cause monetary collapse. Many of you are computer hackers, electronic saboteurs, creative accountants, forgers, and counterfeit artists. You have been handpicked and developed for your individual contribution of talent to form a well-balanced team. Remember, your job is infiltration, and you are the Colombian economic infiltration team. You are to find and report any new deceptive accounting practices, technical innovations, or knowledge that proves useful in furthering our own goals."

"Your first targeted subjects are the Serpa twins, Ramon and Renaldo, the founders of High Green Grow Brokerages SA. The firm is suspected of being a cocaine brokerage for all of Colombia. Their success has rapidly developed over the last year. The Serpa twins are Colombian nationals, twenty-two years old, graduates of SMU in Dallas, Texas, and sons of the infamous Leonardo Serpa, who is serving forty-two years in a Colombian prison for drug dealing and murder. The twins are grandsons of a wealthy American finance broker, Walter Hill. Rene Hill, Walter's daughter and the mother of the twins, is an *Elle* model and a competitive tango ballroom dancer. Our organization is eager to stifle their operation before it gains further momentum, and the twins' case has been put onto the fast track.

"Mr. Rodriguez, please stand for your introduction. I wish to introduce Sergio Rodriguez, who started his career as an army base pool attendant and has worked his way up the ranks to assume this new command. You will respect his position and will stand whenever he enters or leaves your meetings. He is my successor and your commander." I paused and waited for the team to stand as Sergio took his position on the sanctuary platform. The new arrogant team members looked around at each other in disbelief but eventually stood up in Sergio's honor.

"You may be seated," I encouraged.

"Santiago Rojas, will you please stand? You have been appointed team captain. You are responsible for the planning, executing, and succeeding of orders. You will report to Señor Rodrigues regularly on Colombia's economic infiltration progress. I present your team captain Santiago."

Santiago age twenty-eight, a native Colombian, could be Bruce Lee's look-alike, except that he wore heavy black-rimmed reading glasses. He was agile, fast in his movements, smart, educated with a master's degree in computer technology from the University of Texas, and a natural leader. He was also cunning. He had served prison time in Huntsville, Texas, for banking systems hacking where he had been recruited. Santiago was responsible for one of the largest banking fraud cases to date. He successfully siphoned over $10 million into his Swiss bank account, but a disgruntled friend reported him to the FBI, and we hired him for the job.

The youngest man of the team raised his hand. "If you have a question? Stand and state your name," I commanded.

"My name is Diego Martinez. We all know Camilo Vasquez and think he should be the likely choice for our team captain," Diego said assertively.

I felt my blood pressure rise and heat pouring out from under the monks' robe. I shouted, "God dammit to hell! How old are you, Diego?"

"I am seventeen," he answered in a shaking voice.

"Diego, if you want to live to be eighteen and not be pounded into the ground to become any shorter than you already are, you need to learn rule number one. Never buck a superior officer," I shouted. "Do you know the qualifications of Captain Santiago Rojas?" I bellowed.

"No," Diego meekly answered.

"Then sit down and shut your mouth. Being chosen as Captain is about skills and qualifications! The selection is not based on some congeniality contest. Got that?" I shouted. "Diego, stand up again," I ordered. Diego stood up with a frightened face.

"Santiago Rojas please stand," I asked calmly.

"Diego, apologize to your captain," I demanded.

"I'm sorry," he squeaked out.

"You will address him as Señor Rojas from now on! Repeat your apology," I roared.

"I am sorry, Mr. Rojas," he stated firmly.

"I accept your apology, Diego," replied Santiago Rojas. The

chapel was as quiet as a prayer group, and the men sat with bowed heads.

"Mateo Munoz." I paused until he stood up. "Please prepare a detailed personal profile on Ramon and Renaldo Serpa. We need to know their internal business structure, daily habits, friends and family contacts, hobbies, business associates, religious or spiritual organizations, and domestic habits. You also will assist your team if any legal advice is required," I continued.

"Yes, sir," he replied.

Mateo, age thirty-nine, who was a native Colombian and graduated from Bogota Law School, cum laude, had also studied corporate law and finance at Harvard. He was known for his expertise in both Colombian Roman law and US civil law. He had recently become unemployed from a New York law firm after five years. He had had a prolonged illness with cancer. We hired him, paying him a higher salary and his medical bills. We knew he was terminally ill. Mateo was a small man with dark hair and eyes and walked with a slight limp. He was a shy and unsocial man who was married with two children.

"Victor Lee," I said. He stood quickly when his name was called. "Victor, you are responsible for all communications infiltration. You will place recording devices on Mr. Leonardo Serpa. He was the suspected master planner of the twins' business and ran it from prison. You will monitor and gather evidence from the twin's grandfather, Walter Hill, the Santos family, and all electronic devices of anyone suspected of brokering cocaine."

Victor, from Kentucky. age twenty-five, worked for Advanced Micro Devices, Intel, and Dell computers as a technical designer in Austin, Texas. His years of experience outnumbered his years in higher education, but he had natural talents for inventing things. He had been an Olympic gymnast contender in 2012 but had been disqualified after testing positive for drugs. Victor was blond, blue-eyed, five feet ten inches, 160 pounds, and very physically fit.

"Mr. Rodriguez, I present key members of your team!" Sergio Rodriguez took his position of command at the chapel's pulpit. Santiago Rojas quickly stood up, and everyone followed.

"Gentlemen, please be seated. We will meet here on Saturday morning at 10 a.m. When I become better acquainted with you, positions and assignments will be given to more of you. Santiago, I expect you to prepare our entrance- and exit-detailing of the chapel. You will clean evidence of our existence. We will meet here wearing our robes until we become detected. It is our tradition for the orientation of a new team to be given a celebration of its choice. Santiago, huddle with your team and make the request for tonight's event," Sergio instructed.

After ten minutes of intense deliberation, Santiago stood and made his request. "We want a steak dinner at Siete Dieciseis in Usaquen. Eight of us want to meet beautiful girls at the Marriott Hotel," Santiago reported.

I stood and announced, "Your wish is my command. Meet me in the lobby of the JW Marriott Hotel at 19:00. I will arrange everything," I said as I left the chapel and gave a salute. The chapel door closed behind me. I removed the monk's robe and left it in Sergio's car. I called a professional girlfriend that I knew.

"Hi, Sophia, this is Angelo Lopez. It has been awhile since we talked. Are you as adorable as you used to be?"

"Angelo, I have gotten better with age, just like a good wine or cheese, but now I am much tastier," Sophia cooed.

"That's great! I need your help. Is it possible, my sweet Sophia, to have eight, young beautiful girls between the ages of eighteen and twenty-two available in the lounge of the JW Marriott Hotel at ten tonight?"

"Angelo, you have some nerve! This is very late notice to be asking for such specifics," Sophia protested.

"Sophia, for hell's sake! It is only eleven thirty in the morning. You have the entire afternoon."

"How long do you want my girls?" she asked.

"The guys have suites and want the girls all night," I explained.

"Can you afford us?" she asked.

"Come on, Sophia, what kind of question is that?"

"Okay, I will get the girls for you, but it will cost $700 per girl. That will be $5,600 American dollars," she warned.

"You're charging $700 per beautiful girl? Do I get you?" I questioned.

"Sure, if that's what you want," Sophia teased.

"It will be fun. See you tonight! Ciao," I said, clicked off, and then called Siete Dieciseis and made reservations for seventeen people.

I didn't know Sophia's boyfriend was an NPR reporter who had dropped her off at the hotel and had told her to call him when she needed a ride home. Sophia was cute, looked like a present-day Betty Boop in her late thirties, and was atypical of her profession. Sophia spent the day inviting young college girls who needed extra cash for their tuitions to work for her. Sophia went to the hotel lounge early to meet the girls and made sure they fit my requested requirements. Sophia knew most of the girls, but there were three new ones she didn't know. The girls were all beautiful with good figures, and I was pleased with the inventory.

At 9 p.m., I and several of the recruits walked into the lounge. Sophia greeted us and introduced her team to my team. We all stayed in the lounge, drank, talked, and unobtrusively made selections. By eleven thirty, everyone had dispersed and left Sophia and I alone.

"Would you like one more drink before we go upstairs?" I asked.

"Yes, let's do. It has been a long day for me, and now my job of getting everyone tucked in with beddy-byes is finished. I can relax," Sophia sighed.

"You look beautiful, unlike uncorked, aged wine or cheese," I flirted.

"I would like to take care of the business side of things first as it might be hectic in the morning," Sophia explained.

"Sophia, we both are relaxed, and I don't want to spoil the mood you cast over me by thinking about business. I want to make a toast and finish our drinks," I replied.

"We have been friends for a few years, and I am too tired to argue," she stated.

"Here's to our friendship and to your beauty," I toasted.

We finished our drink. We rode the elevator up to the seventh floor and walked to room 007.

"Did you choose this room yourself, James Bond?" she asked.

"No, honestly, I did not! It was what the hotel gave me," I chuckled. The room was Marriott luxurious—always clean and fresh. We sat down on the bed, and I suggested, "Since you had a long day, would you like to sleep for a couple of hours while I work?"

"That would be peachy-keen," she said.

I watched as she slipped off her dress, and I admired her well-toned body. She wore dark blue panties and a bra. When she reached behind her back to unhook her bra, she exposed her plump firm breasts. She lifted the printed duvet and slid under the white sheets. "Are you sure you wouldn't like to join me?" she asked.

"You sleep. I have work, but then I will try to sleep next to you."

Sophia fell asleep in less than five minutes. I envied her. I worked online with strategy for two other teams in Georgia and Brazil. An hour passed. I turned off the computer, removed my shirt and pants, climbed in beside her naked body, and tried to sleep. I hoped that her sleep would seep into me. I lay beside her and searched the black cave for the hibernating soft mound of sleep that I never found.

Sophia had been sleeping for four hours when she awoke, touched me, and pressed her breasts into my bare back. She pushed me over and kissed my face, lips, and ears. She nibbled and massaged every corner of my abdomen while her hands knew the patterns of genital massage. She was good, but I wasn't aroused.

Sophia worked on the art of touch until five o'clock when it became light outside. She gave me pleasant oral sex, tasting, licking, sucking, and cooing, and I responded by touching her but wasn't aroused. She flattered me, told me sexy poems, described my attributes that turned her on, but I simply couldn't become interested. She continued to cuddle me and began conversations she thought I would be interested in. It was now ten minutes after seven, and another long night had passed.

"Sophia, would you like to order room service for breakfast?" I asked.

"Wowzer, yippy skippy," she said as she walked to the desk for the menu, turned on soft music, and danced seductively while she read the menu. She had been in a professional theater's chorus line and was an elegant dancer. I enjoyed watching her, but my body didn't respond. We both ordered mammoth-sized breakfasts, and Sophia continued to perform while we waited for breakfast delivery.

"Let's shower together while we wait for our breakfast," she invited.

We were in the shower when room service announced his arrival. Sophia jumped out, dripped water, and answered the door. She knew I was watching her as she opened the door to admit the waiter. He was stunned and stared at her beautiful body. She pranced and danced while we both watched. The waiter got aroused, but I didn't. I knew her waiter performance was for my benefit.

"Put your tip on my bill," I said as he closed the door.

We ate our omelets, toast, waffles, bacon, and coffee in the nude while the soft music filled the silence, but Sophia knew I had given up on her. She quickly dressed and called her boyfriend for a ride. She confirmed that he was waiting in the lobby.

"Angelo, pay me now so I can settle up with the girls who are waiting for me," she stated assertively.

"Let's go to the lobby so I can check out. I'm tired of being cooped up in this room," I replied.

The lobby was filled with people checking out and managing their luggage. I saw a few of my men from the team and a few of the girls from last night. Santiago waved, smiled, and gave me a thumbs-up.

I waited in the checkout line at the desk while Sophia walked across the lobby to the man who waited for her. When I finished at the hotel checkout, I walked toward her, and she met me halfway in the middle of the lobby. I handed her an envelope with $240. She took it and counted it.

"Where is the rest of it? We were to get $700 each," she screamed in anger.

"That's all you were worth," I retorted.

"It's not my fault you couldn't get it up," she bellowed as the crowd smiled and snickered. Her friend, the NPR reporter from the US, smelled a story and began to take pictures. Santiago grabbed his camera, and Diego pushed him to the floor. Sophia and the scrambling men attracted the attention of hotel security.

A mob of people watched as she screamed. "I did everything I knew how to do to help you get it up. It isn't my fault you were as limp as leftover spaghetti." The watching crowd included my team, and they formed a circle round Sophia like kids on the playground, as they broke out laughing. I pushed my way through the crowd while Sophia continued to be a wild, angry *bruja*, yelling like a *perra* in heat.

"Thirty dollars! Thirty dollars is what he paid us. He is a US agent and can't get his gun to fire," she bellowed to the watching crowd, who roared with laughter. I was humiliated in front of my men. I left the hotel and grabbed a cab and headed to the airport.

The cab ride gave me time to realize my error in strategy. I thought that Sophia wouldn't make a scene in public and that I could easily make my escape without paying her. I didn't think any woman would discredit herself as a prostitute in the middle of the JW Marriott Hotel. I concluded that Colombian women had no sense of dignity.

In the airplane on the way back to the States, I tried to dissolve the humiliating scene into the blackness of sleep, but the scene replayed itself over in my mind. In the eyes of my men, I had been unzipped and exposed. Our NSA identity had been known and shouted all over the Marriott Hotel. I was shamed.

By the time I arrived at my Washington DC office on Monday morning, the Colombian prostitute story was on National Public Radio. The office scuttlebutt had it that the NSA agency was very embarrassed because the incident hadn't shown our country in a positive light. I had some explaining to do.

"Angelo Lopez, what is the meaning of the National Public Radio prostitution scandal?" Mr. Speaker of the Committee asked.

"Oh, sir, it is nothing. In Colombia, prostitution is legal, and some of the men needed to let off a little steam. Americans will forget about this in two days because they are caught up in the entertainment of the republican and democrat budget crises," I glossed over.

"Most of Central American countries, especially Colombia and Costa Rica, have strong laws protecting the identity of agents. It is forbidden to release an agent's photo. Even if he is accused of wrongful acts, he isn't prosecuted. There were no names released, and you are the only people who know it was my men," I explained, and the affair was forgotten.

My world became frantic chaos. I was pulled between catching Edward Snowden, who had taken refuge in Russia, silencing the many journalists who had leaked secret information, and our desperate attempt to cover everything up. The public was the driving force that demanded more of this entertainment news. There were global journalism leaks that threatened our espionage in several countries.

Journalists from Costa Rica had given the courts proof our agents had intercepted and conducted surveillance on their telephone records. According to the evidence given to the courts, the agents responsible for the espionage had been the agents investigating organized crime and narcotics. Our agency lawyers pointed to a weakness in their case, which didn't explain how agents had been able to obtain phone records. The how was locked in our secret of the Xkeyscore.

Journalists denounced the practice of phone record collecting as a violation of international law and contended that it was a threat to their profession and to the rule of law in Costa Rica. Spain, Brazil, England, and Russia made the same contention. Journalists felt the pressure of our censorship. My crime-fighting job changed to include new strategies for media censorship and for covering up our infiltration. My world was like a mouse running on a spinning top. The faster the mouse ran, the faster the top spun. The faster it spun, the faster he had to run until he died of exhaustion. The top eventually slowed down and stopped. I needed to end the life of Angelo Orlando Andres Lopez.

CHAPTER 34

ENTRAPMENT

It had been two years since I had spoken to Sun Wren Richards. I decided to send her an e-mail revealing my location. It was worth the gamble to see if she would come. The message read:

Located: Angelo Orlando Andres Lopez, 4709 Town Lake, Austin, Texas 78704.

Two days after the e-mail was sent, I received word that Sun Wren Richards had arrived at the Town Lake location. Bingo! The embers of my memory ignited the challenge of entrapment and captured her back into my blood. I sprang into control mode.

She expected to find a home or condos and was amazed at the grandeur of the building at the given location. It was a stately old Texan southern mansion constructed from the beige Texan limestone. The building was four stories tall, with the center of the building designed into four stories of open-air balconies. It was a beautiful old building.

Sun found parking in a visitor parking lot and looked out over the walkways of expansive, green St. Augustine grass, dotted with scores of large oak trees, which were typical of the Texan native landscape. An impressive fountain, which was similar to the grand fountain I had given her in Costa Rica, splashed in front of the building. This fountain wasn't as tall, had no graceful bowls, and was surrounded by a railing to keep people out. No, this fountain was certainly not as beautiful as the one from her past. I watched her petite form descend from the 2000 green Toyota truck, which her lack of finances had reduced her to. I felt an electric current of pride at my masterfulness.

She followed the walkway to the entrance and read the large limestone sign: "AUSTIN STATE HOSPITAL." She must have doubted the correctness of the e-mail and wondered if there was a mistake. Sun ambled into the lobby where an older woman with sweptback, greying hair and a pleasant heart-shaped face looked up at her. The receptionist removed her glasses as I watched.

"May I help you?" asked the chatty receptionist.

"Thank you. I hope so. What kind of hospital is this?" she inquired.

"It is a mental hospital for people with acute psychiatric illnesses, and we serve three hundred patients. What hospital are you looking for? Do you have the correct hospital? Are you in the right place?"

"I'm not sure," Sun answered as I listened. "I was given this address," Sun said and showed her cell phone.

"Yes, you have the right location," the receptionist assured.

"Do you know someone by the name of Angelo Orlando Andres Lopez?"

The easygoing and talkative woman behind the desk looked through some papers in a vanilla-colored folder and then at her computer. She looked at Sun perplexed. "We have a new patient who was admitted two days ago by that name. Are you a relative?" she asked.

"No, we were friends when we both lived in Costa Rica," Sun answered.

"What is your name?" she inquired as she filled in a visitation form, which required extensive personal information and Sun's signature. "Costa Rica? This hospital is for Texas patients. Let me take a minute and review his file," she said returning to her computer. "Our files are empty in his regard. Can you contribute any information that may be helpful for a treatment plan?" she asked hopefully.

"I knew him when he worked on highway construction projects in Costa Rica," Sun openly answered.

"Is he married with children or other living family?" she continued to inquire while taking notes.

"No, he only expressed interest in his work. Why are you asking these questions? Are they requirements for a visitation?" Sun asked, unsure as she stood at the reception area of the state mental institution.

"Your friend was committed by a government court, and we don't have any history for him except that he was admitted without designated local mental health authorities. He had an emergency medical screening in compliance with EMTALA in consultation with the LMHA, and the admitting doctor authorized his admission. His history reports everything as unknown: unknown family, unknown employment, unknown level of education, and unknown prior health and mental history. His services were paid by a Washington agency," she said.

"Do you know which agency?" Sun asked, hoping to fill in missing details that I had previously withheld.

"No, I'm sorry. Our information is limited. If he is from Costa Rica, he must speak Spanish, right?" she assumed.

"Yes, Spanish is his native tongue, but he speaks fluent English," Sun tried to augment the file's information.

"Oh yes, he talks constantly in English like a malfunctioning computer. I assumed you wanted a visitation?" Sun nodded assent.

"Your visitation will be monitored by doctors observing you from behind glass where they can see and hear what is said in the hopes of learning something about him," she disclosed.

"Did your hospital send me the text message concerning his location?" Sun asked.

"No, the only thing we know about him is his name and the information you gave me today. We didn't know he had any friends. The only reason for allowing your visit is the hope it may help him. The doctors may want to visit with you following your visit. Have a seat while I arrange for your visit. It may take ten to thirty minutes," the receptionist cordially added.

A bowl of dried flower petals sat on the small table to mask the accumulation of centuries-old collected human stress and misery dating back to 1860 when the building had been known as the Texas State Lunatic Asylum. The feelings of ancient human turmoil and suffering were unnerving Sun, despite the staff's determined efforts. Sadly, the superficial and pretentious endeavors only made the environment worse.

Sun stared into space, and her thoughts were interrupted by a tall slender blond woman who wore casual street clothes and sensible shoes and carried a folder. I watched Sun from a hidden video camera placed above where she sat.

"Ms. Sun Richards, I'm Dr. Sally Hill. I'm glad you've come to visit our patient, Angelo Lopez. We want to observe any recognition he has of you or what his reactions might be. Follow me, please? Leave your purse or any items from your pockets in this locker and leave the key at the front desk. Your visit must be limited to thirty minutes." She cordially directed Sun into the visiting room. Sun walked further down the hall into the observation room the receptionist had described.

Sun forced herself to open the door and to step into the naked room that gripped two lonely rocking chairs. When she closed the door, she saw Angelo as he paced and talked out loud to no one. He was dressed in clean, casual, nice street clothes of khaki pants and a yellow short-sleeved shirt. He turned to face her, and she didn't recognized him! He had gained over 350 pounds. He showed muscle loss and was going bald. His deep chocolate eyes were sunken into the roundness of his fleshy face, and his eyelids fluttered and hid his eyes' color. She looked at his mouth, which she had once thought was beautiful but now seemed to be stretched or misshapen.

Sun sucked in air at the sight of his size as he turned, still talking to himself and pacing toward her. She walked up to him and tried to take his hand in friendship while he continued to talk, but he didn't feel her touch. She released his limp hand and let it drop to his side as he continued to roam and rant.

"Angelo, I am glad to see you again," she said. "Do you remember me? I am Sun Wren Richards, and we were friends in Costa Rica." Sun sank down into the mauve, overstuffed rocking chair while he walked and talked. Sun was so absorbed by the intensity of the moment that she wasn't even distracted by the fact that she was being monitored. A hundred questions must have raced through her mind about what she wanted to know.

He cocked his head like a bird, waddled, and spoke in monologues. Sun continued to talk over his voice, and they were in a miserable, overlapping verbal duet. It must have been impossible for the doctors to understand anything either of them said, and this was good because what Sun had to say to Angelo was intimate and private.

"Our agency team was assigned the secret return to Honduras of President Manuel Zelaya, September 21 of 2009. The country's near revolution was ignited by Manuel Zelaya's attempt to rewrite the constitution of Honduras to allow himself to run for another term. The country was outraged and may have assassinated him without our intervention. Honduras had no clear constitution process for removing a sitting president and planned to do it with violence. We rescued him and later had to take him back. Our team returned him clandestinely to the Brazilian embassy in Tegucigalpa.

"Nikola's poem said:

> I tolerate no betrayal,
> No tarnished loyalty.
> If my trust in you does fail,
> You die like dethroned royalty.

"In 2010, President Zelaya was exiled to the Dominican Republic. Now he represents Honduras as a deputy of Central American parliament. His wife also ran for president. Our work meant nothing and would circle around again." Angelo kept his monologue going continuously, and his higher pitched words were slurred together.

"Did you know you were the second man in my life that I loved? I think you knew it, but I wanted to repeat it again now. I loved you, Angelo, and I trusted in your honor to do the right thing toward me, but I ended up homeless with a financial mess. I was left with nothing because I had given it all to you. I'm not telling you this out of anger or to cause guilt, but I am here today because I hoped you would tell me what happened to you, and why our friendship didn't grow into permanency," Sun said.

"We all knew the USA had oil interests in Nicaragua. The border dispute with Costa Rica intensified daily, and the USA took sides with Nicaragua. I chose to be loyal to my job while I was labeled a traitor to Costa Rica. The issue was under consideration by the judge of the International Court of Justice in The Hague. The Ministry of Foreign Affairs in the lawsuit maintained a decision that granted greater maritime sovereignty to Nicaragua but ruled the power of the keys, including the disputed island of San Andres, and it remained with Colombia. In the coming days, we made a comprehensive review of the judgment to determine the scope it had among the republics of

Nicaragua and Colombia and how that related to the interests and rights that Costa Rica had in the Caribbean Sea. Nikola's poem said:

> I'm going to fight you.
> You know I don't like you.
> I will slam you and strike you.
> I will kick you and bite you.

Angelo recited, paced, and mumbled over Sun's voice, and their dual orations flooded the abused and trodden beige-carpeted floor.

"You knew my thoughts had always been respectful toward you even during the year I was a vagrant, Angelo. I had never harbored ill will or bad thoughts toward you, and I thought you were one of the most interesting people I had ever known. You were a very gifted man with a superhuman mind. You were everything I ever wanted to find in a companion. You were aware of your own abilities, and I believed you were a rare individual whose goal was to use his full potential.

"I continue to purge my pent up emotions toward you, Angelo, but I don't think you hear me. We are both experiencing this strange situation today because I don't understand anything you are telling me, and you can't hear or understand me. Aren't we symbols for all of humanity, who can't understand, hear, see, or feel each other?" she desperately challenged. Sun poured out her discourse uninterrupted, and so did Angelo.

> You will be banished to Lucifer's fiery domain.
> Your soul for love famished,
> Abandoned, dying in the rain.

"That was what the poet Nikola told us. Costa Rica had deplorable overcrowded prison systems where 326 prisoners were stuck in the holding cells of the Judicial Investigation Organization because the national prison system refused to accept new inmates. The OIJ cells were completely full and lacked beds, adequate ventilation, and access to sunlight. The country's prisons were an echo of the holding cells. The courts gave bracelets to prisoners and released them into the streets.

"The US ambassador, Mrs. Andrews, had given money to the correctional segment of the judicial system, but the money was never realized to relieve conditions. Convicts spread terror for tourists in the southern Caribbean zone, and police suspected that a gang of heavily armed convicts were responsible for causing panic in the Caribbean zone of Costa Rica, where in the last two months, there were twelve assaults on foreign tourists. Leaders in the tourism industry related that gangs had become more organized and were better armed than the police were." Angelo paced, ranted relentlessly, and became intense and emphatic.

"Wouldn't it be delightful for us to have experienced the beauty of Costa Rica with its lush greenery, its beautiful waterfalls, its oceans, and its powerful volcanoes. I wanted for us to enjoy those things together, Angelo. Our time together was such a waste of a rare moment, where the universe gave us a chance meeting, but the window of opportunity closed without us seizing its gift." Sun walked with him up and down the small carpeted room while their overlapped word canons continued their volleys.

"Drug lords laundered money and transported drugs in vacuum-sealed packages covered with blue tape inside human body cavities or surgically placed inside the lining of human bellies. Our human race became piggy banks for the drug cartels. The Costa Rican President supported extradition of its nationals who were wanted in other countries for organized crime and drug trafficking, but drug production and transporting became big business to the country's economy. We could clean up this mess, but the country's economy would plummet, and the poor would starve because of our efficient work. The line of right and wrong disappeared," Angelo rambled on, unaware that Sun kept pace with him.

"Why did you put the lien on my property?" she asked. "I really want to know why things turned out as they did. Did you lose the money gambling? Do you still like to play blackjack? I chose to believe you used the money to buy Manuel a home so he could get out of the job because you knew it wasn't good for him. Angelo, I didn't think your job was good for you either, and I wanted you to resign. Did you resign? I wanted to help you find quiet inner peace and feel relaxed. I wanted you to know the beauty of our world, but most of all, I wanted you to experience restful sleep. You never got enough sleep when I knew you. You were always on the edge of turmoil and anxiety.

"I am glad to have this chance to tell you what my heart felt. I wanted good things for you! I loved you, Angelo. Do you not know that we both tried to make our world a better place but had opposite strategies of approaching the problem? I tried to change human behavior at the cellular level through meditation, and you tried corporal force, which seemed to have destroyed your sense of purpose and your great gifts. I begged you to consider other methodologies. I wanted you to resign," Sun orated over his voice.

For a moment, Sun stood and watched him walk and noticed that his heavy body distorted his normally turned-out toe gait. She tried to stop his walking by standing in front of him. She grasped both his forearms, but his stride continued uninterrupted. If she hadn't stepped out of the way, he would have pushed her over, totally oblivious of her presence.

"Can you please stop walking and talking and look at me? Do you see me, Angelo? Do you hear me, Angelo? Do you know me, Angelo? Angelo, do you feel me taking your hand?" She released his hand without receiving any reaction or change in the stream of his words.

Her grief brimmed over because of the void in his mind. Sun grieved that he was unaware of her presence. She felt compassion for the inner turmoil he was going through. Sun knew his stress had existed three years earlier during their first meeting in the Casa Ave Hotel kitchen.

"Angelo, I am sorry for your troubles. I am saying good-bye, and I wish you well," she said as she turned toward the door.

Sun felt the smallness of the room pulsating with the accumulation of centuries of human distress, which oozed into the atmosphere and pushed her toward the door. She had to leave. She walked to the lockers with the key the receptionist had held out to her without speaking. I watched as she retrieved her purse and cell phone and left the building. Her eyes flooded over, and her sobbing body made sounds that told the whole outdoors of her bereavement. She cried while she stumbled down the cement walkway and sat on a bench under the condolence of a large live oak tree.

The live oak tree and the wooden bench on the grounds of the Austin State Hospital helped her regain emotional stability. She was ready to return to her beach cottage when her cell phone interrupted her self-absorbed silence.

"Hello, Sun, this is Angelo. May I join you on the bench under the tree?" his familiar baritone voice rang in her ears. I knew she was stunned and couldn't answer.

"Sun, I am walking toward you now. Do you see me?"

She turned, looked behind her, and saw me as she had known me, walking toward her in my familiar toes turned-out gait. I sat down next to her as if it were yesterday.

"Sun, you look great! How did you like meeting with Angelo Orlando Andres Lopez number two?" I asked and continued without her reply.

"The only way I could resign from the system was to die or become incapacitated. I chose the latter. The man you just met was a longtime operative from one of my teams, who flipped out. The Government paid for his care, and he remained useful to our agency by becoming me. It put me off any criminal's radar and off my job hook where I have a new identity. I can live however I want, and in essence, I resigned as you suggested. Your visit today was our test to determine his believability."

I paused and continued explaining without her response. "I planted a recorder in his shoes before you arrived and heard what was said. We had been apart for a long time, and I wanted to know what you thought about me."

"Angelo, how can you be so cavalier about what you have put me through today. For the last two years, I haven't known if you were alive or dead. I was homeless because of your actions. I traveled around the United States and stayed at Motel 6, with family members, or friends who invited me. You didn't care about the economic hardship your lien and foreclosure caused, and your actions weren't expressions of a caring friend. Everything you have done since our meeting has been self-serving." She enforced these words intensely by standing up.

"What we did today to that poor man walking around inside the Austin State Hospital may have lasting effects on him, and I am concerned for his recovery," she continued.

"I want a companion who is made of a strong moral character. Ours would be an impossible relationship without trust, and I don't have any left. It seems you use the people who love you to further your personal cause. I am tired of being controlled, spied upon, and used for your personal gains. I no longer will be a victim for your opportunity."

I watched as she walked away. My new position and clandestine technology would always have control over Sun Wren Richards. My job gave me control over everyone, and I expanded with her shrinking freedoms. My lifelong training and grooming under the tutelage of the School of the Americas would give me the advantage of civil unrest and achieve goals for world domination.

EPILOGUE

Angelo Orlando Andres Lopez never resigned. He was promoted and continued to work as a strategist operative for the U S government with a new Georgian identity.